THE MIDAS CONSPIRACY

BLUE FEATHER BOOKS, LTD.

To my mother, who has always believed in me and offered her unconditional love.

The Midas Conspiracy

A BLUE FEATHER BOOK

BY

Jennifer McCormick

THE MIDAS CONSPIRACY

Cover design by Ann Phillips

A Blue Feather Book
Published by Blue Feather Books, Ltd.

www.bluefeatherbooks.com

ISBN: 978-1-935627-84-5

First edition: October, 2012

Printed in the United States of America and in the United Kingdom.

Acknowledgements

First of all, I want to acknowledge everyone at Blue Feather Books. I would like to thank my editor, Nene Adams, for all the work she has done to help make my novel the best it can be. I would also like to thank my family, who continue to love and support me in all that I do.

Chapter 1

Ducking behind a colossal stone pillar, Cybil Reynard held her breath for fear of giving away her position. A heavily armed security drone hummed several meters away, its infrared sensors carefully scanning the area where she had just been. After long, excruciating seconds of uncertainty, its readings showed no signs of life, and the drone at last disengaged from attack mode and moved away. She slowly released a sigh. As a space mercenary, she expected a life of peril and unpredictability. However, she did not particularly enjoy taking reckless chances.

She forced herself to move from the relative safety of the cover offered by the pillar and continued her way across the vast, darkened lobby. She kept to the shadows as she moved and constantly glanced over her shoulder for any sign of pursuit. The building was the corporate headquarters of Midas Pharmaceuticals, located in the capital city of planet Turon, one of the most populated worlds in the galaxy. Sneaking into the fortified high-rise had been no easy task, even for someone with her expertise, but although she had managed to breach the outer perimeter, the mission was far from over.

Cybil crept forward in the darkness. The portable scanner secured at her belt indicated movement in the corridors ahead: living flesh and blood, not machine. The man she had been hired to kill was somewhere within the maze of corridors and offices. She had seen him enter the empty building with her own eyes.

That bug-eyed alien bastard. The thought of the malice shining in those strange bulbous eyes made her blood boil. She took a deep breath and proceeded along the course set by her scanner. There would be time for vengeance later, she said to herself. She would not allow her barely contained contempt to interfere with her mission. Cybil Reynard always got her man. Or alien, as the case may be.

Just as she was rounding a corner in the network of hallways, a blazing red light streaked past her head and struck the wall behind her. She smelled charred metal where the plasma blast had melted and warped the wall panel. The dark corridor came alight with pulsing light as similar blasts blazed over the cooling unit she crouched behind.

Apparently, her presence had been expected in the office building in the dead of night, which could only mean one thing: her prey was fighting back. Cybil smiled. She enjoyed a good challenge.

* * *

"Slow down, *Si'rah* Leara," Kitani Veldina called softly as they approached the door leading to the main offices of Midas Pharmaceuticals.

Heeding Kitani's advice, Leara Sorani came to an abrupt halt and spun around. An apparently surprised Kitani nearly slammed into her before she could stop herself. Face flaming with embarrassment, Kitani leapt away, placing a respectable distance between herself and Leara while saying, "Forgive me, but there's no need for us to rush into the unknown."

"This is what we came here to do, Kitani." Leara spoke with cold determination. "Two of our warriors have already succumbed to Midas's treachery. How much longer would you have us wait? And please, don't refer to me with such titles. As long as we're on this mission, your status is the same as mine. Now, what we are searching for is somewhere beyond those doors. Let us not waste a moment more."

We've made it this far, Leara reminded herself encouragingly. *There's no turning back now. Too many lives depend on us*. Somewhere within Midas Pharmaceuticals lay evidence that the corporation was behind a recent series of disappearances. Race and occupation varied greatly from one individual to the next, but all had one thing in common: every last abductee was alien.

Midas Pharmaceuticals was mostly human owned and operated, a fact which did not bode well for the newest species to grace the intergalactic stage. Someone was targeting nonhuman races. Leara had vowed to persevere until she learned the motive behind it.

Leara flattened herself against the wall on one side of the massive door and nodded to Kitani, who had positioned herself on the other side. She began entering a code into the adjacent keypad, which would hopefully override the system and open the door without setting off any alarms. She stepped back to wait as the hatch slid open, expecting to hear the wail of alarm klaxons at any second. When the deserted office building remained silent, she breathed a sigh of relief.

"Don't let your guard down just yet," Kitani warned her. "Security drones patrol this area regularly. Wait here while I scout ahead. If you hear any sounds of conflict, don't hesitate. Run away from here without looking back."

Leara wanted to argue that the success of their mission was far too important for cowardice but remained silent. The golden hilt of the long curved sword sheathed at Kitani's side glinted in the pale light, reminding her sharply that the woman was a warrior, prepared to die in order to fulfill her duty and protect her charge, a truth further emphasized by the plasma pistol Kitani carried in her holster. She hoped Kitani would not have to resort to using the weapon, but she feared completing the mission without conflict was too much to ask.

When Kitani gave her the all-clear signal, Leara rushed forward to join her.

"I don't understand it," Kitani was muttering when Leara reached her. "It's as though every security drone in this place is elsewhere right now. But where? What could possibly have lured the drones away from the executive offices, even for a second?"

Leara shook her head. "I don't know. Perhaps this is the miracle we have hoped for."

"I wish I could believe that." Behind the visor of her helmet, Kitani's eyes glowed like embers in the office's semi-darkness. "But let's not allow it to distract us from our true purpose. I have had enough of this place. The sooner we have our information and are away from here, the better. I have an ominous feeling our adventure is only now truly beginning. This is too easy," she added, her voice low. "Something is about to happen, I can feel it."

"Only a little while longer, Kitani," Leara said. "Then we can go home."

Kitani bowed her head in a noble manner, but her eyes still held a trace of doubt. "I hope you're right."

With Kitani following, Leara crept toward the corridor leading to the executive offices, all the while watching the shadows warily, half expecting an ambush at any minute. One didn't simply waltz into the chief executive's office uninvited without meeting some form of resistance, she thought. She didn't doubt the corporate heads had installed all sorts of safeguards to prevent their valuable data from falling into the wrong hands.

"Please, allow me," Kitani said as they neared the large, round portal at the end of the hall. Taking a small handheld device from her pocket, she plugged it into the keypad next to the sealed entrance and began typing in commands. Leara held her breath in the brief eternity that passed before the light above the door flashed green and the portal opened in a spiral that began at its center and spread outward.

"Nice work, Kitani," Leara said softly.

Kitani squared her shoulders and stood rigid as Leara passed. "It was nothing," she said.

Leara half expected her to salute. Kitani may have been trained for the sole purpose of serving as her bodyguard, but sometimes she wished the woman wouldn't take her duty so seriously. It was disquieting to be treated with such undeserved reverence, especially when all she really wanted was to be seen as an individual.

Once inside the office, Leara sat gingerly in a chair in front of a computer console and produced a small device of her own which she connected to the dormant computer. Holding her breath once again, she awaited the sound of alarms blaring as they were discovered, but nothing happened. Everything seemed to be going according to plan until she and Kitani heard the faint murmur of voices from somewhere much closer than the street far below.

Kitani immediately snapped to attention. "*Si'rah* Leara, please," she whispered imploringly, in her panic clearly forgetting Leara's request to address her as an equal.

Leara's handheld computer would not download the files any faster, no matter how she tried to will it to do so with her mind.

Kitani's hand rested nervously on the hilt of her sword as the voices grew loud and excited. "I am sorry, but we must leave *now*," she said.

Nodding, Leara unplugged her handheld computer, knowing full well she might be jeopardizing the mission with the incomplete information stored inside. Her eyes flew open wide as an alarm wailed in the distance and warning lights began flashing around the office. She was sure their presence had at last been detected.

She didn't expect the sound of gunfire which suddenly erupted from somewhere nearby.

Uttering a mild curse, Leara kept her head low as she and Kitani made their flight from the not-so-deserted office building.

* * *

"So, Kuvair N'arex," Cybil said menacingly. "We meet again." She had at last found her target cowering like a spineless worm in one of the executive offices. The Zulian security guard sat in front of a panel of monitors; each focused on a different area in the Midas Pharmaceuticals building.

"You must be mistaken," N'arex replied. "I don't recall ever seeing you before."

Cybil eyed the Zulian with scorn. Although it was usually difficult to discern one individual from another among the amphibious humanoids, she would never forget this one's face. The long, angry scar marring his scaly complexion was a testament to his crimes.

N'arex misinterpreted her silence as ineptitude, perhaps as a result of the mind-altering drugs he pandered to colonists of Turon, Cybil thought. Smiling, he said, "You don't know me, I don't know you. I don't know how you managed to get in here at this hour, but I am willing to forget I ever saw you if you agree to go away. There might even be a little something extra in it for you." He fished in his pocket and produced a small bottle filled with brightly colored capsules. "What do you say, hmm? Do we have a deal?"

Cybil gave him a crooked smile. "Thank you. That was all I needed to hear from you." She reached behind her back, producing the plasma pistol she had been hiding. "You've made my job much easier by willingly presenting irrefutable evidence of your crimes."

Realizing too late that this woman was no mere junkie, N'arex made a move for his own weapon, but Cybil shot his hand before he could reach it. N'arex shrieked in agony as the hot blast of charged particles seared his flesh.

"Who are you?" he choked.

"This is the end of the line for you, you sadistic, drug-peddling son of a bitch." Confident of her victory, Cybil strolled forward until she was standing only a few feet from N'arex. "I don't expect you to remember me. I've changed a lot in the past twenty years, after all. But I've never forgotten about you, not for a single day. You killed my father."

N'arex's bulbous black eyes widened in recognition.

"That's right," Cybil affirmed, reading his thoughts from his expression as easily as if she possessed a powerful telepathy. "The colony on Fortuna. That was the day you received that scar, if I remember correctly. At least my father managed to get in one good swipe at you before he died. I was helpless back then, hiding and shivering in the shadows while I watched you murder my father, inciting the civil war that wiped out both our colonies. Now," she added, raising her plasma pistol until it was level with N'arex's head, "now I'm not so helpless." Squeezing the trigger, she fired a single shot that struck N'arex squarely in the forehead.

The enormous black eyes froze in shock and disbelief for a brief instant, and then lost their wet gleam, growing as dull as his scaly skin as N'arex collapsed to the floor.

Cybil could not bring herself to pity him. The encounter with the Zulian brought back memories of one of her darkest days. In her mind's eye, she saw her father slump to the ground as a spray of blood danced in the air behind his head, and her own blood ran cold.

A chorus of blaring alarms erupted nearby, prompting Cybil to incline her head so she could speak directly into the tiny transmitter embedded in the collar of her combat armor. She whispered, "Cybil to *Kashmir II*, requesting urgent action. Pick me up at the east side of Midas Pharmaceuticals. I repeat; this is urgent!"

A brief pause left Cybil worrying if her ship's AI program would respond to her call, but she didn't have to wait long before a deeper shadow fell across the darkened window. The *Kashmir II* was hovering just above her location.

She fired a short burst from her plasma pistol to break the glass and leapt into the open port airlock. She heard plasma shots from a group of backup security drones striking the hull of her ship as the hatch slid shut, but the thrusters kicked in, and the ship sped away just as the sun crested the mountains.

"Impeccable timing as usual, Kashmir," she said, unfastening her cloak and tossing it aside as she strode from the decontamination chamber to the bridge to find the fresh change of clothes waiting for her. She could hardly wait to get out of her sweaty combat armor.

After zipping herself into a deep blue jumpsuit and tightening the belt at her waist, Cybil felt like a new woman. The purification process of the decon chamber left her feeling thoroughly cleansed without the need for water and also eliminated any potentially hazardous bacteria she might have unwittingly brought aboard from her last mission. One could never be too careful, especially when dealing with a corporation with a reputation like Midas Pharmaceuticals.

"Could you be any more reckless?" A sensual voice purred from overhead, sounding playful and a bit sultry. Cybil thought the voice of the *Kashmir II*'s AI program was as alluring as the woman after which it had been named, the same woman who had provided her with the information for her last mission as well as many others.

Designed as a personal escort craft with the weapons and maneuverability of an elite corvette, the *Kashmir II* was a state-of-the-art spacecraft employing some of the most advanced technology available, so there was no need for Cybil to remain at the controls. The highly advanced artificial intelligence was perfectly capable of piloting when she stepped away.

“So tell me, captain, do you plan on settling down any time soon?” Kashmir asked. “The perils of this uncertain life are bound to catch up to you eventually.”

“I knew this job was dangerous when I took it.” Even after more than a year of owning the *Kashmir II*, Cybil still found it uncanny how much the AI’s quirks and comments resembled the real Kashmir. Sometimes, it felt as though she was speaking to the woman herself instead of the ship’s computer.

Nevertheless, she decided, the AI had a point. Having a warm, loving woman to return to after each daring, perilous mission wouldn’t be such a bad thing.

The AI made a deep, breathy hum as it sent the mission report to Cybil’s employer. For an instant, Cybil felt a stir of arousal while listening to the seductive voice, and then she gave herself a mental shake. Space could be a lonely place, but that was no reason to begin lusting after a machine, she told herself. Perhaps there would be time to quell her loneliness when she went to collect her payment, which would be soon enough.

Chapter 2

"Thank the Goddess that's over," Kitani muttered under her breath when she and Leara at last reached their ship. After using a hand sanitizer, she removed the contact lenses concealing her natural eye color. When she next met Leara's gaze, her eyes were fiery orange, each split down the middle by a long, elliptical pupil.

Leara was not surprised by the transformation. She took Kitani's actions as a cue to remove her own contact lenses. She blinked a few times, her eyes adjusting to the feeling of being bare. She had been hiding her true identity so long it felt strange to be unmasked and the truth of her species laid bare.

She and Kitani were Valori, an ancient race of humanoids hailing from the planet Aria. In fact, of all the races represented in the Senate, the Valori were closest in appearance to humans except for a few minor cosmetic differences such as the catlike eyes, which could be easily covered. Kitani's natural hair color was outstanding, a pure snowy white which, from what they had heard, was uncommon among young humans. She had been forced to darken her hair to platinum blonde, but after months of working undercover at Midas Pharmaceuticals, the color was beginning to fade.

Leara sighed, exhausted from the night's exertions. Six months working undercover as Midas Pharmaceuticals employees had been trying. Posing as human women was no easy task, either. It was longer than either she or Kitani had ever spent away from their homeworld, but their work was not finished yet. Since the information she had downloaded from the computer in the main office was incomplete, their only option was to resort to the backup plan.

Her thoughts were interrupted by a gentle nudge on her arm. "We must leave now," Kitani said urgently. The orange eyes gazed pleadingly at her. "Turon is no longer safe for us."

"I agree." Leara knew their safety had been compromised the moment they set foot in Midas Pharmaceuticals. Whatever had raised the alarm hadn't helped. She thought it likely that the whole building and its perimeters had been closely monitored from the second their presence was discovered—yet another reason they should make a hasty departure from the planet. In a few hours, they would be two of the most wanted women on Turon, if not the entire galaxy.

Leara quietly strapped herself into the navigator's seat as Kitani prepared to take off. Once she was settled, she pulled a small round disk from the pocket of her jacket.

"All that trouble, all those long months of pretending," she said softly, holding the disk aloft and inspecting it while keeping her contempt carefully restrained. "In the end it was all for naught."

"We did the best we could," Kitani said soothingly. "Had we not escaped when we did, no doubt we would have been overtaken by a horde of angry security officers. Damn it!" She slammed her fist against the console. "Everything was going according to plan until fighting erupted in the other room. Who else could have been in the executive offices besides us?"

"I'm afraid I cannot answer that question," Leara said, wondering who had caused their mission to end so badly.

"To Kronos, then?" Kitani asked, hesitating a little.

"Given the circumstances, what other choice do we have?" Leara slid the disk back into her pocket and placed her hand over it protectively.

The lives of many people, including those of innocent and unsuspecting Valori, were riding on finding the irrefutable proof of Midas Pharmaceuticals' heinous crimes. Two Valori had lost their lives already. Whether or not this was due to Midas Pharmaceuticals remained to be seen.

Leara knew they could not give up if they wished to preserve peace throughout the galaxy, even if that meant venturing into the uncharted wilds of Kronos, braving subzero temperatures in order to locate their goal.

* * *

The interior of the space station Eden IV was hectic and bustling as usual. For a fleeting instant, Cybil nearly balked at the sight of so many people. Accustomed to the lonely life of a space mercenary and the dangers and wariness such a profession entailed, she found large crowds unnerving. The loud voices and smells of so many humans and aliens assailed her nostrils. She couldn't fathom what it must be like for some of the alien races whose noses were supposedly many times more sensitive than a human's. In all truth, she didn't want to imagine such a thing.

Taking a deep breath, she stepped from the platform leading to the docking bay and descended the stairs to the markets. There she was welcomed by a gigantic sign bearing the message "Welcome to Eden." Eden IV was a veritable paradise, she thought. Constructed from a hollowed asteroid, the space station looked every bit as rough as its reputation. Within the deceptively small metal hull, Eden IV was surprisingly like a large city, containing both shops and thoroughfares lined with vendors peddling their wares.

Cybil was not here to shop. Her purpose lay beyond the markets, in the grand casino that towered over the other buildings in Eden IV. Its twinkling lights shimmered like stars against the black rock and metal alloy used to construct the outer walls of the space station.

Cloud Nine Casino was the largest casino in Eden IV, and probably one of the most famous—or infamous, depending on who was asked—in the Milky Way. Cybil exited the elevator on the top floor and glanced around the huge room filled with gamblers and fortune seekers. She didn't have to look long before she caught sight of the person she wanted to meet.

The woman stood on the stage at the far end of the room. Her hair was dyed a very unnatural shade of blue to match the outfit she wore as well as the color scheme of the suite, appropriately called the Sapphire Room. She pursed her lips, also colored blue, and blew a kiss to the audience as she wrapped a long leg around the translucent glass pole protruding from the stage floor and extending to the ceiling. Her hips swayed suggestively. The room erupted in a chorus of cheers and applause as the lights on the stage dimmed until only the blue of the woman's hair, lips, and clothing remained visible, glowing luminously against the darkness before they, too, disappeared.

Cybil stood rooted in place by the elevator. Some of her earlier unbridled longing for female company returned as she watched the erotic dance. By now, other entertainers were taking the stage, but these women, though lovely, did not hold the power and mystique of their predecessor. Still, their supple bodies and sensual movements set her blood boiling and ignited a fire deep within her loins. She was so entranced by the dancers' performances, in fact, that she failed to notice another person coming to stand at her shoulder.

"Enjoying the act?" a familiar voice cooed in her ear.

Cybil jumped, prompting a laugh from the blue-haired woman who had graced the stage only a moment before. As she tried to cover her embarrassment at being caught leering at the performers, the woman ceased laughing, her expression growing serious.

"Come," she instructed in a firm tone. "Let us find somewhere more private so we can discuss business." She turned to make her way through the crowd.

Kashmir was a sight to behold, Cybil thought as she followed the woman. With her long legs and shapely figure, she was one of the most popular entertainers on the space station. Although human, she attracted the attentions of many races and many genders from across the galaxy, which was how she came across much of the vital information she passed on to Cybil and other freelance mercenaries who worked for her.

Exotic entertainer by day, leader of Eden IV's secret underworld of vigilantes by night, Kashmir was perfectly suited to the task, Cybil decided. And she paid well, too, a result of all the clients she received during her business days, some of them rather prominent in society and quite rich. In fact, her ship, the *Kashmir II*, had been obtained from such a man, a Zulian governor who had been so enamored with Kashmir he'd named the vessel after her. Having no need for such a thing herself, Kashmir had presented it to Cybil as a token of her gratitude.

"I see you've survived yet another brush with death," Kashmir said as she and Cybil sat at a small table in the darkest corner of the Sapphire Room. She moistened her full lips with her tongue. Surprisingly, the blue lipstick did not so much as smudge at the contact. She continued, "I take it that Kuvair N'arex has been successfully eliminated?"

"His days of running drugs supplied by Midas Pharmaceuticals are over," Cybil told her. "He won't be troubling you again."

"And were you met with any opposition?"

Cybil paused. "Only a few security drones. What you would expect from a corporate office building like Midas Pharmaceuticals. Why do you ask?"

"No reason. Only it would seem that you were not the only one sneaking around the executive offices last night. You always have been one to charge headlong right into the heart of danger, Cybil. I must commend you for your tenacity." Kashmir gave her a seductive smile as she slowly crossed her legs, the skin tight fabric of her short skirt stretching until Cybil thought it would come apart at the seams.

Her staring did not go unnoticed.

"Would you like a free lap dance?" Kashmir asked. "In addition to your usual payment, of course."

Averting her gaze to the floor, Cybil quickly cleared her throat. "That won't be necessary. The payment we agreed upon will suffice."

Kashmir's sudden appearance and the bustling crowd in the Sapphire Room had been sufficient to quell Cybil's raging libido. Her only interests at the moment were collecting her payment and returning to the quiet solitude of her ship.

"You're not much fun," Kashmir said, pouting. "But you don't let anything stand in your way of completing a mission. That's why I value your services above those of my other mercenaries, Cybil. So, how would you feel about undertaking another such daring mission immediately?"

Cybil leaned forward on her elbows, her curiosity piqued. "I'm listening," she said.

"Now that I have your undivided attention," Kashmir said as she uncrossed her legs in another purposeful distraction, "I have something very interesting to tell you."

Cybil didn't so much as bat an eyelash at Kashmir's deliberate attempt, so the blue-haired woman went on.

"Remember when I said you weren't the only one at Midas Pharmaceuticals last night? Recently I received information of a security breach in one of the executive offices. Apparently someone infiltrated their headquarters last night and gained access to some top-secret files."

"What kind of files, exactly?" Cybil asked, not liking where this was heading one bit. Midas Pharmaceuticals had a rather notorious reputation. Kuvair N'arex had been just one of many corrupt individuals hiding in the corporation's shadow.

Shaking her head, Kashmir said, "Sensitive intel was compromised, and as a result, many at Midas may lose their jobs. I know this isn't along the lines of your usual missions, but it would be much appreciated if you would track down the infiltrator and retrieve the information. And as always, it pays very well."

"I thought you were against Midas Pharmaceuticals and all it stands for," Cybil said carefully. "Why, just a minute ago you were practically cheering at my disposal of one of its top security officers. Just how much is this mysterious client of yours paying?"

Smiling coyly, Kashmir said, "There's more to this than you realize, Cybil. Much more. I have no interest in protecting Midas Pharmaceuticals or its employees. However, the fact that someone acting on behalf of Midas would resort to hiring a mercenary to retrieve the information intrigues me. If I could get my hands on the missing information, I might finally be able to see just what Midas Pharmaceuticals is up to. What about you? Are you game?"

Cybil knew her eyes must be shining with interest. Smiling slightly, she said, "So you intend on betraying them and keeping the information for yourself? Count me in. Something about Midas Pharmaceuticals makes my skin crawl. Just tell me what I need to do."

"Excellent," Kashmir said, sighing in what sounded like relief. "My client will be pleased. Well, for a while, at least. Surveillance equipment captured an image of two women leaving Midas Pharmaceuticals early this morning, just before daybreak."

"This client of yours must have come to you immediately after the breach occurred," Cybil said.

"Yes. As I said before, this information could be devastating in the wrong hands. Anyway, my network of spies and informants has been tracking the targets' vessel across the galaxy and has successfully pinpointed its location. At the time of their last checkpoint, the ship was orbiting near Kronos."

"Kronos?" Cybil asked incredulously. "Why would they take such valuable information to that frozen wasteland?"

"Your guess is as good as mine. Kronos's unforgiving climate makes it the perfect place to deal in all sorts of shady business without fear of intrusion. Perhaps the targets have agreed to meet a buyer somewhere on this frozen world."

"If that's the case," Cybil said, rising from her chair, "then I should go to Kronos as quickly as possible, before the targets have the chance to meet this alleged buyer. It will be easier to retrieve the information if it doesn't change hands."

"Precisely the kind of fast thinking I need on a mission like this, Cybil. I will contact you if my spies detect a change in their course, or if any new information presents itself."

"Fair enough. You know where to reach me." Cybil stood, extending a hand across the table to Kashmir before departing.

Exiting Cloud Nine Casino, Cybil started to return to the docking bay and then reconsidered, taking a quick detour through a side alley. She had been adrift in space for a while with only her ship's AI for company. A quick rendezvous with some old friends might be just what she needed before setting out on her next adventure. And the Midnight Suns might have intel on the recent activities on Turon.

The Dark Star Tavern seemed as formidable as ever, nestled in an isolated location in the lower wards of Eden IV. A frequent haunt of the Midnight Suns and other mercenaries, the tavern was as good a place as any for her to search.

The atmosphere inside the tavern was dark and oppressive. As soon as she stepped over the threshold, Cybil found herself feeling like a kid again, as if she didn't belong in such a place. Aware these thoughts were silly, she couldn't help feeling that some of the stares her sudden appearance garnered were not entirely welcoming.

Ignoring the sensation and the way it made her hair stand on end, Cybil made her way to the bar and ordered a drink. An unexpected thump on the back nearly caused her to fall off the stool. She whirled around, her hand on the butt of the plasma pistol concealed beneath her cloak.

"Easy, Reynard." Riley gave Cybil a goofy grin as she raised her hands, keeping them in front of her in plain sight. "Is that any way to greet a former shipmate?" she asked.

"She probably thought you were a space scoundrel looking to start trouble," Ashley chimed in, stepping out from behind Riley. "And the sad part is she wouldn't be that far from the truth."

"Come on now. I'm not that bad." To Cybil, Riley said, "So, runt, how has the freelancing business been treating you?"

Cybil relaxed, leaning back against the bar and propping herself up with her elbows. "Can't complain. A job is a job, no matter who you're working for." She recalled that at one point, she had contemplated joining the Midnight Suns. She had grown so close to Ashley, Riley, and the others during her childhood that it seemed inevitable. Her decision to go solo had surprised everyone, including herself. Even now, she was tempted to don the black armor that Ashley and Riley both wore to represent their fierce pride and passion. The emblazoned circle of orange adorning the breastplate symbolized their strength as well as their unity.

In many ways, the mercenary group was like a family, but Cybil's tragic past had kept her at a distance. To belong to something greater than herself had been a luxury that she couldn't afford… until now.

Although the Midnight Suns claimed there were no hard feelings, Cybil sensed her decision had somehow distanced her from them. She had hoped that by going to the Dark Star, she could dislodge the invisible wedge between them.

"I hear you recently took down Kuvair N'arex," Riley continued cautiously.

Word traveled fast among the mercenary groups, so it was no surprise that news of this event had reached the ears of her friends, Cybil thought.

Riley must have known she was treading in dangerous territory since she worded her next question with obvious care. "How did it feel to pull the trigger on the guy who betrayed your colony and murdered your father?" she asked.

Cybil remained silent for a long pause before smiling broadly. So much uncertainty filled her mind that smiling was the only way to hide her feelings from her friends. "Like having a weight lifted off me," she said. Killing N'arex had been one of the greatest, most fulfilling moments of her life, which made her worry and wonder if it was a normal reaction for a mercenary to feel when taking a life. Was she truly so devoid of joy that she was beginning to enjoy the act of killing? She felt her smile waver as she continued, "It's like everything holding me back has finally been removed. Like I can at last move on."

"Look out, universe," Riley said cheerfully. "Cybil Reynard is off her leash. So what do you plan on doing next?"

"That's the problem. I haven't really ever given it much thought. I've been commissioned for another job, but after that, it's anyone's guess."

"Have you considered settling down?" The question came from Ashley, who leaned affectionately against Riley as she spoke.

"Have you?" Cybil countered.

Both women looked uncomfortably at each other and glanced away. "After years of serving Captain Jarvis, domestic life wouldn't suit us," Ashley replied.

"Hanging out all day sounds dreadfully boring to me," Riley added.

"So I take it that neither of you are planning on retiring any time soon?" Cybil asked.

"A Midnight Sun does not retire," Ashley said with pride.

"They just fade away," Riley said jokingly and winced as Ashley elbowed her in the ribs.

"Where is Captain Jarvis?" Cybil asked, looking around as if noticing his absence for the first time. In truth, she was well aware of the captain's apparent aversion to company. Given Ashley and

Riley's reluctance to retire, she thought she understood why. A veteran of the First Contact Wars which had ended thirty-eight years before, Captain Jarvis must be well into his seventies, if not older, she thought. She recalled thinking he was an old man when she first met the Suns twenty years ago.

Nodding towards the corner, Ashley said in a near whisper, "Over there."

Cybil looked. Jarvis sat at a booth in the darkest corner of the tavern, hunched over the table, and leaned on his elbows with his head hung low. When she approached him, he raised his eyes, met her gaze, and smiled, surprising her.

"Welcome back, Cybil," he said kindly. "You hardly ever visit us anymore. It's good to see you again." He spoke more like a doting father than a rough and tough space mercenary, Cybil thought, but in the absence of her own family, she *had* come to view him as a surrogate father. "Did you finally take care of that unfinished business that has been plaguing you since we first met?" he asked.

"Yeah," Cybil replied, taking a seat across from Jarvis. "N'arex will never betray anyone again. And he won't cause any more children to become bitter orphans, either."

"Then justice has been served."

She and Jarvis sat for a long while in silence before she asked, "Have you heard anything from Sierra?"

"Not a word," he answered.

Cybil had suspected as much. Eight years earlier, her childhood friend and fellow orphan, Sierra Callaway, had suddenly vanished without a trace. Neither Cybil nor any of Sierra's former allies had heard from her since.

"I suppose that's gratitude for you," she joked but fell silent when she recalled her own decision to go solo when the Midnight Suns had expected her to join. The mercenaries had practically raised Sierra and her. Was sudden defection any way to repay them? She felt a little guilty. Even when she and Sierra had spent time in an orphanage on a backwater planet, the Midnight Suns had ensured they were well looked after, and the members had visited often.

"I'm sure Sierra has her reasons," Jarvis said. "I only wish I knew what they were."

"She vowed to go after the ones responsible for her mother's death, but never once have I run across Sierra in the mercenary business," Cybil said.

Nearly twenty years before, the genetic engineering laboratory where Sierra's mother worked, Touchstone Cybernetics, had been destroyed, incinerated by an explosion that completely obliterated all traces of the facility's research. Popular speculation concurred that the research the scientists were working on had proved too volatile and the explosion was merely an accident that occurred as a result of their boldness. However, there were some who believed Touchstone Cybernetics had been a target due to some controversial, secret research. Sierra was one of those people.

There were times when Cybil had wondered just what those scientists had been doing that could've attracted such negative attention, but if Sierra knew, she had never let on.

"Do you think she changed her name?" she asked as an afterthought.

"Didn't you vow to avenge her mother's misfortune as well?" Jarvis asked. Cybil accepted the sudden subject change and nodded. He went on, "Have you come any closer to learning the truth about what happened to those scientists? Because in finding the culprits behind the catastrophe at that genetic engineering lab, you may very well find Sierra."

"My resources are continually scouring the galaxies for information, but so far I haven't come across any real leads. Whoever planned the incident knew what they were doing and covered their trail effectively."

"Are you guys talking about Sierra?" Riley asked, displaying a keen interest in the subject. She joined Cybil and Jarvis, followed by Ashley. "It's like she vanished into the inky blackness of space without even offering a proper farewell."

"Sierra's trail is almost as difficult to follow as that of the culprits behind the incident, if not more so," Cybil agreed. "But I will find her, mark my words. And when I do, I'll bring her back and see what kind of excuse I can drag out of her for going so long without contacting us."

That seemed to alleviate some of the tension in the room, as well as placate Riley's irritation. "See you later, runt," Riley said when Cybil rose from the table. "Oh, but I can't rightly call you runt anymore, can I? Especially not when you're taller than I am." She made a show of measuring the difference in their height with her hand, and then her expression grew more serious. "See you later, Reynard. May you have the best of luck on your next mission."

"Thanks, Riley." Cybil turned to go, but not before offering a last salute to her friends and former comrades. Walking out the door, she headed down the narrow side street, her mind already focused on what lay ahead.

Somewhere out there, she needed to find two women who knew too much about the shady dealings of Midas Pharmaceuticals. Perhaps when she apprehended them and reclaimed the information, she would be one step closer to understanding what was really happening with Midas Pharmaceuticals.

Chapter 3

The sky above Kronos was overcast as the dark, low-lying clouds promised a blizzard to come. As soon as Leara set foot outside the warmth of the ship, she found herself wishing she could remain within the metal hull, protected against the harsh elements of the frozen world. Instead, she pulled the collar of the insulated jacket closer around her neck and trudged after Kitani.

The insulated clothing she and Kitani wore gleamed silver in the bright sunlight, providing ample camouflage against the intense white blanketing the surrounding landscape. The internal heating units located in hidden pockets of their jackets also helped somewhat, since the insulated outfits worked as conduits for the warm air to circulate.

As a safety precaution, she and Kitani had decided to land their ship far away from the outpost facility, not realizing this decision would entail walking nearly two miles through knee-deep snow to reach their destination. To make matters worse, they couldn't even count on better weather to relieve their torment. The clouds threatened to cover the world with another layer of fresh snow at any moment.

"Damn this Kronos weather," Kitani mumbled as she walked ahead of Leara. Her words were muffled as if her mouth had frozen—not entirely impossible since they were walking headfirst into the biting wind. "No wonder Midas chose this planet for its outpost. The terrain itself is a safeguard against anyone accidentally stumbling upon its heinous research. It's quite possibly one of the most ingenious plans I've heard of." She sneezed and muttered a mild curse.

Leara paused, gazing out across the snow-capped mountains that sprang up from the earth like jagged fangs. "This world is actually quite beautiful, in its own right," she said, knowing her soft voice would barely carry over the roaring wind and Kitani would have to strain her sensitive ears to discern her words.

"I suppose it does contain a certain charm," Kitani conceded. "But it is one that is best enjoyed as a work of art, preferably one displayed in a warm gallery."

"Be grateful for this opportunity, Kitani," Leara said, laughing "Not all Valori have the chance to embark on an adventure such as this. I certainly never would have believed I would receive such a chance."

"What makes you say that?"

"You're a warrior, Kitani. It's not so unusual for someone like you to be sent on a dangerous errand to prove her worth. But for me, the daughter of High Matriarch Dallia Sorani, a Valori whose only duties in life are to be groomed to become a great matriarch herself someday… for me, this is the chance of a lifetime. An opportunity to set out, see the galaxy, and meet all manner of people may never present itself to me again. That is the bane of being destined for something *greater*." She spoke the last word with slight disdain.

"I never thought of it that way," Kitani admitted, sounding shy.

Lost in thought, Leara did not reply. Although she had known Kitani since they were both very young and Kitani was being groomed to become a Matriarchal Paladin, she only now realized her friend didn't know her very well at all. Though sworn to protect her at all costs for as long as she lived, Kitani was a stranger to her.

Matriarchal Paladins were an ancient Valori custom, one that dated back even before the elders of the current High Matriarchs were children. Like so many Valori customs, the Paladins were likely to endure for as many more centuries. Being a long-lived race, with some individuals even reaching the age of a thousand or more, the Valori saw many new things come and go in their long lives and so cherished such old traditions that withstood the test of time. As a result, many of the buildings on their homeworld were the remnants of the generations who came before them, and some were now crumbling to the ground. Despite the many advances in space exploration they now possessed, the Valori remained clannish, shying away from colonizing worlds alongside other species in the past. However, if Midas Pharmaceuticals had its way, the Valori might not have another chance for colonization in the future

Leara shivered despite the protection of the insulated jacket. She brushed past Kitani, lowering her head to avoid the worst of the cold wind. She had delayed their progress long enough. Somewhere within the frozen mountains lay the proof of potentially the worst threat her people had ever faced. Even if no one believed her suspicions, she could not sit idly by and allow a slumbering beast to awaken.

* * *

Immediately after making landfall on Kronos, Cybil found herself wishing she was anywhere else in the universe other than the frozen planet. The howling wind was fierce enough to penetrate through her insulated clothing and the thermal underwear she wore beneath her combat suit. The biting cold did nothing to ease her already foul mood. *Damn those blasted women! Couldn't they find someplace warmer to conduct their business*?

Despite her irritation, Cybil couldn't blame the women for choosing Kronos. The world's harsh, almost uninhabitable climate provided the isolation required to make a secret transaction without fear of being followed. After all, who in their right mind would willingly land on such an unforgiving planet? *I suppose that makes you a lunatic, Cybil*, she chided herself, which didn't make the cold go away, but did help take her mind off the fact she could no longer feel her fingers inside the thick gloves she wore.

Reaching into the inner pocket of her jacket, she pulled out a handheld thermal scanner and began checking the nearby wilderness for signs of life. According to Kashmir's spies, the enemy vessel had touched down somewhere close to where her own ship was currently hidden, but she had difficulty believing anyone or anything could survive long in this weather.

A blip flickered faintly on the scanner's small screen, and then disappeared completely. Cursing, Cybil waved the device in the air above her head. When she lowered the device to examine it again, a round white shape appeared on the screen, soon joined by others of its kind.

Cybil looked at the sky in time to see a flurry of soft white snowflakes drifting silently to the ground. Zipping up the jacket to her chin, she turned and trudged through the deepening snow in the direction of her target, which, to her utter confusion, happened to be in an outpost facility owned and operated by none other than Midas Pharmaceuticals itself. Why in the worlds would the women be taking the stolen information back to the very people they had obtained it from in the first place?

Shaking her head, she exhaled and her breath formed a cloud of mist in the air. Sometimes her targets' actions were unfathomable, but luckily, she wasn't being paid to understand why people did the things they did. Her job was simply to apprehend these two women and retrieve the stolen data, she reminded herself for what seemed like the thousandth time that day. When she dealt with the targets, she would have to make sure she did not damage the disk if she could help it. Kashmir wanted desperately to get her hands on that information, and she would likely pay a generous sum if Cybil could deliver it to her intact.

And now to find the mystery women, she thought. But this time, finding her target was only half the problem. Infiltrating the heavily guarded research facility without being blasted to bits by security drones constituted the other half of her dilemma.

The remainder of her brisk hike through the mountains proved uneventful and cold. By the time Cybil reached the base of the massive hill, she felt frozen to the bone. The outpost facility was in sight now, but the most difficult part of her journey was only beginning.

No sooner had Cybil come in sight of the colossal compound than she came under fire from two enormous gun turrets mounted on either side of the main entrance. A searing blast of energy struck the left shoulder of her combat armor before she could take cover. *The women had the right idea by taking an alternate route*, she thought wryly as she ducked behind a rock and listened as the boulder was pounded into gravel by rapid-fire blasts from the gun turrets. Bits of rock rained down on her, striking her helmet and armor before cascading to the ground. Wondering how she could escape the situation, she hunkered down behind the diminishing boulder, contemplating her next course of action. The answer presented itself in a most unlikely way when, as if by some miracle, the gun turrets suddenly and unexpectedly disengaged, retreating into their domed coverings.

Not wasting a second of the reprieve, Cybil approached the facility's door and used a tiny handheld computer to decrypt the entrance code. She pressed herself flat against the side of the building as the door raised, keeping her plasma pistol ready. Though she could not understand her lucky break with the gun turrets, she knew the danger was far from over.

* * *

Leara strode silently past the inert guard, treading lightly for fear of attracting any unwanted attention. The guard had stepped through an emergency door located at the back of the building only to be met by Kitani's fist. So far she and Kitani had been able to infiltrate the outpost facility without any problems save for this one guard, but one careless mistake could alter their good fortune.

Kitani stepped over the prostrate guard and through the open door to where Leara waited. "We should hurry. He won't be out very long, and when he wakes, he'll undoubtedly set every guard in this place on our trail. It would be easier to just kill him, but—"

Leara gave Kitani a knowing smile. "But that is not the Valori way," she finished. "There's no need for unnecessary violence. As soon as we reach the labs and retrieve the crucial bit of evidence needed for our quest, this will all be over. We'll sneak out the back door without even being noticed. It will be easier now that we've deactivated the gun turrets mounted around the compound."

"And if we're noticed…" Kitani said, waving a plasma pistol in the air to call attention to it. "Such a cowardly weapon, completely lacking the honor and grace of a sword. I don't particularly enjoy the idea of using one of these on an unsuspecting person, but drastic times demand drastic measures."

"Only a little while longer." Leara kept her voice calm and reassuring, completely the opposite of how she truly felt. "Do you have the equipment ready?"

Kitani pulled a small camera from her jacket and showed it to her.

Leara nodded approvingly. "Good. I believe we're almost to the labs. Get ready, Kitani. Anything could be waiting on the other side of that door." She motioned to the sealed door at the end of the dark corridor.

A look of apprehension crept into Kitani's stern and proud features. *So headstrong and bold, yet so innocent*, Leara thought as they pressed onward. Indeed, beneath the warrior's dashing and prideful exterior beat a heart of gold. She only hoped Kitani's kind heart and gallantry weren't forever tarnished during this mission.

Leara was beginning to wonder if it had been a mistake to bring Kitani along, but she knew she would have had it no other way. She understood that as a Matriarchal Paladin, it was Kitani's life ambition to protect the Sorani family, even if her induction into the ancient order had not been as traditional as others. She knew about the "wild blood" flowing through Kitani's veins, the blood of the forest dwelling apostates who refused to bend to the Supreme Matriarchy's rule.

Kitani's mother had paid with her life for the crime of nonconformity, Leara had been told, the execution order given by none other than Dallia Sorani herself. Was it any wonder the Sorani family was looked upon by so many Valori with terror as well as awe?

Leara sighed. Sometimes being the only daughter of a living legend made her life a living nightmare. She didn't like feeling this way and even felt some degree of shame for having such dour thoughts regarding her destiny, but she couldn't help it. Her mother was the most powerful—and some would say the most beautiful—woman on her home planet. Dallia's strength and courage didn't come merely from her honored position. Living up to her mother's fame and fierce reputation wasn't going to be easy. She didn't look forward to trying.

Leara remained silent while she and Kitani proceeded through the lab area until they rounded a corner and came upon a brightly lit area.

"By the Goddess," Kitani mumbled, a pallor spreading beneath her olive-toned skin.

For a moment, Leara feared the Valori warrior would faint from the sight in front of them. "Get the camera ready," she instructed Kitani in what she hoped was a steady voice. "The Supreme Matriarchy must see this."

* * *

Hearing alarms blaring, Cybil cursed silently. She checked her scanner, which had been malfunctioning since landing on Kronos, and saw a faint blip flashing intermittently at the top corner. The blip was moving rapidly in her direction and, though she couldn't be sure, she thought she briefly saw a second blip trailing close behind the first. The two blips could be her targets, but she wasn't holding her breath. She reminded herself that the two blips could be guards, or even security drones locked in on her location, and prepared accordingly. Whatever was heading her way with such speed would have to cross the large observatory ahead of her. She would be waiting, tucked securely away in the shadows.

She moved swiftly into position at the end of the corridor and aimed her gun at the center of the room. She checked the scanner lying on the floor next to her just in time to see the blip disappear. She waited for the target to appear, but there were no signs of life, neither ahead of her nor on the radar screen.

Slowly, carefully, Cybil rose from her crouched position. Stepping just inside the open area, she was nearly taken down by a dark shape moving around the perimeter of the room. She brought her gun up defensively, but there wasn't enough room to fire. However, having a plasma pistol aimed at its head was enough to stop the fleeing figure in its tracks.

Cybil took an assertive step forward, then another, and continued until she had successfully backed the figure into the center of the room, where silvery moonlight streamed in through a vast skylight. Beneath the three moons' illumination, she could clearly discern the features of a woman dressed in insulated clothing similar to her own, a woman who appeared very unlikely to be either a guard or a scientist at the facility. She believed she had found one of her targets at last, but when she took one step closer, she froze.

The woman's eyes were wide in shock, giving Cybil a clear view of the elliptical pupils, even through the visor of her helmet. She watched in dazed fascination as the pupils constricted to narrow slits until they nearly faded entirely into the woman's almost luminescent blue irises.

"You're a Valori?" Cybil asked, barely finding her voice. The meeting was unexpected, since the Valori were typically a peaceful race. In all her years as a mercenary, she had never once been hired to assassinate a Valori. Indeed, this was her first time standing so close to one.

The Valori merely stared at her, the elliptical pupils narrowed to hairline slits from fear as she awaited her fate. Cybil tried desperately to regain her composure, but before she could do so, a sharp pain erupted in her right side and she was sent flying across the room.

A control panel along the edge of the opposite wall stopped her flight, and the force of her body's impact left a large dent in the metal console. A burning sensation erupted along her right shoulder, leaving her unable to feel the pain of the surprise attack for the intense fire coursing through her body. Before she could stagger to her feet, her assailant appeared, standing over her. A second Valori, she realized, stood before her in the pale moonlight. The new Valori twirled around in midair, striking her again with a powerful kick to the ribs. She coughed as she struggled to her knees, feeling certain that something was broken.

The second Valori looked down on her with disdain. "Stay in your place, human," she said coldly, "unless you wish to die."

Determined not to be fazed by the Valori's threats, Cybil pulled herself to her feet to stand on wobbly legs, staring proudly and defiantly at her assailant.

"I warned you," the Valori said, drawing out a plasma pistol and aiming it at Cybil's head.

"Enough." The voice, soft as silk yet powerful enough to stop the tall Valori in her tracks, came from across the room where the blue-eyed Valori stood. "We didn't come here to randomly kill innocent bystanders," the Valori continued in a calm, cool tone. She sounded as cold and unfathomable as her icy eyes, yet her voice evoked sensations of peace and tranquility within Cybil.

The orange-eyed Valori, whom Cybil had heard named Kitani, looked at her companion in apparent bewilderment. "But she was pointing a gun at you, Leara. If not for my intervention, she surely would have killed you."

"But she didn't, even though she had ample opportunity. That's what truly matters." The calm, almost angelic voice seemed to soothe the edgy Kitani, but the implications behind the softly spoken words abraded Cybil.

Raising the gun with a shaky hand, she aimed it directly at Leara's heart. Before she could even contemplate pulling the trigger, however, Kitani grabbed her arm and twisted it until she was forced to drop the plasma pistol at her feet.

The look of mild amusement never left Leara's face. "Although your aggression toward me is unfounded," she said to Cybil. "Your tenacity is admirable."

"Foolish," Kitani muttered under her breath. Giving Cybil's arm a final twist, she released it. "Forgive my insolence, Leara, but we don't have time to deal with this human riffraff. Our objective has been accomplished. The entire complex is set to self-destruct in less than ten minutes."

Cybil felt her breath catch when she heard Kitani speak. "Self-destruct?" she managed to choke out. "You set the complex to self-destruct?" As if to confirm the truth of Kitani's words, a voice, most likely the facility's AI program, began rattling off a series of warnings over the intercom.

"Attention all Midas employees, this station's security has been breached," intoned the artificial female voice from the intercom. "The self-destruct order has been issued and will be executed in nine minutes, thirty-six seconds. For your safety, please evacuate to the nearest emergency escape craft." The voice began repeating the warning.

That explains the lack of guards, Cybil thought, trying to remain calm despite the severity of her situation. Into the built-in microphone inside her collar, she said, "Cybil to *Kashmir II*, requesting immediate evac. I'm now sending you my coordinates." She knew the coordinates weren't necessary, but it was a precaution worth taking. Although the *Kashmir II* automatically kept track of her using a microchip embedded in her suit, she felt safer giving the ship her exact location using the small scanner.

Ignoring the two Valori and their curious glances, she strode over to the wall console she'd slammed into earlier and began entering data. Filled with the desire to live, she almost failed to notice the scarlet stain spreading outward on the shoulder of her jacket. The plasma blast from the gun turret earlier had scorched through her armor. She had been so preoccupied with tracking her target that she had not noticed the blood—and the pain—until now. A few drops of blood spattered the console as she leaned over, but this was neither the time nor the place to dress her wounds, she decided. With just a few minutes until the whole place erupted in a burst of flame, survival was the only thing that mattered.

Just as she'd hoped, the massive glass ceiling began sliding slowly to one side, giving the *Kashmir II* ample space to make the pickup. A cascade of white flakes streamed in through the open skylight. She noticed the snowfall had increased drastically since she was last outside. Shivering, she zipped up the front of her jacket. All she could do now was wait and hope that the *Kashmir II* would be able to pinpoint her location in the blizzard.

"Pardon me," Leara said from behind Cybil. "If you have an escape plan, we'd like very much to be a part of it."

Of all the nerve, Cybil thought. Actually, during all the excitement, she had all but forgotten about her mission to apprehend the Valori and retrieve the data. But with so little time remaining before the facility self-destructed, she was in no mood to carry out the orders and possibly become involved in another altercation with Kitani, who still glared challengingly at her. Such unnecessary bickering could cost all of them their lives. But how was she to obtain the missing information?

In a gust of wind that nearly knocked Cybil and the Valori to the ground, the *Kashmir II* appeared, a dark shape amidst the white hovering just inside the open dome.

"Three minutes, twenty seconds until detonation," the facility's AI announced.

"Your assistance would be most appreciated," Leara continued hopefully, though the look in her eyes said she was resigned to her fate. "And I can pay you handsomely for your services, of course. I have in my possession some rather sensitive information—"

"Leara, no!" Kitani said in urgent tones.

This was the opening Cybil had been waiting for, the chance for her to obtain the evidence against Midas that Kashmir needed. Now, if only Kitani would come to an agreement with her companion, the matter would be resolved.

"What other choice do we have, Kitani?" Leara asked, her voice holding not a trace of scorn or regret at having to part with the data she had risked life and limb to obtain. She turned back toward Cybil, her blue eyes shining luminously in the eerie light. Although she spoke not a single word more, the look in her alien eyes was so imploring, so profound, that Cybil found her resolve weakening.

"Eighty seconds until detonation," the AI continued counting down the seconds remaining until the complete obliteration of the research facility and everyone in it.

Cybil's shoulders sagged as she began to feel the toll the mission had taken on her. There wasn't enough time to conclude this business in the research facility. She sighed, saying, "Come on. We don't have much time."

She ran up the ramp extending into the *Kashmir II*'s open hatch, all the while acutely aware of the presence of the two Valori following close behind. *Should've let them go first*, she thought as the decon chamber purified her and the other two of any possible contaminants. She didn't like the idea of turning her back on the Valori for a second. Aliens were different than humans, and she couldn't bring herself to trust them. *No matter*, she decided. Settling matters with the Valori would have to wait until later. At the moment, she was more concerned with escaping with her life. Shoving the two Valori into the cargo hold once the decon procedure was complete, she rushed toward the front of the ship.

Taking control of the *Kashmir II* once she reached the cockpit, she manually engaged the turbo thrusters as the complex beneath them shuddered and erupted in a torrent of fire reaching into the sky. She steered the ship through the licking flames and swirling debris until she heard the slight clink of metal striking metal as a piece of detritus grazed the hull of the ship. Such a small interaction was enough to cause her to veer dangerously to one side. Their situation was only worsened by the fact she couldn't see where they were going through the storm. Matters became further complicated when the ship struck something hard and unyielding and came to an abrupt halt, causing her to pitch forward against the pilot's seat's restraining harness.

The view screen in front of her was black. Switching the canopy to transparency did nothing to aid her vision. All around her, she saw nothing but darkness save for the occasional soft white snowflakes that drifted past.

"Kashmir, give me a damage report," she ordered.

"Affirmative, Captain."

Cybil breathed a sigh of relief. Her future would not look very bright if the AI program had been damaged in the crash.

"A foreign object has pierced the outer hull and breached one of the internal compartments, causing minor damage to the primary propulsion system," the AI continued. "I shall begin making repairs immediately. Estimated time for propulsion systems to be operable is three hours."

Cybil unbuckled the safety harness and rose stiffly from the pilot's seat. *Three hours*, she told herself, looking through the view port. It seemed as though the ship was stuck in a deep snowdrift. She sighed, exited the cockpit, and crossed the bridge, discarding the insulated jacket as she passed a chair. She slowly descended the curving stairs leading to the cargo hold where she had left her unwanted guests. The Valori were still in the hold, looking rather worse for wear after being tossed around during their hasty retreat.

Kitani was the first to speak. "What sort of pilot are you? You nearly killed us."

"There's been a technical problem," Cybil said matter-of-factly, though talking to aliens always made her uneasy. "The ship has taken some damage, but the AI program is currently in the process of repairing it. The procedure should take no more than three hours. Until then, we must remain here and use as little power as necessary."

Leara nodded. "Understandable."

Cybil crossed her arms in front of her chest. "I believe we had an agreement. I rescue you; you return to me the information you stole from Midas Pharmaceuticals."

"Yes. Of course," Leara said as she nodded in Kitani's direction. Kitani stomped over to Cybil and roughly shoved not one, but two, data disks toward her. One disk appeared to be a visual data disk, like a video log.

"Here," Kitani said, disdainfully averting her eyes. "Take it, greedy human." She returned to her position next to Leara and went on, "Now that you have your precious information, what do you plan on doing with us?"

Cybil rubbed her hand over her side, grimacing when she reached the area where Kitani had kicked her during their altercation. Now that the adrenaline burst from her near death experience had worn off, she was in a considerable amount of pain. She dared not imagine how serious the injury could have been if not for the extra padding provided by her armor.

"You have some rather interesting moves, Valori," she said. "Tell me, are you some sort of warrior?"

"I don't have to tell you anything, human," Kitani replied firmly, "but, yes, I am indeed some sort of warrior."

Kitani spoke in a decidedly proud manner, and no wonder, Cybil thought. If Kitani was one of the fabled Valori warriors, then she would undoubtedly have endured years of rigorous training. In all likelihood, the tall, powerful Valori could probably best her in physical combat in a few heartbeats, especially with her current injuries.

"Impressive," she said, careful not to provoke a reaction "But unfortunately, I have no need for someone such as you." She aimed her plasma pistol at Kitani. "I suppose I should kill both of you here and now," she said.

Kitani growled, obviously prepared to draw her own plasma pistol, and equally confident that Cybil would prove no match for her quick Valori reflexes.

Such arrogance will be your downfall, Cybil thought and froze, stunned, when Leara brushed past Kitani, continuing to advance until the barrel of Cybil's gun touched her chest.

"Do what you must," Leara said, the lights overhead glittering in her icy blue eyes like starlight on frost. "I have fulfilled my purpose. The information on those disks and the decisions you choose to make regarding it are in your hands now."

For a long, awkward moment, Cybil stood with her gun pressed between Leara's breasts. Kitani seemed to be holding her breath, her hand hovering near her plasma pistol. The Valori certainly had more nerve than Cybil would have given her credit for. Something in Leara's forlorn expression touched her, and for a second she almost felt pity for her two captives.

Finally, Cybil lowered her gun with a sigh. She had the information. There was no need to kill these two just yet, not when they offered no threat. "All right, you two," she said. "I can't have you wandering around as you please. Accompany me to the bridge while I await the repairs being made to my ship."

Leara, whose gaze had never left Cybil during the entire confrontation, smiled slightly.

The Valori's warm expression made Cybil more than a little uncomfortable.

"You're injured," Leara said softly, indicating the crimson stain on the shoulder of Cybil's armor "If you want, I could take a look at it for you—"

"That won't be necessary," Cybil said, jerking away from Leara's hand. The erratic movement caused a new wave of pain to wash over her. She grimaced as the world threatened to fade to black and quickly turned away, hoping to hide her agony from the two Valori. She couldn't let them see how weak and exhausted she was.

After a few minutes of leaning her forehead against the cool metal of the cargo hold's wall, she no longer felt like she was going to faint. Even the pain in her shoulder dissipated somewhat. She turned back to face her guests.

Apparently satisfied that she and Leara were safe for the moment, Kitani removed her helmet, letting it drop to the floor with a loud thud. Cybil was startled to see the short, mussed, pale blonde hair that had been hidden beneath the helmet, but not as startled as she was when her gaze fell on Leara, who was following Kitani's example and removing her helmet.

Leara's shaggy hair was darker than the farthest reaches of deep space and slightly longer than Kitani's. The feathered edges mostly covered her ears and reached just to the nape of her neck. The two Valori were polar opposites in their coloring, Cybil thought, Kitani with her caramel skin and pale hair, and Leara with her alabaster skin and glossy obsidian hair. Even their eyes were opposites: Kitani's like fire and Leara's like ice. She had always believed the eyes were the windows to the soul, and from what she'd seen and experienced so far of the two Valori, her theory of fire and ice seemed correct.

Cybil could only stare as Leara ran the fingers of her gloved hand through her hair. She had not expected the aliens to so closely resemble human women. True, she had seen Valori before, but only from a distance. They were generally an aloof race, refraining from mingling too much with other species.

She sighed in exasperation. First she'd been lusting after a computerized voice, now she was gaping at an alien. Although she had to admit Leara was a very attractive alien, nevertheless aliens were different from humans. She knew these beautiful Valori were no exception. Members of a race consisting of only one gender, Leara and Kitani were not truly women, not in the same sense as Cybil herself. How could they be?

Perplexed by her unexpected company, as well as the many secrets the Valori no doubt held, Cybil drew a deep breath and let it out slowly. She had a feeling these were going to be the longest three hours of her life.

Chapter 4

Kitani and Leara proved surprisingly calm and quiet despite the potentially grim outcome of their situation. Cybil was certain that if she'd been held as something of a prisoner aboard an alien's vessel, she wouldn't have accepted her condition so peacefully. Perhaps, as Leara had earlier claimed, these Valori were truly resigned to their fate. She couldn't say she was ungrateful for their cooperation, especially after such a long and trying mission. Nearly being blown to bits was enough excitement for one day.

Sitting in a chair, Cybil wrapped her injured shoulder in thick bandages as Leara continued to watch her every movement with interest, making her shift uncomfortably. Leara's eyes were the palest, purest blue she had ever seen, but the expression within them remained alien and unreadable.

Cybil refocused on her injury. Her armor had warped and melted where the blast from the gun turret had struck her left shoulder, allowing the searing heat to burn through to her skin. She had seen this type of injury before, but it was the first time she had been hit by a blast powerful enough to take down a small assault craft. Despite the amount of blood and singed flesh, the wound was only superficial and would heal easily.

As Leara stared, Cybil gingerly pulled the upper portion of her jumpsuit over her shoulder and the sleeveless shirt she wore beneath, grateful for the cover from Leara's prying eyes. It felt as though Leara had never seen a human before, a concept that made her wonder if the Valori felt as uneasy around her as she did them.

Kitani sat to one side, a constant scowl on her face as she engaged in a silent battle of wills with Cybil. Every time Kitani caught her looking too intently at Leara, the frown deepened and those fiery eyes seemed alight with an internal flame. When Cybil's gaze darted away, Kitani folded her arms over her chest and leaned back in the chair with a look of satisfaction.

Unable to bear the cycle of staring and awkward silences any longer, Cybil at last spoke. “It shouldn’t be much longer.” Not much in the way of starting a conversation, she thought, but in all truth, she just wanted to break the silence before she went stark raving mad. “And the weather is letting up some as well,” she continued. “By the time Kashmir finishes with the repairs, visibility should be good enough to take off.”

“Your ship is incredible,” Leara said. “From what I understand, these AI-based models are the latest in interplanetary travel and quite expensive. It must have cost you a small fortune to purchase it.”

“It was something of a gift from my employer,” Cybil replied.

“And what sort of work do you do?” Leara asked.

The question was meant innocently enough, Cybil decided, but she dreaded making a reply. Fortunately, she didn’t have to answer due to a sudden outburst from Kitani.

“Isn’t it obvious?” Kitani said. “This woman is undoubtedly a ruthless, opportunistic space rogue. Or worse, maybe she’s an employee of Midas Pharmaceuticals, in which case we’ve found ourselves in the hands of the enemy. At any rate, she can’t be trusted. Every credit she has to her name probably came from another’s misfortune.”

Leara ignored Kitani’s accusations, saying to Cybil, “What’s your name? I fear I’m at a loss without it. Especially after you saved our lives.”

“Cybil Reynard. And I am most certainly no employee of Midas Pharmaceuticals. Nor am I as cruel and heartless as your friend seems to believe. I’m a mercenary. I don’t go around killing just anyone with a price on their head. I only agree to undertake a mission if the universe’s best interests are at stake. I’ve only ever taken a life when the individual in question was beyond redemption,” Cybil added, recalling her latest mission. The Valori apparently had taken the information from Midas Pharmaceuticals as Kashmir’s anonymous client claimed, but she couldn’t help feeling that there was more to the matter than they let on.

Kitani seemed to detect an uncertainty in her voice and didn’t hesitate to take advantage. “Do you believe Leara and me to be beyond redemption, as you so tactfully put it? What business would a mercenary have on Kronos?” she asked, her eyes boring into Cybil’s for a scorching moment before she turned away. “Unless, of course, you were hired by Midas to eliminate us. Greedy, bloodthirsty human,” she muttered under her breath.

Kitani was certainly a suspicious one, Cybil decided. Given the Valori's situation, she couldn't say she blamed her.

"Now, Kitani," Leara said soothingly, "Captain Reynard hasn't heard our side of the story yet."

"Don't bother," Kitani said. "She has all the information she needs on those two disks we gave her. It's up to her how she decides to use it."

Pulling the disks from her pocket, Cybil examined them as if she could see their secret knowledge with her naked eyes. "You've mentioned some sort of dreadfully important information contained on these disks before. What exactly did you find out at Midas?" she asked.

Leara and Kitani shot each other grave looks. Cybil noted how Kitani's dark complexion paled considerably.

"What the hell is on these disks?" she demanded.

"Perhaps you should have a look and see for yourself, Captain Reynard," Leara said. "Mere words cannot convey the grim evidence we gathered against Midas."

Cybil hesitated, and then said, "I'm under orders to bring this information back to my employer, who will return it to its rightful owner—"

"You mustn't," Leara interrupted, desperation underlying her usually calm voice.

It was almost enough to make Cybil recoil from the disks and whatever horrid information might be stored upon them.

"If you return it to Midas Pharmaceuticals, you will surely die," Leara warned.

"As will everyone involved," Kitani added. "There's no way Midas would allow anyone who came in contact with such sensitive information to walk away. I believe that more than ever after witnessing the willing sacrifice of one of its own facilities simply because of a security breach."

Cybil held the disks aloft for a moment more as she stared thoughtfully at them. "Well," she said at last, sliding one disk from its protective cover and inserting it into the computer console in front of her, "if our fate is already sealed, as you claim, then I suppose there's no harm in having a look, is there?"

Leara noticed many expressions crossing Cybil Reynard's face as the human examined the files taken from Midas Pharmaceuticals' headquarters on Turon: shock, dread, and finally, an intense, brooding anger.

"I'm afraid the information on that disk is incomplete," Leara explained. "During the final stage of our mission there was a security breach of some sort, and Kitani and I were forced to depart rather hastily."

"So the rumors are correct," Cybil said. "Midas Pharmaceuticals is behind the recent disappearances across the galaxy. I'd heard as much before. Wait." She suddenly leaned forward in her chair, staring intensely at the monitor in front of her. "This file mentions a genetic engineering lab located on one of Earth's prime colonial worlds. Touchstone Cybernetics."

"You mean used to be located," Kitani corrected her. "That laboratory was completely destroyed in an explosion twenty years ago."

"I'm aware of that," Cybil replied. "What I'm getting at is… why is it mentioned in Midas Pharmaceuticals' files? As far as I know, the two companies were in no way affiliated."

"Isn't it obvious? Midas is responsible for the unfortunate 'accident' that befell the research lab," Kitani said. "The research being conducted at Touchstone Cybernetics was too much for Midas to resist, so they infiltrated the facility, took the data, and destroyed the crime scene."

"Inhuman bastards," Cybil said under her breath. She pounded her fist against the control panel, and then sat in silence for a long moment, clearly trying to regain her composure.

"You think that's bad," Kitani said, "wait until you find out what else Midas Pharmaceuticals has been up to over the years."

Cybil looked at Leara. "What does she mean?"

Unable to meet Cybil's questioning glance Leara looked away as she said, "It's not knowledge for the faint of heart. I'm sure those who were abducted by Midas wish they had been so fortunate as to meet as swift a death as those who worked within Touchstone Cybernetics. Theirs was not a pleasant fate."

Cybil was quiet for a few minutes, obviously considering. At last, she said, "What are those Midas bastards up to? What are they trying to hide that's so important they would be willing to take innocent lives in order to ensure their secret remains hidden?"

Leara felt somewhat anguished by the hopelessness of her situation. "We believe that Midas intends to develop a biological weapon to be used against alien races such as ourselves. That's precisely what Kitani and I were sent to investigate."

Cybil looked thoughtful. "And you infiltrated the outpost facility in the hope of catching Midas in the act?" she asked. "What did you learn before the place exploded?"

Kitani looked away rather pointedly as the pallor returned to her features at the mention of the secret laboratories. "You'll find the answers to all your questions on the second disk," she said. "It's a video log we made during our infiltration of the Kronos complex." Her vision clouded over with unshed tears as she spoke. Embarrassed, she turned away from Cybil. "Though I must warn you that you won't like what you see."

Silence fell behind Leara, as though Cybil was uncertain if she wanted to learn the absolute truth behind the conspiracy. Soon she heard a soft rustling as the human inserted the disk into the console and waited for playback to begin.

She and Kitani had been present for the filming of the material. It had pained her so much to film the footage that she did not wish to view it again. She was sure Kitani felt the same. Instead, she stared around the room during the disk's playback, trying to focus on anything that would help drown out the pitiful cries of the test subjects locked away in the outpost facility's labs. She noticed Kitani doing the same

She assumed Midas's purpose in obtaining test subjects and performing such cruel experiments was to study the secrets of alien anatomy firsthand and use the knowledge to create devastating weapons to be used against them. That was where the hapless colonists came in. The highly addictive substances Midas had been distributing throughout the universe ensured a constant supply of test subjects, and because of the victims' addictions, their disappearances were often overlooked. In addition, two space-faring Paladins had died, the victims of apparent substance abuse. The incident reeked of Midas's influence.

Many species had already fallen victim to Midas's nefarious plot. How much longer, Leara wondered, would it take for the Valori to become infected with one of Midas's pathogens? Their resistance to diseases had protected them for centuries, but the Valori reproductive cycle was a delicate process. An unknown strain of bacteria or a widespread fever could cause permanent sterility among her kind, forever endangering the fragile balance of Valori society. So far the debilitating effects of the pathogens were caused by so-called "medicinal" drugs manufactured and distributed by none other than Midas Pharmaceuticals, but within the secret labs, Leara and Kitani had discovered evidence that attempts at an airborne variety were being made. If Midas succeeded in making its horrible weapons airborne, the effects on intergalactic society could be devastating.

The experimental subjects seen by Leara and Kitani had been in such a terrible state that it proved difficult to discern their species. The disease had been allowed to run its course, causing the subjects' bodies to deteriorate. However, the unfortunate subjects' minds seemed very much intact, leaving them aware of their appalling circumstances. She'd found that awareness most disturbing to her and thought it likely Cybil would feel the same.

At the sound of plasma pistol fire, Leara turned around rather abruptly. The sound was followed by alarms blaring, heralding the end of the video log. She noticed immediately that Cybil was nearly as pale as the snow falling outside the ship.

Cybil turned a questioning gaze on her. "You killed them?" she asked.

Leara knew the ending of the video log would raise questions from whoever viewed it, but what else was there to do except tell the truth?

"Yes," she answered. "I couldn't bear to leave those sad and misfortunate beings to suffer any longer. It was our firing at their cell doors that triggered the alarm, which in turn caused the explosion. I'm deeply sorry for any inconvenience our actions might have caused."

Cybil said nothing. Her complexion paled by the minute.

Leara found Cybil's paleness troubling. "Are you all right, Captain Reynard?" she asked, taking a tentative step forward. For an instant, Cybil remained silent as stone, then she spoke in a shaky whisper choked with unimaginable rage.

"That's close enough," Cybil said, rising stiffly from her chair. The hollow tone of her voice and the emptiness in her eyes made Leara shudder. She went on, "I have many things to do before takeoff, so if you'll excuse me..."

Leara backed away. "Of course, Captain."

"You can use the crew's quarters for now," Cybil continued, her complete lack of emotion making her sound eerily like an automaton. She ushered Leara and Kitani down a narrow corridor to a room with two bunks fastened to the walls on either side.

"There's a lavatory beyond that door over there," Cybil said, motioning to the door at the opposite side of the room before turning to leave. "Please, make yourselves comfortable for the time being. I'll alert you before we take off."

After the door closed and the sound of Cybil's footsteps receded in the distance, Kitani snorted indignantly. "How are we supposed to be comfortable while locked in a room like prisoners?" She tried the door to prove her point.

"I'm sure this is a lot for Captain Reynard to process all at once," Leara said.

"Likely too much for her tiny human brain to ever comprehend." Kitani stripped off the more cumbersome pieces of her armor and let them drop on one of the lower bunks.

Despite the subzero temperatures outside, it was rather warm on board the *Kashmir II*, Leara suddenly realized. She removed her layers of insulated clothing while Kitani busied herself in the lavatory. She secretly hoped Kitani would be quick about her business. In all the excitement, she hadn't noticed how badly she needed to use the facility.

Moments later, Kitani emerged from the bathroom and plopped down on the bunk she'd claimed for herself, pretending not to notice as Leara swiftly rushed past her. When Leara returned, she found Kitani lying rather rigidly on the bottom bunk on the opposite wall.

"Well, what are we to do now?" Leara asked, sighing.

Kitani rolled over on her back and placed her arms behind her head. "What else is there to do but wait until this human arrives at a more hospitable place, and then escape? She can't keep us locked in here forever."

"I don't believe Captain Reynard intends to do such a thing," Leara said.

"Listen to yourself, Leara. Did you see the way she stared at us like we were some sort of hideous monsters? I'm telling you, the woman is a xenophobe like most humans. Our kind frightens them; they think us unnatural. The sooner we're away from her, the better." Kitani turned her head toward Leara. "What is it?" she asked, sitting up on the bunk.

Deep in thought, Leara shook her head. "I can't explain it, but I felt an unspeakable sadness emanating from Captain Reynard as we viewed the files," she said. "She holds herself proud and rigid, much like you, but deep down, I believe she's frightened."

Kitani crossed her arms over her chest. "Well, I'm not frightened. Not of her, anyway." The statement prompted Leara to smile faintly. Kitani went on, "So what's this Captain Reynard so scared of? She certainly doesn't appear to fear death or pain, not after the way she foolhardily rushed into that heavily guarded complex armed only with her wits and a plasma pistol. And definitely not the way she defiantly stood against me in the observatory."

"I couldn't say," Leara replied. "Perhaps her fears aren't as tangible as you might think."

Kitani clearly didn't understand Leara's newfound fascination with a human woman, but said no more. Leara wondered how she could explain what she felt when she herself was confused by the fluttering sensation she felt in her chest every time she laid eyes on Cybil Reynard. Cybil wasn't a physically stunning woman, certainly not by Valori standards, but the human had an inner strength, and beyond that, a beauty not even the most striking Valori possessed. Deciding she must be drawn to that factor alone, she lay down on the bunk, wishing Kitani could understand without the need for Leara to lay herself bare.

Chapter 5

After locking the two Valori securely in the crew's quarters, Cybil returned to the main computer console on the bridge, hesitating only briefly before inserting the first disk again.

As she waited for the files to load, she shuddered at the thought of those poor dying creatures she'd seen in the video. Leara's heart had been in the right place when she'd brought an abrupt end to their torment, but that didn't make the test subjects' cruel fate any easier to accept.

Only when the list of missing persons appeared on the computer screen was she able to banish the disturbing thoughts from her mind. She scrolled through the list, scanning each name more carefully this time, until she came to an entry that made the blood freeze in her veins.

Callaway, Melinda.

Cybil shivered despite the relative warmth of the ship's interior. Could this woman possibly be the mother of her childhood friend? Sierra Callaway's mother had been a scientist at Touchstone Cybernetics at the time of the explosion, which could only mean one thing, she decided: Midas Pharmaceuticals was responsible for her death.

The official report had stated that the explosion was an accident, but Cybil knew differently now. Thanks to the meddling Valori, she understood the truth behind Sierra's mother's death, as well as the disappearances and deaths of many others. She owed the aliens a great deal of gratitude, certainly more than she was currently showing them, but bringing herself to trust another species was a trying task. Her parents had once placed their trust in their Zulian neighbor, Kuvair N'arex, only to have that trust betrayed in the worst possible way. She refused to be so gullible.

Although she thought she had detected a trace of sympathy in Leara's unfathomable eyes, she decided that was nonsense. Why would a Valori sympathize with her over the loss of a few human lives? Besides, those eyes, so alien and catlike, were impossible for her to read. The thought made her simmering anger and resentment begin to boil.

What exactly were those two trying to prove? she asked herself as she slipped the disk back into its protective cover and tucked it safely away in her pocket. True, Midas Pharmaceuticals had done plenty to arouse suspicion, but Cybil refused to believe that anyone would be as cruel and conniving as the Valori suggested. Rising from her chair, she stalked down the corridor toward the crew's quarters, resolved to find out.

The two Valori were awaiting her as the door slid upward. No doubt they had been alerted to her coming by the clinking of her boots against the metal floor. Valori were known for their acute senses. She saw Leara sitting patiently on the edge of the bunk at the farthest side of the room, while Kitani was perched on the bunk next to the door, looking like a cat ready to pounce.

"I've been reviewing the information on the data disks you gave me," Cybil began, hoping that all signs of tears and sorrow were gone as she met the gaze of each Valori in turn. "And I'd like to ask you a few questions before takeoff, if I may."

"Who are we to refuse our captor's request?" Kitani said mutinously.

Better keep an eye on that one, Cybil reminded herself. "I only wish to acquire more knowledge of Midas Pharmaceuticals' scheme," she said. "After we leave Kronos, you'll be free to go."

"Anything to be of assistance," Leara replied, politely bowing her head. "I am afraid you already know as much as anyone about Midas's experiments. Kitani and I were sent to investigate the corporation based on a mere hunch. We were just as shocked as you at what we found."

"What is Midas planning?" Cybil asked.

"The complete and utter annihilation of intelligent life as we know it," Kitani replied darkly. "What humanity doesn't understand, it seeks to destroy. That's the way it's always been, if your kind's history is any indication."

Leara waved a hand at Kitani for silence. "Unfortunately, what Kitani says is the truth. Midas intends to create and release a deadly biological weapon. If it succeeds, all alien life will be affected in one way or another."

"I had already figured as much." Cybil shook her head in disbelief. "I know Midas has had some shady dealings in the past, but the destruction of intergalactic civilization? I don't know. It seems a bit too farfetched for me."

"Are you implying that we're liars?" Kitani's tone was as sharply honed as the sword sheathed at her side.

"I never said that," Cybil replied carefully. But what if what they said was true? How would Midas's actions reflect on humanity as a whole? If word of this got out, it could be the First Contact Wars all over again. Except this time, humanity wouldn't be able to count on the Federation for support.

Shrugging off the unpleasant thought, she added, "I was merely stating that this tale seems disproportionate to the facts. You stole some rather disturbing and highly classified information from Midas, and I was hired to track it down. Although I admit the corporation's deeds are nothing short of atrocious, there have been no implications that Midas intends to launch a full-scale genocide campaign."

"Because you haven't searched deeply enough," Kitani said. "You haven't seen what we have. There were a few alien employees at Midas's offices on Turon, although I cannot fathom why they would choose to stay. Discrimination runs rampant within Midas, and its top officials make no effort to hide it. I have my suspicions that the alien employees are not there of their own free will. Maybe those employees know too much about what's really going on. Midas will keep the universe in the dark until it's too late, and those fools in the Senate are too blind and content with their positions to do any probing unless the fate of the universe has been threatened. At that point, the damage will already have been wrought. Who knows if the effects of Midas's plot can be undone?" She shook her head. "Your people's limited knowledge and even greater intolerance of those different than yourselves has made humanity a thorn in our side ever since your kind first appeared."

Cybil realized that Kitani distrusted humans about as much as she trusted aliens, which led her to the conclusion that the intergalactic races' mutual tolerance of one another was not as solid as it appeared. Seeing Valori so far removed from the safety of Valori space, on an expedition to uncover the dark secrets of an insidious plot, seemed far from common. She wondered if there was perhaps some truth to the Valori's outrageous claims.

"That's another thing I wanted to ask you about," Cybil said, breaking the tense silence that had fallen. "The data on the files makes no mention of Valori being used in Midas's experiments.

Why become involved in something that doesn't concern you? I thought you Valori were supposed to be a xenophobic race."

Kitani rose from the bunk and strode briskly over to stand in front of Cybil, her glowing orange eyes inches away from Cybil's own. "We aren't xenophobes, as you say, but peacekeepers of the galaxy. And in case you haven't been listening, the Midas conspiracy *does* concern us. Just because no Valori have been affected yet doesn't mean Midas will continue to ignore us. If it succeeds in developing an airborne version of its affliction, it will affect the Valori as well." She backed a few steps away, but her eyes still smoldered. "Remember this, Reynard. We Valori are the galaxy's peacekeepers and keep the peace we shall. Now if you'll excuse me, I don't wish to be a part of this conversation any longer." Pivoting on her heel, Kitani stormed into the lavatory and sealed the door behind her.

"Please forgive her," Leara said from across the room. "This has been a trying ordeal for Kitani, and she isn't acting herself lately. Perhaps it's merely homesickness. Neither of us has ever been away from our homeworld so long."

Cybil looked at Leara. Something in Leara's calm demeanor caused some of her tension to fade away. "I didn't mean to offend you," she said, the apology more sincere than she intended. "It's just that I haven't met any Valori before, not personally anyway. I've seen a few on my travels, but I've never spoken to one until now."

Leara's expression lightened a little. "No wonder you look at us so strangely," she said, her pupils narrowing as her smile faded. "I'm sure you've heard all sorts of bizarre rumors concerning the Valori. I can honestly say I don't blame you for your reservations toward us."

Cybil cleared her throat, feeling uncomfortable that Leara would talk to her at all after how badly she had been treated. "I know that your race consists entirely of females. That fact alone is enough to cause wild speculation among some of my kind."

Despite the long, difficult struggle for equality among the human colonies, Cybil knew there were some who still considered same-sex relationships to be unnatural. To those narrow-minded individuals, a race such as the Valori would be the ultimate kick in the face.

"That's not entirely true," Leara replied. "Outwardly, we may very much resemble human females, but we're not female in the same sense as a human woman. Actually, Valori are neither male nor female, and the idea of a dual-gendered society is rather difficult for us to grasp." She looked uneasy, possibly searching for words to explain a difficult subject. "I suppose you could say we're neutral. Most of the time, anyway. There are, of course, certain times when we become fertile and our bodies produce the necessary hormones and generative cells."

Leara was clearly suffering under her scrutiny, Cybil thought. To alleviate some of the tension, she asked, "So you're sequential hermaphrodites?"

Some of the warmth faded from Leara's eyes. Cybil had heard that Valori could communicate with their eyes as easily as they used spoken words, but unfortunately, she did not understand such subtle nuances.

"Not exactly, but the comparison will have to do," Leara said, the resentment in her tone taking Cybil completely by surprise. "We don't particularly enjoy being labeled as hermaphrodites by other races," she added, narrowing her eyes ever so slightly. "The term is used to refer to creatures that are both male and female when, as I said before, Valori are neither."

Flustered and embarrassed, Cybil didn't know where to look.

Leara cleared her throat. The indignation fading from her tone, she added more softly, "I probably shouldn't be telling you any of this. Valori prefer to keep knowledge of our physiology from other species. As a safety precaution." She shuddered slightly.

"I understand your reservations," Cybil said. "I was merely curious." When Leara remained silent, she added, "I hope I haven't offended you."

"Not at all," Leara reassured her. Some of the tension between them dissolved as she spoke. "It's refreshing to meet one of another race who is genuinely interested in our culture. Unfortunately, I'm afraid I'm not at liberty to provide you with more of the information you seek about my species. Perhaps someday..."

Cybil's curiosity was nearly eating her alive, but she nodded politely in agreement. If the Valori were indeed the targets of potential genocide, then Leara had every right to safeguard her people's secrets.

She glanced at Leara, who was regarding her with interest. It was difficult for her to imagine the lovely Valori playing a masculine role in a relationship, and even harder to think of Leara as anything other than a beautiful young woman, perhaps one of the most beautiful she had ever seen.

"Kitani and I were sent on this mission by the Supreme Matriarchy," Leara said suddenly, bringing Cybil back to the present with a start. "Or rather, I received permission to embark on this journey after pleading with the High Matriarchs."

Cybil stood gaping for a second. "The Supreme Matriarchy?" she asked, trying to recover her composure. The abrupt change in subject had completely thrown her off course, but it was something of a relief after their earlier awkward conversation.

"Forgive me," Leara said with a bow. "The Supreme Matriarchy is the chief ruling branch of Valori government. It consists of three of the oldest, wisest matriarchs,, seasoned warriors who have passed their prime, and other incredibly powerful and well-respected Valori chosen to carve the path to the future in their golden years."

"Which, from what I understand, can be a very long time," Cybil interrupted.

"Correct. Valori often live a millennium or more, and the Supreme Matriarchy represents the best of what can be achieved in those long years."

"So in other words, you were sent on this perilous mission by very important officials. Does that mean you can expect backup from your matriarchs in the fight against Midas?"

Leara lowered her gaze. "I'm afraid they're awaiting our report. Until our return, they'll be powerless to act. You see, that hunch I mentioned before was my own. Valori have developed resistance to most diseases, so I became suspicious when two perfectly healthy Valori Paladins turned up with an unknown and seemingly incurable ailment after returning from an interplanetary mission. It was my idea to conduct this investigation, Captain Reynard. I only needed clearance from the Supreme Matriarchy to do so."

Cybil latched onto Leara's words. "What sort of mission were these two Paladins on, exactly? According to the files you obtained from Midas, the pathogens can only be introduced in drug form at the current stage."

"Valori are not exempt from temptation," Leara said. "Sometimes during long missions, space-faring warriors have been known to be influenced by outside forces. The two Paladins exhibited symptoms of an overdose. At this time, we're unable to conclude whether or not this substance abuse was voluntary or forced upon them."

Outside forces, Cybil thought, meaning elements beyond the Valori's control. Aloud, she said, "Your companion said that no

Valori has been affected so far. Don't try to tell me she wasn't aware of this information."

Leara shook her head. "Kitani is wary, perhaps too wary. She mistrusts everyone, but it's the Valori way to deal with our kind's matters privately. I often wonder if it is relevant in modern society. After all, Midas's plot will affect everyone. Perhaps we could use the insight provided by other species."

Cybil fought to contain the emotion in her voice. Was Leara asking for her help? "So a couple of Paladins got hold of some bad drugs. Seems like a lot of trouble to go through just to protect your own interests," she said.

"My actions do not ensure the safety of the Valori only, but help ensure the survival of all the sapient races. If this plot continues unchecked, how long do you think it will be before Midas extends its reign of terror across every settled region of space? Including humans?"

"But Midas Pharmaceuticals is an Earth corporation, both owned and operated by humans. Do you truly believe it will resort to using these tactics against its own people as well?" Cybil found the idea very disturbing. To be on the receiving end of such hatred and discrimination... she couldn't imagine how that might feel.

"Perhaps it's begun already," Leara said, interrupting Cybil's thoughts. "I believe the genetic engineering lab mentioned in the files was manned by a human research team. If Midas isn't stopped, then I fear for everyone."

"I suppose you're right there. It's best to eliminate the problem at its source. Luckily, eliminating problems just happens to be my specialty," Cybil said, finally convinced.

"So you'll assist me on this quest?" Hope lighted Leara's eyes, making them glow luminously in the low light.

Cybil had to avert her gaze from Leara. A pang of guilt stabbed at her for treating Leara like a criminal. But for all she knew, Leara and Kitani could be criminals, perhaps from a rival faction currently at odds with Midas Pharmaceuticals. "I'll return you and Kitani safely to your homeworld so you can confer with the High Matriarchs," she said stiffly. "But first I must rendezvous with my employer, during which time I'll need you to stay out of sight."

"Your kindness is most appreciated, Captain Reynard."

"I'm merely doing my job," Cybil said. She exited the quarters, this time leaving the door unsealed. She didn't believe the Valori would try anything mutinous, especially after she had volunteered to help them when it would be much easier just to dump them off the ship and leave them in the snows of Kronos. If they did try anything, she would have her plasma pistol ready.

At the moment, her main concern was to escape the close confines of the crew's quarters with at least a shred of dignity intact. Although she would never admit it except to herself, she was more than a little turned on by Leara. With her knowledge of the race, she was disconcerted by the way she felt.

Leara was not like her, Cybil thought, neither female nor male, man nor woman. The Valori existed on an entirely separate plane from dual-gendered species when it came to sex.

Cybil had only been attracted to human women before, yet she couldn't deny that Leara was quite lovely She held her head in her hands, gently massaging her aching temples. The sooner she returned to civilization and was relieved of the Valori's company, the sooner she could return to her solitary existence. She hoped her sanity would endure until then.

Cybil sighed and sat down in the chair facing the main computer console. She began chewing on her fingernail as she watched the *Kashmir II* count down the remaining minutes until repairs were complete.

Only ten minutes, fifty seconds more until we can get off this frozen world, Cybil told herself. *Kashmir is going to love this*. She held the two data disks aloft. Clearly her employer had some inkling of the truth before assigning Cybil to this mission. Cybil hoped that Kashmir was prepared to face the consequences of double-crossing Midas Pharmaceuticals. The only remaining question was: what was she going to do with the Valori? Leara and Kitani didn't deserve to be locked away like criminals in her crew's quarters and then abandoned on Eden IV to fend for themselves. If anything, Leara's actions had unearthed the truth behind the long mystery of Sierra's tragic childhood and brought her at least some closure in the matter.

Melinda Callaway was dead, although not by the same unfortunate circumstances that she and Sierra had imagined. Midas Pharmaceuticals appeared to be the ones responsible for her death, along with so many others. Even though she longed to see her childhood friend again, Cybil did not look forward to giving Sierra the devastating news.

* * *

“I thought she’d never leave,” Kitani said as she emerged from the lavatory. “The human certainly is a curious one. What did she wish to know of the Supreme Matriarchy?”

“She only asked about the High Matriarchs and the role they play in Valori government,” Leara said, quickly averting her gaze. She felt confused and inordinately embarrassed after her conversation with Cybil Reynard. She did not wish for Kitani to see the emotions roiling within her.

“You didn’t tell her anything about yourself, did you? That woman is a ruthless mercenary, Leara. If she knew your true identity, she could hold you for ransom. Or worse.”

“I don’t think we have anything to worry about. After she concludes some important business of her own, Captain Reynard has agreed to see us safely home—”

“Reynard is nothing more than a cunning rogue who would do anything for a few measly credits,” Kitani interrupted. “We cannot, under any circumstances, allow her to learn of your mother’s identity and position among the Valori.”

“Understood.” Leara still didn’t suspect Cybil of malicious intent, but she was tired of arguing with the headstrong Kitani. She sat in silence on the edge of her bunk.

“Since you apparently detest Captain Reynard’s company so,” a sudden passion made her announce after a while, so suddenly Kitani sat bolt upright on her bed, “you should be delighted to know that we’ll be clear for takeoff soon.” She was the daughter of a High Matriarch, one of the most influential women in Valori society. Although she wanted to be seen as a person and not just the heir to the legendary Sorani dynasty, Kitani’s incessant surliness was starting to annoy her.

“Not soon enough,” Kitani said as she lay back down on the bunk. “Mark my words, the sooner we’re away from this woman and her strange ship, the better. And that’s another thing that bothers me. How can a mere human come into possession of such a marvel of modern technology as a completely self-sufficient, AI-based vessel? It’s even capable of performing its own repairs! When all the High Matriarch’s daughter is provided with is an old relic that has seen far better days. I simply can’t understand it.”

Leara opened her mouth to respond, but before she could utter a word, her attention was diverted by a high-pitched whistling from somewhere outside the ship. A loud crash resounded nearby. The *Kashmir II* rocked dangerously back and forth.

Kitani cursed under her breath. “What’s happening now?”

As if on cue, Cybil appeared in the doorway, her complexion ghostly pale.

"We're under attack," she said, rather calmly considering the severity of their situation. "You were right, Kitani. Midas has sent someone to find and eliminate any survivors who might be left after the explosion. That's the only explanation for the attack."

"Have the repairs been completed?" Kitani asked.

Cybil nodded. "*Kashmir II* is preparing for takeoff as we speak. If we can hold out a little longer, we should be in the air, where we'll likely be able to outrun our enemy."

Kitani didn't seem completely satisfied with Cybil's proposal, which Leara knew would sound cowardly to the Paladin. "Doesn't this thing have any weapons?" Kitani asked. "Surely a ship capable of functioning on its own has some means of defending itself."

"The *Kashmir II* is both heavily armed and armored," Cybil agreed, "but the explosion you heard just now came from a heat-seeking missile, and there's no telling how many other nasty surprises our foes are packing. Although I don't recognize the insignia on the attacking vessel, most likely they're mercenaries hired by Midas to clean up the mess left behind after the explosion. As long as we're grounded, there's nothing we can do to retaliate. Some degree of damage is inevitable. We can only pray enemy fire doesn't hit the propulsion system. Now, would you still rather stay here and fight instead of making a hyper-jump to safety?"

Kitani growled softly. "Do as you see fit, Reynard. I'm not the captain here."

For several seconds, Cybil and Kitani glared at each other in a silent showdown. Leara broke the maddening stand-off.

"Whatever you decide, we'd best do it quickly," she said, letting them both hear the urgency in her tone. She heard the faint whistling of another heat seeker approaching them. "Now is not the time for petty squabbling and posturing. We must first escape this frozen wasteland with our lives, then you may bicker to your heart's desire."

Cybil and Kitani turned towards her, their expressions softening as they met her gaze.

"You're right," Cybil said in a tone softer than any Leara had heard her use before. It gave her an odd thrill to hear the human say her name in such a gentle manner. "Let's put all our differences aside for now and focus on getting out of here alive."

"Ten seconds to takeoff," the *Kashmir II* announced over the intercom. "Initiating ignition procedure."

The propulsion system roared to life. The steady humming was the most beautiful music Leara had ever heard, but it was music intermittently interrupted by the pounding of missiles striking somewhere close by. The brunt of the bombardment missed. The ship suddenly jerked, and Leara felt it beginning to rise.

"This is it," Cybil said, bracing herself by grasping the metal bars securing the bunks to the wall. "We were lucky enough to avoid most of the missiles because the ship has been stuck in a snowbank and running on auxiliary power for the past three hours. With the propulsion system at full capacity, those heat seekers will be drawn to us."

"Engaging hyper drive," *Kashmir II* announced.

Leara barely had enough time to wonder why an AI would be programmed with such a sultry, sexy voice before the warp drive kicked in. She was pitched forward as the ship lurched violently beneath her feet. For a moment, she was aware of nothing but the passage of time and great distance as the ship blazed through Kronos's orbit and beyond at tremendous speed. At last, she noticed warmth around her. She was certain it was not generated by her own body.

"Are you all right?" Cybil asked, so close Leara could feel hot breath tickling her ear.

She opened her eyes, realizing she felt the heat from Cybil's body. The human held her tightly, strong arms encircling her as the ship sped through the stars. Indeed, she thought, Cybil's support was the only thing keeping her on her feet.

The hyper drive disengaged, and the *Kashmir II* ceased to tremble. Leara regained her balance as the ship's speed stabilized, but Cybil continued to hold on. *Her eyes are the same color as the sky on a bright and clear day*, Leara mused. The genuine concern she saw in Cybil's gaze gave lie to the human's cold and callous behavior from earlier.

With a shudder, Leara righted herself, pulling away from Cybil's embrace. She felt oddly cold outside that strong grasp. She shivered, saying resolutely, "I'm fine," though her legs still felt wobbly and unstable beneath her. "Thank you." She could not bring herself to look into those sky-blue eyes while standing so close to Cybil. Cybil was a human, an alien; there was no reason for her to feel this way.

Kashmir II slowed drastically. Leara swayed as a result of the sudden change in speed.

"Did we lose them?" Cybil asked the ship.

"Negative contact. No sign of pursuit." For a brief instant, *Kashmir II*'s voice sounded as stoic and serious as any AI program, Leara thought, then the coquettish manner returned. "It looks like you narrowly averted disaster yet again, Captain," the AI teased. "Should I transmit your mission report?"

Cybil shot a quick glance at Leara. "Not just yet, Kashmir., I believe I'd prefer to consult with my employer personally this time."

"Aye, Captain."

Cybil turned back to Leara and Kitani. "It seems we're out of immediate danger, for the time being anyway," she said, her manner distant, her tone clipped. "Your sense of foreboding has proven correct so far, Kitani. I only hope we don't encounter too many altercations between here and the space station where my employer operates."

"It's rather audacious of you to address me so familiarly, Reynard," Kitani said, giving the human a smile more closely resembling a baring of teeth than a friendly expression. "Especially when I don't recall granting you permission to do so." Kitani grinned so broadly, Leara plainly saw her sharp, slightly elongated Valori canines, and she bet that Cybil noticed them too.

"I was only offering my gratitude for your keen foresight," Cybil said, sounding slightly insulted. "Now if you'll excuse me, I have some important business to attend on the bridge. I would appreciate it if you would kindly remain here and avoid roaming too much about the ship."

When Cybil had moved out of earshot, Leara turned to Kitani. "I do believe you've insulted the captain," she said. "Surely she meant no harm."

"You're being awfully protective of this woman," Kitani said, her eyelid trembling in what might have been a wink.

"What exactly are you implying, Kitani Veldina?" Leara pressed her lips together, giving Kitani a stern look.

Kitani averted her gaze submissively, much to Leara's satisfaction. She only used Kitani's full name when she was thoroughly and genuinely upset with her, cause enough for her friend to refrain from making any more accusatory remarks.

Leara sat back down on the bunk she'd selected for herself. She leaned against the wall, the corners of her mouth curving into a smug smile. Her self-satisfaction faded as she recalled the sensation she'd experienced while in Cybil's arms. Kitani had a valid point. Why was she protecting this human woman, a complete stranger?

Hugging her knees close to her chest, Leara leaned her head against the wall, nearly allowing herself to be lulled to sleep by the purring of the ship's propulsion system. However, every time she closed her eyes she was haunted by an array of images of the day's events, from the tortured expressions on the lab experiments' faces to their unexpected meeting with Cybil Reynard. Their meeting with the human woman had been most fortuitous, but she wondered how long their luck would hold out. It didn't take an expert on alien behavior to see that Cybil was prejudiced against nonhumans.

As Leara lay awake, staring at the bunk overhead, she wondered why Cybil had even bothered to rescue them in the first place. Did the mercenary somehow know of her connection to the Supreme Matriarchy? If so, then Kitani's worst suspicions might prove true.

She drifted into an uneasy sleep as she worried about what the future held in store for her.

Chapter 6

Cybil stood patiently at the head of the bridge as the *Kashmir II* pulled into the docking bay of space station Eden IV. Huge mechanical arms extended to anchor the ship in place. A bell chimed to signal it was safe to exit to the station.

She allowed herself a quick sidelong glance at Leara, who was standing next to Kitani. Ever since her disconcerting encounter with the Valori during their hasty retreat from Kronos, Cybil had thought it best to avoid keeping company with Leara. However, no amount of physical distance could erase the warm tingling sensation she experienced at recalling how nice Leara had felt in her arms. She was so soft and warm Cybil had barely been able to tear herself away.

As if sensing her thoughts, Leara's dazzling blue eyes met hers for a fleeting instant, and then became hidden beneath the folds of the hooded cloak she wore as she shyly glanced away.

Both Valori had donned their disguises: oversized woolen cloaks Cybil had found in the back of a storage closet. It wasn't much, but hopefully the cloaks would be enough to conceal the women's identities.

After the attack on Kronos, she had agreed that Kitani and Leara had best accompany her to the space station instead of remaining aboard the ship as originally intended. The inconvenience came with advantages, such as being able to keep an eye on her guests at all times without fear of offending them again. Someone wanted them all dead, and if she knew Midas Pharmaceuticals, she knew they wouldn't give up until that objective had been accomplished. She and the Valori were being hunted by an unknown foe. The realization of how quickly the hunter can become the hunted deeply displeased her.

Cybil drew a deep breath and pulled up the hood of her own cloak as she, Leara, and Kitani prepared to exit the airlock. The space station was full of all sorts of shady characters and even shadier dealings. She hoped a trio of mysteriously clad figures wouldn't be enough to attract much attention.

Nothing appeared amiss as Cybil and the Valori strolled casually along the docks and through the lower sections of the city-ship. If they could only make it to the Cloud Nine Casino without further incident, Cybil thought. *Then what?* Her mission had not turned out the way she'd imagined. If that wasn't bad enough, she was bringing her targets with her to this meeting. As well, she hoped she could somehow obtain the mystery employer's identity from Kashmir so she could set out on another personal vendetta and, at last, fulfill a childhood promise to her friend, Sierra.

All that would have to wait, of course, until after she saw Leara and Kitani safely home, Cybil decided. She had made a promise, after all. She had never been one to break her word although her promise to Sierra went back much further than the vow she had made to the Valori.

Shortly after setting foot on the inappropriately named space station, Leara became withdrawn, lost in her own thoughts as she followed Cybil through the congested streets. Never in her life had she seen so many unsavory characters in one place. There was something about Eden IV, a dreadful feeling she just couldn't shake, although she couldn't quite place it.

She was beginning to wonder if perhaps Kitani's assumptions about Cybil were correct, that Cybil was no more than a bloodthirsty assassin. Dismay crept into her heart at the thought, and that dismay was not entirely due to the possibility that Cybil would betray them. Being in Cybil's company was exhilarating, but perhaps her excitement came from the constant peril in which she and Kitani found themselves.

When the group entered the spacious lobby of a massive building, Cybil turned to face Leara and Kitani, her expression worried. "You two should wait here," she said. "My employer is a bit skittish around strangers."

"And where exactly is here?" Kitani asked, surveying her surroundings.

"It's the Cloud Nine Casino," Cybil replied. "The largest casino within Eden IV, and perhaps the most famous in the galaxy. Don't worry. You should be safe waiting here as long as you don't do anything to draw attention to yourselves."

Leara nodded, noticing that Kitani, who was watching the gamblers milling around the casino, had a distant look in her eyes.

"You can count on us to be here when you return," Leara said to Cybil, taking Kitani lightly by the arm. The gesture proved enough to get Kitani's attention and elicit a grunt of affirmation.

Cybil turned and began to ascend the huge, curving staircase leading to the upper levels of the casino.

"As if we have anywhere better to go," Kitani grumbled. "I certainly wouldn't want to tarry long in the streets outside while unarmed."

What sort of place had Cybil taken them to? Leara wondered, glancing around the casino. The casino's patrons looked even more cutthroat than Cybil, she decided. But something else was troubling her, a strange sense of foreboding she could not quite name had been worrying her ever since they docked at the space station.

Although Leara was certain Cybil carried her own plasma pistol with her, the human had insisted that Kitani leave her weapons behind. After much protesting from Kitani, she had ordered Kitani to comply with the demand. At the time, agreeing with Cybil had seemed the sensible thing to do. Now, as she stared around the vast lobby, feeling the weight of many curious glances, she wasn't so sure she had made the right decision.

"We'll be fine," she said, as much for her own assurance as Kitani's. "Cybil won't leave us unattended for long. I'm sure of it."

"You're probably right there," Kitani said, a smile softening her hardened features. "That human doesn't trust us at all. In fact, I would almost say she's as suspicious of us as we are of her. Or rather, as suspicious as *I* am." She gave Leara a knowing wink.

"Now isn't the time for silly accusations." Leara tried to sound stern and reprimanding, but her voice barely came out as a shaky whisper. "We must wait here until Cybil returns for us."

"I wonder if she'd mind if I tried my hand at gambling," Kitani said, her gaze returning to the casino's patrons. Leara gave her a bewildered look. "Not to worry," Kitani added with a grin. "Unfortunately, I don't have a single credit on me. I left all our funds on our own little ship, which is still buried in the snow somewhere on Kronos, I assume."

Leara rolled her eyes at Kitani's flippancy. "I only hope we don't find ourselves in dire need of those credits."

While Leara was chastising Kitani, it finally dawned on her just what was amiss. She scanned the lobby once more to confirm her doubts. Not a single alien face could be seen among the crowds patronizing the slot machines or lounging by the bar. Cybil had claimed that this was one of the most popular casinos in the galaxy, so why weren't there any non-humans?

"Are you all right?" Kitani asked, waving a hand in front of Leara's face to get her attention.

"Have you noticed anything unusual about this place?" Leara asked.

"If by unusual, you mean that we're standing in a casino on a space station whose population is comprised mostly of rogues and scoundrels, then yes, I have."

"That isn't what I'm referring to. Look around us and tell me what you see."

Kitani did as she was told, taking a moment to carefully examine the casino. "Like I said earlier, nothing but a bunch of human ruffians."

"Exactly," Leara pronounced with satisfaction.

"What?"

"Everyone in this room besides us is human. Now that I think about it, I don't recall seeing any other species as we made our journey across the city. Don't you find that a little odd?"

Kitani nodded. "Perhaps that explains why some of this casino's occupants are giving us such dirty looks. Too bad we didn't bring our contact lenses with us to conceal our eyes. I'd prefer not to use my combat skills here, but if any of these rogues gives us trouble..."

"Calm down," Leara said. "Perhaps there's a rational explanation as to why this space station appears to be completely devoid of aliens. Do you think we should ask?"

"Ask? One of these galactic lowlifes?"

"What other choice do we have?"

Their conversation was interrupted when a young woman from the bar approached them.

"Excuse me," the woman said nervously—a bit too nervously, Leara thought. "You two wouldn't happen to be Valori, would you?"

"What do you think?" Kitani arched an eyebrow, purposefully drawing attention to her long, catlike pupils.

"Well," the woman stammered, dropping her gaze, "I only thought it fair to warn you. There seems to be some sort of virus that only affects aliens going around. One entire ward of Eden IV has been quarantined until further notice. You know, to help control the spread. But I wouldn't have a clear conscience if I didn't inform you of the situation."

"Thank you," Leara said with a gracious bow. "You've been most helpful." When the woman was out of earshot, she rounded on Kitani. "Did you hear that?"

"Sounds like Midas has been doing a little research here as well," Kitani said. "Do you think the space station's water supply has been tainted, or has Midas succeeded at developing an airborne version?"

"I don't know. We can only pray to the Goddess that the latter hasn't yet come to pass." *Not now, not ever*, Leara added mentally. "We should inform Cybil of this at once."

"Does she even care what happens to us? So far Midas hasn't targeted humans, so why should it bother the mercenary if we're in danger here?"

Leara frowned but could not find it in herself to argue. Too much was at stake for them to be at each other's throats. Instead, she asked, "What do you propose we do?"

"What can we do? Just being here has already compromised our health. Even if Reynard does intend to honor her promise and return us to Aria, it isn't safe for us to be among other Valori until we know what we're dealing with. It looks like we're stuck with Reynard, at least until we can be examined by a physician."

"You're right. It would be selfish for us to return to Aria now and possibly expose our people to the very thing we wish to protect them from. Still," she added casually, "Cybil deserves to know of our change of plans. Only she ordered us to wait here until she returns."

"We aren't her lackeys to be ordered about," Kitani said. "I say we track her down and barge in wherever she's holding this important meeting."

Leara chuckled at Kitani's rashness, finding it a small comfort to have something to take her mind off the very real danger she and Kitani were in.

"If you wish to get on Cybil's good side," she said to Kitani, "then I'm afraid you are going about it the wrong way."

As she and Kitani continued to make distracting small talk, Kitani casually pulled her to the side. "Don't call attention to yourself," she said, "but I believe we're being watched." Nodding in the direction of the gamblers, she indicated a group of darkly clad figures located at each corner of the room. "They've been tracking our movements for some time. Be ready. I think they're about to make their move."

Leara nodded her agreement, her mind barely registering Kitani's words. Who were these people? Were they the same mercenaries they had encountered on Kronos? And why would they choose a crowded casino to close in on them? Leara had little time to prepare herself before she noticed movement out of the corner of her eye. There were more of the figures clad in black armor than she realized. Kitani tried to place herself between Leara and the unknown stalkers as best she could, but the enemy had them surrounded on all sides. Leara could only watch from Kitani's shadow, trembling in spite of her efforts to remain calm as the dark figures closed in.

Where was Cybil? As much as Leara hated to admit she needed help from a human, the mercenary might be their only hope now.

* * *

Cybil kept her head lowered as she fidgeted with the long-stemmed glass on the table in front of her. She had explained to Kashmir how the research facility on Kronos had self-destructed, obliterating everything caught inside it or in its path—which, she'd added, had almost included herself.

"I know I completely botched this mission," Cybil continued, "so I don't expect any payment, nor would I accept it for such lousy work. By setting off the catastrophic chain of events at the research facility, I could have jeopardized the mission." She didn't mention that she might have mercenaries following her. In all truth, she'd be grateful if she could put this mission behind her and get on with her life, she thought.

Kashmir didn't appear in the least surprised that Cybil was rejecting payment for her efforts. Cybil knew why. Kashmir considered her an honorable woman who would never be satisfied with herself for leaving a job half done.

Kashmir turned the disk—the one taken from Midas Pharmaceuticals' headquarters on Turon—over in her hands once again. Since Kashmir had only requested the one disk, Cybil thought it best if she left the video footage shot on Kronos aboard her ship.

"On the contrary," Kashmir said, "causing Midas's outpost facility to self-destruct may turn out to be a strike in our favor in the long run. You did well, Cybil."

Cybil, playing the part of a downcast and disheartened mercenary just returned from a failed operation, kept her gaze focused on the table.

"So there's no need to be so glum. Here, have another drink with me," Kashmir said, refilling Cybil's glass with a sweet red Korvallian wine. "Maybe this time, you'll even have time for that lap dance before you leave. It's the least I can give you for your valiant efforts."

"I already told you," Cybil said as she rose from her chair, "I can't accept payment for an unfinished job. I wouldn't feel right about it." Despite the allure of Kashmir's feminine charms, Cybil found herself far more interested in the lovely Leara waiting for her in the lobby downstairs. The sparkling red wine didn't help, since Korvallia was the capital city of the Valori homeworld, Aria.

Kashmir laughed softly. "As uptight as ever, I see," she said with a smile, and then all signs of merriment faded from her countenance as she slowly uncrossed her legs and stood. She crossed the spacious dressing room in several elegant strides until she stood next to Cybil. "I have a remedy for that," she purred, her lips next to Cybil's ear.

Cybil flinched when Kashmir reached up to stroke her hair. "I must go," she insisted. "Someone is waiting for me downstairs."

"You mean those two Valori you came in with?" Kashmir's smile turned smug as Cybil looked to her in astonishment. "I have surveillance equipment set up all over this casino, Cybil," she went on. "The thermal scanner picked them up as soon as you set foot on the premises. Did you know that the body temperature of a Valori is noticeably higher than that of a human?"

Cybil had not known that fact and felt a fool for her lack of knowledge. While it was true that Leara and Kitani were probably not endangered by detection from Kashmir's equipment, the same could not have been said had she led them into hostile territory.

"I must admit, Cybil, I've had you pegged all wrong," Kashmir continued. "All this time, I thought you were something of a xenophobe. But now that you're traveling with two aliens..."

Cybil scowled. Did she really seem so anti-alien to those around her? Admittedly, she had expressed reservations toward other races in the past, mostly Zulians, but this was an entirely different matter. Kuvair N'arex was dead, justice was served, now it was time for her to move on.

"Two very attractive aliens, I might add," Kashmir said as she arched an eyebrow, dyed cobalt blue to match her hair, lips, and attire. Her attitude grew serious once again. "There's something I must tell you, and it's not in the least pleasant. A mysterious illness has been cropping up among the alien residents of Eden IV."

Cybil felt her heart stop when Kashmir relayed the grim news. Irrefutable proof, it seemed to her, of Leara's accusations against Midas.

"I've had my men closely monitoring every person entering the station for any sign of illness," Kashmir continued. "That's how I concluded your two companions were either aliens, or humans with high fevers."

"So it affects humans as well?"

Kashmir shook her head. "Not that we know of. So far only aliens have come down with symptoms of this mysterious ailment. Most reported cases have been Zulians, or species with similar physiology. A dangerously high temperature, followed by fatigue, paralysis, and in the most extreme cases, death. It doesn't seem to be very communicable, however, and that's something we can be thankful for. Only a handful have been infected, mostly residents of the east ward."

"The east ward? Isn't it mostly inhabited by aliens?" So it was a targeted attack, Cybil said to herself.

As if reading her thoughts, Kashmir nodded somberly. "My sources seem to think an amphibious humanoid such as a Zulian infected with the disease entered the station several days ago, but I can't know for sure. At any rate, this is serious. Considering the Zulian population on Eden IV, this could quickly become an epidemic if left unchecked. And the fact that it seems to be spreading to other species so soon doesn't bode well for us, I'm afraid."

There it was, Cybil thought, proof that the Valori's fears were not unfounded. Many of the test subjects mentioned on the data disks were Zulians, as were many of the buyers of Midas's drugs on Turon. She hesitated. Kashmir was bent on combating corruption in the galaxy. Millions of innocent lives were at stake, and she might be one of the few individuals with knowledge of Midas's threatened genocide. If she could trust anyone with the information she had, shouldn't it be Kashmir?

"I may have some inkling as to the truth," she said slowly, gauging Kashmir's reaction with each word. "I have a confession to make. That isn't the only data disk I obtained from Midas Pharmaceuticals."

"I already suspected as much, but go on."

"While infiltrating the outpost facility on Kronos, I stumbled across some information that would expose the corporation for the horrible monster it truly is."

Kashmir listened attentively as Cybil described in full detail the atrocious plan to launch a deadly array of biological weapons aimed at the galaxy's nonhuman population. When she concluded her story by recounting the pitiful condition of the test subjects in the video log, Kashmir frowned.

"It's worse than I imagined," she said. "If Midas achieves its goal and successfully creates an airborne version of these afflictions, no alien will be safe."

"No human either, I'm afraid," Cybil added, recalling Leara's warning.

"You may be right," Kashmir agreed. "At its current rate, Midas is on its way to becoming an intergalactic nightmare."

"I agree. We must crush it before it can grow too strong." Cybil suddenly gasped as she realized her two companions were currently unsupervised in a lobby filled with food and drink that could very well be toxic to them.

"You said the water might be contaminated?" she asked. "If that's so, I should really return to my guests before they have a chance to sample anything."

"Go right ahead," Kashmir said, "and the best of luck to you on your travels."

Cybil turned to go, but halted when Kashmir placed a hand on her arm.

"You have a new mission, Cybil," the woman said. "Protect your new friends at all costs. Don't let Midas get to them."

Cybil froze for a second, realizing that Kashmir had seen right through her. At last, she replied, "Understood."

"There's a secret emergency elevator at the back of the closet," Kashmir said. "I only reveal this knowledge to my most trusted friends."

"If this isn't an emergency, then I don't know what is." After another pause, Cybil decided to further confide in Kashmir. "You said this incident with the aliens began a few days ago, right? In that case, the timing would be accurate."

"Tell me, Cybil," Kashmir said with a wan smile, "what have you deduced?"

"Your client, the one who presented the information of the breach in Midas Pharmaceuticals' security and hired you to commission a mercenary to retrieve the data, could be the one who introduced the contaminants into the water supply. The information on that data disk was more confidential than you can imagine. I don't believe Midas intends to allow anyone with knowledge relating to this incident to survive, Kashmir, including you."

Kashmir appeared unfazed as she stared solemnly at Cybil. "I had already guessed as much," she said. "In fact, I've spent the better part of the last two days preparing for an emergency evacuation. Most of my possessions have already been loaded aboard a vessel waiting in an undisclosed location." She glanced around the spacious dressing room affectionately. "Eden IV has been a great base for operations, but in my line of work, one can never grow too settled. Come on, Cybil, I'll show you that secret exit."

Cybil followed, waiting impatiently while the secret elevator took her down to the casino's level. The doors opened, letting her out into an alcove designed to appear as no more than an elaborate flourish in the lobby's decor. Hidden in plain sight, she thought approvingly.

Her heart sank. The situation downstairs was much the same as before. The lobby was still filled with the laughter and boisterous talk of gamblers and adventurers, but the two Valori were nowhere in sight.

Thinking perhaps Leara and Kitani had come into contact with the tainted water, Cybil stalked across the atrium and sat down at the bar. Leaning forward on her elbows, she asked the bartender, "You didn't happen to serve any Valori earlier, did you?"

The woman looked up from the tumbler she was filling. "Valori? I saw a couple of Valori a short while ago. Warned them about the strange virus that's been infecting aliens."

Cybil breathed a sigh of relief. "Thank you. You've been more helpful than you can imagine." She left the young woman a generous tip and departed from the bar.

Where could those two have wandered off to? she wondered. Alarmed at the sudden desire to find and ascertain if her companions were safe, she pushed onward. She couldn't help thinking that the two women roaming aimlessly through Eden IV were at risk, even if they were armed with the knowledge of the unseen dangers lurking within the space station.

Could Leara and Kitani have been so frightened by the news of the sickness that they had decided to hide themselves? *Perhaps they're hiding from you*, a voice teased in the back of her mind. She had certainly provided little comfort or hospitality since collecting them on Kronos, and hiring a vessel to escort them to their home planet wasn't so difficult. Did they have the money to do such a thing? She wasn't sure. She'd had the decency not to rummage through their things during their brief stay on board her ship.

Cybil frowned. She was in no mood to pat herself on the back for her small generosity.

When she rounded a corner on the street outside Cloud Nine Casino, she found a pulse rifle aimed directly at the center of her forehead.

"Halt!" a gruff female voice commanded. "Throw down your weapons and keep your hands where I can see them. Who are you?"

Cybil dropped her pistol but didn't answer the question. Instead, her mind was racing with every possible alternative to getting shot by this accursed woman.

"I asked your name," the woman said as she closed the distance between them, the rifle's aim unwavering. She wore a heavily armored combat suit and a helmet that obscured most of her face. "I don't intend to ask you again," the woman continued. She came to a halt several paces in front of Cybil and then began studying her features with intense scrutiny.

"See something you like?" Cybil asked, knowing it was foolish to taunt someone pointing a pulse rifle at her head, but unable to refrain. Something in the woman's arrogant manner bothered her.

The woman guffawed. "Nothing here I'm interested in," she replied. "But you match the description I was given. Are you Cybil Reynard?"

"What's it to you?" Cybil remained defiant. She may have reached the end of the line, but she'd be damned if she was going to face her fate whining like a coward.

"I have orders to take you into custody. Your two accomplices have already been secured on my ship, and I've impounded your vessel." She kept the rifle trained on Cybil. "Either you be a good little girl and come along quietly, or we do things the hard way. The choice is yours to make. Personally, I'd prefer the second option. It's more fun." The woman bared immaculate white teeth at her in a feigned smile. "So what's it going to be?"

Sighing, Cybil turned in the direction of the docking bay. "Lead on," she said in a defeated tone. What else was she to do with the *Kashmir II* in this woman's clutches?

Letting her enemy believe she had been defeated, Cybil allowed herself to be herded through the busy streets of Eden IV. Considering the crime rate on the station, no one bothered to look twice at someone being ushered through the docking bay at gunpoint. It was one of the things Cybil had loved about Eden IV in the past. Now that the tables were turned, she was beginning to loathe the residents and their indifference to these types of situations.

Looking to the dock workers for help was pointless. She currently had bigger issues to worry about. Somehow, she had to devise a plan to get Leara and Kitani, as well as her ship, away from this woman. Once she regained access to the *Kashmir II*, she would be able to elude her captors easily. Now she only had to think of some way of getting back to her ship, hopefully with the two Valori in tow.

That wasn't going to be easy, but then, in Cybil's line of work, nothing ever was.

Chapter 7

Upon boarding her captor's vessel, a star frigate large enough to hold several ships the size of the *Kashmir II* in its shuttle bay, Cybil was reunited with Leara and Kitani. She breathed a sigh of relief when she saw they were unhurt. The two Valori were closely guarded by several armed men and women, obviously waiting until their apparent leader returned. As she went over to her friends, the woman shouldered her pulse rifle and removed her helmet.

Cybil thought the woman was in her early or mid-thirties, her brown hair cropped short—a common style for soldiers and mercenaries. After running her fingers through her hair, the woman's deep brown gaze fastened on Cybil with an intensity that hadn't been visible through the helmet's visor.

"Now," she said, her speech slow and deliberate, "what am I supposed to do with you, Cybil Reynard?"

Cybil scoffed. "Please, if you're going to kill us, then hurry up and get it over with. Otherwise, I might grow bored and restless."

"Kill you?" the woman said with barely contained amusement. "I imagine you're worth far more alive to me than you would be dead."

"Aren't you mercenaries sent to assassinate the three of us?" Cybil asked.

The woman looked offended at the question. "What do you take me for? A common assassin? Although I must admit, sometimes assassination proves the only way to accomplish a mission." She raked her gaze over Cybil rather pointedly as she paced in front of the group.

As the woman turned to the left, Cybil's eyes suddenly fastened on a crest she had failed to notice before, emblazoned high on the arm of the combat armor: an eye divided down the middle by a long, catlike pupil. A Valori eye.

"Then that makes you an excellent candidate for doing others' dirty work," Kitani said. "If you can truly assassinate someone for the sake of a mission, then why should we trust you? From what I've seen so far, you don't appear to be any better than a common bounty hunter."

"Don't antagonize her, Kitani," Cybil said, feeling her expression grow dark. "I know of her kind. She's far more dangerous than either of you could ever imagine." Turning to the woman, she said, "Who are you? What do you want with us?"

The woman smiled, offering a bow in clearly feigned politeness. "How very perceptive you are. I'm Commander Eris Duran, an agent of Cipher, and the commanding officer of the *Sentinel*. The order for your capture was issued to me by Enigma."

Cybil went rigid as Eris Duran confirmed what she had already known in her heart. She noticed the armed guards training their weapons on her as every muscle in her body tensed for an attack.

"Cipher?" Leara seemed incredulous. "As in *the* Cipher?"

Duran turned to Leara. "That's correct." She offered Leara a stiff bow before continuing, "When you failed to contact the Supreme Matriarchy after the Kronos incident, they assigned the task of learning of your fate to me. You can only imagine my surprise when I learned you had been taken into the custody of the same mercenary Enigma ordered me to capture. I knew I had to act fast, lest this opportunity should escape me."

"Were you the one firing on us back on Kronos?" Cybil asked, filled with burning hatred for the commander.

"Of course not," Duran said. "I was hired to bring Leara back alive, if at all possible. It seems you've picked up a new friend during your adventures on Kronos, Reynard. Whoever it is, they must really want you dead. You're lucky I found you when I did, so why not try to show a little gratitude?"

"Gratitude for what?" Cybil scowled as she spoke. "You've plucked me from one dilemma and dropped me right in the middle of another. So you've been hired to return these Valori to their homeworld. Where exactly does that leave me?"

"That, my friend, depends on High Matriarch Dallia. Although you have the protection of Enigma regarding your life, you did commit a pretty serious crime against the Valori and must expect to pay some price for it. You've been accused of kidnapping Leara Sorani, daughter of High Matriarch Dallia Sorani. Just so you know, the High Matriarchs do not treat such offenses lightly."

"Kidnapping?" Cybil said. "That's absurd! Do you realize that, if not for me, these two Valori would very likely be dead? I would never harm an innocent person. For all you know, I might have been hired as a bodyguard for the Valori," she added, remembering that Kashmir had, in fact, issued the order for her to protect Leara and Kitani at all costs.

"That's not for me to decide," Duran replied. "I'm not saying I don't believe you, but the Supreme Matriarchy has requested to meet with you in person—"

"Do I not have any say in this?" Leara interrupted hotly, her usually soft voice filled with resentment. "My mother isn't here right now, so this doesn't concern her."

Cybil was surprised by the way Leara's eyes flashed with anger at the mention of her mother. All this time, she had thought Leara meek and demure. Seeing the sudden fire in the petite Valori made her feel a grudging admiration.

"Cybil Reynard rescued Kitani and me from the consuming fires of the explosion on Kronos," Leara continued. "She doesn't deserve to be sentenced to a cruel fate at the hands of my overbearing and overprotective mother."

"Leara," Kitani interjected, "you shouldn't speak so harshly of High Matriarch Dallia."

"Please, Kitani, let me finish." Leara turned her icy gaze on Duran. "If anything bad befalls Cybil, do not count on the peaceful cooperation of Kitani or me. Either she goes free, or we revolt." She gave Kitani a slight nod to confirm her words. Kitani returned the gesture with a sigh of exasperation.

Kitani's weariness was echoed in Duran's words. "Very well," she said, motioning for her crew to lower their weapons. "Reynard is free to go. But she doesn't leave my ship before we dock on your homeworld," she added sternly. "Her involvement in this matter is too great to overlook. I won't have a price placed on my head for allowing this rogue to escape."

"Of course, Commander Duran," Leara said with a polite bow. "I will personally see to it that Cybil is on her best behavior."

Cybil, who had been listening to this exchange with keen interest, focused her attention on Leara. Why was Leara so concerned for her safety? She hadn't been particularly nice to Leara and Kitani since taking them aboard her ship.

"See that you do," Duran said, eyeing Cybil rather coldly. Her attention returned to Leara. "I'll send someone around shortly to escort you to our medical bay. I'd like to run a few tests on you, *Si'rah* Sorani, as well as your Paladin. A simple precaution," she added, holding up her hands as Kitani glared at her, "and one that may very well save lives. My superiors have informed me of the mysterious illness infecting alien citizens on Eden IV. Medical officers have been assigned to stay on the space station to deal with the situation. So far, the illness only seems to affect Zulians and other amphibious races, but we can't take any chances. We must ascertain that whatever is affecting the residents of the space station doesn't travel back with us to Aria."

"Agreed," Leara said, nodding briskly before Kitani had the chance to complain.

"I understand your reservations toward being examined by a human doctor, so I brought along a Valori physician particularly for this purpose." Duran inclined her head in a slight bow before walking away, leaving her three guests to discuss matters in semi-privacy.

"I'm glad that both of you are all right," Cybil said quietly when the Cipher agents became engaged in their own conversations. She found herself surprised by the depth of her concern. "I was worried. My employer informed me of the mysterious illness among the alien residents. When I couldn't find either of you, I assumed the worst."

"Perhaps now you finally believe the threat to our people is real?" Kitani said, folding her arms over her chest as she glared at Cybil.

Cybil shrank beneath Kitani's fiery gaze. She deserved that barb and many more. "I'm sorry for doubting you before. I should have known the Valori wouldn't send two undercover agents unless the threat was on an intergalactic level."

Obviously satisfied, Kitani relented, her gaze softening somewhat as she diverted her attention to the Cipher operatives surrounding them.

"How do you know of Cipher?" Cybil asked.

Leara replied, "Cipher was originally a Valori organization. When intergalactic expansion became a reality and dealing with other species an inevitability, the High Matriarchs decreed that an organization be formed to protect Valori space and maintain a level of peace among the other inhabitants."

"In other words, Cipher was created as a sort of reconnaissance network, so you could efficiently monitor your interstellar neighbors?" Cybil said wryly. When Leara began to shift uncomfortably, she added, "A brilliant idea once the possibility of interplanetary conquest became real. Of course, there are those who would take advantage of their own power in order to exploit others' weaknesses."

“Let them try,” Kitani said in evident challenge. “Cipher has been collecting information on the various species for centuries. Not a single detail escapes its watchful eye.”

Cybil made no attempt to negate Kitani’s boastful claim. In fact, she was familiar enough with Cipher’s reputation to know that Kitani spoke the undeniable truth. Cipher was everywhere. It was the eyes of the universe. Although it might have started as a Valori organization, it had grown and spread until it now encompassed every corner of the known universe. The very human Commander Duran’s presence was testament to the organization’s reach.

Also notorious was Cipher’s ambiguity regarding intergalactic issues. Somehow, the organization had come to be associated with every major conflict in the past, including the First Contact Wars which had nearly driven humanity to extinction. Cybil couldn’t believe that was mere coincidence.

“Cipher is on our side, I presume?” she said, hoping to glean any information she could from the two Valori.

Kitani made a derisive snort. “Cipher will always be on our side, even if it has started allowing other species in its ranks. However, your fate may not be so certain, Cybil Reynard. Perhaps you should start praying to whatever deity your kind believes in.”

“Enough, Kitani,” Leara said. “Don’t taunt Cybil so. Not after all she’s done to help us.”

Rolling her eyes, Kitani turned her back on Cybil.

“I can handle myself,” Cybil said. “But I’m delighted that I could be of assistance, however little it may have been.” Leara’s smile prompted her to go on. “Midas Pharmaceuticals cannot be allowed to reach its goal. This battle isn’t over. Justice will prevail.” *Even if I am forced to sit out the remainder of it*, she added mentally.

Leara said nothing, but continued to smile warmly at Cybil, who knew she had left herself exposed by searching for Leara and Kitani as soon as she learned of the tainted water supply. She had placed her life in danger, which ultimately meant that she cared about them and that she was not as coldhearted as she would have them believe.

Duran and her crew began to disperse, leaving Cybil to ponder this new twist in her fate. One of the Cipher officers approached the group. Kitani tensed as the woman stepped too close to Leara’s personal space, but Cybil was the person the agent watched closely.

“As quick-tempered as ever, I see,” the stranger said.

At the sound of the voice, Cybil’s head jerked up.

"Long time, no see, Cybil." The woman removed her helmet, revealing a cascade of rich brown, shoulder-length hair and a pair of deep brown eyes to match.

Kitani staggered back a half step when the woman brushed past her, but Cybil paid little attention, instead exclaiming exuberantly, "Sierra! Is that really you?"

"In the flesh," Sierra replied.

"How have you been? *Where* have you been? Captain Jarvis and the others were beginning to believe you'd left the galaxy." The strangeness of their meeting hit Cybil all of a sudden. She stepped back to examine the pitch black armor Sierra wore. "You're one of them, aren't you? A Cipher dog. That would explain why I couldn't find a trace of you anywhere. Almost like your existence had been erased completely." She narrowed her eyes, not hiding the pain she felt. "In a way it was, wasn't it? Why did you do it? Why did you sell your soul?"

Sierra grimaced at the slight. "I have my reasons," she replied. "Just as you have your own reasons for becoming a freelancer instead of joining the Midnight Suns."

"So you've heard?" Cybil was not surprised. "Cipher really is everywhere and anywhere, apparently."

"We have a lot to talk about, Cybil. Perhaps it would be best if everyone was settled in and comfortable." Sierra motioned for the group to follow her.

Cybil complied with Sierra's suggestion, but her mind was racing every step of the way. For years, she had both looked forward to and dreaded this day, but now that it had finally arrived, she knew the reunion wasn't going to be like old times.

Sierra regarded Cybil thoughtfully as she sat on the edge of a bottom bunk in the crew's barracks. Her friend had changed over the past eight years, yet it was obvious that the fire driving Cybil burned as brightly as ever.

"I see you decided to change your style," Sierra said as she gestured toward Cybil's short blond hair. "Nice. It makes you look tough." *But not as nice as your Valori friend*, she wanted to say, but refrained from doing so. The white-haired Valori had been watching her ever since she removed her helmet. Even now, she could feel those fiery orange eyes on her. "It suits you," she said to Cybil.

Cybil glanced away in apparent embarrassment, rubbing the back of her neck. "You didn't turn out so badly yourself," she countered. "But that should come as no surprise. You always were the pretty one." Her smile looked genuine. "It's great to see you again, even if you are a Cipher bastard."

"Don't be so judgmental. As I stated earlier, I have my reasons for joining Cipher."

"Such as?"

Sierra chewed her lower lip as she pondered confessing the entire truth. "I'm not at liberty to tell you. Not right now, anyway. Boss's orders."

"Boss as in that arrogant buffoon Eris Duran, or boss as in Enigma?" Cybil asked.

Sierra sighed. Of course, Cybil wouldn't let it go. To be protected by Enigma, the most elusive figure in the known universe, was too grand an honor to be dismissed.

"You shouldn't be so quick to insult the commander," she said rather sharply. "She's the first human commander of Cipher, an alien organization, not an easy task to accomplish. To answer your question, it was Commander Duran who ordered us not to disclose the details of our plan to anyone under any circumstances. And the rest, well, you'll find out for yourself soon enough."

Sierra knew she was being huffy, but she couldn't help it. There was no reason for Cybil to be so critical of her new life. Why did she always have to be so difficult? True, Cipher had the tendency to show up at some of the most controversial and devastating events in known history, giving it a rather bad reputation among the general public, but there were reasons for its convenient appearances at high profile tragedies. Cipher was dedicated to promoting peace and harmony among the races throughout the universe, and even more so, it was dedicated to preserving that peace at all costs, she thought. The paramilitary organization was secretive about its actions, preferring to operate in the shadows, which also contributed to its mysterious and somewhat sinister image. She believed Cybil had been spoon-fed the malicious rumors about Cipher, rumors that linked the organization to terrorism, murder, and mayhem. In that case, it was little wonder why her old friend would look on her decision with such disdain. It was up to her to change Cybil's opinion.

"You've probably heard all sorts of terrible things about us," Sierra added. "Remember, Cybil, you can't believe everything you hear."

"That's true," Cybil said, her gaze drifting to her two Valori companions.

Sierra cupped Cybil's shoulder in what she hoped was a gesture of camaraderie, and then looked at the two Valori, who had been watching their exchange with eerie, catlike alertness.

"Make yourselves at home," she said cheerfully "It looks like we'll be roommates for a while."

Her gaze met Kitani's for the briefest instant, but in those few fleeting seconds, Sierra saw a myriad of emotions flicker in the alien eyes. Curiosity was the most prevalent, she decided, accompanied by resentment, though whether it was resentment for her curiosity or for her capture and containment, she couldn't tell.

One thing she knew for certain: Kitani was the most gorgeous woman she had ever laid eyes on. Assuming, of course, a Valori could be accurately described as a woman. She saw no reason why they should not. The Valori often referred to themselves as mothers, daughters, and sisters, and their society was governed by a matriarchy—all terms used to describe females, although during the breeding season, Valori were capable of taking on what would be labeled as a male role by a sexually dimorphic species.

Sierra allowed her gaze to linger on Kitani just slightly longer than necessary, but Kitani noticed the staring and met her gaze as if issuing a silent challenge.

Backing down, Sierra looked away as she walked past, but not before giving Kitani one last playful wink. Kitani's olive skin colored slightly, and she looked away. Surprised, Sierra stifled a chuckle. She had supposed Kitani must have had plenty of passes made at her by humans while working undercover, but it seemed she was wrong.

Oh, she was so going to enjoy being bunkmates for the duration of the journey!

The room to which Leara, Kitani, and Cybil had been escorted was similar to the barracks on the *Kashmir II*, but with more than twice the space. After Sierra's departure, Leara watched as Kitani and Cybil collapsed cheerlessly on separate beds located on opposite sides of the room. Cybil seemed disheartened because Commander Duran had forbidden her access to the *Kashmir II* until they arrived at their destination. Kitani was likely upset because, due to Leara's promise to keep an eye on Cybil, they were forced to share a room with the mercenary.

Leara remained standing in the center of the room for some time, unsure which side of the room she should choose for sleeping. She had just begun to walk toward Kitani's side when it struck her that it would be entirely appropriate to take temporary residence next to Cybil. After all, the captain was her ward for the duration of the journey.

The thought obviously never occurred to Cybil, however. As Leara selected the bunk next to hers, the human's expression reflected utter surprise, mingled just slightly with suspicion. Across the room, Kitani rose from her bed and strolled briskly into the lavatory.

Leara edged closer to Cybil's bunk, sliding all the way to the foot of the bed where only a crisscrossing set of metal bars holding the structures in place separated them. Cybil turned to look at her, her pale eyes glittering in the light from the overhead illumination.

"Won't your friend be jealous?" she asked Leara. "She may misinterpret your actions as choosing me over her."

"Kitani and I have a strict business relationship." No matter how she tried, Leara could not hide her resentment at having someone forced to protect her against her will. She preferred not to speak about her relationship with the quick-tempered Paladin. Having someone dedicate their entire life to her for the sake of tradition alone did not seem right. "She is my bodyguard, nothing more. I have every right to make decisions for myself. I'm a grown woman of one hundred and twenty-three years."

"A hundred and twenty-three?" Cybil repeated, the darkness fading from her eyes.

Leara smiled. She knew revealing her age would lighten the mood as well provide a quick subject change. Humans were always fascinated by the longevity of the Valori.

"Yes," she replied. "I've lived for more than a century measured in human years, yet Kitani and my mother treat me as no more than a child, even when Kitani herself is but two years older than I."

Cybil's gaze turned serious again. "Your mother," she said, "is a High Matriarch of your people. That's a pretty high position among the Valori, isn't it?"

"Perhaps the highest," Leara said, feeling depression seeping into her. Thinking of her mother's and her people's expectations always fatigued her.

"Why didn't you tell me this before?" Cybil asked.

Panic filled Leara's mind as she recalled Kitani's warning of possible treachery on Cybil's part if the human ever learned her identity. She took the time to frame her reply carefully.

"Kitani thought it best if I kept my identity secret during this voyage," she said at last. "No one was to know of my lineage or of my connection to Valori government. But then this business with Commander Duran came along, and you know the rest."

"Duran," Cybil said, her voice dropping several octaves when she spoke the name, making it almost a growl instead of a word.

"You don't much care for her, do you?" Leara asked.

"You can't trust Cipher. Over the years, it's been present at almost every interracial conflict, every pivotal battle in humanity's fight for autonomy. And without fail, each time Cipher rears its head, thousands turn up dead. How could I trust an organization with a reputation like that?"

"What about Lieutenant Callaway? Isn't she an old acquaintance of yours?" Leara tried to mask her curiosity. She'd noticed the way Sierra looked at Cybil. Was she a former lover of Cybil's? Could such a relationship even exist in human society? She supposed it was really none of her business, but even so, she wanted to know the details of the history between the two.

"Sierra and I were childhood friends thrust together by unfortunate circumstances. Sierra was always the smart one. Why she'd do something as idiotic as joining Cipher is beyond me." Cybil sighed, rubbing her forehead. "Anyway, I'm certain Sierra knows what she's doing. She usually does."

"You sound concerned for her. Do you doubt your friend's judgment? Or are you merely worried that her decision will place you on opposite sides?" *Or are you afraid that whatever was once between you will never be again*? Leara wanted to ask, but she held her tongue.

Cybil answered as if she had read Leara's thoughts, "Sierra and I have been through too much together for a minor detail like this to drive us apart. We may not be on the same side, precisely, but we'll always remain allies, no matter who our employers may be. Speaking of which," she added, "I'm certain Duran wished to have me locked away in the brig, and she most likely would have, if not for your intervention." She paused and looked away. "I want to thank you for that," she continued.

Leara thought she detected a hint of embarrassment in Cybil's demeanor.

"It's only appropriate that I repay your kindness," Leara said. "Without your hospitality, Kitani and I would surely not have survived the Kronos incident. It was very noble of you to take in two strangers, especially with a story as wild as ours. You could have just taken the data disks and left us to die. Our presence has brought you nothing but grief from the beginning, I fear. And besides," she added, feeling somewhat shy, "I rather like you, Cybil Reynard."

Cybil's cheeks burned as she met Leara's gaze fleetingly and looked away. "No problem at all," she mumbled to the floor. "On the contrary, I'm glad I met you. Otherwise, I wouldn't have learned the truth about Sierra. This is the first I've heard of her in eight years. It was almost as though she vanished into thin air. Also," she added, her expression growing grave, "I've cornered some of my own demons. When I was a child, I watched my father coldheartedly murdered before my very eyes."

Leara felt her eyes widen in shock, but she remained quiet, listening to this glimpse into Cybil's past with keen interest.

"A Zulian," Cybil continued, "a man he thought he could trust pulled the trigger. From that day onward, I couldn't bring myself to trust others, especially aliens. Then I met you. I realize I haven't been very friendly," she added. "I'm sorry for the way I've treated you and Kitani. It's just that trust doesn't come easily for me. I'll try to be more understanding in the future."

Filled with pity for Cybil's loss, Leara said nothing. She couldn't imagine what it must be like for Cybil to carry around this burden. She no longer blamed Cybil for her prejudices. If she had been betrayed on such a deep level, she would have a difficult time trusting anyone as well.

Cybil apparently mistook her silence for disinterest. "I suppose I shouldn't bore you with all this," she said. "My childhood is my own burden to bear. I've come to accept that truth over the years. I only wish there was some way I could communicate with *Kashmir II*."

"Oh! Your ship," Leara said, snapping out of her daze and realizing for the first time that Commander Duran and her crew could possibly gain access to all the information stored in *Kashmir II*'s computer, including the very sensitive data obtained from Midas.

When she voiced her fears, Cybil didn't appear concerned.

"Don't worry," she said. "*Kashmir II* is undoubtedly aware of our situation, and has more than likely gone into a complete systematic lockdown to avoid having her systems breached. Artificial intelligence is really useful sometimes."

Her mind at ease, Leara steered the conversation into more lighthearted territory. "It will be wonderful to return home to Aria after such a long and trying journey," she said. "I only hope Mother won't make a big deal over my homecoming. I'm exhausted and in no mood to be flaunted around."

Cybil grew reflective and quiet, so Leara followed her example and sat in silence, listening to the hum of the ship's propulsion system. Truth be told, she dreaded making landfall on her world, for doing so would bring her adventures with Cybil to an end. Traveling through space with a tough mercenary was exciting, she had to admit, and things were just starting to get interesting. Cybil was a fascinating woman. She could only regret that she would not have time to learn more about her.

While Cybil was too preoccupied to notice, Leara admired her profile. Cybil was an attractive woman, Leara would openly admit as much. Up close, human women didn't appear very different from Valori, a discovery she found both unsettling and something of a relief. She didn't know how she would have coped with coexisting alongside the Midas employees those long months if not for the familiarity associated with human females. Without that, infiltrating the corporation would certainly have been much more challenging, she thought, for Valori looked nothing like human males or Zulians.

Casting another admiring glance at Cybil, Leara felt a curious sensation within her, a sort of warm tingling in her belly. The warmth spread along her abdomen before settling between her legs, where a pleasant thrumming startled her from her thoughts.

Apparently, she found Cybil more attractive than she would care to admit, she thought, fidgeting absently with the coverlet on the bunk. What was she thinking? Cybil was practically a stranger, and an alien at that.

Never in her life had Leara considered herself a lustful person. Back on Aria, she was content to lounge around the Sorani estate, mostly keeping to herself. She found the social events her mother forced her to attend excruciatingly awkward. Having to constantly turn down the eligible suitors her mother sent her way was not her idea of a fun evening.

She had certainly never felt this way for any of those high-ranking Valori or their daughters. This feeling, this longing, was new to her, but she decided it was not altogether unpleasant. How a human mercenary had managed to awaken such want in her was a mystery, but it was definitely there.

Even as she watched Cybil stare into nothingness, she had to struggle to keep her hands from straying to her hair or skin, which looked so pale and soft in the dim light. She gave herself a mental reprimand for thinking such things, reminding herself how inappropriate Cybil would likely view such an action.

Humans are not like us, she had to keep telling herself. They were a race consisting of two separate and distinct sexes. Cybil had claimed that she did not find this aspect of the Valori repulsive, but Leara feared she was only being polite.

She gave a mental shrug. She had too little experience with humans to fully comprehend their behavior, and with Cybil withdrawn into herself again, she dared not voice her questions. Cybil had been far more generous than usual when she'd shared the details of her youth. It would be rude and inconsiderate for her to ask any more.

The almost omnipresent sadness had returned to Cybil's features shortly after she became lost in thought, which made it all the more difficult for Leara to believe that Cybil was nothing other than an interstellar rogue. *You aren't a cold-blooded murderer, are you*? But of course Cybil did not answer her probing thoughts and instead remained as silent as the stars.

Chapter 8

Cybil woke from a restless sleep, shivering beneath the thin coverlet provided on her bunk. Sitting up, she looked around, but neither Leara nor Kitani had stirred. *Must have been a dream*, she told herself, but the reassurance did nothing to ease her frayed nerves. It was impossible to relax while she was being held captive aboard a Cipher frigate, even if her best friend was a member of the crew.

Former best friend, that irritating little voice in the back of her mind reminded her. Cybil scanned the rest of the bunks in the women's quarters. Sure enough, Sierra was still absent. Probably a high-and-mighty Cipher lieutenant didn't want to share quarters with a lowly prisoner, she thought bitterly.

Rising from the bunk, she tiptoed to the lavatory, closing the door behind her. The door made a faint hiss as it slid down to the floor. She waited a minute to see if she had wakened the Valori. Their hearing was far keener than a human's, and she doubted either of them were sleeping very soundly under such strange conditions. When she heard nothing on the other side of the hatch, though, she moved next to the sink, staring into the mirror above.

She looked a total wreck. With a blackish half-circle under each eye, and her short blond hair matted and sticking out in all directions, she looked as though she hadn't slept in weeks. She felt a wreck, too. It seemed her life of violence, peril, and mayhem was finally catching up to her. She wasn't thrilled with the toll her lifestyle was taking on her physical appearance.

Perhaps a period of rest and relaxation is in order before I embark on my next journey, she decided. That thought brought Sierra to mind once again.

She wondered how she was going to relate to Sierra the grim news of her mother's true fate. It would have been difficult enough sharing the knowledge with her friend, but conveying the message now that Sierra was a Cipher lieutenant seemed next to impossible.

These thoughts and more had been troubling her ever since she was brought to the *Sentinel*.

She shrugged. That would have to wait. She had heard that the Valori homeworld of Aria was a veritable paradise, especially in the equatorial regions where the capital city, Korvallia, was located. She doubted her stay on the planet would be entirely peaceful, though. There remained the matters of the Midas files and her alleged kidnapping of Leara Sorani to be dealt with.

A shudder racked her body as Kitani's earlier words rang out, unbidden, in her mind. She had warned Cybil that, despite being a generally peaceful race, the Valori could swiftly convert to violence. There were many stories of Valori warriors told throughout the galaxy, but until she'd met Kitani, Cybil hadn't taken a word of them to heart, believing the Valori to be pacifists, and thus, no threat. Now she hoped that Leara's protection would extend to Korvallia and right into the heart of the council chambers where the High Matriarchs held their meetings.

That was another thing troubling her, warding off any chance of sleep. Baring her soul so freely was very uncharacteristic of her, yet something in Leara's gentle demeanor had prompted her to do so. Leara was so easy to talk to it made Cybil want to open up and confess all her deepest fears, her innermost secrets. *Am I growing soft*? Not as soft as Leara had been when she held her in her arms...

Cybil tried to shake the thought from her mind, even splashed cold water on her face from the sink, but it was no use. It had been some time since she last afforded herself the pleasure of female company. Leara might just be the most gorgeous person she had ever met.

I rather like you, Cybil Reynard. Leara's words reached in and touched a place Cybil thought she had sealed off long ago. A thrill ran over her body as she envisioned Leara speaking those same words in a much more suggestive way. In her mind, she imagined how soft and warm Leara's skin would be beneath her fingertips, against her mouth.

She mentally reprimanded herself for having such thoughts. *Time for a cold shower. Or two.* Stripping off the thermal underwear, which she wore as night clothes in the absence of anything else, she stepped into the cylindrical shower stall, activating the cold rinse. She felt droplets of recycled water spray against her skin. The carefully rationed water did not last nearly long enough, but it served its purpose in driving out thoughts of the beautiful Valori sleeping in the next room.

Cybil shuddered, stifling a moan. Such thoughts were becoming more frequent with each day she spent with Leara, no matter how she fought to resist her most basic desires. Leara was quite lovely. Her glossy black hair looked invitingly soft, and Cybil could hardly resist the urge to run her fingers through the silken mane. And Leara's eyes were a wonder, the irises icy blue yet passionate enough to melt ice. Those eyes were deeper than the ocean and broader than the sky, and they managed to speak volumes even when Leara herself did not utter a single word. Yet Leara was a Valori, an alien very different than a human woman. Her age and reproductive capabilities proved that truth.

Valori reproduction did not disgust Cybil as it did some humans. On the contrary, living in a society that consisted entirely of women seemed a pleasing prospect to her. What would Leara think if she came out to her as a lesbian? She'd had such thoughts over the past few days, but Leara had spent little time among humans in her long life and likely had never heard of such a thing before.

If only she could bring herself to enlighten Leara of the world beyond Valori space... but that was wishful thinking. She was too embarrassed to discuss the topic of human sexuality with Leara. She dared not imagine Kitani's reaction if she tried to broach the subject with her. *The Paladin would likely kick me across the room again*, she decided with a smile, and then her smile faded. She never would have dreamt it possible, but she was growing fond of both Valori and didn't look forward to parting ways with them so soon.

After pressing a button on the shower control panel, a blast of cool air dried her and she stepped out of the stall. Cybil quickly donned her discarded thermals, eager for the warmth they would provide, and returned her attention to the mirror. Her hair had lost the greasy, matted look and was now as soft and fluffy as down, but the bluish black patches remained beneath her eyes. *I suppose no amount of scrubbing can remove those*. Sleep was the only cure, but unfortunately, she didn't imagine she'd be able to sleep, not when Leara lay so close to her.

Dimming the lights to avoid waking her roommates, she opened the hatch and quietly walked back to her bed. On her way there, she couldn't help pausing to admire the sleeping Leara. The Valori lay with her face tilted up, the low light in the room barely enough to illuminate her fine features.

Cybil's heart pounded as she hovered inches above Leara, whose lips were slightly parted. Her mouth looked so soft and delicate that, for a moment, Cybil wondered what it would be like to kiss her, and then Leara's long black eyelashes fluttered.

Fearing Leara had felt her staring, swiftly and silently Cybil returned to her bunk, pulling the covers to her chin, but sleep was the furthest thing from her mind. She tossed and turned for what seemed like hours, the image of Leara sleeping peacefully vivid in her mind. Finally, the weight of sleep fell on her eyelids, making them heavy, and the world around her grew dark as she dozed.

Cybil was almost asleep when she felt a gentle nudge on her shoulder. She opened her eyes to find Sierra standing over her, a worried look darkening her usually bright and pleasant face.

"We're under attack," Sierra said in a hushed whisper, as if afraid the alleged attackers might overhear her. "I don't know how the enemy managed to elude us this long, but it seems like they've been trailing us for quite a while. We'll have to shake them as soon as possible."

Cybil sat up, her mind trying to process the information Sierra was giving her. Leara and Kitani were already up, she noticed.

Kitani hadn't wasted a second donning her armor. The Paladin looked as though she was aching for a fight, fidgeting restlessly while Cybil continued to stare quizzically at Sierra.

"Rise and shine, Cybil," Sierra repeated. "When the commander says all hands on deck, she means everyone. Commander Duran expects every person on this ship to pull his or her weight, regardless of that person's status among the crew." She looked pointedly at Cybil.

"Who's attacking us?" Cybil asked, now fully awake.

"Who would be foolish enough to launch an attack on a Cipher vessel?" Kitani added.

"Given there's no insignia on the ship, I can only surmise they're mercenaries. As to why mercenaries would be attacking Cipher, I have no idea."

"I have an idea," Cybil interjected. She wondered briefly if she should tell Sierra of her predicament with Midas. Could she trust her childhood friend now that she was a lieutenant in a shadow organization?

"Any information you have could be useful," Sierra said.

Sierra would never ally herself with the bad guys, Cybil decided. *No matter what her reason for joining Cipher, Sierra must sincerely believe she's doing the right thing.*

"We're being hunted," Cybil said, indicating herself, along with Leara and Kitani. "We've acquired some rather sensitive information on a notorious corporation, and it appears these people are willing to go to any lengths to get it back."

"Who's hunting you, Cybil?" Sierra appeared genuinely concerned. "What sort of information do you have, exactly?"

"Incriminating evidence," Cybil said in a matter-of-fact tone. She crossed her arms over her chest. "In the wrong hands, this information could be detrimental to one of the largest corporations in the universe."

"Midas Pharmaceuticals."

Cybil nearly fell over from shock when Sierra accurately guessed their enemy's identity.

"How do you know about Midas?" she asked once she regained her composure.

Sierra looked offended. She said, "Cipher has been tracking Midas for years, carefully monitoring its actions across settled space. We've known about Midas for some time. The conspiracy to develop and employ carefully constructed biological weapons against our alien allies is nothing new to Cipher. I must admit, I'm surprised that you'd find yourself embroiled in such a high-profile case."

"Then you know about..."

"About what Midas did to my mother? Sure. That was one of my reasons for joining Cipher in the first place." Sierra shook her head. "So young and naïve, I never realized there were far bigger problems in the universe than my own frustrations."

"So you've known all along?" Cybil was secretly grateful that she wouldn't have to be the bearer of bad news, yet she felt strangely isolated at being the last to know.

Sierra nodded. "The research they were conducting at Touchstone Cybernetics was considered highly controversial at the time, research that included everything from genetic modification to cybernetic implants. Needless to say, it attracted a lot of undesired attention, including the attention of Midas Pharmaceuticals. Perhaps Midas saw my mother's research as a rival to its own, or maybe it just wanted to eliminate the facility. Whatever the reason, I won't let the corporation get away with the crimes it has committed."

A barrage of enemy fire struck the hull of the *Sentinel*, bringing Cybil's mind back to the current problem. Swinging her legs over the side of the bunk, she grabbed her combat armor, struggling into it before following Sierra and the others. By the time the group reached the bridge, she was fully dressed and as ready for a fight as

Kitani, although she had her doubts whether any of them would be granted access to weapons.

"I've brought our guests," Sierra informed Commander Duran.

With her cooperation, and that of the two Valori, the commander's crew would be increased to fourteen, including the commander herself, Cybil thought. If they didn't cooperate, she, Leara, and Kitani would likely be locked away in the brig.

Sierra turned to Cybil, asking, "Can we trust you with a gun? You won't try to shoot any of us in the back, will you?"

Cybil glared past Sierra at Duran for a moment before replying, "I'll be on my best behavior, Sierra. Given the circumstances, it doesn't look like I have much of a choice. Now what do you want me to do?"

"Excellent. Do you know how to operate a plasma cannon? One of our gunners was wounded during a previous battle."

"I thought you were going to give me a gun, not assign me a station at a plasma cannon."

"You didn't actually think we would return your weapons to you while we are under enemy fire." Duran pinned her with the weight of her gaze. "It would be the perfect opportunity for you to try to run. This way, you have the chance to make yourself useful without causing harm to me or my crew. I expect everyone aboard my vessel to pull their weight."

Cybil was speechless. She hadn't really known what to expect, but being asked to play gunner for a Cipher vessel had been the last thing on her mind. And Sierra questioning her loyalty when she knew there was no possible way for her to commit mutiny in such a position… well, she didn't know what to think. She looked at Sierra, who had a wide grin on her face as she awaited an answer.

Sighing, Cybil decided there was no way out of the situation. "Very well," she said. "Show me the cannon, and I'll see what I can do."

Kitani bristled slightly when Sierra asked Cybil to take control of the *Sentinel*'s guns, but she doubted any of the humans noticed. Beside her, Leara stared after the two human women while Sierra gave Cybil a brief overview of how the cannon functioned… a touch grudgingly, she thought. Kitani begrudged Cybil her position as well, but her jealousy stemmed from the humans choosing Cybil over her for the replacement of the injured gunner, or so she told herself. She watched Cybil sitting at the controls with Sierra leaning very close as she explained their functions and felt a tremor of envy shake her body.

Leara must have sensed her discomfort. She momentarily tore her attention away from Cybil. “Are you all right, Kitani?” she asked. “You’re shaking.”

“It’s nothing,” Kitani said, rather more harshly than she intended. She turned her back on the human women, adding in a softer tone, “Only annoyed at how these blasted humans continue to overlook our presence as if we didn’t exist. Can a race be truly so narcissistic and conceited? I mean, I have far more experience with manual weapons than Reynard. Everything about her ship is automated.”

“Now who’s being conceited? If you wanted to help so badly, why didn’t you volunteer your services earlier?” Leara asked. Before Kitani could say anything, she added, “It’s frustrating, I know. To be left out of the loop as these humans go about their daily routines. Perhaps they only want to protect their own interests. Being assigned escort duty to a High Matriarch’s daughter isn’t a task to be taken lightly.”

“That’s exactly what keeps them at a distance,” Kitani said. “They see us as a liability. Never mind you and I are capable of holding our own in combat.” She knew Leara had been thinking the same thing, only she dared not speak of it lest she insult Cybil Reynard.

The Valori were outnumbered on the Cipher vessel, Kitani thought. She hadn’t failed to notice that every single member of the small crew was human, except of course for the Valori medical officer who had examined her and Leara earlier. How could a great Valori organization like Cipher have become overrun with humans in so little time?

“Our starboard engine’s been hit,” the navigator called out. As if to confirm his words, the *Sentinel* suddenly veered dangerously to the port side. Kitani held tightly to Leara and braced herself against the wall.

“I want a full damage report, Jacques,” said Duran, who despite the very real peril her ship faced, seemed unnaturally calm and collected. Navigator Jacques was clearly trying to match her composed demeanor as he framed his reply, but failed terribly.

“The main propulsion system remains operable, but we’ve lost our starboard engine.” Kitani heard a very evident tremor in the man’s voice.

"Then we'll have to make an emergency landing," Duran said. "What's the nearest terrestrial world?"

"That would be Cerulean, commander."

"Set course for Cerulean. Perhaps we can give our adversary the slip when we enter restricted space."

Kitani doubted that. Now that they possessed knowledge of Midas's heinous plot, she suspected the mercenaries would track them all the way to Aria, if they made it that far, which at the moment did not seem very likely.

She was forced to hold fast to a secure object when the ship turned sharply in its altered course toward Cerulean. The blue planet came into sight within minutes and, just as Kitani had hoped, granted the *Sentinel* permission to enter its atmosphere. Once the crippled frigate was caught in Cerulean's gravitational pull, it began descending rapidly toward the planet's surface.

Having strapped herself in a chair after seeing to Leara, Kitani gripped the armrests, watching the viewport as the ground rushed up to meet them. The ship was currently over one of Cerulean's many seas, the sparkling blue water looking anything but welcoming as it threatened to submerge the *Sentinel*, swallowing all life aboard.

"Steer us toward the beach beyond those trees," she commanded, nearly pushing the startled pilot out of her seat. She reached for the controls. "Anywhere away from the bay."

The pilot complied with the commander's order. The *Sentinel* grazed the tops of the trees, toppling a line of scraggly conifers in its wake as it skidded to a halt in the sandy soil.

Immediately after impact, Kitani checked on Leara, who remained buckled into the chair next to her. "Are you all right?" she asked.

Leara gazed at her, clearly dazed, her pale blue eyes wide and unfocused. "A little shaken up," she replied, "but otherwise I think I'm fine."

Around the bridge, people were helping their comrades to their feet or tending to the wounded, but Duran seemed unfazed by the rough landing, Kitani noted.

"Any landing you can walk away from," Duran said, laughing heartily.

Cybil, on the other hand, didn't appear to find the situation the least amusing. "You might want to postpone the celebration for a while. We have company," she said.

Kitani's heart sank as she looked out the ship's port observation window. Cybil was right. The *Sentinel* may have landed on Cerulean, but the Midas assassins were still tailing them. Three small assault craft had clearly launched from the battleship, fast approaching while the frigate sat helpless on the ground.

"Everyone, brace yourselves," Duran shouted, but the dreaded attack never occurred. Instead, one of the fighters suddenly burst into flame, promptly followed by another. The final assault craft tried to make its escape. Kitani watched as a Cerulean photon cannon blasted the remaining enemy out of the sky. The Ceruleans had saved them, twice if one included letting them make an emergency landing on their world.

Kitani sat back in the chair and drew a deep breath. It had been a long night, but if her intuition proved correct, their troubles were far from over.

Chapter 9

Pacifica, the capital city of Cerulean, was breathtakingly beautiful, Leara thought. Its sandy beaches and crystalline waters were every bit as wondrous as those found on Aria, if not more so. She was glad that after their harrowing escape, the crew of the *Sentinel* had been invited by the Ceruleans to their magnificent city while repairs were made to the ship.

She had learned the Ceruleans were a kind and hospitable race in general—their architecture reflected a laid-back lifestyle and incorporated themes of the planet's oceanic nature—but like the Valori, they wouldn't hesitate to take action when threatened. The Ceruleans were an amphibious race, living as easily on land as in water, a fact she found evident throughout the capital. The streets and courtyards contained enormous pools and fountains, not merely as decorative elements, but intended for swimming as well.

Leara took in every detail with wonder as she explored the vast courtyard in front of the embassy building in which she and her companions were housed. It was the first time since her departure from Aria that she'd had the leisure to admire an alien landscape and she intended to do so with relish.

Having spent most of her life in the coastal region of Korvallia, located on the main continent of Aria, she felt quite at home by the sea. She was surprised when she learned this was Cybil's first time viewing an ocean.

"I spent most of my childhood on colonized worlds," Cybil had said when Leara voiced her surprise. "After my parents' death and the Midnight Suns rescued me, I stayed in a little orphanage in the colony of Cornelia's Hope. It seemed there was never any time to take a vacation."

She couldn't imagine how lonely Cybil's life must have been. Although Dallia's matriarchal duties kept her busy much of the time, there had always had someone around, usually Kitani or one of the other Paladins, to take care of her daughter.

Leara walked around the courtyard, recalling that Cybil was currently with Duran and the rest of her crew, negotiating with the Ceruleans to decide a form of payment for the damages their ship's emergency landing had caused.

The commander no doubt didn't trust leaving Cybil to her own devices, Leara thought, and had left her under the supervision of her old friend, Sierra—another source of grief.

Cybil and Sierra seemed awfully close. Cybil might have made it painfully clear that she loathed Cipher and everything it stood for, but she was still willing to trust Sierra. That much seemed obvious. Could she ever hope to obtain that level of confidence from Cybil? Perhaps only time could answer that question.

She and Kitani were free to wander about the city as they pleased. Kitani, weary of the confines of the various ships and space stations they'd been forced to live in on their mission, had told her earlier she wanted to have a closer look at the ocean, and now Leara wanted to join her.

Leara found Kitani standing on the curb of a cobbled street leading to the water, where dry land met the sea. Kitani was focused on the area of shallow water before her, pools of sapphire-blue shimmering beneath the afternoon sun.

"Maybe I was wrong about Eris Duran after all," Kitani said suddenly. "I thought she had no regard for life unless it was human, but look over there."

Leara obeyed, gazing with curiosity and fascination at the strange pools. Upon closer inspection, she saw they were constructed of coral formed along the sides of the highway in the same stretch of ocean the *Sentinel* had nearly plummeted into. Many of the indentations in the reef were filled with round, shiny objects that resembled bubbles.

"What are they?" Leara asked, fascinated.

"This is the Ceruleans' spawning ground," Kitani said. "By diverting the *Sentinel*'s path, Commander Duran saved many young lives, even though in doing so she risked the lives of herself and her crew. Perhaps humans are not completely without honor." She smiled, a thin, tight-lipped smile, but Leara knew it meant Kitani was pleased. Clearly, the commander had raised Kitani's estimation of her and perhaps of humanity in general.

"And those shiny objects are Cerulean eggs?" Leara's previous knowledge of the galactic races consisted mainly of Valori, which, despite their unique reproductive systems, were still mammals. This was her first encounter with an egg-laying race. It was hard to believe that the luminous orbs would someday mature into the humanoid Ceruleans.

"They're amazing," she added. Beside her, Kitani nodded.

"I've heard the humans refer to the Ceruleans as mermaids," Kitani said, "after an old legend which originated from their homeworld. Mermaids were beings with the upper body of women and the tails of fish. Ceruleans don't have tails, not that I've seen anyway, but their ability to thrive both on land and in water certainly explains this association."

Mermaids? Leara mused as she continued to gaze out at the ocean. She wondered how humanity viewed her own kind and, more importantly, how Cybil viewed her. She was so immersed in her concerns that her mind did not register the sound of other people approaching until she heard Cybil's voice.

"When will the ship be ready to take off?" she was asking Lieutenant Sierra Callaway as they walked along the seaside road.

"The repairs should take a few days," Sierra answered. "Ceruleans may not look it, but they're very nimble at performing such tasks."

"Never would have expected that. Not with their webbed fingers and all." Cybil paused, a bit uncertainly it seemed to Leara, and then asked, "You're familiar with the Ceruleans?"

Sierra laughed. "Our hosts are from the Cerulean branch of Cipher. I've worked with quite a few of them over the years. Let me tell you, they're an asset to have around."

"The Ceruleans are working with Cipher?" To Leara's ear, Cybil's voice contained a hint of incredulity. "I suppose that shouldn't come as such a shock. The Ceruleans are a peaceful race, and Cipher exists to promote unity throughout the galaxy. Or so it claims."

"You still don't believe we're fighting for the greater good? Cybil, do you honestly think I would fight for anything else?"

Leara stared at Cybil in expectation as Sierra awaited an answer. At last, Cybil said cryptically, "Perhaps, in time, we shall see just how honorable Cipher's intentions really are. Until then, for your sake, I'll reserve judgment."

Leara continued to watch as Sierra and Cybil stared each other down. Only the sound of someone else nearby tore her gaze away from the two women. Duran had moved to join her and Kitani by the water and had begun speaking to them in a low voice.

"Glad to see the little ones are all right," Duran said with evident relief as she gazed out over the Cerulean spawning ground and the shiny orbs within the pools. "It looks like they'll be ready to hatch soon."

Despite having so many questions about Ceruleans and the development of their young, Leara held her tongue. Something in the way Duran and Kitani stared at the ocean mesmerized her. Perhaps it was the serenity of the moment that took her breath away, but whatever it was, she decided her questions could wait until later. It seemed they would be spending a few days on Cerulean. There would be plenty of time to learn more about the planet's culture while the *Sentinel* was undergoing repairs.

Cybil wasn't thrilled at the prospect of remaining a prisoner of Cipher for longer than originally planned, nor was she pleased by the fact that Commander Duran seemed intent on restricting her access to the *Kashmir II*. She would have liked to examine the files taken from Midas's headquarters again, perhaps even share the information with Sierra, but there was a good chance the Cipher lieutenant already knew everything contained on the disk and more. What infuriated her was Sierra's refusal to impart any exclusive information to her. Sighing, she rolled over onto her back.

Without access to her own ship and with all the restrictions placed on her actions, there was little to do while she awaited repairs to the *Sentinel* to be completed. She could either go into the courtyard, enclosed on all sides by the massive embassy building, or lie around her room all day. Since she was currently in no mood for a stroll through the gardens, she had opted for brooding in the relative privacy of her room.

Lying on her side gave her a view of the outside world through the small window. All that was visible from the third floor, however, were the tops of the tall, palm-like trees lining the court. The window had been left partially open. She was thoroughly fascinated by the continuous roar of the surf, and the cool breeze was refreshing.

Through the noise of the ocean, Cybil heard a faint murmur from the courtyard below. She thought she recognized a few of the voices. Rising from her bed, she padded barefoot over to the window and looked out, seeing Leara and Kitani talking to a Cerulean.

She thought the Cerulean might be female, but from such a distance, it was hard to tell. Discerning gender among the blue-skinned humanoids was difficult enough at close range, since even the males possessed very effeminate features. The long flowing garments favored by both genders did little to help distinguish the sexes.

Cybil remained surprised at how well the Ceruleans maneuvered on land, but this was her first encounter with them. With their pale blue skins, she imagined they would be nearly invisible in the water—the perfect camouflage for an aquatic life form.

She recalled how she had often joked with Kashmir that her hair color matched the mermaid people. Thoughts of her old life reminded her just how seriously she had botched her last mission, so she preferred not to dwell on them, instead wondering how Kashmir was faring after her departure from Eden IV. As far as employers went, Kashmir was one of the best, and she had even come to think of the blue-haired vixen as her friend.

Thoroughly dismayed by her thoughts, Cybil sank into a chair next to the window, continuing to watch the three figures in the courtyard. She wondered if her life would return to normal now that she had met the Valori, then she wondered just how normal that life had been in the first place. Most of all, she wondered if she should go down to the courtyard and join the group. She considered this option a second longer before deciding that perhaps a stroll through the courtyard would do her good. Lying around reflecting on her past accomplishments and failures was depressing, and, furthermore, she had some things she wished to discuss with Leara and Kitani while Sierra was occupied elsewhere. After informing the two guards posted outside her room of her intentions, she made her way to the enclosed courtyard.

When Cybil drew near the assembled group in the courtyard, she recognized the Cerulean Navetrian, Cybil believed she was called, for she had made it clear at an earlier meeting that she was female when Cybil made the dreadful mistake of referring to her as male.

The Cerulean was the first to notice her arrival. Bowing in the stiff fashion of her people, Navetrian said curtly, “Good evening, Miss Reynard. I trust you are finding your accommodations satisfactory?”

Navetrian had been put in charge of ensuring proper lodging for the unexpected guests. Cybil thought she obviously took her duty quite seriously, despite the earlier faux pas.

“Couldn’t be better,” Cybil replied, returning the bow. “After spending so much time in cramped ships recently, your planet is like a little piece of paradise.”

Navetrian seemed pleased. After politely excusing herself to Leara and Kitani, she took her leave.

"Such charming people, the Ceruleans," Cybil said once Navetrian was gone. "And the planet is just beautiful. If I ever find time for a vacation, I believe I'd like to return here someday." She meant every word in spite of the hint of sarcasm leaking through.

"Was there something you wanted to say, Reynard?" Kitani asked, narrowing her eyes. As usual, Kitani appeared in favor of skipping the niceties and getting right to the point.

"I've been thinking about the situation with Midas, and I've come to fear for this planet's safety. Are the Ceruleans aware of what they risk to provide us safe harbor?" Cybil asked. "Their ecosystem is a fragile one. If Midas happened to release one of its pathogens here—"

"I'm sure Cipher knows what it's doing," Kitani interrupted. "As do the Ceruleans. Commander Duran seems committed to her promise of ensuring the safety and harmony of the galaxy. Don't worry about these things, Reynard. When you're distracted by unfounded fears and vague possibilities, you're of little use to anybody."

Cybil glared at Kitani. "You have a point, but are you really so sure we can trust Commander Duran's intentions?"

"What does it matter? Currently, our opinions make little difference in decisions made by Cipher." Kitani glanced away, suddenly turning sullen and withdrawn.

"This grim talk chills me to the very core," Leara said, diverting Cybil's attention from Kitani. "So much has happened. Perhaps it's left us all on edge."

"You couldn't be more right," Cybil said. Feeling the stares of the Cipher guards, she added, "Maybe we should discuss this some other time. I..." she began, letting her voice trail off uncertainly. She cleared her throat before trying again. "I was actually hoping to talk to you again, if you would permit it?"

Kitani's gaze seemed to burn holes in Cybil's skull as she glared, but Leara appeared pleased by Cybil's offer. "I'd like that," she said, smiling radiantly.

"Maybe tomorrow?" Cybil asked.

To Kitani's visible horror, Leara agreed to meet her the following morning. Walking back to her room on the third floor, Cybil wondered what had possessed her to extend such an offer. True, Leara was easy to look at, and the fact that she was pleasant to talk to didn't hurt, either. But good looks and engaging conversation weren't everything, she had to remind herself. Leara was still an alien. She was different and always would be. So why did she find herself looking forward to their next meeting? It felt almost like a date, but she knew that was silly. Even though she was attracted to Leara, it was ridiculous to think the Valori would ever be interested in pursuing a relationship with a human.

With a sigh, Cybil shoved her hands in her pockets and entered her room to resume her position by the window. She stared up at the bright blue sky outside. A brilliantly colored bird soared overhead, making her long for freedom, and making her long, also, for a time when everything had been less complicated.

Taking a deep breath, Kitani lunged forward, abruptly cutting her stride short and bringing her sword up in a smooth arc as she turned on her heel. After making a full circle, she charged once again, running through her imaginary foe's body with her gleaming blade.

For some reason, she was becoming increasingly restive, although she couldn't explain the source of her newfound energy. Hearing the quiet sound of Leara's laughter as her charge sat conversing with Cybil Reynard on the far side of the courtyard, she brought her sword up for another lunge. Leara's obvious attraction to the human woman was troubling, but that wasn't what had her worried. Cybil had grown fond of Leara, and the human had also proven herself somewhat trustworthy. She was certainly not the bloodthirsty assassin Kitani had initially taken her for. Cybil appeared to be genuinely interested in the safety of the Valori and nonhumans in general in relation to the blight being developed by Midas.

Perhaps her restlessness stemmed from her own reservations, Kitani thought. Returning to Aria was not high on her list of priorities right now, not with the experience of the limitless freedom of space life so fresh in her mind. She'd been rather pleased to hear their departure would be delayed for several more days and decided to make the most of it by honing her skills as a warrior.

It was very generous of Vanadrien, the Cerulean ambassador and commander of the Cerulean branch of Cipher, to allow her the leisure to stroll around with her sword so freely.

When the image of Sierra and the brazen way she had winked at her crept into Kitani's mind, she stumbled, nearly losing her balance as she twirled around to face another adversary. Muttering a mild curse under her breath, she lashed out, using the pommel of her sword to strike at her pretend foe's head, a blow which would have stunned an actual opponent and granted her enough time to gain the upper hand. Bringing her sword around in a lethal slash, she delivered a blow that would have gutted her imaginary enemy. The short, broad-leaved shrubs some distance away trembled and swayed from the force of the strike, and one leaf was neatly cut in half.

She noticed that across the courtyard, the two Cipher guards in charge of Cybil were watching her display.

"They're as deadly as they are beautiful," Kitani heard the female guard mutter to her male companion.

At this, the man swiveled his head around to look at her. "You think they're beautiful?" he asked incredulously.

"Don't you?"

He stammered before saying, "Sure, the Valori may look pretty on the outside. Wild, exotic, mesmerizing... Like a woman from your wildest fantasy." With a smirk, he added, "But you know their plumbing has to be different in order for their species to survive."

The two shared a laugh, completely unaware of the fact that Kitani could hear every word they said with perfect clarity. When she looked up to glare at the two guards her eyes settled instead on a figure in the background. Lieutenant Callaway had rounded the corner and was standing behind her two subordinates, listening to their insensitive prattle. The sound of her voice made both of them jump.

"Any problems with our guests?"

"None, ma'am," the male guard said, his face reddening as Sierra surveyed him.

"As operatives of Cipher, your mission is to promote unity and understanding of the many races," Sierra added, narrowing her eyes at her underlings.

"Yes, ma'am," both guards said in unison.

"Have you forgotten that it was the Valori who founded our great and noble organization?"

"No, ma'am."

"Since you're apparently already under the impression that you're on break, you're relieved until further notice."

"But, Lieutenant, the mercenary—" the woman began, but Sierra dismissed her with a wave of her hand.

"I know Cybil, and I assure you that she won't try anything as long as I'm here."

Kitani watched with satisfaction as the two Cipher guards complied with Sierra's order and left the courtyard.

Pretending not to notice the exchange, Kitani lunged forward with her sword. A high-pitched whistle drifted to her from across the courtyard. With incredible fluidity, she halted her attack, whirling around to face Sierra as if she had only now become aware of her watching.

"Whew! Such impressive fighting," Sierra said, moving out from beneath the shadows of a cluster of trees. "That last move, it was *val'tali*, wasn't it?"

"It was," Kitani answered, stunned that a human would be familiar with the ancient and revered discipline. *Val'tali* was taught only to the greatest of Valori warriors, and its secrets had long been safeguarded against outsiders.

"I've never seen a move executed so gracefully, so perfectly," Sierra continued.

"Well, I am a Paladin, one of the highest orders of warriors among the Valori," Kitani said without a trace of modesty. Sheathing her sword, she sat down on the ground.

"Did you train long?" Sierra asked, moving closer to take a seat next to Kitani on the soft patch of grass next to the tall, fan-leaved trees.

Kitani let out a sharp bark of laughter that rang out across the courtyard. "Two long decades I studied the discipline, and it was two long decades of torture."

"Surely it wasn't that bad."

Kitani recalled the long evenings spent under the tutelage of Raniya Drace, the senior Paladin to the Sorani family at the time. Raniya had been her instructor as well as her mentor, and her fierce reputation as a warrior was reflected in her teaching methods.

Owning a great deal of respect for her teacher, Kitani doubted anyone could have felt the pain of abandonment sharper than herself when Raniya had suddenly decided to leave the Paladins without a word to anyone. At the time, she'd sworn to herself that she would become stronger, training until she could best even the skills of her former instructor.

"I suppose there was some good in it all," Kitani replied after a long silence. Without Raniya's intense training, she wouldn't be the powerful warrior she had become, a Valori whose fierce passions often dictated her style.

Sitting with her knees hugged close to her body, she felt the power surging within her legs and arms. Her body was akin to a well-honed blade, partly due to Raniya Drace.

Sierra's next words cut through her thoughts like a sharpened knife. "Is it true that Valori warriors sometimes use a display of their fighting skills as a courting ritual?"

Kitani stifled a low moan. She had hoped the lieutenant would be uninformed in this aspect of the dance, but she could see that Cybil was right about one thing: however Cipher gathered its information, its sources were quite accurate, perhaps disturbingly so.

"It is," Kitani said slowly, avoiding Sierra's curious gaze. Perhaps she had said too much already. Revered almost religiously by the Valori, the ancient discipline was not a casual subject for discussion, especially not with a foreign species. Pausing, she made not a sound, afraid even to breathe for fear of further compounding her error.

In a sudden exhalation of breath and laughter, Sierra asked, "Did it ever work for you? If your knowledge of the subject is as you claim, then surely you must have quite the social life."

Kitani lowered her gaze to the ground to hide her expression. "Some Valori warriors use their *val'tali* skills in courtship, but not Matriarchal Paladins," she said, a little embarrassed about her limited freedoms. "Paladins are forbidden to take mates. Our role in society is a sacred one, upheld through the centuries since the Supreme Matriarchy was established. We have but one mission in life, and that is to protect and serve the High Matriarchs obediently and faithfully. Having a mate waiting at home or a life of our own would only distract us from that goal."

"So the Supreme Matriarchy decrees that its humble servants should remain celibate, loveless. Does that make it right?" Sierra asked, glaring hotly.

Kitani raised her head, unsure if she'd heard correctly. Finally, she replied, "Whether it's right or not doesn't matter. It's our way."

"And you're content with that?" Sierra asked, unmasked fire in her challenge and a flicker of something else in her chestnut brown eyes. Kitani thought she recognized something sultry and forbidden, making Sierra seem all the more exciting.

Kitani felt her body react to the unmistakable twang of desire that hung in the air between them. Swallowing hard, she carefully regarded Sierra. The human woman seemed to shimmer beneath her scrutiny. No Valori had ever roused such feelings within her and no

Valori would ever dare, being familiar with the law forbidding Paladins from having mates. Any guilty party was susceptible to the punishment of permanent sterilization, including the accused Paladin's suspected lover.

She inhaled the fragrant air deeply. For the first time in her memory, she was blatantly discontent with the inhibitions hanging over her like a dark cloud. She remembered also that the Supreme Matriarchy would rain down devastating retribution upon those who dared disobey its laws. That knowledge alone ultimately brought her to her senses.

After swallowing past the lump that had formed in her throat, Kitani said, "I don't know what you're searching for, but I assure you, you won't find it within me. I'm not like you. I am a Paladin whose life is devoted to the protection of the High Matriarchs, nothing more. There is nothing else for me." The words sounded dreadfully harsh to her ears, driving home the fact that she would never be anything other than a Paladin.

Sierra continued to stare, some of the heat dissolving from her gaze. She looked sad, Kitani thought. Whether the sadness came from being rejected or was due to sorrow for a Paladin's fate, she didn't know, nor did she intend to linger long enough to find out.

Kitani still felt the passion Sierra had roused in her. She could not bear to remain in Sierra's company a second longer. Valori might be infertile most of the year, she said to herself, but infertility did nothing to affect their sexuality. She feared the consequences for both of them if she didn't leave at once.

She rose from the grassy knoll, collected her sword, and retreated without another word, leaving Sierra alone. One thing she knew for certain: Sierra's questions were making her all the more reluctant to return to Aria and leave her life of intergalactic adventuring behind.

Chapter 10

A soft rasping against the marble tile floor alerted Kitani that something was amiss as she lay dozing on her bed. The faint but unmistakable scent of fresh blood accompanied by the smell of flesh burnt by the heat of a thermal weapon brought her completely to her senses. In a single fluid movement, she was on her feet in a crouching position, unarmed but not wholly defenseless. She had not been merely bragging to Sierra earlier that day. Her vast knowledge of *val'tali* made her as deadly as if she had been packing a missile launcher.

She detected no signs of danger in her room, making her even more worried. Dashing across the room as silently as a shadow, she opened the door which connected her room to Leara's via an adjoining passage.

After moving down the passage she paused, knowing her presence was obscured by darkness. Leara lay sleeping in a pool of moonlight filtering in through the open curtains, apparently unaware of the danger that must surely be lying in wait nearby.

Kitani scented the air once more to make certain her nose had not deceived her, but the odors of blood and burned flesh remained—fainter now, but still detectable, which could only mean one thing: whatever had happened, it had occurred somewhere farther along the hall, likely near where Cybil was being closely guarded. Was she wrong about Cybil, after all? The possibility left her with a disturbing new thought. Who had been assigned guard duty on Cybil that night? Might it be Lieutenant Callaway?

Sounds of a struggle could be heard from a few rooms down the hall, prompting Kitani into action. In a few quick strides she was beside Leara's bed, gently shaking her awake.

"Leara," she called softly as she knelt next to the bed. When Leara opened her eyes drowsily, she continued, "I believe some tragedy has befallen the Cipher agents." She wanted to mention her suspicions about Cybil being involved, but knowing Leara's feelings toward the human woman, she said no more.

Leara sat bolt upright, no doubt awakened fully by Kitani's words as well as the smell of blood. "What can we do?" she asked. "Without weapons, we're defenseless against this unknown enemy."

"Not defenseless." Rising from her kneeling position, Kitani strode over to the door. "Not as long as I'm around." The sounds had ceased, but then they heard a blast from a plasma pistol. Acting nonchalant, Kitani tried to mask her eagerness to rush to the source of the turmoil. She was about to ask Leara what she thought they should do when Leara leapt out of bed.

"That sounded like it came from Cybil's room," she said, panic rising in her voice.

Kitani slowly averted her gaze. "It most likely did."

"We have to help her!"

Before Kitani could say anything, Leara pushed past her and out into the hall. She followed at once, every muscle in her body tensed for a fight, but when she came to a halt beside Leara, she knew the action was already over.

Just as she had suspected, two guards lay dead in puddles of their own blood outside Cybil's room. To Kitani's relief, neither of them was Sierra. Her unaccountable concern for the human woman was troubling, but not as troubling as the scene they found inside Cybil's room.

On the floor lay the corpse of an unknown human male shot at point blank range with a plasma blaster. Kitani saw Sierra was also there, her arm draped affectionately across Cybil's shoulders. When Sierra saw the two Valori, she quickly disentangled herself from Cybil and walked briskly over to join them.

"The assassins have somehow infiltrated Cerulean's barriers," Sierra said, launching into the current situation without preamble. "They would probably have succeeded in their mission had it not been for my intervention. Even so, they managed to take out two of our agents." She looked saddened by the loss of her teammates.

Kitani wondered if she could have prevented their deaths if she had only acted sooner.

"We don't know how many more of them there could be," Cybil said loudly.

Sierra turned to face her. "I know. That's why Commander Duran has ordered me to escort the three of you off Cerulean, in secrecy if at all possible."

"Escort us? How?" Cybil asked. "The repairs to the *Sentinel* haven't been completed yet."

"That's why I'm commandeering your vessel, Cybil. The *Kashmir II* is locked in the *Sentinel*'s cargo hold and suffered only minor superficial damage during the altercation with our enemy. And I'm doubtful all of those nicks and scratches are a result of our battle. More than likely some of them are evidence of your lousy flying." Kitani struggled to stifle a chuckle as Sierra continued. "I have to admit, I'm rather looking forward to piloting an AI-based model. Cipher has access to such technology, but it's seldom seen."

"So where are we fleeing to this time?" Cybil asked, clearly unwilling to argue.

"Where else? Aria, of course," Sierra replied. "I believe you have a trial awaiting you there. Does any of this ring a bell? Look, Cybil, I know you didn't kidnap Leara, but the High Matriarchs won't rest until they've had the chance to question you themselves."

Cybil ground her teeth while Sierra laughed.

"Not to worry. No serious harm will come to you, Cybil. Enigma's word will guarantee that," Sierra said. "And Commander Duran will be joining us shortly. She can't have her prize prisoner roaming around the universe with only a lieutenant to guard her."

Cybil stood and walked across the room with her shoulders slumped in what Kitani read as a defeated manner. "When do we leave?" she asked.

"The sooner, the better. Does everyone have everything they need?"

Kitani nodded. She noticed Leara and Cybil nodding along with her. None of them had many personal possessions. Even the sword she had used in her training earlier that day had been taken back into the custody of Cipher.

"Great," Sierra said. "We leave immediately."

Kitani brought up the rear when the small party exited the embassy. She constantly scanned the bushes and anywhere else an assassin might be hiding. They were heading home at last, she thought, knowing she should have been delighted to hear the news. Instead, she felt only regret. She was disappointed that she had no time to learn more of the universe and the vast knowledge it contained, and, perhaps most importantly, she was regretful that she probably would learn no more of Sierra and the seemingly omnipotent power that was Cipher.

Once their little party was safely aboard the *Kashmir II*, Cybil made herself comfortable in her private quarters, thankful that at least this privilege had not been compromised. Time to reflect on the whole situation was precisely what she needed. At long last, she would have the peace and solitude she craved.

The mysterious Enigma had decreed that her life should be spared, no matter what the Valori High Matriarchs or anyone else said against her. But why would the elusive, almighty figurehead of Cipher go to such lengths to protect one mercenary? Surely it would be easier to simply allow her to fall victim to Midas's assassins. Was her testimony against the corporation truly so valuable? Even without her, the information contained on the disk retrieved by Leara and Kitani and the video footage they'd shot would be invaluable for the prosecution.

Cybil shook her head as if trying to physically dislodge the unpleasant thoughts from her mind. Nothing made sense anymore, especially Cipher's actions. Whatever happened next, her fate was in Enigma's hands.

A soft knock on the door made her rise swiftly from her bed to answer it.

"Have a minute?" Sierra asked brushing past her without an invitation. She strolled into the quarters, brazenly seating herself on the edge of Cybil's bed. "We haven't really had time to talk since our reunion. You know, to catch up on all that's happened during my long absence."

"Is that what you came here for? To talk?" Cybil felt annoyed that she couldn't find a moment of peace even in her own cabin.

"Absolutely," Sierra replied. "You may think I abandoned you and the Midnight Suns, but not a day has passed that I haven't thought about our time together. So how is everyone? Are the two lovebirds still behaving like a couple of honeymooners?"

Cybil knew that Sierra meant Ashley and Riley. She nodded.

"Is Riley as annoying as ever?"

Laughing, Cybil said, "Perhaps even more so." She moved to join Sierra on the bed.

After an awkward pause, Sierra asked, "How is old Jarvis?"

"Older than ever. He asks about you every time I see him," Cybil replied.

"Is that so? Well, it's no surprise really. In a way, we were like daughters to him."

"What should I tell them?" Cybil felt herself grow cold. "That you ran off and joined the ambiguous Cipher in its fight for justice and peace?"

"Maybe it would be best if you told them nothing. Go on pretending you never found me. Assuming we manage to survive this mission, of course. Somehow, I don't think the others will be as understanding as you, Cybil. You've seen the nightmare Midas has in store for us with your own eyes." Sierra looked away, but not before Cybil noticed her brown eyes brimming with tears. "And like me, you've known the pain of loss."

"I killed the man responsible for betraying my colony, the one who killed my father," Cybil said, no longer cheered by the thought of the Zulian's death. "My long vendetta is finally over. Vengeance is won."

"Let me have mine," Sierra whispered, sounding sullen. "That's all I ask of you."

"I promised I'd help, remember?" Cybil asked, giving Sierra a gentle nudge with her elbow. "None of that has changed. I'll honor my promise, so don't try to stop me."

Sierra raised her head, a warm smile on her lips. "You always were a stubborn one."

"Some things never change."

"And some things do. About your friends," Sierra began, a mischievous twinkle in her eyes. "I couldn't help but notice how lovely that Leara is. Are the two of you close?"

Cybil knew Sierra was enjoying making her squirm.

"Fear not, dear friend," Sierra added reassuringly, "I wouldn't dream of coming between you. In fact, I find Kitani most striking, even more so than your raven-haired beauty."

"Well, if you're into that sort of thing," Cybil said through clenched teeth. Why did Sierra insist on teasing her? "Which I'm not, if you must know. I have little time enough for human women, and I certainly have no intention of dating outside my species."

"Truly? Does our little matriarch know of this? Poor Leara will be heartbroken, what with the way she follows you around with that dreamy expression."

"You're imagining things. As usual."

"Quite the contrary. Leara speaks very fondly of you and of your heroic deeds."

Cybil shook her head in disbelief. "What use could a High Matriarch's daughter have for a mercenary like me?"

"I could think of a few," Sierra replied, waggling her eyebrows suggestively.

"You haven't changed at all, have you? Still a dirty old man trapped in the body of a beautiful woman."

Sierra laughed. "And your remarks still scathe, as always. I'm flattered that you find me beautiful, though."

"Did I say that?" Cybil teased.

"That's what I heard."

"That sounds uncharacteristically nice of me," Cybil said. "Maybe you misunderstood."

"Or maybe your mind was simply straying to Leara again." Sierra smirked when Cybil flinched. "Lighten up a little. Where's the Cybil I knew long ago? She would never allow her mixed emotions to stand in the way of true love."

Cybil wanted to tell Sierra that she was afraid to get close to anyone. The universe was a perilous place filled with uncertainty and heartache. It was far safer to remain cold, callous, unfeeling so that she could be certain she would never be hurt again.

She didn't tell Sierra these things, choosing instead to remain silent. So much had changed in so little time, she thought. Even the bond of her friendship with Sierra had been tested, a bond she had once believed was unbreakable.

Chapter 11

The sky over Aria's bustling capital was clear and blue when Cybil and her companions exited the *Kashmir II*. Groups of chattering Valori lined the streets, no doubt to get a better view of the procession making its way to the Matriarchal Council Chambers, Cybil thought. She was aware Sierra had contacted High Matriarch Dallia Sorani's secretary earlier to notify her that the ship was en route with her daughter aboard.

"This is nonsense," Cybil muttered to Sierra so no one else would hear. "You know as well as I do that I meant no harm to these two. You already said my life would be spared due to Enigma's influence. Besides, you know I'm no kidnapper. If anything, I saved the Valori's lives. Why do you insist on putting on this charade?"

Sierra gave her an elusive smile. "Boss's orders."

Sierra was in another of her tight-lipped moods, it seemed, a fact that did nothing to alleviate Cybil's foul mood. Gone was the warm and familiar visage of her dearest friend, replaced by the calculating and analytical Cipher lieutenant.

Walking ahead, Leara turned, giving Cybil an apologetic glance.

She refused to meet the Valori's gaze. Her situation on Aria was tremulous enough. She couldn't afford to be distracted, not at such a crucial moment.

The weather on Aria couldn't have been more pleasant, Leara thought, wishing the sun could brighten her companions' dispositions. Kitani appeared to cheer up a little as the familiar sight of the Council Chambers came into view. The Paladin's wariness returned when her eyes fell on the crowd of Valori gathered outside the round building.

Leara followed Kitani's gaze. Among the crowd, she noticed two heavily armed Valori Enforcers. She grimaced. Although many hunters and warriors carried swords and daggers the Enforcers were specially trained to deal with hostile alien visitors and were permitted to arm themselves with more modern defenses. These two possessed pulse rifles. They held the weapons rigidly, as if awaiting further commands. Beyond the Enforcers, she saw three Valori whose elegance and regal bearing spoke more clearly than words of their important positions. These Valori stood proudly at the top of the of stairs leading into the Council Chambers.

As Leara and her group approached, the central Valori stepped forward, the pupils of her pale green eyes narrowing to slits as she surveyed every member of the little group with disdain. Leara had been concealing her features in the hood of a cloak borrowed from Cybil. She threw the hood back under the close scrutiny. The Valori's eyes widened in recognition.

"Dear Leara," she said with a sigh of relief that Leara knew was false. "I feared I had lost you forever."

Valori were known to age gracefully. Even at the age of eight-hundred and sixty-four, Dallia Sorani was an exquisite beauty, Leara thought. Her alabaster skin was as smooth and flawless as a Valori in her bicentennial years, and accentuated by deep auburn hair barely covering the nape of her neck. Her mother was a lovely sight to behold.

Leara stepped closer. "But you haven't lost me, Mother," she said meekly, feeling as lost as always within the ray of blinding sunshine that seemed to accompany Dallia's presence. "There's no need to make such a fuss over my return. I'm here now. That's all that matters."

"I only received the information that you were alive a few days ago," Dallia said, casting a dark look toward the two human women. Obviously, she was trying to decide which one was the mercenary and which was the Cipher agent, Leara thought. "You must forgive me if I'm overreacting a bit. I'm just so overjoyed at having my baby returned to me unharmed."

Leara's scowl deepened. She wouldn't feel so bitter if her mother meant what she'd said, but a hundred and twenty-three years was more than enough time to learn that Dallia's main concern was for herself and the image she held in the public eye. Dallia only ever showed off her maternal instincts when surrounded by a group, as they were now. When she and Leara were alone, Dallia became distant toward her.

"I was never in any real danger, Mother," Leara said, determined to show nothing of the hurt her mother's indifference continued to cause her. "Even when our actions caused the research station on Kronos to self-destruct, we were promptly provided with a solution to our plight by Cybil Reynard—"

"Reynard?" Dallia arched an eyebrow. "As in the human mercenary who kidnapped you after you infiltrated Midas Pharmaceuticals' headquarters? Where is this woman now?"

"She did not kidnap me," Leara began, but her mother would hear nothing of it.

"Which one of these humans is Cybil Reynard?" Dallia asked, paying little heed to Leara's protests.

Sierra Callaway was the first to speak up. "This is Cybil Reynard," she said after clearing her throat nervously. She waved her hand in Cybil's direction. "Commander Duran thought you might wish to speak with her in person, so she ordered me to escort her here while she was occupied with other matters."

"An impressive and accurate assumption on behalf of your commander," Dallia said.

Leara raised her head ever so slightly as the two Enforcers ushered Cybil toward the center of the crowd, the barrels of their pulse rifles trained on her. Just as she was about to protest this unnecessary precaution, what her mother said next drowned out all coherent thought.

"Bring her inside," Dallia said. "Too long have the Valori awaited with uncertainty the fate of their future High Matriarch. After the mercenary has had an opportunity to speak in her defense, we, the Supreme Matriarchy, shall pass judgment."

Leara noted the finality with which her mother spoke, as if the High Matriarchs had already decided Cybil's fate before she even arrived on Aria. Knowing her mother the way she did, that might very well be true, she decided. Gathering her thoughts and composure as quickly as she could, she followed the procession inside the massive marble structure.

The tall wooden doors slammed shut behind Cybil, the resounding bang a reminder of the dire situation in which she now found herself. Two heavily armed Valori kept their pulse rifles trained on her back as they continued to herd her into the building.

While proceeding through the middle of the amphitheater, a statue at the far end of the room caught Cybil's eye. The statue quite clearly depicted a Valori warrior, a great double-bladed axe raised above her head as she looked impassively at the people brought before her. The sculpture bore a perfect likeness to an actual Valori, despite being at least three times the height. Every detail had been finely carved to match its subject. The realism and majesty of the statue nearly took her breath away.

Her progress finally came to a halt before a raised dais.

The same Valori from before had gathered on the dais, two beautiful, yet almost feral women seated in elegantly carved chairs. The red-haired Valori to whom Leara had been speaking now joined them on the dais, taking the seat in the center. Although the redhead bore little physical resemblance to Leara, she knew this imposing woman had to be Dallia Sorani. Something in the way Leara flinched in her presence told her this was true. Dallia's chair was the tallest of the three, a subtle detail that spoke volumes of her influence among the Valori.

Cybil hadn't been overly concerned about her fate on the journey to Aria, but as she stood in front of the august assemblage beneath the stately stone warrior, she began to be afraid. She chided herself silently. Hadn't Sierra told her that Enigma's interest in her would keep her alive no matter the outcome of her trial? She could only hope her friend's assumption proved correct.

The High Matriarchs gazed down on her from their elevated pedestals, the cold, murderous looks in their eyes sending an icy chill down her spine.

"Well, human," Dallia began, the boom of her voice reverberating around the vast chamber and making Cybil jump, "do you have anything to say that will perhaps redeem your actions?"

Cybil pushed her fear aside. "I do," she said, hoping she appeared steady and unmoved to those listening. "You may think me a scoundrel with murderous intent when in fact, it was I who rescued your daughter and her guardian from the explosion of Midas's research outpost."

"Do you seriously expect us to believe a story like that?" Dallia sounded cold, emotionless, her expression as unreadable as the statue towering above her. "What would a mercenary be doing at a remote outpost facility like the one on Kronos? What business could possibly have brought you to the frozen wasteland?"

"I fight corruption," Cybil stated, meeting Dallia's gaze boldly. "And if anyone wishes for Midas's failure, it is I."

"Enough," Dallia said, sighing deeply. "My mind is too preoccupied with other recent and more pressing matters to listen to your pathetic rambling today." She took another deep breath and spoke the words that Cybil had dreaded hearing since landing on Aria. "Cybil Reynard, on behalf of the House of Sorani and the

Supreme Matriarchy, and the power which they both hold, I, Dallia Sorani, place you under arrest."

"But I'm innocent!" Cybil protested. The two armed Valori guards shifted uncomfortably when she took a defiant step forward. "Maybe if you didn't take such delight in the sound of your own voice, you could actually hear what I'm trying to tell you."

That did it. The room fell into a shocked silence after Cybil's tirade. All eyes focused on the human, this alien who dared speak to the Supreme Matriarchy so intemperately.

Dallia Sorani appeared flustered for a fleeting instant, and then said, "Take her away. I do not have to sit here and listen to her insolence. There's no reasoning with these ruffians. Guards!" she shouted to the two Valori who had been keeping their pulse rifles aimed at Cybil during the entire exchange. "Get this riffraff out of my sight."

Cybil shrugged away from the Valori's reach as the guards prodded her away from the High Matriarchs. There was little more she could do. Even she knew better than to put up a fight now, so soon after insulting one of the most powerful women on Aria. The two pulse rifles pointed at her back also played a part in her decision to go along with the Valori for now.

"Don't worry," Sierra whispered into her ear.

If she were being honest with herself, Cybil wasn't worried. She had better things to do than worry over what the Supreme Matriarchy thought of her. First of all, she needed to devise a plan to get away from the armed Valori and back to her ship. The sooner she was away from Aria and the Valori, the better.

Leara watched in horror as the two Enforcers began to lead Cybil away. During the brief hearing, she had been hanging at the back of the crowd, waiting for the perfect moment to testify on Cybil's account. Cybil's unexpected outburst had taken everyone by surprise, not in the least Leara. She was so shocked by Cybil's audacity that for several minutes she could only stand, gaping as the Enforcers shoved her along in front of them. At last, she regained her voice and stomped over to the raised dais where her mother still sat.

The statue of Arilan, the legendary Valori warrior and prophetess, watched them in silence, just as she had done through countless trials over the centuries, Leara thought.

"You're arresting her?" she asked. Perhaps it was the echo of her heavy footfalls, or perhaps the note of desperation in her voice, but something stopped the Enforcers—and Cybil—in their tracks for a moment longer. “Whatever for? If not for her presence on Kronos, Mother, you might have truly lost me forever, after all. I requested her aid when the last remaining seconds until detonation were counting down. I offered her payment in exchange for safe passage from Kronos. Cybil has told you of her innocence, and so have I. Why do you refuse to believe a word either of us tells you?”

“I’m sorry, Leara, but that is the law.” When Leara looked as if she might offer further protest, Dallia added, “You should be grateful that I’m only arresting her. After the way she dared speak to me, I should order her tongue cut out. How can you protect such a scoundrel? Why would you even want to?” She motioned for the Valori Enforcers to continue escorting Cybil away.

What could she say? It wasn’t as though she could tell her mother, the other two High Matriarchs, and the entire crowd of spectators that she actually cared about the welfare of a human woman. She wanted to appeal to the compassionate aspect of their natures but being too friendly with an alien might inspire revulsion and speculation, she thought, dismayed by the conflicting emotions in her heart.

“No fears,” Dallia continued once the Enforcers obeyed. “Reynard is merely to be incarcerated until she can receive a fair trial. No harm will come to her unless she is found guilty of plotting against the Valori government or the Sorani family. If her words are true, then she has nothing to worry about. And neither should you,” she added.

In that instant, Leara finally found the courage to face her mother directly, though her eyes brimmed with unshed tears. It seemed to her that her rage was as obvious as if she’d shouted her frustrations across the amphitheater. Wasn’t Dallia listening to a word she said? If Cybil had wanted to harm her, she could have done so on numerous occasions. Why did Dallia refuse to accept the truth?

“Don’t waste your tears on her, Leara,” Dallia said, her voice devoid of emotion. “If she’s innocent, you have nothing to worry about. Furthermore, it is unseemly for a Valori of your status to raise such a fuss over a member of another species.” She narrowed her green eyes at Leara.

Perhaps her mother sensed something more behind her fondness for Cybil. Lusting after an alien her first time away from Aria would not look good for her, nor would it help Cybil. Leara felt her blood run cold at the silent warning, reminding herself this was neither the time nor place to broach such an argument, not with so many Valori watching them. Cybil's safety was, for now at least, out of her hands.

Her heart sank as she watched Cybil cross the vast chamber. She thought the presence of the Valori Enforcers formidable enough to prevent the human from making a scene. Cybil was tough. She should be able to handle herself just fine until Leara could prove her innocence.

Cybil cast a last hopeful glance over her shoulder at Leara before being ushered through the huge doors. Or perhaps she was looking at Sierra, Leara thought. The Cipher lieutenant remained standing before the dais. How could Sierra just stand there, watching calmly while her supposed best friend was sentenced to unjust incarceration? Sierra's recent actions erased any thoughts she might have had about the two humans being former lovers.

She recalled that Sierra had claimed no one could touch Cybil as long as she had this mysterious Enigma's protection. Glancing at Sierra, she saw that the human did indeed sport an unconcerned and smug smile despite the fact her friend was being imprisoned on an alien world.

Determined to prove Cybil's innocence, Leara made a mental note to enlist Sierra's help. The only question remaining was how to gain entry to the prison without her mother learning of her intentions.

Sierra caught up with Leara on the stone stairs outside of the Council Chambers. The Valori's flawlessly smooth brow was furrowed with concern, doubtlessly over Cybil's fate. "You don't have to look so glum," she said, causing an unsuspecting Leara to jump. "Cybil will be all right. She's a fighter." She recalled the angry little girl Cybil had been when she first met her and smiled fondly at the memory. "A few days in a Valori prison will be like a vacation compared to some of the things she's been through."

"Will your Enigma truly be able to protect Cybil, even here on Aria?" Leara asked.

"Enigma is everywhere, just like Cipher, and like Cipher, Enigma's influence extends even to the farthest reaches of the universe." Sierra paused to consider her next words. It seemed strange to talk about Enigma to anyone, especially since she had no idea of Enigma's true identity.

As the governing body of Cipher, the omniscient, ever watchful Enigma was perhaps the most prestigious position in the known universe, therefore, the identity of the person or persons behind the title remained unknown, Sierra thought. She doubted even Commander Duran knew their elusive boss's real name or location.

"It's hard to explain," she said finally, "but rest assured. Cybil is in good hands."

Leara visibly relaxed. Sierra decided to press her luck and question her further.

"It has come to my attention that you're deeply concerned for Cybil's safety. Is this true?" she asked.

Leara's alabaster skin reddened. "Cybil saved my life. I've little enough experience with humans, but in the short time I've known her I've come to think of her as a friend."

"That's good. Cybil needs all the friends she can get. You know," Sierra said, "if you wish to see Cybil, perhaps I can be of assistance."

"How?"

"Maybe I can keep your mother and the other High Matriarchs busy while you're visiting. I am a foreigner on your world, after all. In spite of my Cipher status, your mother wouldn't want an alien visitor unsupervised and left to run amok in the streets."

"That would be most generous of you. I don't know how I can ever repay you."

"No payment is necessary. Cybil is an old friend of mine, whether she still believes it or not, and I would do everything in my power to help her. Maybe your presence will cheer her up while we're waiting for Commander Duran to arrive."

"Thank you so very much, Lieutenant Callaway. I was wondering how I could sneak away without drawing my mother's attention. Your suggestion has provided me with just the solution I was looking for."

"Give me a few minutes while I go back inside and create a diversion. Hopefully, you'll be able to get away while the High Matriarchs are busy dealing with me."

Leara nodded. Sierra prepared to enter the Council Chambers.

Now, what should I do to cause a distraction? Sierra touched one of the standard issue flash grenades secured to her belt. The loud noise and blinding light would be perfect for causing chaos, while the explosion itself would do no real harm.

Making sure no one was looking, she tossed the grenade behind the topiary in the main lobby before making herself scarce.

Chapter 12

Cybil sat on the cot in the small prison cell, contemplating how she was going to escape this unforeseen predicament. Her only apparent option was to strike some sort of deal with the Valori using the data disks, which were still in her possession and only accessible by her. The information on those disks was crucial in justifying their actions against Midas. The Valori needed the disks, of that much she was certain.

She never imagined the High Matriarchs would actually lock her away in a prison, not after the way Sierra had so convincingly promised no harm would come to her. Yet Sierra had done nothing to prevent this outcome. Even Leara had raised more of a fuss than her former best friend.

Perhaps Leara's wishes didn't matter when they conflicted with the orders of the High Matriarchs. *Or perhaps Leara simply doesn't care what happens to you now that she's returned home*, her nagging little mental voice chided her. And why should she? Now that they had presumably eluded the assassins sent by Midas, and Leara and Kitani had been delivered safely to Aria, there was no need for Cybil's protection, as dubious as it might have been.

Cybil felt like kicking herself for being attracted to Leara. Her infatuation had led her right into a trap she might not be able to walk out of again.

She took a minute to take in her surroundings. The cell was immaculate. The metal walls, ceiling, and floor had been polished until they gleamed beneath the harsh light of the illumination system in the ceiling. *At least I haven't been locked away in a dank and grimy dungeon*, she thought with mild relief.

There were very few furnishings in the cell. The cot on which she sat was the most prominent and covered by a thin quilt, which, like the rest of the cell, appeared surprisingly clean and unused. Against the opposite wall, tucked away in the back corner, stood a metal toilet.

The only possible exit from the cell was the same metal door the Enforcers had shoved her through earlier, and that held very little promise of escape, being sealed fast against anyone entering or leaving the room. The narrow slit used as a window was not large enough to crawl through, even without the vertical steel bars. The only other view of the outside world was through a similar window at the back of the cell, positioned so high in the wall she could barely see out of it while standing on her toes. This window was also reinforced with steel bars similar to those on the door. Through it, she heard the sounds of the ocean in the distance, the roar of the waves as they crashed against the sandy shores of an alien beach.

She leaned back against the wall, enjoying the coolness of the metal. She closed her eyes, reminiscing about her past and wondering how Leara's gentleness had cast light into the darkness of the demons that still haunted her.

Lost in her thoughts, she almost missed a faint tapping sound alerting her to a presence at the door. She rose cautiously from the cot and approached the door. Peering through the narrow slot, she saw, to her surprise, that Leara stood on the other side, her face mere inches away as she leaned forward to whisper through the bars.

"I hope you didn't think I abandoned you," Leara said. "I would never do such a thing, not after all you've done to help Kitani and me."

Cybil noted that Leara still wore the dark cloak she had borrowed, as though she wished to keep her identity hidden from onlookers. Clearing her throat, she replied, "I suppose I didn't make it any easier on myself by lashing out verbally at the High Matriarchs. Honestly, do you think I'll ever see the light of day again after such a blatant display of disrespect?"

Despite her effort to remain calm and collected, her voice gave away how genuinely nervous she was. She mentally cursed herself for being so emotional, chewing her lower lip and averting her gaze from Leara.

In all her twenty-nine years, Cybil had never felt so awkward and unsure of herself in someone else's company, like her world was spiraling out of control into an uncertain future. It wasn't a feeling she particularly enjoyed, yet it wasn't entirely unpleasant, either.

"You've done nothing wrong. You merely spoke your mind," Leara said with a smile. "If only more people could find the courage to dispute my mother like you did. I apologize for not doing more.

But you see, when my mother gets an idea in her head, it becomes quite difficult to convince her otherwise." The way Leara's gaze kept darting to the corridor beyond the cell door gave Cybil the notion that Leara had come against her mother's wishes.

"And your mother believes that I'm a threat to you and all Valori everywhere, and that it would be for the best if I'm locked away in a cage until further notice?" Cybil asked. She wasn't sure, but it seemed as though Leara's eyes grew darker.

"That's correct," Leara said with obvious reluctance, lowering her gaze to the floor.

"Well, out of sight, out of mind, I suppose. Precisely how long do you think I'll have to wait before I receive a trial? I have a life of my own to get back to, and we humans are short-lived and impetuous, you know," Cybil said.

Leara's expression lightened a little at Cybil's attempt at humor. "You should be here no more than a few days. This case is a rather important one, after all." Her pupils narrowed and her expression darkened. "Cybil," she hazarded, the human name sounding unfamiliar and exotic on her tongue, "what were you doing when I first met you on Kronos? What was your true purpose in visiting a research outpost in a frozen wasteland?"

Cybil felt a darkness creep into her own features as well. So far, the subject of her most recent mission had not been broached, but now, with her impending trial regarding her alleged kidnapping of Leara Sorani, it seemed unavoidable.

"I was hired by an anonymous client of my employer." There was no way to avoid the ugly truth any longer, so Cybil blurted it out. "My objective was to track down the infiltrators and retrieve the data taken from Midas Pharmaceuticals."

Leara's reaction was neither shock nor dismay, but instead one of fulfilled expectancy, as if she had known the truth all along.

"You mustn't say this at your trial," she said calmly. "It sounds too much like you were working with Midas."

Cybil could think of nothing to say.

"About the data disks," Leara continued.

"They're still safely locked away in the *Kashmir II*'s computer," Cybil replied. "In fact, I was just wondering if I should bring them into play. Maybe I could use the information to bargain with the High Matriarchs."

"Wait a while longer. I'll speak with my mother. Hopefully, I can talk some sense into her when she's out of the public eye. I really shouldn't be telling you this," Leara continued, "but I couldn't sit idly by while you were being led into an elaborately woven trap. I've seen how the High Matriarchs conduct their trials. You'll become more entangled in their web with every word you speak. If Mother learns that I have spoken to you and warned you of her intentions..."

The statement confirmed Cybil's earlier suspicion that Leara had been forbidden to visit her. The Valori was risking much for her benefit with very little to gain. She felt foolish for believing Leara had abandoned her to her fate so casually.

Leara reached up to the steel bars in the narrow window and gently placed her hand over Cybil's. "We never got around to our talk," she said. "It seems that we're always too busy running for our lives. I regret not being able to spend more time with you, Cybil." Her fingers were soft and cool.

Cybil relaxed somewhat as Leara lightly massaged her trembling hand. It would be nice to get to know her better, she thought. Leara was sweet and kind. In a universe filled with people only looking out for themselves, Leara seemed to genuinely care about protecting those around her.

She had come to admire that quality, but she had caused enough distress in Leara's life as it was. Leara was too good, she decided. Her only option was to end this and let Leara walk away before Cybil became too fond of her company.

"You shouldn't be here," she said, her voice gruff. Her next words made Leara's eyes widen in shock. "Kitani and your mother are right, Leara. I'm a dangerous woman, a ruthless and cruel mercenary who earns her living at the cost of others' lives. You shouldn't associate with me anymore." She turned her back to the cell door and to Leara. "Now, go," she said coldly. "You don't belong in this prison, nor do you belong with me."

There was a moment of almost unbearable silence, a short stretch of time that seemed to linger for a small eternity. Already regretting her harsh words, Cybil nearly turned around to face Leara, and would have done so if not for the sudden rustling which punctuated the painful quiet. Behind her, she heard a sharp intake of breath, followed by a soft sobbing sound and the patter of footsteps moving away. When she cast a glance over her shoulder, Leara was gone.

Too bad forgetting her won't be so easy, Cybil thought.

She sat back down on the cot with a heavy sigh, tears flowing freely down her face at the hurt she had caused. She didn't want to forget Leara as long as she lived, but at the moment, perhaps it would be better if she tore her mind away from the beautiful Valori and the bitter, but inevitable, end of their companionship. Instead, she should concentrate on her survival.

Leara stormed away from the prison cell. She wiped at the tears streaming down her cheeks with the back of her hand as she hurried up the stairs leading to the street. Why had Cybil lashed out at her that way when all she wished to do was help?

Leara quickly dried her eyes and stepped into the bright sunlight. She walked hurriedly down the street on the opposite side from the prison. No one must know she'd been visiting the prisoner, though she was unsure why she still insisted on protecting Cybil.

She had given Cybil fair warning, she reminded herself, far more than most prisoners received. Whether or not she took the friendly advice was entirely up to her. If the human spoke those horrible words in front of the High Matriarchs, in front of her mother, then there would be nothing more she or anyone else could do to help her.

Cybil's confirmation of her business on Kronos had not been shocking to her. In all truth, she had already suspected as much. Cybil was a mercenary, after all, and mercenaries were often hired to track down and obtain valuable information.

She guessed her true disappointment came from the fact that Cybil seemed to have no interest in her feelings and her demeanor was all business. Cybil couldn't care less that she was truly concerned for her well-being or that she was the closest thing Cybil had resembling a friend on Aria.

Her heart aching, Leara shuffled along the street aimlessly, her gaze focused on the ground and little else while her mind raced. When she came upon a grove of trees, she almost failed to notice the dark figure standing in the shadows. It wasn't until the shadow raised a hand and beckoned her to come over that she realized she was being watched. She had hoped she was anonymous in her borrowed cloak, and it would be difficult for her mother to recognize her. Accordingly, she was caught off guard at being identified by a stranger across the street.

"I thought I'd find you here," a familiar voice said when she came closer.

Leara found herself confronted by Kitani, the Paladin's fiery eyes shining with mirth despite her scolding tone.

"Couldn't bear being separated from your dear Reynard for too long, could you?" Kitani asked with a touch of caution underlying the playful teasing.

At the mention of Cybil, Leara's surprise at being followed faded, quickly replaced by the anger and frustration she felt toward Cybil. For a moment, it felt as though a fire burned within her, then taking a deep breath, she gathered her composure.

"As if I would waste my time courting that galactic scoundrel. Besides," she added in a slightly softer tone to ease the shock Kitani must feel at her outrage, "I'm a Valori and she's a mere human." The memory of Cybil's rejection rang painfully in her mind. "It would never work between us," she concluded, falling silent.

Rubbing the back of her head, Kitani shifted from one foot to the other in clear discomfort. At last, she spoke. "High Matriarch Dallia sent me to search for you upon finding your quarters vacant," she said in a dreadfully professional manner.

The mention of her mother's name and Dallia's feigned concern for her safety were enough to regain Leara's attention.

Kitani went on, "Also, Commander Duran and her crew have arrived, which is causing great excitement among the Valori. It's not every day that a human Cipher commander pays a visit to Aria. Some Valori are still having difficulty accepting that other species are now allowed in the organization, much less one who's risen to the rank of commander. With all the humans about, one begins to wonder if it is safe to walk the streets anymore," she added in evident good humor.

Leara gave her a slight smile. "Surely by now you know better than to suspect these humans of malicious intentions."

"So far they've been helpful, but I do worry."

"I do hope Mother isn't too terribly worried," Leara said, unable to conceal her bitterness. "I've been confined in ships for so long. I thought a breath of fresh air would be nice."

"It is nice to be back on Aria," Kitani agreed. Although Kitani's words seemed genuine, Leara could not help suspecting she seemed slightly disappointed at returning to the confines and traditions of a Matriarchal Paladin.

Upon returning to their homeworld, she noticed Kitani had shed her combat suit in favor of the traditional attire worn by Paladins: a sleeveless tunic in shimmering gold covering a long-sleeved shirt the shade of midnight. Black trousers and knee-high boots completed Kitani's wardrobe. Coupled with the formidable sword sheathed at her side, she made quite an intimidating sight standing in the golden-green sunlight flickering through the tree leaves. Kitani's hair had also been returned to its natural color, a dazzling shade of moon-white.

"Tell me, Kitani," Leara asked, "is my mother expecting me soon?"

Kitani shifted awkwardly, returning her attention to Leara. "She did make it rather clear that she would prefer if I found you quickly. Something about some urgent business she wishes to discuss with you. You'll find her waiting in your family's ancestral home. Go easy on her, Leara. She's recovering from the near loss of her only daughter, after all. I know your mother can be difficult to read at times, but I think she means well."

"If only that were the case," Leara mumbled. She strode past Kitani, walking in the direction of Sorani Manor.

She feared the reason her mother wished to speak with her so soon after her return to Aria entailed far more serious matters than mere dread over her nearly disastrous mission. With the threat of Midas Pharmaceuticals still looming on the horizon, the High Matriarchs had far more to be concerned about than the safety of one Valori, even if that Valori was the daughter of their esteemed leader.

Chapter 13

Leara drew her lower lip between her teeth, chewing it thoughtfully as she gazed out the enormous window covering most of a wall in her family's ancestral home.

Surviving through countless millennia, the stately stone mansion was a symbol of the Valori's long history and a constant reminder of the immense power and respect held by the Sorani clan. Each generation had added mementos of their achievements to its library. It also served as a visual representation of just how much the Valori loved to preserve old ideas and objects. Indeed, Sorani Manor was much the same as it had always been, excluding some of the necessary renovations made from time to time.

She believed the interior of the mansion was every bit as impressive as the exterior, if not more so. With its vast airy rooms, ancient furniture, and priceless antiques, the house felt more like a museum than an actual home. She had always felt this way, especially as a child, when her mother constantly sent her outside to play for fear she would damage some irreplaceable old relic.

Of course, Leara had spent barely a moment alone in her entire life. Kitani, who was only two years older, had been no more than a rambunctious child herself at the time. Before Kitani, her childhood guardian and ever present shadow had been the former Matriarchal Paladin to the Sorani family, a courageous and dashing Valori named Raniya Drace.

A true warrior, Raniya was as bold and fearless as they came. She had loved Leara as much as if she were her own child—which might very well be true, Leara thought. According to rumor, there had been a time when Dallia was quite smitten with Raniya, but neither ever publicly acknowledged their relationship, if one even existed. The speculations might be no more than wild gossip, but that didn't stop her from wondering.

Matriarchal Paladins were absolutely forbidden to have mates, much less a mate of such high status as Dallia Sorani. For a Paladin to take a mate was a crime punishable by the permanent sterilization of both parties. Over the years, she recalled, the sentence had been carried out from time to time. However, no accounts existed of a High Matriarch suffering the penalty of one of the Supreme Matriarchy's own laws.

If there was truth in this tale, it could cause a scandal among the Valori government. Perhaps that was why Raniya had suddenly and unexpectedly left the service of the Sorani estate, vanishing in the night without a trace and breaking her young heart.

Tilting her head back, Leara continued gazing out the impressive window as she had done many times in the past. The various sections of colored glass were arranged to form a depiction of the Goddess. When light filtered through the panes, it bathed the parlor in a rainbow of colors. Leara had always loved the window. Looking through it now brought back many fond memories from her youth.

Her mind was drawn back to the present as a shadow flickered across the window. The sun was setting over the vast expanse of vineyards stretching for miles on the south side of Korvallia, making the newcomer's outline rather clear in the fading light.

"Good evening, Mother," Leara said, as politely as possible given her solemn state. She turned around to find Dallia standing behind her. Memories of her youth and her other parent's unknown identity had succeeded in taking her mind off the current crisis with Cybil, but reminiscing had done nothing to improve her mood.

"Good evening?" Dallia looked completely taken aback by Leara's casual greeting. "Is that all you have to say to your mother after returning from a treacherous journey to alien worlds, and then disappearing without a word? Honestly, I thought I raised you better than that."

You didn't raise me at all. The thought came unbidden to Leara's mind. She found herself unable to restrain the question dancing on the tip of her tongue. "Mother, why is it that you never entered into a life union with anyone? I'm sure you must have been propositioned many times when you were younger."

The words had the desired effect on Dallia. The haughtiness faded from her features, if only for a second. "I've explained it to you many times before, Leara," she said with an exasperated sigh. "I've never met anyone worthy of my attentions. Now, come and sit by the hearth with me. We have much to discuss."

Leara did as she was told, but she thought she detected a trace of unease in her mother's posture and in her voice. As always, she had struck a nerve by questioning her mother about the issue of relationships. Her small victory made her bolder.

"What about Raniya?" she asked, unconcerned about the ramifications of the question.

Dallia looked up from the stack of papers in her lap. "I beg your pardon?"

"You said you never met anyone who deserved your attentions. I was merely inquiring if that included Raniya Drace. There are rumors that you two were once lovers." Leara felt her breath catch at the absolutely murderous gleam in her mother's eyes, but it was too late to retract her words once they had been spoken.

"Where did you hear such utter nonsense?" Dallia began ranting. "My heart belongs to no one, least of all that selfish rogue Paladin." She clutched fiercely at the arms of her chair at the mention of Raniya's name, but Leara noticed how her gaze seemed to cloud over with sorrow, or perhaps unshed tears. Immediately regaining her composure, Dallia added in a knowing tone, "And it would be best if you followed my example, dear Leara, and never allow your heart to dictate actions best left to the mind."

Leara's heart froze. She feared Dallia was speaking of the situation with Cybil. Could her mother have guessed her feelings for the human woman? Was her infatuation with Cybil so obvious?

"You've grown into a fine young woman, Leara," Dallia continued, "but you shouldn't be in a hurry to forge any serious relationships, especially without first considering the repercussions of your actions."

She must know. There was no other explanation for the direction this conversation was taking. The Valori were a xenophobic and clandestine race, so choosing a partner from another species would be greatly scorned.

Leara felt her face grow hot. This was the first time she had acknowledged her feelings for Cybil for what they truly were. Somehow admitting she was actually considering Cybil as a potential mate made her more uncomfortable than the feelings themselves. Beneath Cybil's tough outer shell was a kind, caring woman with a heart of gold, but did she possess the courage to pursue her heart's desire? If she did, what would be the consequences of taking a human woman as her lover?

"But enough small talk," her mother said, interrupting her troubled thoughts. "I trust you're intelligent enough to weigh the consequences of your decisions and not go rushing haphazardly into anything that might sully your reputation. Now back to business.

The objective of your mission was to obtain incriminating evidence on Midas Pharmaceuticals, as I recall. What did you find out? I certainly hope it was worth risking your life and my sanity over."

For once, Leara ignored Dallia's attempt to play the doting mother. *The data disks*! In that instant, she remembered that the information she and Kitani had risked life and limb to obtain was still stored in the *Kashmir II*'s computer. With the ship shut down for security reasons and Cybil locked away, there was currently no way of extracting the information.

"We learned much," Leara said, "but unfortunately, due to unforeseen circumstances, the data disks are not available to us at the moment. I hope this isn't too much of an inconvenience, Mother. Do you think the council will believe the testimonies of Kitani and myself?"

"This is most unusual, but as you're the daughter of one of the High Matriarchs as well as a Sorani, I don't think there should be any problem." Dallia went quiet for a moment, finally adding, "Unforeseen circumstances? Was the information compromised by that mercenary or one of the other rogues at the space station?"

Leara didn't respond at once, instead considering her next words very carefully. This could be her chance to tell Dallia that the data disks were in Cybil's possession, perhaps opening a bargaining channel for the human. After a few thoughtful moments, she said, "The mercenary, Cybil Reynard, may also be able to testify. She was at the research outpost on Kronos and also witnessed the atrocious acts Midas committed. Also, the disks are currently in her possession, stored in her ship's computer where only she can access them." Leara's mouth felt dry as she spoke.

There, she had said it. Her mother now knew Cybil held the data disks, and the ultimate outcome of Leara's mission, in her hands. It wasn't easy speaking to Dallia Sorani in such a bold manner, but she had learned from Cybil how to be bold and audacious, especially when important matters were at stake.

Dallia remained silent for an excruciating moment, and then said, "And how, may I ask, did the human come into possession of this information?"

"I offered it to her as a sort of payment," Leara replied. "In exchange for safe passage from Midas's outpost facility. A wise trade, I would think."

"I suppose it can't be helped then," her mother said thoughtfully, tapping her index finger on the low table in front of her. "Have the human brought to me at once. We need that evidence in order to take action against Midas."

Leara breathed a sigh of relief. At least she had managed to lengthen Cybil's life, even if only for a few more days. Despite Cybil's harsh words to her earlier, she didn't want to see the brave space mercenary sentenced to death. Perhaps Cybil could somehow prove herself invaluable to the investigation and clear her name.

"It's settled then," Dallia said resolutely. She rose from her chair. Her actions were not in the least slow or deliberate, despite the fact she was nearing her nine hundredth year. "I'll summon a Paladin to fetch the mercenary. If she proves willing to cooperate with us, I may reconsider my judgment. If not, I pity her."

Leara gulped in apprehension. Surely the High Matriarchs would see that Cybil was no threat to the Valori. She hoped Cybil had been listening to her advice earlier and wished she could offer a second warning. She would have to trust Cybil's instincts and cunning to prevent her from incurring the wrath of the High Matriarchs.

Cybil sat on her bunk, picking at a few slices of prickly fruit closely resembling a pineapple in taste and appearance, the only remnants of food left on the metal serving tray a Valori guard had brought to her earlier. A somewhat tropical world, Aria boasted ideal climes for growing and harvesting citrus fruits. The warm seas covering the planet were also home to many species of fish and marine life, another major export. Cybil knew much of the food and wine exported from Aria was served in the galaxy's finest restaurants. Being served such food while locked in a Valori prison seemed one of the perks of her situation. Still, it was ironic that she was eating a dish in a prison cell that she usually couldn't afford while free.

Sighing, she sucked the juice from a wedge of fruit. The hurt expression on Leara's face had been replaying in her mind over and over again since that afternoon. Her concern was for Leara's safety, but had such harsh words been necessary?

Valori live for a thousand years or more, she reminded herself. *In a few decades, Leara will forget all about me. I'm unwanted here, an outsider on this world. I must find a way out of here. Besides, Leara deserves someone better than me.* Surprisingly, these thoughts burned more than a blast of hot plasma.

Soft rustling noises from somewhere outside the cell drew Cybil's attention to the door. She sat obediently on the bunk, waiting for the guard to return to collect the serving tray, but when the corridor outside fell silent, she grew suspicious.

"Who's there?" she asked. The silence was nearly unbearable. Evidently, someone had decided it would be amusing to play a trick on the new prisoner, she thought, hating being made to look like a fool. Or perhaps the situation was far more serious. Could the assassin hired by Midas have found her, even after Duran's ruse and traveling all the way to Aria?

Cautiously rising from the bunk, Cybil picked up the serving tray. She had nothing else to use as a weapon, and the tray was made of very sturdy and solid metal. She stood on her toes to get a better view through the narrow opening and was met by a pair of familiar orange eyes.

Kitani Veldina stood on the other side of the door, her moon-white hair standing out in spiked tufts to reveal a silver headband with a sparkling orange gemstone embedded in the center. Cybil had noticed such headgear among the Valori. It seemed popular. Unlike Leara during her previous visit to the prison, Kitani wore no unassuming garments to better conceal her identity, but instead had donned the traditional black and gold uniform of the Paladins. Somehow, the attire made her look more lethal than any combat armor ever could.

"What are you doing here?" Cybil asked, trying and failing to keep the fear and confusion out of her voice. Suspense and tension filled the air, so thick she could have cut it with a knife.

Kitani glared at her, her expression as disdainful as ever. "What do you think? I'm here to free you, you fool," she snapped.

Cybil grew warier. "Why would you do that?" she asked. "You certainly have no reason to. You and I haven't exactly been very close."

"You're right on the latter point," Kitani said with a slight smile. "However, your former assumption is incorrect. I do have a reason to free you, Reynard. High Matriarch Sorani wishes to speak with you. I would advise you to be on your best behavior."

The High Matriarch, Cybil mused. Leara's mother. What could possibly be behind the powerful Valori's decision to have her released and brought to her at such a late hour?

"Do you know the reason for this meeting?" Cybil asked as Kitani unlocked the door.

Kitani gave her an unreadable look. "Let's just say that you have something the Supreme Matriarchy needs. Now stand back while I open this door. I warn you, if you try to escape, I won't hesitate to use this." She placed her hand on the hilt of her sword.

Although Cybil didn't believe Kitani would kill her after being ordered to bring her to Dallia Sorani, presumably alive, she wasn't about to take any chances. Something in Kitani's demeanor said that she was in no mood to play around.

"One other thing," Kitani added, so suddenly it took Cybil by surprise. "Commander Duran has also requested an audience with you."

"That rotten Cipher commander?" Acid dripped from Cybil's words, though she barely knew Duran. Only half of Kitani's face was visible through the narrow slot in the door, but that was enough for her to notice how the usually assertive Paladin averted her gaze. "You shouldn't be so quick to judge, Reynard. Commander Duran is one of the few people on Aria who believe you should be set free," Kitani said. "Never take your allies for granted."

Cybil was quiet while she considered Kitani's words. "You know that I'm innocent," she said. "I know you don't like me, but surely you can't stand by and watch as an innocent woman suffers an unjust fate. I thought you were too noble for that."

"Maybe I'm not as steadfast in my duty as you believe," Kitani said.

Cybil wondered at her words, but said no more. There wasn't enough time to voice her opinion before Kitani opened the door and grabbed her by the arm, roughly hauling her out of the cell. She could almost feel the emotional tempest raging behind the alien eyes as Kitani shoved her along in front of her. She didn't know what had triggered the change in Kitani's attitude, but one thing was for certain: Kitani clearly wanted to drop the subject.

In the council hall outside the grand chamber where the Supreme Matriarchy had passed judgment on so many, Leara waited for Kitani to return with Cybil. Although this was an informal meeting, Dallia had suggested using the council chambers to conduct their business since inviting Cybil into their home would seem too hospitable. Leara didn't argue. At least Cybil was going to be free, even if that freedom might only be temporary.

She was pacing in front of the planter holding an elaborate topiary at the entrance of the building when Cybil appeared, followed closely by Kitani. Cybil seemed surprised to see Leara waiting for them. Kitani, on the other hand, only nodded in greeting.

This was Leara's first encounter with Cybil since the mercenary had so blatantly stated that she wanted nothing more to do with her. For an instant, she had to struggle to maintain her composure. What was wrong with her? There was no reason for her to feel so agitated every time she saw Cybil.

"My mother is waiting in the council chambers," she said, trying to remain calm and detached as she met Cybil's gaze. The fate of one human was really insignificant when she thought about it. The outcome of their plight with Midas was momentous. If they failed, billions of lives could be lost. There was absolutely no reason for Leara to care what happened to Cybil Reynard.

But she did care.

With the data disks stored securely in her ship's computer, Cybil held the fate of the universe in her hands. Leara and Kitani had spent long months working undercover at Midas Pharmaceuticals and risked their lives for this mission. Now it was all riding on Cybil's decision.

That wasn't the only reason why Leara felt so concerned about Cybil. The mercenary was distant, cold, and abrasive, but she did not actually believe Cybil would be willing to sacrifice the entire universe for her freedom. Somewhere beneath that callous exterior, Cybil *must* care about what happened to the universe. Otherwise, she would have collected her payment and left them to die on Kronos.

Kitani leaned against the curved marble staircase leading up to the council chambers. "This is it, Reynard," she said, crossing her arms over her chest. "Try not to make a spectacle of yourself like you did earlier." She watched Cybil for a moment longer and added, "Good luck."

When Cybil was through the double doors and beyond earshot, Leara turned to face Kitani. "What a strange thing to say," she said. "Did you mean it?"

"Because of Reynard, you and I are still alive. For that, I'm grateful. Why is it so strange that I would wish her well in her meeting with the High Matriarch?"

"It's just unexpected, I suppose." Leara thought about what Kitani had said. Although she wanted to be angry at Cybil for being so harsh and insensitive, she couldn't deny the immense gratitude she felt toward her for saving their lives.

Kitani watched her, curiosity gleaming in her orange eyes. "Don't you hope for Reynard's success at bargaining with your mother? It could make a world of difference in her case."

"Negotiating with my mother isn't easy. Besides, if Cipher has its way, Cybil will go free either way. Remember, Cipher doesn't need the word of the Supreme Matriarchy to act."

"You don't have to remind me," Kitani said. "The organization fascinates me. To be completely above Valori law, even Federation law, must be a freedom like no other. It's a shame we won't be able to learn more of Cipher, assuming Commander Duran successfully gains custody of Reynard. It's ironic, really. We're Valori, yet we know next to nothing about the shadow organization we created."

Leara listened politely while Kitani spoke, but the words barely registered in her mind. She was too preoccupied reflecting on how, if Duran had her way as Kitani suggested and Cybil was released into Cipher's custody, Cybil would be leaving Aria. She would likely never see her again. As much as she wanted to convince herself it was for the best, she found she couldn't bring herself to walk away. The thought made her uneasy.

Ever since Cybil had first shown up in her life, it seemed things had been becoming increasingly complicated. Now, with the possibility of Cybil's departure, Leara wished for some reason to keep the mercenary around for a while longer.

High Matriarch Dallia Sorani waited for Cybil in the grand amphitheater along with Commander Duran, who stood off to the side like a statue clad in midnight armor. Cybil hardly looked at the commander when she passed, her gaze focused instead on the red-haired Valori seated on her throne in the center of the raised dais. Dallia's reasons for arranging this meeting in the council chambers, Cybil thought, were likely so she could appear every bit as intimidating and regal as she did during a formal hearing. In a way, she *was* on trial here. She told herself not to forget that.

Dallia wasted no time with formalities, addressing Cybil immediately.

"It has come to my attention that you have something which belongs to the Valori," she began. "It would be in your best interests to return it without delay."

Cybil knew Dallia's words were meant to still any notion she had of raising a complaint, and reinforce the idea that she should be frightened for her life, but damned if she was going to turn over her trump card without a fight.

"If you're referring to the files obtained from Midas Pharmaceuticals, then yes, I do have something that once belonged to the Valori," she said, meeting and holding Dallia's gaze. "But your daughter offered it to me as payment, which I readily accepted. My services aren't cheap."

Dallia leaned forward in her chair. "Stop toying with me, mercenary. I don't have time for your games. What would you have in exchange for the information?"

"My freedom, since I've committed no crime."

The High Matriarch grew thoughtful for a moment, and then said, "Why should I grant you your freedom? My daughter risked her life infiltrating Midas Pharmaceuticals. That information belongs to the Valori!"

"Actually, it belongs to Midas Pharmaceuticals," Cybil said. "Your daughter hacked into a corporate terminal in order to obtain it. But that no longer matters. It's mine now, and unless you agree to my terms, you'll never get your hands on it."'

Cybil continued to stare Dallia down, never once letting her courage waver. This might be her only chance. If she couldn't win this battle of wills with Dallia, she might not be fortunate enough to receive a second chance.

"You're in no position to negotiate," Dallia said, baring immaculately white Valori canines. "Hand over the evidence, or I'll see to it that you rot in prison. I was a fool for ever believing Leara's suggestion that you might actually be reasonable. You're a human, impetuous and irrational."

Cybil nearly lost focus at the mention of Leara's name. Did Leara truly have so much faith in her? How could Leara believe that she would put the fate of the universe before herself, especially after how indifferently she had treated her? It was almost enough to make her regret her selfishness, but on the other hand, she could do nothing to help the universe if she was locked away in a prison cell.

"If I wasn't brought here to discuss my freedom," she said "why was I summoned?"

Duran, who had been silent until now, cleared her throat. "Actually, you were brought here so we could discuss the terms for your release. If you'll only be patient, we will come to that."

Dallia sighed and said, "The commander is correct. Were these ordinary circumstances, you would be required to undergo a proper trial. But since Cipher is involved, I have little say in the matter."

Cybil could hardly believe her ears. "You're really letting me go?"

"I don't have much of a choice." Dallia looked like she did not agree with this decision at all, Cybil thought. "The situation is beyond my control."

"I'll give you the data disks," Cybil said, hoping to alleviate some of the tension between herself and the Valori. "I have no use for the information myself. It would be much better off in the hands of someone who can make a difference."

"Your offer is most generous," Duran said, "and it makes my job much easier, since my first order would have been for you to hand over the data disks."

"Your order?" Cybil didn't understand.

Duran smiled. "You didn't think you were free to do as you please, did you? Aren't you forgetting that Enigma's protection is the only thing keeping you from harm? Enigma's immeasurable power goes far beyond the government of Aria."

"Once again, Reynard, the commander is correct." This came from Dallia, smiling sarcastically from her throne. "Cipher is highly revered among the Valori. And since I have no desire to be at odds with Enigma, I am hereby placing you in Cipher's custody."

Out of one prison and into another, Cybil said to herself, somewhat dismayed that her plan didn't work out as she'd hoped. How could she have forgotten about Enigma and the strange power this almost mystical figure held over her life?

Slowly, she turned to face Duran—her new master, for the time being—her heart sinking as she was faced with the prospect of being conscripted into the services of Cipher. Duran met her gaze unflinchingly.

"Well," she said, "it would be for the best if you returned the data disks immediately, then we can be on our way. I'll radio ahead and notify Lieutenant Callaway to accompany you, should you have any ideas about escape."

"I'll send one of my Paladins with her as well," Dallia said. "If that's all right with you?"

Duran agreed, probably, Cybil thought sourly, so the High Matriarch would feel that she still had some power in the matter. Or maybe, she added as an afterthought, the commander wanted an extra escort to better quell any hopes she had of escaping.

Sierra was waiting for Cybil in the lobby, just as Duran had promised, along with Kitani and Leara. The two Valori regarded her with curiosity as she descended the curving stone steps, but remained silent. Sierra stepped forward to greet her once she reached the bottom of the stairs.

"Well, old friend," she said, "it looks like we'll be seeing a lot of each other for the next little while." Despite the apparent hopelessness of the situation, her smile seemed genuine. "Commander Duran informed me that you have something you'd like to return to the Valori."

Cybil looked away. She thought she saw relief flicker in Leara's eyes at Sierra's words. "I guess you could say that," she said. "The way I see it, the information in those files will be put to better use by the Valori than it could ever be in the hands of a space merc."

"We'd best be going then," Sierra said. "We wouldn't want to keep the High Matriarch waiting."

"I've been instructed to accompany you as well," Kitani said, stepping forward when Cybil neared them. "After all, I was in Midas Pharmaceuticals when the data was obtained. I would know the real thing from a fake."

"I would never betray you." Cybil tried to keep the emotion from her voice and features, but Kitani's obvious mistrust of her hurt all the same. It was to be expected, she supposed, after the way she had treated Kitani and Leara while they were in her care.

"I never said you would," Kitani replied, "but I'm going with you anyway."

"I think it best if I came as well," Leara announced suddenly. "I've had a personal interest in this mission from the start."

Sierra saluted Leara in the traditional Valori fashion by clenching her fist over her heart. Cybil had seen Kitani perform this gesture countless times, but she hadn't realized it was also practiced among Cipher agents.

"It would be an honor to be graced with your presence, *Si'rah* Sorani," Sierra said, using the same title Cybil had heard Kitani use to address Leara many times before.

Laying it on a little thick, aren't we? Cybil fought the urge to shake her head at her friend's fawning behavior toward the Valori.

Leara paid little attention to Sierra, Cybil noticed, somewhat surprised to find the Valori's gaze fastened to her. Leara followed her every move with an intensity she immediately recognized as hunger. Those pale catlike eyes burned with desire for a fleeting instant before Leara realized her staring hadn't gone unnoticed.

"Time to be going," Leara said, returning her attention to Kitani. "The Supreme Matriarchy needs those files." Her gaze drifted briefly back to Cybil. "And I need you… ah, that is, *we* need you in order to access them."

Cybil nodded, but her mind remained focused on the memory of Leara from a moment ago. Was Leara even aware of the raw feelings she must surely be experiencing? Cybil didn't think so.

I need you. The words played over and over in Cybil's mind as she walked with Sierra, Kitani, and Leara to her ship.

The expression in Leara's eyes ate away at the wall she had constructed around herself. Maybe Leara was truly concerned for her safety. Why had she been so blind to this truth before?

The *Kashmir II* was docked in the Korvallia spaceport, just where they had left it on their arrival on Aria. Cybil had told them the main computer had gone into precautionary lockdown upon the ship's impoundment by Cipher, but the files could be accessed easily enough.

Cybil placed her hand on a square indentation on the control panel, and a light scrolled by beneath her palm, scanning her unique fingerprints.

Once the *Kashmir II* confirmed the captain's identity, the sexy voice of the ship's AI greeted them. "Welcome back, Captain Reynard. How may I be of assistance to you?"

Why must that blasted AI sound so sultry and alluring? Kitani wondered. She briefly imagined how the woman who provided the voice for the AI might look and immediately scolded herself for her behavior. The voice, no matter how flirtatious, belonged to a machine. There was no sense in acting like a rutting adolescent during the height of breeding season. Only it wasn't the AI that had her on edge. That honor belonged exclusively to the Cipher lieutenant standing next to her.

Sierra was currently focused on Cybil, her dark eyes trained on Cybil's every move as she retrieved the files and copied the information to a new disk. Kitani found herself wondering what sort of relationship had existed between Sierra and Cybil in the past, although she had no idea why such a thing should concern her.

Sierra brushed her rich sable hair back with a quick movement of her hand. For a moment, Kitani's keen nose caught the scent of shampoo and a hint of something else, something mysterious and musky beneath the flowery sweet smell. The scent of human arousal, perhaps? She hadn't been among humans long enough to be certain. For a few seconds, the scent nearly drowned her senses in a wave of desire. She edged away from Sierra, all the while keeping her gaze fixed on the woman.

Sierra's attention remained fixed on Cybil. She probably didn't even realize the effect she was having on her, Kitani thought, struggling to regain her composure and feeling envious of Cybil. Not envious of the human's access to such modern technology or how she had so easily managed to earn Leara's trust. No, it was Sierra's attention causing her to narrow her eyes at the mercenary.

"There, it's done," Cybil said, producing a data disk similar to the original and handing it to Sierra. "I hope the Supreme Matriarchy knows what it is getting itself into. Midas won't go down easily."

"Don't worry too much about the High Matriarchs," Sierra replied, taking the disk and inspecting it casually. "Commander Duran will want to view this. We've been tracking Midas for months, but somehow we keep coming up with dead ends. The information on this disk could justify any action we take against Midas in the future."

"I thought Cipher had free run of the universe and could do pretty much whatever it wants," Cybil said. "Not even the Federation intervenes when Cipher is involved."

Kitani had been listening to the conversation intently. She decided now was the time to speak up. "Attacking a corporate giant like Midas Pharmaceuticals with apparently no provocation would be foolish, not to mention such an action would be detrimental to Cipher's reputation."

"Cipher is a shadow organization," Cybil countered. "What little information is known about it doesn't exactly illuminate it in a positive light."

"Cipher is legendary among my people," Kitani said. "Its long list of contributions to the Valori is proof enough that it exists to serve us, not to harm us."

Leara turned to look at her in astonishment. "I never knew you were so keen on Cipher lore," she said.

Calming herself, Kitani said, "Cipher has benefitted the Valori greatly throughout the centuries. I don't wish to see its name tarnished on account of the more mysterious aspect of its nature."

"I meant no offense," Cybil said.

Although Kitani found Cybil's apologetic manner uncharacteristic, she believed Cybil meant no harm. If she suddenly found her fate resting in the hands of a predominantly alien organization, she supposed she would have some reservations and misgivings of her own, and Cybil didn't hesitate to express such reservations aloud.

"Well," Leara said, breaking the awkward silence that had fallen, "I'm sure my mother will be willing to allow your commander access to the material on the disk. As Kitani said, Cipher has been most beneficial to the Valori, and we respect all for which it stands. It would be difficult for Mother to refuse a request issued by such a revered organization."

Obviously, Kitani thought, still surprised at how easily Duran had negotiated Cybil's release into her custody. No one spoke to Dallia Sorani the way Cybil had done and simply walked away.

Things were becoming increasingly complicated every day, she mused. Not even the harsh justice system of the Supreme Matriarchy could be counted on any more. She longed for something more in her life, something beyond her position as a ceremonial guard at Leara's side.

Kitani gave a mental shrug. This yearning was not like her. Her status as Paladin had always been sufficient before, and she was content with the path chosen for her, if not entirely pleased.

"We should be heading back," Sierra said, pulling Kitani out of her reverie. "Commander Duran is waiting."

Kitani found that she was a little disappointed that Cipher would be leaving Aria now that Duran had Cybil in her custody. Just because this particular unit of Cipher was composed of humans did not belittle the organization in her eyes.

Cipher was legendary, and its elusive leader was almost a mythical figure in the tales surrounding Cipher's noble actions. She wished that she could be a warrior of that magnitude, a defender of the universe, but she knew she would never be able to leave her old life behind. Tradition forbade it.

On the way back to the council chamber, Leara stayed at the back of the crowd, her mind racing. Cybil would be leaving soon. Although there was no reason for her to feel sorrow at Cybil's departure, she didn't want their friendship to end on a sour note.

Also, the business with Midas remained. This mission had been hers since the beginning, and she felt no desire to give it up now, not even to Cipher.

Looking at Kitani, who had been unusually solemn since their return to Aria, she said, "It would seem Cipher is at last satisfied." She spoke softly so Sierra and Cybil would not overhear. "But unfortunately, I'm not."

"What do you mean? Reynard is in Cipher's hands, and so no longer our problem. Life should return to normal."

"That's exactly what I mean," Leara replied. "How can we expect everything to go back to the way it was when you and I know the truth? Midas Pharmaceuticals won't stop just because a few secret files were compromised. You heard what Sierra said. Cipher has been pursuing Midas for months, looking for that bit of crucial evidence which could pin the rash of unexplained disappearances on them. Given its ample supply of resources, Midas could move its operations elsewhere before Cipher has the time to act."

"What do you think we could do about it?" Kitani asked. "Let it rest, Leara. It's in Cipher's hands now."

"Do you want to let it rest?" Leara rounded on Kitani. "Could you ever truly rest knowing that Midas is still out there? We've been in this from the start. I only want to see our mission through to the end, for the sake of the Valori. Everything we know and care about hangs in the balance."

"What are you planning?" Kitani asked.

Leara smiled, aware that Kitani knew her well enough to deduce she had concocted a clever scheme. "Let's just say that I'll be having a talk with my mother when we return."

Hopefully, her mother would be willing to listen to her request. Dallia Sorani had once been one of the greatest warriors in Valori history. Even now, daring tales of her youth were told in fables. Maybe she would understand Leara's desire to stay close to her mission, to follow it through until she had attained victory.

As much as Leara hoped her mother would accept her proposal, she wasn't holding her breath. Dallia was proud, stubborn, and inclined to reject any idea of her daughter's unless she was the first to think of it. Perhaps that was the key to winning her mother's approval, she thought. Make Dallia believe it was her idea to send her daughter out on another space-faring mission that would help Leara develop character.

Yes, Leara decided, Dallia would want her to become stronger, so that she would one day lead the Valori with the skill required of a High Matriarch. She would convince her that accompanying Cipher would be the best means to gain this experience.

And then there was Cybil. Although Leara knew she shouldn't be having these feelings, she couldn't deny the sensation she experienced every time Cybil was near. Electricity danced in the air between them, an energy that flowed through her and set every nerve tingling.

She wanted Cybil. Leara was aware of that now. The only thing that bothered her was the intense longing she felt whenever Cybil was around, like the remotest part of her subconscious was attempting to reach out and establish some sort of connection with the mercenary. Such was the Valori way when it came to courtship, but Cybil was no Valori and probably didn't sense a thing. That's what hurt Leara the most, knowing that her desire was destined to go unreturned. Life was becoming so complicated. She was beginning to miss her days of lounging around Sorani Manor with only her thoughts and the ever watchful Kitani as her companions.

She shot a glance at Kitani, who still regarded her warily out of the corner of her eye. The faithful Paladin would be there beside her, no matter how treacherous the journey might be. That was the one constant she could count on in her ever changing world.

Leara watched with disinterest when Sierra reunited with Duran. Her mind was locked on Cybil, who stood quietly, if a little impatiently, to the side while the commander discussed viewing the material on the disk with Dallia Sorani.

She longed for Cybil to look her way, but Cybil seemed interested only in concluding this business and being on her way.

That settled it, she decided. One way or another, she simply must accompany Cipher on its mission. Her mission. Broaching the subject with so many people present would be reckless. It would be best to wait until she had her mother alone, so Dallia could devote her undivided attention to the matter.

Later, Leara thought, confident that she could do this. She *would* do this, even if doing so meant she would alter her fate forever. Destiny was waiting.

* * *

Leara found her mother sitting alone in her bedroom, just as she had hoped. She had had a long day and an even longer night, so it was no surprise finding her here now. Dallia would want to get in as many hours of sleep possible before morning, when the whole hectic schedule started all over again, except for one detail, of course: there would be no humans and no Cipher to deal with. Once Cybil was transferred to Commander Duran's care and a copy of the data disk made for Cipher's use, the Cipher agents had set out abruptly for the *Sentinel*.

Leara hoped that Kitani, whom she had personally sent as an escort, could stall them long enough for her to convince her mother that she needed to be on the ship.

She paused just inside the door of the room, waiting politely for Dallia to acknowledge her before she went any further. The largest, and by far the grandest, private room of the house, Dallia's bedroom was even more impressive than the spacious parlor. Like the sitting room, this room also had a wall of stained glass, giving a view of the north side of the estate overlooking the sea and the sandy beaches of Korvallia. Another image depicting the Goddess was formed by the many panes of glass, the figure accompanied by the fabled warrior Arilan—the same Arilan whose likeness adorned many statues and carvings like the one in the Council Chambers. Aside from the impressive stained-glass display, a huge four-poster bed was the centerpiece of the room, its wood posts elaborately carved in the lithe forms of Valori Paladins, their proud and regal forms supporting the canopy overhead.

Like all Valori art, Leara felt the decor of Sorani Manor was too steeped in Valori history and legend to be relevant in the modern age. Perhaps that was why so many other races didn't understand the Valori and thought them estranged and standoffish. She was sure Cybil felt this way, too.

To be suddenly dropped into a society where she was the alien must be truly traumatic for her. Leara couldn't begrudge Cybil her foul temper at all when she considered the situation from her perspective.

Readying herself for bed, Dallia glanced over her shoulder. "Do you need something?" she asked. "It's very late. I'd like to get at least a few hours of sleep this night, if possible."

Her mother was in an irritable mood. She would have to tread lightly if she wanted to accomplish her objective successfully.

"This won't take long, Mother," she said. "I just wanted to bring to your attention that Cipher is departing with sensitive knowledge of Midas's atrocities."

Sighing, Dallia said, "I'm aware of that. I granted them permission to make a copy of the files you obtained during your covert mission. To be perfectly honest, I'm just glad to see them go. And as an added bonus, they're taking that insolent mercenary with them."

So you're trying to convince yourself that by ordering Cybil's release, Cipher is doing you a favor? Leara mused.

"Cipher is powerful," Leara said. "Even the Supreme Matriarchy cannot rival its immeasurable power, since Cipher is ungoverned by the politics that keep us here while Midas is free to continue its heinous research. Cipher doesn't need to go through all the right channels, nor does it need to answer to anyone." Leara could tell her mother was fuming even though she had her back to her. "We're in good hands," she continued. "Our cause is in good hands. Cipher won't fail."

"*Our* cause," Dallia said. "This was our investigation from the beginning. Who does Cipher think it is, dismissing us so casually after all our hard work? Two of our own are dead because of Midas. I should contact the Aria branch of Cipher and let them know how a human officer is making a mockery of our investigation."

"Maybe you should have voiced your concerns to Commander Duran," Leara suggested. "In fact, it's not too late. I believe Kitani accompanied the commander and her crew to the spaceport. As of yet, she hasn't reported back."

"Your Paladin?" Dallia asked. "What business does she have in this matter?"

"I asked her to escort the Cipher agents to the spaceport. This episode with the mercenary has been taxing on us all," she added. "I only wanted an eyewitness account to confirm Cipher's successful extraction of the human."

"How very cautious you're acting," Dallia said, clearly suspicious of Leara's intentions. "But back to the matter at hand. This is our investigation and I won't have anyone, not even Cipher, ordering us to stay out of it."

"We were never ordered to stay out of it," Leara reminded her. "If you were to send someone to join Cipher on its mission right now, Commander Duran wouldn't be likely to refuse you. As I mentioned before, Kitani is already at the spaceport. All I have to do is radio her with your orders."

Dallia grew thoughtful for a moment. Finally, she said, "And who might I send on a mission as perilous as this? A Paladin would be the wisest choice, for given Cipher's fierce reputation, they are likely to face combat. Do you have any suggestions?"

This was it, the moment Leara had been waiting for. "Don't forget that it was Kitani and I who obtained the data in the first place. After successfully infiltrating Midas Pharmaceuticals' headquarters and blending in as humans for six months, I might add. I think the choice should be obvious."

"You?" Dallia seemed taken aback by Leara's suggestion. "Leara, this mission is going to be filled with peril and uncertainty. Two of our young Paladins have died already at the hands of Midas. You're so frail and delicate. How could I send you?"

"I'm your daughter," Leara said. "The daughter of Dallia Sorani, one of the greatest warriors known to the Valori. Doesn't that count for something?"

Giving Leara a tight smile, Dallia said, "I suppose it does. Radio your Paladin and let her know of our change in plans. I must admit, Leara," she added, "you're turning out to be a rather impressive young adventurer."

Leara was at a complete loss for words. This was the first time her mother had ever complimented her. Usually, she just dismissed her and treated her as no more than another instrument to improve her status in the eyes of her people. Was Dallia finally beginning to see her as a person instead of her pampered, over-privileged daughter? As much as she wanted to believe it, she surmised her mother's reasons involved her training as a future matriarch.

Whatever the reason, Leara decided, her plan had worked. Now she hoped that she survived and returned to Aria with her mission accomplished.

Chapter 14

"This is highly irregular," Commander Duran said, looking first at Leara, then at Dallia.

All the while, Cybil watched the unfolding scene with dazed fascination. Leara was asking permission to accompany the crew of the *Sentinel* as they faced Midas once and for all, and her mother was actually backing her decision. She wanted to ask if the Valori had lost their minds, but her current status among Cipher prevented her from doing so. She was little more than a prisoner here. There was no need for her to get herself in any deeper over the reckless decisions of a couple of Valori.

For a moment, it felt to Cybil like the world slowed down, and all the chaos and confusion faded into the background when Leara stared right through her with penetrating blue eyes. She detected a slight reproach in Leara's expression, but after the way she had spoken to her during their last meeting, she couldn't say she didn't deserve it. She wouldn't have been at all offended if Leara exacted some small act of vengeance, such as a slap across the face, but the quiet Valori said not even a terse word to her as she stepped onto the boarding platform.

"Does Cipher protocol prevent you from taking willing volunteers aboard your vessel?" Dallia asked.

"No," Duran began uncertainly. "Actually, I've never had such a request before. Usually, people are content to avoid Cipher as much as possible. Are you absolutely sure about this?"

Leara nodded. Dallia, on the other hand, hesitated a moment before giving her consent.

"This has been my daughter's investigation since the start," she said. "Our personal interest in the outcome is too great to back down now. I've granted Leara permission to accompany you, Commander Duran, along with her Paladin, if you'll have them."

Cybil waited, probably as eager as Leara herself, while Duran considered her answer.

"I have no right to deny your request," the commander said finally. "If you believe your daughter will make a valuable addition to my team, High Matriarch Sorani, then I graciously accept your offer." To Leara, she said, "Welcome aboard, *Si'rah.*"

Cybil could hardly believe what was happening. Leara was going with them into the heart of danger. She was embarking on a mission from which she might have no hope of returning. Leara was no warrior. Any fool could see that.

What did Dallia Sorani hope by allowing this nonsense? Leara had been delivered safely to her homeworld, just as Cybil had promised. It was her decision whether or not she preferred to stay there.

Sneaking a glance at Leara, Cybil was met with a shy smile. Certainly not the wanton look from before, this expression didn't seem so alien on Leara, she decided, though she hardly knew enough about the Valori to say what was strange and what was normal. Maybe it was her physical appearance. Leara seemed so pure and ethereal, almost angelic in a way. But that was silly, of course. She knew that Leara was a person. Like all people, she had desires, though seeing those desires reflected so openly in Leara's pale eyes had surprised her. To imagine, even for a second, that she might be the object of those desires was enough to send her mind reeling.

She looked again at Leara, who had now returned her attention to Duran. Leara listened intently while the commander spoke to her, nodding every so often in response to whatever Duran said. Cybil didn't hear a word of the commander's speech. She assumed Duran was laying down the ground rules for the Valori before takeoff. Her attention was focused solely on Leara. She admired how soft and smooth Leara's creamy alabaster skin looked. It caught the light from the glow of Aria's three moons and appeared as flawless as marble in the moonlight.

Cybil continued to stare in open admiration for a few minutes before catching herself. *Now who's looking so wanton and full of desire*? The next time she looked, Leara was coming her way, striding purposefully toward the open hatch where she waited with two Cipher agents. Leara met her gaze openly.

"It looks like we'll be traveling together," she said.

Unsure if she had any right to speak to Leara at all after the way she had treated her during their last conversation, Cybil nodded in response.

"Don't forget about me," Kitani said, stepping in line behind Leara. She bared her teeth at Cybil in a feral grin.

Groaning inwardly, Cybil watched as the two Valori boarded the *Sentinel*. But the prospect of being with the Valori was not an unpleasant one. At least she knew Leara and Kitani. Commander Duran and her crew, with the exception of Sierra, were complete strangers to her, strangers in an alien organization with a somewhat shady reputation.

Cipher was a mysterious and terrifyingly powerful organization, its agents given the authority to handle situations as they saw fit, even if that meant blasting an entire area to bits, and then covering it up as though it never existed, or so she had heard. The rumors were partially the reason why she still could not bring herself to trust Duran or Sierra, not even after Cipher freed her from the Valori prison. Sierra was a good friend—she couldn't ask for a more loyal ally—but there had to be more to Cipher's part in the rescue than anyone was letting on, of that much she was certain.

Obediently, Cybil allowed herself to be ushered onto the ship by the ever present Cipher agents. Her plight with the Valori had been solved rather neatly, but the solution itself opened up new avenues of complication. No longer a prisoner of the Valori, she was now once again in the clutches of Cipher, and she still had no idea what Enigma wanted with her. Not to mention Commander Duran. Trapped aboard a ship with a woman whose intentions she didn't trust wasn't unlike being locked in the Valori prison. At least she had known where she stood among the Valori, she thought wryly. With the commander, the possibilities were endless. One thing she understood for certain: Enigma must have something important in store for her, otherwise Duran wouldn't have gone to so much trouble to free her.

Once the *Sentinel* left the spaceport and was in orbit over Aria, Kitani ventured to the third deck via the ship's elevator. She recalled some of the crew mentioning a training room on this deck during her previous stay aboard the *Sentinel* and thought that now was as good a time as any to investigate. Leara was on the bridge under Commander Duran's supervision, and safe for the time being. She didn't need to shadow her every move, not on a Cipher vessel.

Being on a strange ship filled with humans and embarking on another perilous mission so shortly after returning from the previous one had left Kitani's nerves frazzled. Since Leara didn't need her at the moment, and since Duran had granted them free run of the ship and its facilities, she decided she could use some time to herself. A proper workout would do her good, and go a long way in alleviating some of the anxious energy she felt building up inside her.

Cybil lurked in the corridor outside the crew's quarters. She seemed genuinely surprised to see Kitani outside of Leara's company.

"What are you doing here?" she asked, looking around—probably for any sign of Leara, Kitani conjectured.

"Relax, Reynard," Kitani said. "I'm not here to start trouble. If you must know, I was on my way to the training room."

Cybil followed her gaze to the door at the end of the corridor, but remained silent.

"Some exercise would feel great right about now," Kitani continued. "I've been longing for a chance to stretch my muscles for what seems like ages." She returned her attention to Cybil suddenly, pinning the mercenary with her gaze. "Perhaps you would join me? I'm aware of how brittle human bones are, and I promise to go easy on you, Reynard," she teased.

For a moment, Cybil's blue eyes burned, and then a thin smile curved her lips. "Let me fetch my combat armor and I'll show you just how brittle I am," she said.

Kitani grinned. She was going to enjoy teaching Cybil how strong a Valori Paladin could be. Practicing her *val'tali* skills on her own was fulfilling in its own way, but having a sparring partner—or in Cybil's case, a target—was far more satisfying.

When the bout began, Cybil could barely keep up as Kitani leapt around the large room with ease, unhampered by her armor's added weight. She didn't think she actually needed armor, but she wore it so Cybil would feel she had a sporting chance at landing a blow. So far, Cybil hadn't been able to land a single hit. A Paladin simply moved too fast for human reflexes.

Kitani paused, her hand drifting automatically to the place where her sword was usually sheathed at her hip. Since there were no training swords in the *Sentinel*'s arsenal of practice weapons, and since Cybil had likely never even held a sword before, she'd had to settle for a wooden pole which she was using as a staff.

Misinterpreting Kitani's hesitation as an opening, Cybil lunged forward. Kitani easily sidestepped her attack. Twirling the wooden staff in the air, she brought it down hard against Cybil's back. The wood struck the composite material of Cybil's armor with a loud crack. The staff splintered and a large section of it broke off.

Dismayed, Kitani held the staff up for investigation. Cipher should have better quality weapons, she thought, even practice weapons. Anything employed by Cipher in the training of its agents should be able to stand up to more abuse than she had applied. Much more. Having the staff break under the strain of her attack was dissatisfying.

"Well, Reynard," she said, swinging the broken staff casually to and fro, "it looks like no more practice for us—" Her words were interrupted as a flash of movement rushed at her from the side. She spun to face her opponent, but it was too late. A weight struck her squarely in the chest with a force so great, she was knocked off her feet.

"Never turn your back on your opponent," Cybil said, her weight pinning Kitani to the floor. In her hand she held the broken fragment of the staff, which she pressed firmly across Kitani's throat. "I thought someone like you would definitely know to never underestimate your adversary, no matter how weak and useless you believe they are." She relaxed her grip on the fractured staff and removed her knee from Kitani's chest.

Kitani laughed as she rose. "You're a cunning foe," she said. "I should have been more cautious. As it is, I feel a fool for allowing myself to be so easily beaten."

"You think it was easy?" Cybil panted between words. "My victory was no easy win, I assure you. Any longer and I would have collapsed from exhaustion."

"Glad to see you two are getting along." Sierra strolled into the training room, followed closely by Leara. Kitani noted how Cybil immediately locked her gaze on Leara. Strangely enough, Leara seemed intent to avoid Cybil's stare at all costs, focusing instead on Sierra.

"On the other hand," Sierra continued, "I'm not really sure if you're getting along or trying to kill each other. Cybil, you look awful."

"Thank you. As always, Sierra, you know just what to say to a girl to make her feel better," Cybil responded with a smirk.

Kitani was confused. How did Sierra telling Cybil she looked awful make her feel better? She shook her head. Understanding the nature of humans was no easy task. She wondered if she would ever figure them out.

"So what are you doing down here?" Sierra said, coming over to stand next to Kitani and Cybil.

"I thought I could use a good workout," Kitani replied. "I've spent too much time in cramped ships lately. My muscles were getting stiff."

"I decided to come along so I could get the stuffing kicked out of me," Cybil said, wiping the sweat from her brow with the back of her hand. "Imagine my chagrin, getting my butt kicked by someone ninety-six years older than I am."

"No need to be embarrassed," Sierra said, "especially when your opponent is a highly trained Valori Paladin. Besides, you have some moves of your own, Cybil. I saw that last maneuver."

Kitani's chest constricted, a stab of humiliation striking deep into her gut. Sierra had been watching and had seen her suffer defeat at Cybil's sneaky, underhanded moves. She felt like sinking through the floor, anything to be away from Sierra, who regarded her closely.

Sierra must have sensed some of the distress her compliment to Cybil had caused Kitani.

"Those were some slick moves," she added to Cybil, "and efficient when it comes down to it. But your style isn't nearly as polished as Kitani's. She's a truly valiant warrior. Sort of like a knight."

Rolling her eyes, Cybil brushed herself off. "Don't you think you're piling it on a little thick?" she asked. She made a ridiculous face at Sierra when she walked past her, headed toward the open hatch.

Kitani could make no sense of the exchange. What was Sierra piling on so thickly, and why was it a concern to Cybil? She had been watching the entire time and had seen her do no such thing. Nor did she understand why Cybil had wriggled her eyebrows so strangely at Sierra in passing. What were the human women trying to say to each other? Sometimes, it felt almost like she was traveling in a ship filled with lunatics.

"What brings you down here, anyway?" Cybil asked Sierra. "I know it's not so you could reprimand me for my sneaky and somewhat desperate tactics in a fight. Were you looking for me for a reason, or am I to be under constant supervision by you and your shipmates?"

"Actually, Commander Duran is the one looking for you," Sierra responded with a smile. Clearly, she enjoyed the unease her news caused Cybil, Kitani observed. "She wants to have a word with you on the bridge. You don't want to keep her waiting long, Cybil. I told her you would be prompt."

"Thanks for your consideration," Cybil said, going through the hatch. Kitani heard her grumbling to herself as she walked along the corridor, undoubtedly believing herself out of her companions' earshot.

Leara pointedly avoided making eye contact with Cybil, Kitani noted, until the mercenary was out the door. Once her back was turned to them, Leara stared after Cybil.

Kitani thought she detected a trace of longing in Leara's watchful eyes, and sadness, too. As of late, Leara was becoming nearly as difficult to read as the humans, she mused. Each new quirk in her behavior was more confounding that the last.

As though sensing someone's gaze upon her, Leara turned and looked squarely at Kitani. Her pale skin reddened slightly. Her eyes widened.

"Hope you feel like going a second round," Sierra interjected, stepping purposefully into Kitani's line of sight.

Kitani found herself completely and utterly baffled by Sierra's unusual statement. "Pardon?" she said, trying to look past Sierra to Leara.

"That was quite a workout you gave Cybil," Sierra explained. "I was wondering if you had any energy left after such a display."

Kitani scoffed. "As if a little skirmish like that would affect me. I'm not even out of breath."

Sierra flashed Kitani a broad smile. "Then maybe you'd be interested in engaging a more worthy opponent," she said, leaning in close.

Kitani felt Sierra's warm breath against her face. Why did these humans insist on allowing themselves to be bested so? she wondered. Did all humans share a tendency toward masochistic behavior, or was it a trait found solely in Cipher agents and mercenaries?

Behind Sierra, Leara still watched them with a baleful expression. Something was definitely troubling her, Kitani was sure of it.

"As much as I'd love to show you my skills," she said, "I'm afraid it will have to wait until later."

"Oh." Sierra accepted her statement without inquiry—a huge relief to Kitani. She didn't feel like explaining herself every time she made a decision, although a part of her wished the humans would take time to explain some of their incomprehensible actions.

Sierra watched Kitani strolling past her. Before Kitani was out the door, she called out, "I'll be looking forward to our match."

Kitani thought she heard an underlying meaning in Sierra's words, but after some of the things she had just witnessed the humans say and do, she was ready to admit she was no expert in alien behavior.

She followed Leara along the corridor at a respectful distance. For now, she remained silent. Whatever was bothering Leara, she knew she would open up about it when she was ready.

Chapter 15

"What have we gotten ourselves into?" Kitani asked Leara for what seemed like the thousandth time that day. Ever since boarding the *Sentinel,* Kitani had been unusually quiet and contemplative. While it was not uncommon for the Paladin to become withdrawn and sullen, Leara sensed a whirlwind of thoughts raging just beyond those fiery eyes.

"I'm fully aware of the danger I've placed myself in," Leara said as she sat back on the bunk. Once more, they'd been set up in the women's quarters of the ship, probably because they more closely resembled human women than men. She found the gender specific facilities aboard the vessel confusing and alien. "I thought you felt the same."

Caught off guard by the question, Kitani sat in thoughtful silence for a few minutes. "I want to be here," she said. "I—we belong here. This mission has been the Valori's from the beginning. It's just that… well, I'm not so sure I feel comfortable with our shipmates."

"You seemed perfectly at ease with Cybil only a moment ago," Leara said. "I've never seen you so relaxed during a training session, not even when you were sparring with the other Paladins."

Kitani made a derisive snort. "I wouldn't exactly describe that as a training session."

"Did you enjoy beating Cybil senseless?" Leara quirked an eyebrow.

"Did *you* enjoy watching?"

Leara felt the smile fall from her face. Immediately, Kitani pounced.

"Aha! Seems I've found a touchy subject. What's going on with you and Reynard, anyway? Until a short while ago, I believed the main reason you wanted to come on this journey was so you could be closer to Reynard. But you've hardly said a word to her since we boarded."

Were her innermost thoughts so easy for Kitani to read, Leara wondered. Was her pain truly so obvious?

Kitani's gaze softened. "What's wrong, Leara? I know something is bothering you. It's as plain as if it were written on your face. Tell me, please. This brooding isn't like you."

Clearing her throat, Leara said, "It's as you said before. Humans aren't like us. They don't understand us, and we don't really understand them. Cybil and I have differences, and it's a cultural gap I don't believe can be easily bridged."

"But you would try, wouldn't you?" Kitani smiled warmly when Leara whirled around to meet her gaze. "You care for Reynard. I've been aware for some time."

"Too bad the feeling isn't mutual."

"What makes you so sure? Have you seen the way Reynard follows you with her eyes like a lovesick adolescent?" Kitani laughed. "At first, I thought it some sort of threatening alien behavior. It wasn't until recently that I recognized it for what it truly is." She paused a minute while Leara held her breath in anticipation. "She likes you, Leara."

"Preposterous." Leara recalled how Cybil had turned her away, even when she only wanted to help her. It seemed like Cybil had refused her help many times. "Why would you even think a thing like that?" She shook her head, not wanting to listen to this nonsense any longer. But on the other hand, Kitani was not one to engage in idle talk. She wouldn't have broached the subject unless she believed it was true.

"Cybil likes me?" Leara repeated.

"Only one way to find out," Kitani replied, shrugging.

"She's at a meeting with Commander Duran."

"The meeting won't last forever. Given Reynard's feelings toward the commander, I'd say it'll be over before you know it. Hopefully she won't mouth off to Duran and find herself locked in the brig for the duration of our journey. Reynard can be a bit brazen at times."

"Go easy on her, Kitani," Leara said. "Cybil has been through a lot recently. The stress and uncertainty of our situation would tax anyone's patience."

"She does have a way of finding herself at the top of everyone's Most Wanted list."

Leara arched an eyebrow in silent inquiry.

Kitani added, "Surely you didn't believe Commander Duran rescued her out of the goodness of her heart? No, I overheard

Commander Duran talking earlier. She wants to keep Cybil close for an evaluation of some sort."

"Why would she want to evaluate Cybil?"

"Your guess is as good as mine. I simply cannot comprehend the ways and behaviors of these humans. If you wish to learn the truth, I'm afraid you'll have to come right out and ask."

Leara was silent for a moment, and then asked, "Are you sure about what you said earlier? If Cybil likes me so much, why doesn't she say anything?"

"Maybe she's afraid."

"Afraid? Of what?"

"Rejection, perhaps. Or maybe she's merely waiting for you to make the first move."

What Kitani said made sense. Leara had sensed a great uneasiness in Cybil ever since they first met. Could her nervousness really stem from physical attraction?

Once again, Kitani was right. There was only one way to find out.

Commander Duran leaned against the metal railing that encircled the bridge, her arms crossed over her chest in an arrogant pose.

"That was some impressive work you did back on Turon," she said to Cybil. "Not many have the blind ambition you possess when it comes to executing a mission."

"It wasn't ambition that motivated me to pull the trigger," Cybil said, glaring daggers at the commander as she stood before her on the raised platform. It deeply insulted her honor that anyone would even think she would murder another living creature for the sake of ambition alone. Kuvair N'arex's crimes were too severe, and the wounds he had caused too deep to ignore. How this Cipher commander had found out the details of her supposedly confidential mission was beyond her. In addition, Duran's attitude was starting to infuriate her.

"I see," Duran said, rubbing her chin thoughtfully. "You're one of those self-righteous types. I never would have guessed that. Well, whatever motivates you, I suppose."

"Listen, you worthless, cold-blooded Cipher rogue," Cybil said, charging forward until she stood close to the commander. "I have no desire to be labeled as a ruthless assassin by such as you, nor do I wish to be known as some sort of dark angel on a personal crusade. I'm a mercenary. Nothing more, nothing less." She backed away, putting a respectable distance between herself and Duran, fully aware that half of the crew present on the bridge had their hands on their holstered weapons, ready to take action at a moment's notice.

Cybil fought back bitter tears at the memory of her parents and the pain she had felt when she lost them. She didn't enjoy reflecting on those dark days, nor was she comfortable discussing her past with a Cipher agent. Deep down, she did care about the importance of this mission, and she really did want to help, but damned if she was going to let that cheeky Cipher commander see her softer side.

The bridge seemed to breathe a collective sigh of relief when Cybil retreated a few paces from Duran and adopted an insulted pose.

Duran chuckled. "Yes, I'm familiar with your employer's reputation. Kashmir trains her mercenaries well in order to carry out her vigilante work across the universe. So it's your work as a mercenary that fuels your passion for the hunt, eh?" Duran asked, growing serious once again. "If that's the case, then you should be more than willing to assist in bringing about the downfall of Midas. But I must warn you, you'll see more of the suffering you have witnessed thus far, perhaps worse. Are you prepared for that?"

Cybil swallowed hard past the lump in her throat. Shuddering, she squared her shoulders determinedly. "I'll do whatever it takes to put an end to these nefarious experiments," she said.

"Excellent, Reynard. It just so happens that my next assignment involves the complete obliteration of Midas Pharmaceuticals, a command issued to me by none other than Enigma."

"When do we start?" Cybil asked, hiding her uncertainty beneath a mask of bravado.

Duran laughed heartily, and then her amusement faded, her expression growing grim. "Right away. You're aware of the situation on Eden IV, and so must know how evolved these biological weapons are becoming. The effects initiated by exposure are sometimes permanently debilitating. And that was probably nothing compared to what Midas has hidden away in the laboratories of its main base. We haven't a moment to waste. If you have business to take care of, I suggest you do it now."

Cybil hesitated before hazarding the request that had been on the tip of her tongue all day. "I'd like to be given access to my ship. There are files stored on her computer that I need to review again."

Duran smiled. "Consider it done. Report to the weapons and training room when you're finished. We need to get you outfitted with better equipment before the operation commences."

The thought of getting her hands on some of Cipher's exclusive weapons and armor gave Cybil a tingle of excitement, but before anything else, she had to visit the *Kashmir II*.

Cybil had no trouble getting to her ship, just as Commander Duran had promised. It felt good to sit in her own captain's seat and bask in the comfort that she was still in command of her own vessel, at least. She placed her hand on the console, on the square area designed to check her fingerprints.

She heard humming, buzzing, and other sounds of the ship coming to life, and finally the sound of *Kashmir II*'s sultry voice as she welcomed her back.

"Greetings, Captain Reynard. I trust everything is all right now that you've returned?"

"Yes," Cybil responded automatically. She pounded on the holographic keyboard displayed beneath the main monitor. "I'd like to review the files regarding Midas Pharmaceuticals again."

Kashmir II immediately opened the files she requested. Within minutes, Cybil found herself staring once again at the list of atrocities Midas Pharmaceuticals had committed. So much pain and suffering had been wrought by the nefarious corporation, yet all this would be nothing compared to the consequences should Midas execute its completed plan of alien genocide.

During this period of dark brooding, Cybil became aware of soft breathing somewhere behind her, a steady rhythm calming enough to soothe her frayed nerves. She knew the identity of her uninvited guest without looking. The Valori's lightly sweet scent gave her away, but she also felt the inexplicable peace that seemed to accompany Leara wherever she went.

"Cybil." Leara whispered softly.

"How long have you been following me?" Cybil asked, still refusing to face Leara as she rose from the chair. "You know nothing good will come from associating with me."

"Not this again," Leara said with a sigh. She sat down in a chair. "I don't want to hear such things. I came here to find you. We need to talk." She paused as if unsure what she wanted to say next and went on, "I overheard your conversation with Commander Duran. It was brave of you to volunteer yourself, but you don't have to fight this battle anymore if you don't wish. It is in Cipher's hands now."

"This is my battle as much as it is anyone's," Cybil said, more harshly than she intended. She found it difficult to control the tone of her voice with the war of emotions raging within her mind. She wanted to fulfill her promise to Sierra, but she wanted so much more, and Leara's presence reawakened those desires. She was torn, her longing to be near Leara conflicting with everything she had ever believed about aliens. But Leara was not at all like the aliens she had known in the past.

Had she ever truly known any aliens? She had encountered many on her journeys, but she had never taken the time to get to know any of them. Until Leara. At one time she had been so sure of herself and of her beliefs, no matter how prejudiced they were. But Leara had changed her opinion of galactic society. Had changed her. She wasn't even sure when this change had occurred, but she felt it now. There was no turning back. She wanted this fight. She wanted to end Midas's plot so that she could help people like Leara and Kitani.

Had she always felt so awkward and nervous around the lovely Valori? Did Leara also harbor these same longings, carefully hidden behind her unfathomable blue eyes?

After an uncertain pause, Cybil stammered, "I'm s-s-sorry, I didn't mean to sound so harsh. With my disagreeable disposition, I can't imagine why you would even want to talk to me." She turned slowly to face Leara, feeling suddenly naked beneath Leara's intense scrutiny. "I said some horrible things to you on Aria," she continued. "Things I regret. So much has happened lately. It feels like my whole world has been turned upside down. I realize that's no excuse to be such a boor," she added with a nervous laugh. "After the way I've treated you, I wouldn't blame you if you slapped me across the face."

Leara was quiet for a moment, the faintest traces of a smile playing at the corners of her mouth. "That won't be necessary," she said at last. "Kitani has already given you a proper trouncing once today." She stood and took a few steps toward Cybil. "Besides, I think you've learned your lesson."

Cybil felt her cheeks flush. Leara had witnessed her sparring match with Kitani, and judging by her expression, she wasn't kidding about enjoying it. Oh, well. She supposed she deserved this cool treatment after giving Leara the cold shoulder when she only wanted to help.

"I also saw how you somehow managed to emerge victorious in the end," Leara added. "Impressive. I don't think Kitani has ever lost a match before."

"Should I be watching my back from now on?" Cybil joked. To her, Kitani seemed the type to hold a grudge. "Can I expect to be ambushed by Kitani at every turn?"

Leara continued to regard her with an unreadable expression.

Cybil was undaunted by the fearsome Paladin. Facing down an army of armed security drones didn't faze her in the least. Yet something about this small Valori made her want to shrink away. Her face burned. Leara seemed to stare right through her.

"I should be going," Cybil said awkwardly, but she made no move to go. Leara was currently blocking the only exit, and she obviously had no intentions of stepping aside.

Should she try to pass, even when doing so would bring them uncomfortably close?

"You're doing it again," Leara said, her soft words amplified by the silence that had fallen. Taking another step forward, she said, "Stop avoiding the issue, Cybil. I came here to talk." She continued forward until she stood toe-to-toe with Cybil. "I have questions and I'm not leaving until I have answers."

Something brushed against the back of Cybil's leg. She sank rather ungracefully into the chair she'd occupied a moment before. Leara hovered over her, a hand on each armrest preventing her from escaping.

"Answers?" Cybil knew nothing else to say as she stared up at Leara. Her brain could no longer function properly with Leara mere inches away. "What do you want to know?"

Leara's eyes darted nervously to the side. "I don't understand what's happening," she said. "Something is changing. I have this feeling." She lifted a hand from the armrest and placed it over her heart. "In here, inside myself. It confuses me. And yet, no matter how confounding it is, I still yearn for more. I enjoy feeling it."

Leara removed the hand from over her heart and reached tentatively forward. Taking Cybil's hand in her own, she lifted it. Her grip was strong, yet so soft and so warm, Cybil mused.

"Do you feel it too?" Leara asked, placing Cybil's hand on her chest. Beneath her palm, she felt Leara's heart racing wildly.

Gasping, Cybil looked up from where her hand rested between Leara's breasts.

Leara met and held her gaze. "You *can* feel it, can't you?" she insisted. "Please tell me you can. Let me know I'm not crazy."

Before Cybil even knew what she was doing, she reached forward and wrapped her free arm around Leara's waist. Bringing the startled Valori down to sit in her lap, she captured Leara's mouth in a fierce kiss.

Leara was sweet. Her scent, her taste, was intoxicating. Cybil passionately explored her mouth with her tongue. Leara yielded to her, parting her lips invitingly as Cybil claimed her.

Wrapping her arms around Cybil's shoulders, Leara seemed to melt into her lap. Their tongues met for a fleeting instant, entwining sensually as Cybil fought to remain in control. Leara was flooding her senses. It felt almost as though someone else was dictating her actions, yet something about the sensation felt so indescribably right.

The trance was broken when a sharp metallic tang filled Cybil's mouth. In her moment of heated passion, she had raked her tongue over the sharp tip of one of Leara's canines. The taste of her own blood brought her to her senses at last. Reluctantly, she ended the kiss and pulled away.

Leara sat half on her lap, half hanging over the edge of the small chair. She watched Cybil expectantly, which did little to help Cybil formulate the words to explain her actions.

"I shouldn't have done that," she said at last. Her tongue still stung from the intimate encounter and felt heavy inside her mouth. "What's wrong with me?" she demanded of herself. "Every time I try to atone for my harsh treatment of you, I end up doing something even more insulting and insensitive. You must think I'm crazy. I wish we could just start over."

"Maybe we can." Leara leaned forward and brushed her lips over Cybil's ever so lightly.

The tenderness behind the action made Cybil shiver in anticipation, but in spite of how her body ached for Leara's touch, her mind knew she should not allow this to go any further.

Taking Leara gently by the shoulders, she said, "I don't think we should be doing this." She looked at Leara, and for a brief instant was nearly overcome by the hurt in those blue eyes. "Now isn't a good time. I gave my word to meet Commander Duran in the training room, and if I tarry any longer, I'm afraid she'll think I'm trying to escape." Mortified at the thought of a worried Duran barging in to find her in a compromising position with Leara, she added, "Perhaps you'd like to accompany me?"

Some of the pain seemed to evaporate into thin air. Leara smiled. "I'd like that."

Cybil breathed a sigh of relief before realizing that she still held Leara in her arms. Helping the Valori to her feet, she wondered what had possessed her to react in such a way. She'd been longing for some female company as of late, and was attracted to Leara, but she didn't usually give in to her desires so easily. There was something between them, some kind of intangible force, as if she and Leara had been caught in each other's gravitational pull. She wondered how much longer they could continue to revolve around one another without colliding.

Chapter 16

The weapons and training room was an impressive sight, Leara thought. During her earlier visit, she'd been so preoccupied with watching Cybil and Kitani's sparring match that she'd failed to notice the sheer size of the room. The chamber was large enough to accommodate several small ships, and its walls were covered in a substance that would absorb the energy blasts of any stray shots without causing damage to the metal beneath. Cybil was in her element here, she observed, watching the mercenary saunter over to where two Cipher agents waited.

Acutely aware of Cybil's every movement, Leara stood to one side of the room. She needed time to think about what had happened, what was still happening, within her own body. Cybil had kissed her, she had kissed Cybil, and through it all there had been no holding back.

She was drawn to Cybil. Her body yearned to be near the human, but there was something else that went beyond the mere physical aspect of the attraction. She had felt it for a fleeting instant when Cybil held her close, an inexorable force that seemed to pull at her insides, urging her to move even closer.

Rah'xenoji, the passion in the heart. It was the bond that united all Valori couples and drew them together, both physically and emotionally. Leara had heard of the phenomenon, but had never experienced it herself. Nor did she particularly understand why she would feel it now. Cybil was a human, an alien. She wasn't supposed to have these feelings with an outsider. She'd been introduced to many attractive Valori during her lifetime, but had never before established such a link. Cybil had a way of getting under her skin. Her every word and action had some profound impact. There was something about Cybil, something wild and enticing, and it was driving Leara wild.

The sound of Cybil's excited chatter brought Leara back to the present. Cybil was examining a very large pulse rifle and carrying on a discussion with one of the Cipher officers on the benefits and inconveniences of carrying around such a cumbersome weapon.

Leara mentally chastised herself for ever thinking that Cybil's features were unremarkable. Although Cybil lacked the exotic charms of a Valori, the woman was truly magnificent. In profile, her features were proud and strong, accurately reflecting the boldness of her warrior's heart. Gazing upon Cybil now, as she prepared to risk life and limb so that many innocent lives would be preserved, made her heart flutter in her chest.

Footsteps approaching from the far end of the room interrupted Leara's admiration of Cybil. Duran strode through the chamber with her usual pride and arrogance, the ends of her long jacket billowing in the breeze stirred by her passing.

"Glad to see you could make it, Reynard," Duran said to Cybil.

Although Duran didn't say much, Leara felt Duran's words implied that she had believed Cybil would try to escape once she regained access to her ship.

Cybil gave her a warning glance, and Leara didn't speak her objection aloud.

"I see you even managed to convince *Si'rah* Sorani to come along with you," Duran continued, ignoring Cybil's intimidating stare. She moved on to Leara. "It's an honor to have you in our presence this evening, *Si'rah*," she said, giving a deep and overly flamboyant bow.

"It's an honor to be here," Leara replied, returning the gesture graciously. "From what I understand, it isn't often that Cipher allows guests aboard its vessels."

"You're quite right. However, we do make exceptions from time to time." Duran turned back to face Cybil and the few crew members who had gathered before she continued, "I believe you know why we're here."

"To put an end to Midas Pharmaceuticals' plans once and for all," Cybil said as she stepped forward. "So where are these highly advanced weapons you promised me?"

"I was just getting to that." Duran nodded at one of her crew. The man immediately rushed away, returning after a moment carrying a large metal case.

"Is this what you've been waiting for?" Duran asked. The crew member opened the lid of the case, revealing its contents.

Cybil stood awestruck for a moment before kneeling to investigate what lay within the metal box. Leara saw two guns nestled snugly on a cushion of red satin: a rapid-fire plasma rifle similar to the one she had seen Cybil carrying, and a smaller, yet still imposing plasma pistol. Cybil gingerly lifted the pulse rifle from the cushion and cradled it in her arms.

"The T3-9000 Banshee," Duran informed her. "It's the most powerful pulse rifle in its class, one of the most powerful ever made. Highly illegal—unless, of course, you happen to work for Cipher. And the pistol is nothing to laugh at, either. It may lack the rapid firing capabilities of a pulse rifle, but it can emit an energy blast strong enough to pierce even the protective barrier in this room. I would prefer you take caution when aiming it."

Leara thought Cybil seemed so enthralled with the guns that it hadn't occurred to her to try them out on the targets provided. While Cybil fired a volley of white-hot energy with remarkable precision and speed, Duran turned back to her.

"I have a gift for you, as well," the commander said, motioning for the crew member to bring a second case over to them. This case was smaller than the one given to Cybil and contained only a single plasma pistol inside.

Stricken speechless, Leara struggled to find words to express her gratitude and hide her dismay. "Thank you," she said, "but I cannot accept this gift." She had no idea how to use a gun, having never held one in her life. The Matriarchal Paladins accompanied the High Matriarchs and their families wherever they went. There had never been any need for her to learn to fire a gun… until now.

"Nonsense," Duran said. "We have firepower to spare. There's no need to be so modest. Take it."

Leara wanted to explain her situation but kept her thoughts to herself. If she confessed her inexperience in combat now, would Duran regret granting her passage aboard her vessel? She had wanted so badly to be part of this mission, she hadn't considered that she might actually be expected to fight. *It isn't modesty. I just want to make it through the day without injuring myself or anyone else.*

Obediently and politely, she took the gun from Duran when it was presented to her, and joined Cybil at the firing range. By remaining some distance behind Cybil and the other Cipher agents present, she hoped she would go unnoticed, therefore avoiding making a complete fool of herself. Overjoyed with her new gun, Cybil didn't appear to notice her for a while, until Leara began taking a few steps backwards. The slight movement caught Cybil's eye, for she turned at last to see Leara with the pistol in her hands.

"Oh, I'm sorry," Cybil said. "I didn't realize you were waiting back there."

Leara swallowed hard. The pistol felt uncomfortably heavy in her hands. There was ample space for more than one person to fire at the targets at the same time, only she had a vague fear that she would miss her mark entirely and puncture the hull of the ship, jeopardizing not only herself, but the entire crew as well. Hadn't Duran warned Cybil about aiming the pistol given to her? Surely the plasma pistol she held was not so powerful, but in any case, it would probably be capable of singing flesh and causing a nasty burn.

"Oh, no," Leara said, not quite a lie, "I was merely admiring your marksmanship."

Cybil must have sensed her increasing discomfort and hesitancy to fire her gun, and chose that moment to promptly change the subject.

"So where does our next objective lie?" Cybil asked Duran.

"You'd never guess in a hundred years where Midas has set up its main facility," Duran said, and paused.

Cybil snapped impatiently, "In case you've forgotten, we don't have a hundred years."

"Quite right," Duran agreed. "We've traced the corporation to a distant world, located on the other side of the Milky Way. The world to which I'm referring is, of course, none other than Earth, the planet from which humanity originated."

"The main base is on Earth?" Cybil asked, sounding incredulous.

"Yes," Duran replied. "Are you familiar with the planet?"

"I've heard of it before, but I've never actually been there."

"Not many have, at least not in recent years. Since humanity began colonizing other worlds, Earth has become a thriving epicenter for galactic corporations such as Midas Pharmaceuticals. The planet will literally be crawling with security officers and battle drones. That's why we need to take every necessary precaution."

Duran continued lecturing as combat suits were presented to them, but Leara did not listen. Her attention was focused on Cybil, who had become unusually quiet. So quiet, in fact, that she nearly jumped when Cybil spoke again.

"Is Kitani to take part in this operation?"

"Yes," Duran replied with a wry smile. "But she's already been outfitted with the appropriate equipment. That's why she isn't here with us now."

Cybil's concern for Kitani was almost as shocking as the sound of her voice after the long silence, Leara thought. Cybil and Kitani had been at each other's throats since they met, but she recalled that Kitani had developed a sort of admiration for Cybil of late. Perhaps they were finally seeing the similarity each had to the other, both containing a warrior spirit she had recognized right away. Still, never in a thousand years would she have envisioned herself accompanying those two warriors into the very heart of danger.

Leara stared at the plasma pistol in her hands. Her dismay trebled. What was she doing here? She was no fighter. If she infiltrated the base on Earth, there was no hope of her surviving. When the battle began, she would only get in the way. What bothered her most was that she could do nothing to help Cybil.

"We make landfall in approximately nine days," Duran said very loudly, bringing Leara's attention back to the matter at hand. "You have over a week to rest and make whatever preparations you need before the real danger begins. Don't waste it," she added, shooting Cybil a cautionary glance. Her gaze softened when it drifted to Leara, and then she pivoted on her heel and began walking away, two underlings following close behind. The group's footsteps echoed loudly in the silence that followed.

Once Duran had gone, Cybil turned to face Leara. She regarded her thoughtfully, but remained silent. After a moment, she began the task of returning the pulse rifle to its case.

"Well, I should be going," she said, still fidgeting with the metal cases. "It's getting late, and I really want to try on this new combat suit. The weave feels amazing and the armor plating is so finely crafted." She ran her fingers over the suit. She closed the lid of the armor case and looked up at Leara, her blue eyes glittering in the light. "Are you coming with me?"

Leara thought she detected a trace of unease in Cybil's voice. It was highly possible that Cybil still felt as awkward and uncertain as she did over the events that had transpired earlier. Even now, she could still feel Cybil's mouth on her lips. But as much as she wanted to remain by Cybil's side, she knew she had unfinished business at the firing range. The plasma pistol in her hands glinted mockingly at her in the light.

"I'll be along shortly," Leara replied, searching the darkest recesses of her mind for some excuse not to join Cybil. "I must first have a word with Commander Duran," she said finally, knowing Cybil would likely pass on enduring another confrontation with the Cipher commander. She wasn't disappointed.

"Then I suppose I'll see you in the crew's barracks."

Smiling, Leara nodded. "Yes," she said quietly.

Cybil exited via the same door Duran had taken, leaving her alone with her depressing thoughts.

With Cybil gone, her complete attention was drawn to the light, yet solid weight of the pistol in her hands. She ran her finger along the barrel. The metal was cold against her skin. If she could somehow learn to use the firearm, she thought, it might bring her a huge step closer to Cybil. Impressing Cybil might help in getting her to return her affections.

Slowly, steadily, she raised the plasma pistol until it was level with the target's head.

Upon returning to the crew's quarters, Cybil found she had the room completely to herself—not entirely good news, since she'd been hoping she could talk to Kitani before Leara returned. The Paladin had been behaving strangely since their sparring match earlier, and she wanted to ease the tension between them.

She turned, staring at her reflection in the small mirror positioned above the bathroom sink. The combat suit was a perfect fit, she thought, not at all surprised since Commander Duran probably had a complete file on her with every detail from the foods she ate to her boot size. Such close monitoring annoyed her, but at least Cipher was granting her access to some of its toys.

She examined herself once again in the mirror. The combat suit felt a bit heavier than she normally preferred, but she would adjust to the extra weight in time. What mattered more was that it employed the latest barrier technology, generating a force field around its wearer that could withstand penetration from a point blank pulse rifle blast while allowing a full range of flexibility and movement thanks to the steel-reinforced armor weave.

Clad in her new armor, she sat on her bunk to wait. When, after a couple of hours, neither Valori had returned, she grew tired of doing nothing and resolved to find the elusive Paladin.

Kitani wasn't an easy person to find, especially since she'd been behaving more strangely than usual since boarding the *Sentinel*, but Cybil had a vague idea where she would find Leara, and the two were rarely apart.

The last place she had seen Leara was the weapons and training room. There was a good chance Kitani might be there with her. At any rate, matters needed to be discussed between her and Leara, even if she couldn't locate Kitani.

Cybil felt like a fool for her earlier behavior, but she couldn't get their shared moment of intimacy out of her mind no matter how she tried. Something within Leara seemed to be speaking to her, calling her. She knew how ridiculous that sounded, but she felt it nonetheless.

She stalked quietly along the ship's corridors, constantly scanning her surroundings for any sign of Leara or Kitani. She reached the training room without drawing any undue attention to herself and found exactly what she was searching for—or more precisely, *whom* she was searching for.

Leara stood in the center of the room, completely unaware of Cybil's presence as she fired shot after shot at the target. Some of the energy blasts struck the target in random places. Others missed the mark entirely and instead hit the thickly sheathed metal walls. Oddly enough, Kitani was not with her, which caused Cybil to wonder. It seemed to her that the Paladin wasn't taking her duty very seriously lately.

Leara was so absorbed in her activities that Cybil was able to approach her without being noticed. As she drew nearer, she could see beads of sweat on Leara's forehead, matting strands of thick black hair to her brow as she fired repeatedly at the target.

The Valori's barrage only ceased when the weapon became overheated and would fire no more, which was when Cybil noticed how badly Leara was trembling. Leara must have been firing continuously in the same manner ever since Cybil left the firing range earlier, and she had now reached the point of exhaustion.

As soon as the plasma blaster had cooled down enough for another round, Leara leveled it at the target, squeezing her finger on the trigger. Cybil held the shaking gun steady.

"You'll never hit it like that," she whispered softly in Leara's ear.

She stood behind Leara, her arms around the lithe Valori, her own hands covering Leara's while she steadied the gun. Gently, she applied pressure to Leara's finger, squeezing the trigger and causing the gun to discharge. A blast of ghostly blue energy erupted from the pistol's barrel and struck the target dead center.

"Relax," she said, still speaking in Leara's ear. "Stay calm and cool. Don't let your muscles tense up, it ruins your aim. Did you see how well you did when you were relaxed?"

"That was only because of you, Cybil," Leara replied quietly, relaxing further into Cybil's embrace. "I never would have made that shot without your guidance," she purred, arching into Cybil's embrace even more and tipping her head back.

"I wanted to talk to you," Cybil said. "I kissed you."

"And I kissed you," Leara replied. "Cybil, you don't have to apologize—"

"I didn't come here to offer an apology," Cybil interrupted.

Still enfolded in her arms, Leara looked at her curiously.

Cybil continued after a deep breath, "I may be way out of line, but I wanted to see you again." Gazing into Leara's eyes, she sighed. Leara felt so soft and warm in her arms. How long had it been since she allowed herself the simple pleasure of holding a woman so close?

"Why do you look at me like that?" she asked. "Like your world is on fire and I'm the only one who can extinguish the flames?"

"Because that's how I feel," Leara answered gently. "Whenever I'm around you, I feel as though my very soul is ablaze. In order to provide such an accurate description, you must feel it, too."

"I do." Cybil didn't know what possessed her, or why she felt compelled to answer Leara's probing so honestly. That odd sensation engulfed her again, like Leara was calling to her on a subconscious level.

Leara continued to regard her. "What should we do?" she asked, pressing her body against Cybil's.

Cybil gulped. She became acutely aware of Leara's firm buttocks against her groin, of the heat emanating from the Valori as she held her in her arms. Leara was so warm, almost like a furnace. It was nearly too much for her to bear.

A wave of confusion seemed to ripple in the space between them, and the strange bond shattered. Cybil regretted the invisible link between them breaking. The world around her suddenly seemed cold and lonely. What was that all about? Never in her life had she experienced such a calm and serene feeling. So alien, yet at the same time oddly welcome.

Still disoriented from the severed bond, she managed to choke out, "Right now, we should focus on this mission. In spite of her arrogance, Commander Duran needs all the help she can get. We should practice and hone our skills for the trials to come."

"Cybil," Leara said, "I never could have hit that target without your guidance. I don't even know what I'm doing here. Do you know that I've never even held a gun before today? How can I expect to be any help in the coming battle?” Blue eyes filling with tears, Leara pulled away from her grasp.

“There’s plenty you can do,” Cybil offered reassuringly. “If you really want to learn how to use a gun, I’ll teach you. Honestly, in all the galaxy, there’s no one else I’d rather have as my crew.”

“You want me to accompany you even when there’s so much at stake?” Leara sounded touched as well as baffled by Cybil’s invitation. “I’d be delighted, if that’s truly what you wish.”

“I mean it.” Cybil reached forward, reclaiming Leara in her arms. To her delight, Leara did not resist. “We’ll get through this,” she said, breathing in Leara’s sweet scent. “Together, we will prevail. I promise.”

Leara rested her head on Cybil’s shoulder.

Cybil held her, wondering what would happen when they reached Earth. Would whatever was between them continue to strengthen, or was the pleasant sensation destined to wither away?

Chapter 17

Earth was an industrial giant. The entire planet resembled an enormous, sprawling metropolis, the expanse of human cities interrupted only by the planet's oceans. Kitani shuddered to think what it must be like to live so closely among so many others. As the Valori were only fertile during their breeding cycle, the Valori population was in no danger of growing out of control due to raging adolescent hormones of or increased sex drives of mature adults. Both the breeding cycle and the deep bond formed between a mated pair ensured that the Valori did not overpopulate to the point of depleting their world's vital resources. This had been a major factor in the Valori's decision not to colonize worlds alongside other species. So far, intergalactic expansion had not been necessary.

Humans, on the other hand, apparently had no such biological luxuries as a breeding cycle to determine fertility. When the ship entered Earth's atmosphere, Kitani began to understand why some species feared allowing humans too much freedom. With their greater numbers, they could easily overthrow some of the races if they could achieve unity among their ranks. Fortunately, according to her understanding, such mass cooperation seemed rare where humans were concerned.

She was glad when their journey ended at a small, relatively uninhabited outpost town, located just beyond the borders of the enormous industrial metropolis. During the trip, she had learned that Duran had contacts at the outpost.

"Easier to sneak up on the enemy when you have the element of surprise," Duran said when the *Sentinel* touched down in an overgrown landing field.

Disembarking from the ship, Kitani found a large tree stump and sat down as she surveyed the alien landscape. Earth was not so different than Aria, she decided.

The area around the outpost was littered with copses of deciduous and coniferous trees, the former in full bloom—not surprising, since she'd been told this region of Earth was at the height of spring. Shoots of untended grass shot up between the cracked pavement of the landing field and the roads leading through and around the town.

One thing greatly differentiated the human world from Aria: the choking miasma hanging in the air. With her keen sense of smell, Kitani was acutely aware of the smoke and gasses emitted by the nearby industrial city. She found the stench almost suffocating. Leara doubtlessly detected the polluted air as well, but her charge was currently paying the source of her discomfort no mind.

Leara had heeded her advice and sought out Cybil on the *Sentinel.* During the days preceding their arrival on Earth, the two had become nearly inseparable. Cybil now stood behind Leara, her arms encircling her as she gave instructions on how to properly aim a plasma pistol.

Kitani was tempted to rush over and shove Cybil away from Leara. She would have done so, if not for the fact that she knew how dearly Leara enjoyed the human's company. As if to prove her point, Leara turned to look at Cybil, and Kitani saw how she beamed with joy.

Kitani drew in a breath of the noxious air, letting it out in an exasperated sigh. She continued to watch the two a bit enviously as they laughed and talked in hushed whispers that not even her sharp ears could pick up. She was so deep in thought that she almost failed to notice the soft crunch of booted feet on grass until the person stood right behind her.

Her nostrils flaring, she caught a whiff of a familiar scent over the choking miasma. It was light and sweet, like a spring day. She immediately recognized the scent of Sierra's perfume. When she turned around, it came as no shock to find Sierra standing behind her, grinning widely at her apparent success in startling a Paladin.

Having gone out of her way to avoid Sierra since their uncomfortable encounter in the training room, Kitani directed her attention elsewhere, hoping to deter the lieutenant.

"What's on your mind?" Sierra asked, sitting down uninvited on the stump beside Kitani.

The close contact caused Kitani to shift about uneasily until she was nearly hanging over the side of the tree stump. She hesitated a moment and finally said, "Nothing important." She hoped her dismissive attitude would discourage Sierra's curiosity, but she wasn't so lucky.

"I don't believe that for a second!" Sierra said. "You were so immersed in your daydreams that you didn't even notice I was standing behind you."

"I'll have you know that I was perfectly aware of your presence the whole time. Your perfume leaves a trail that even a fool could follow. The fact that you're about as stealthy as a stampeding herd of mammoth beasts doesn't work in your favor either."

"Mammoth beasts, you say? Well, you should be grateful that I'm not a mammoth beast, otherwise you'd have been trampled just now."

What could she say? The lieutenant had a point. In allowing herself to become so entranced with Leara, she had made herself vulnerable. Still, Sierra irked her in a way no other had before. She was most surprised to find the sensation not entirely unpleasing.

"And I won't bite," Sierra added, leaning close and brushing her shoulder against Kitani's. Apparently, Sierra had noticed her very obvious discomfort and decided to make it worse. "There's no need to be afraid of me."

"I'm not afraid," Kitani said, although in truth she was aware that if she slid over any farther, she'd end up sitting on the ground.

Sierra laughed merrily, withdrawing to her own side of the stump. "Of course not. I wouldn't expect a Paladin to be scared of a harmless human."

I definitely wouldn't describe you as harmless. To Kitani, the mild spring day suddenly seemed to grow almost unbearably hot, especially since she was encased in the heavy Cipher combat armor.

"I wanted to apologize for before," Sierra said unexpectedly. "There seems to have been some sort of misunderstanding, and lately the tension between us has been so great you could cut it with a knife. I'm an alien to your world and its customs and have no right to criticize the ways of the Paladins. I was out of line, and I'm sorry if I offended you."

So Sierra was aware of the developing tension, Kitani thought, but she remained silent, wondering how perceptive the human might be when it came to the subtle ways of the Valori.

"Well," Sierra said, stretching her legs out in front of her, "I suppose I've bothered you enough for now."

Kitani noticed sadness in Sierra's eyes when she spoke, and reluctance too, as though she didn't actually want to leave.

You weren't bothering me, nor do I find your brazen behavior particularly offensive, Kitani wanted to say, but the words simply wouldn't come. All she could do was remain on the stump as Sierra rose to go.

"I should check whether Commander Duran has any use for me. See you later, Kitani."

At Sierra's use of her name, Kitani felt her body go rigid and her breath catch in her chest. Never in her life had the sound of her own name had such an effect on her. She exhaled slowly, her entire body relaxing—all but one part of her, which remained quite stiff and swollen as she watched Sierra's retreating back.

Kitani was slightly alarmed at the pleasant thrumming between her legs. In the past, she'd managed to control her arousal quite well—a good thing, since letting her libido get out of control could be detrimental for a Paladin. Controlling sexual urges was the primary reason why Paladins were required to take Pompeilo extract.

However, she was currently far away from Aria and the watchful eyes of the High Matriarchs, so those old laws should no longer affect her, she decided. Besides, there was no harm in looking, was there? She could allow herself that much. She sat and stared after Sierra as the lieutenant disappeared inside one of the low buildings.

Suddenly, her mind reeled back to the present. Why would she feel this way with this burning desire threatening to overwhelm her? Retracing the steps of recent events in her mind, she came upon the event that had started the whole complicated situation for herself and Leara, the turning point. Kronos. The explosion at the outpost facility and the abandonment of their own ship. That was where they had met Cybil Reynard, and that was where she had left her supply of Pompeilo.

Doing the math in her head, Kitani calculated that enough time had passed for the effects of Pompeilo to wear off, but she didn't think she should be so easily aroused yet.

During her brief stay on Aria, it had completely slipped her mind that she would need to restock before setting out again. Everything had happened so fast. Just as she was coming to terms with the fact that life would return to normal for her, High Matriarch Sorani had ordered her to accompany Leara when she ventured out with Cipher. Now she was billions of light years from Aria, the only planet in the universe known to sustain the Pompeilo flower.

The realization made her panic. What would happen if her sexual potency was allowed to surface and she became fully capable of breeding? She decided she shouldn't worry so much. The two were not definitely linked. Many Valori were sexually active while remaining sterile. But she was a Paladin and had never been allowed such a privilege. This new power, this raw emotion flooding through her was frightening.

The air outside was suddenly smothering, so Kitani rose from the stump to seek shelter from the Earth's glaring sun.

Cybil sat at the end of one of the long tables in the compound's mess hall where the crew ate their dinner. As usual, Leara was present at her side. She and Leara were growing closer, and so was the indescribable bond between them. Although she still had no name for what was happening, she felt it all the same. It was something of a relief for her that Leara understood and returned her feelings, but not everyone was pleased with their budding relationship.

Shortly after the *Sentinel* left Aria, Kitani had withdrawn into a dark, brooding state. Of course, she'd always found Kitani more than a little standoffish, but lately, the Valori refused to talk even with Leara, her closest friend among the crew.

In the few short hours since making landfall on Earth, Kitani had become even more sullen. Cybil didn't dare approach her, since something in Kitani's expression said more clearly than words that the Valori was itching for a fight. Cybil didn't want to find herself on the receiving end of one of Kitani's kicks. Even now, her side ached when she thought of the powerful blow that had sent her flying across the room in the research station on Kronos.

How long ago that seemed, Cybil mused. She, Leara, and Kitani had been through so much since their first encounter that it was becoming difficult for her to imagine a time when the two Valori had not been in her life. She rested her gaze on Leara, who was examining the contents of the plate of food in front of her. Never had she laid eyes on a woman more beautiful, human or otherwise. She was truly fortunate to have won the attentions of such a wonderful and caring person.

Just as she leaned over to whisper to Leara how much she appreciated her company, a sea of murmurs drifted over to her. She looked up to see Kitani standing in the center of the large room.

There was an intensity about the Valori warrior that had not been there before, Cybil noted, watching Kitani survey the faces of the room's occupants before storming off to a find a seat at a small table at the back of the room. The tension emanating from Kitani was almost palpable and seemed to reverberate around the room like an echo. She noticed everyone averting their gazes as the Valori passed, seemingly not wishing to challenge her.

Leara's shivering attracted her attention.

Cybil leaned closer to Leara, muttering in a voice she hoped was too low for Kitani to overhear, "What's wrong with Kitani? I've never seen her look so savage. She looks ready to explode into violence at any moment."

"I think I may know what's happening," Leara said, her eyes downcast, a tremor underlying every word. For the briefest instant, Leara tensed almost as much as Kitani. "I think it would be best if we leave now, Cybil." It sounded more like a command than a suggestion.

Cybil had to hurry to catch up to Leara as she strode quickly from the mess hall.

Once outside, Leara became noticeably more relaxed. She leaned against the metal hull of the long, domed building, and stared up at the sky.

Cybil desperately wanted to question Leara about the scene inside the mess hall and the very obvious discomfort it caused her, but she held back out of respect for Leara's feelings. Clearly, something had upset her deeply. She knew that Leara would explain it in time. For now, she was content to merely hold Leara's hand, giving it a light squeeze to reassure her that she had a sympathetic listener close by.

"Cybil," Leara said, turning to her. She looked uncertain, as though she wanted to say more, but was unsure how to start.

Cybil nodded encouragingly, but just as Leara opened her mouth, Duran rounded the corner of the building. Instinctively, her grip on Leara's hand loosened, her own hand falling limply to her side when Duran stopped before them.

"Ah, Reynard," Duran said, a trace of annoyance in her voice. "I've been looking for you. I figured if I found *Si'rah* Sorani, I'd also find you." She paused to give them a leering smile that made Cybil want to punch her. "Anyway, the reason for my interruption is quite simple. You have a message waiting for you aboard the *Sentinel*. One of my crew should be able to patch it through for you."

"Who could be contacting me?" Cybil asked. Receiving a message seemed too suspicious for her taste. Aside from Leara, Kitani, and the Cipher officers she was currently traveling with, she could think of no one who might know where to find her.

Duran arched an eyebrow, making a show of looking Cybil over. "Although I cannot for the life of me fathom why, Enigma seems to have taken a strong interest in you." She shrugged. "Maybe Enigma's tastes run a little differently than mine. Certainly there's nothing overly impressive about you on the exterior."

"Enigma?" Cybil gasped. Duran had claimed earlier that Enigma's interest in her was keeping her alive, but she had taken the information rather halfheartedly. Now the elusive figure wished to speak with her in person, which seemed unbelievable.

"Enigma has been concerned about you since your departure from Aria," Duran continued with a nod, "and has some advice to offer before our next mission, I believe. Go speak to our leader, Reynard. That's not a suggestion; it's an order."

Cybil glared at Duran for a long moment before finally conceding. "Fine," she said gruffly. In a more pleasant tone, she added, "Let's go, Leara."

"*Si'rah* Sorani wasn't invited to take part in this conversation," Duran said, offering a bow to Leara. "I mean no offense by my refusal, *Si'rah*, but it's Cybil with whom Enigma wishes an audience."

"I understand," Leara said amiably, but Cybil caught a glimpse of thinly veiled distress still lingering in her expression.

What was it she wanted to tell me? Did Duran interrupt us intentionally? No matter, Cybil reassured herself. If what Leara wanted to confide in her was truly important, she was sure to learn of it later. What bothered her now was her unexpected appointment with the mysterious and secretive Enigma. What could Cipher's high command possibly want with her? There was only one way to find out.

Squaring her shoulders, Cybil turned to march in the direction of the *Sentinel*, glancing back over her shoulder only once to offer a reassuring smile to Leara.

Chapter 18

Cybil didn't know what to expect as she paced impatiently in the *Sentinel*'s communications room. Enigma, the mystery enshrouded figurehead of Cipher, wanted to speak with her, a lowly space mercenary. What was there to say? At present, she was uncertain whether she should be honored or offended by the exclusive invitation.

A buzzing heralded the opening of a communications channel. The room was suddenly filled with the boom of a thunderous voice, so electronically scrambled it was difficult to discern the speaker's gender. "Are you Cybil Reynard of the Midnight Suns mercenaries?"

The answer to that question should be obvious, Cybil thought, especially since she was the one who'd been summoned, but she kept the smart comment to herself. Instead she said, "Yes. And are you Enigma, the living shadow that envelops the universe?"

The ominous voice remained silent for a long pause, and then it said, "Yes."

When it appeared that Enigma wished to say no more, Cybil took it upon herself to ask the question that had been plaguing her mind since her whole ordeal began. "Why did you spare my life? What interest could the head of a secret and dangerous organization such as Cipher possibly want with someone like me?"

"Dangerous?" The voice, which had sounded deep and gruff until now, made no attempt to hide its amusement. "Is that what you think of me?"

Cybil was certain that the voice had taken on a completely different pitch, which led her to believe that perhaps Enigma was composed of several different persons. However, it could be a trick to further perplex anyone who might be listening to their conversation.

"Aren't you?" she responded cautiously. "Cipher is a collection of the deadliest warriors in the universe, all of whom are at your disposal. Surely you aren't going to try to persuade me that you're benign. Your word surpasses even the strict boundaries enforced by the Senate. Now, I'll ask you again: why have I been spared?"

She heard chuckling from the communications channel, a rumbling sound rather like distant thunder. "You're every bit as bold and audacious as they say," Enigma said. "Very well, I'll answer your question and hopefully satisfy some of your curiosity. You've been brought here by Commander Duran for evaluation."

"Evaluation?"

"Your skills have attracted the attention of Cipher, Reynard, not an easy task, I assure you. I wanted a chance to assess these abilities for myself. If I'm satisfied, you may be considered for a position among the prestigious ranks of Cipher… if you wish to join us, that is."

For the first time during the interview, Cybil found herself struck speechless. Her, an agent of Cipher?

Most of her life had been spent believing that Cipher was the ultimate evil bent on secretly controlling the universe through tyranny and threats, and many of those beliefs had been instilled in her by the mercenaries. Only now, she thought, she was beginning to see that Cipher was not the terror people made it out to be. Duran might be obnoxious, but the woman seemed genuinely dedicated to ending corruption and saving lives, and all with the knowledge that she would never be thanked for her contributions.

In addition, there was Sierra Callaway. She frowned. As much as she had originally wanted to believe otherwise, she knew her old friend would never involve herself with a band of galactic scoundrels. But how could she abandon her ideals, becoming the very thing which she'd been taught to fear and hate?

Her conflicting thoughts were interrupted by the sound of Enigma's laughter. "It seems I've presented you with a rather troubling offer. Take some time to think it over. I'll be here when your decision is made. Until then, the best of luck to you and your allies."

Enigma ended the communication with a sudden crackling noise followed by silence. It was over, Cybil thought. The conversation she had dreaded was finally over, yet in some ways it had only just begun.

When she returned to the building housing the crew of the *Sentinel*, she found Leara waiting anxiously for her. Undoubtedly, Leara was curious to know the reason behind the mysterious conference. However, she wasn't sure if she was ready to completely confide the details to anyone, even Leara.

"How did the meeting with Enigma go?" Leara asked. Her pupils had widened to dark orbs in the dim light, which gave her an unsettled appearance, like a nervous cat.

With the rest of the crew still outside enjoying the pleasant weather, Cybil noticed that she and Leara had the building to themselves. They sat side by side on her bunk as she mentally prepared herself for the onslaught of questions likely on the tip of Leara's tongue, but the questions didn't come.

Instead, Leara withdrew into herself, becoming quite melancholy as she apparently waited until Cybil was ready to begin her account of the evening. Recalling how disturbed Leara had behaved in the mess hall earlier, she quickly dismissed her recent conversation with Enigma in favor of hearing Leara's story.

"It seems that our help will be invaluable to Cipher on this upcoming mission," Cybil said. "However, I am currently more concerned with your well-being. What happened earlier? Is Kitani okay?"

Fastening her gaze on the floor, Leara hesitated before saying, "Kitani is fine, although she may be feeling a certain degree of discomfort. You see, before we left Aria for Turon, Kitani was given an ample supply of an herbal extract called Pompeilo, taken from the flower of the same name."

"Pompeilo? I don't recall hearing of it before."

"You wouldn't. The Pompeilo is indigenous to Aria. The nectar of its large and beautiful flowers is harvested and used to ensure sterility even during the breeding season. Paladins are kept in a constant supply of Pompeilo. As you may know, Paladins are not allowed to breed or even take mates. Pompeilo keeps them sterile, and it's also been proven to help repress sexual urges," Leara said solemnly.

Cybil found it obvious that Leara disapproved of this practice, and with good reason. She shuddered to imagine what it would be like having a government deny her freedom to love and being made a neuter to ensure unwavering service to those who oppressed her.

"What troubles me most, though," Leara continued, "is that the timing isn't right. The way I figure it, Kitani hasn't taken any Pompeilo since before we left Turon. That doesn't seem like enough time for the effects to wear off completely. She might be going through a sort of withdrawal."

"That would certainly explain the increased aggression we've been seeing in her," Cybil said.

"Yet Kitani is exhibiting all the signs of sexual potency awakening in her. I just don't understand it. Unless," Leara added, her face lighting up as a thought struck her. "Maybe something happened to trigger the change. I worry for Kitani, though. The whole experience will be alien and confusing for her."

"Will she be all right?" Cybil wondered if the Valori underwent any physical changes during this stage. Considering the Valori's secrecy regarding their physiology, she doubted Leara would tell her if any changes did indeed occur. "What will happen if Kitani does become a sexually potent Valori?"

"I don't think you need to worry about that," Leara said reassuringly. "Not for a while, anyway. Kitani is most likely experiencing withdrawal symptoms from the sudden lack of Pompeilo. Even if Kitani does begin to feel sexual urges, it's highly improbable that she'll enter into the stages of the breeding cycle. It is too soon."

Now that Cybil's curiosity was piqued, she couldn't hold back. "What are breeding Valori like? I mean, do they look any different than usual? Are there any noticeable changes?" She noted that Leara was looking at her, her eyes wide with shock. "Forgive me if I've overstepped any bounds. You must think me incredibly rude."

Oh, how Cybil wished she could learn to keep her mouth shut, but there were just so many secrets about the Valori, and she had so many questions. Her genuine interest in the subject surprised her. A short while ago, she never would have believed she would care enough to want to learn about an alien society—just another thing that had changed since meeting Leara.

"They're more irritable," Leara began slowly, bringing Cybil back to the present with a jolt. She appeared uncertain whether she wanted to continue or not. Finally, she went on, "And on occasion they may become more aggressive and competitive. The stress brought on by the fluctuation of hormones can be mentally taxing as well. The breeding cycle is similar to your species' menstrual cycle, I suppose. Well, not exactly, but the emotional effects are comparable." When Cybil shot her a surprised glance, she added, "I studied a little about human culture and anatomy before our covert operation on Turon. I hope I haven't offended you."

"No. No, not at all." Cybil shook her head to further emphasize her point. "It's just a little startling, that's all."

Kitani had a notorious temper. Cybil didn't want to imagine what she would be like with PMS. No one would be safe from her wild mood swings, she thought, somewhat amused at the idea that the Valori were not so different from humans, after all.

"So can we expect many more sparring matches like the one between Kitani and me?" she asked, getting back to the matter at hand. It was a wonder in itself that Leara was willing to share this intimate knowledge with her. She didn't want to ruin it for herself by making immature jokes.

Other than Leara, there were no other Valori present, Cybil recalled suddenly. Would Kitani attempt to mate with a human should the opportunity present itself? Her thoughts went immediately to Sierra. Her friend's interest in the Valori warrior was painfully obvious. Would Kitani be able to read Sierra's desire so clearly?

Sierra knows how to take care of herself. There was no need for her to worry over Sierra like an overprotective older sister.

"Is there anything we can do to help?" Cybil asked, feeling the heat from Leara's body as the Valori sat quietly on the edge of the bunk. Leara's proximity made her shudder. The beautiful woman sitting next to her might appear human except for her eyes, but Leara was very different. Perhaps the boundary between their races had never been crossed before, and maybe, she thought rather solemnly, it shouldn't be.

Leara shook her head. "I'm afraid not. Without Pompeilo, our efforts would be useless. Also, I think it might be best if I kept my distance from Kitani for a while. The burgeoning sexuality of one Valori has been known to start a chain reaction among others. In fact, when one Valori enters into the stages of the breeding cycle, it triggers a change in her partner. The mate will respond and develop according to her partner's sexuality."

"Is that how Valori are able to breed?" Cybil asked, startled that Leara would give her this much information about her species' reproductive capabilities. "You say the Valori are one gender. I wonder how breeding is even possible among a single-gendered race. So you aren't asexual, as some people believe?"

Leara shook her head. "No, during the breeding cycle, each individual plays a separate role. Those roles may change depending on the needs of a partner, or due to factors in the developmental period. Most Valori have preferences, of course, but the same Valori who birthed a child during a previous breeding may sire one in the future."

"Fascinating," Cybil said, not wanting to give Leara the impression that she was repulsed by the revelation. Actually, she really did find the information intriguing.

"You're not revolted?" Relief washed over Leara's features. "I was afraid you'd find the truth disturbing."

"Not at all. One thing does concern me, though," Cybil added. "Before, you mentioned keeping your distance from Kitani for a while."

"Until she learns to cope with her new sexuality," Leara clarified. "Right now, Kitani is giving off many signals. It's most likely unintentional, but any mature Valori would be able to pick up on them just the same. Even though Kitani and I aren't mates, and I have no particular interest in becoming so, prolonged exposure to her during these stages may awaken a change in me, as well."

Cybil started at Leara's words. As much as she wanted to reach out and console her, she couldn't bring herself to move a muscle. She felt as though her limbs were made of lead.

Leara noticed the change in Cybil's demeanor. "Does this information frighten you?" she asked. "Are you having second thoughts now that you're witnessing firsthand the true nature of the Valori's unique physiology? I suppose there's a reason my people want to protect these secrets."

Meeting Leara's gaze Cybil said adamantly, "Not at all. You're a wonderful person, Leara. Nothing you could tell me of Valori biology could ever change the truth in that." She drew Leara to her in an embrace and rested her chin atop Leara's head. "You worry too much. I'm not so easily frightened."

Although Cybil had claimed she understood the strange new emotions fluttering in her heart, her mind was filled with confusion and uncertainty. In one day, she'd had some of the ideals firmly ingrained in her since childhood thoroughly tested. Enigma wanted her as a Cipher operative, and it was becoming increasingly obvious that Leara wanted her as mate.

Deep inside herself, Cybil acknowledged that she didn't know if she was ready to make such huge commitments. Not to Enigma and, sadly, not even to Leara.

After going to the mess hall and realizing she had very little appetite, Kitani had returned to the eerily silent ship. While the rest of the crew, Leara included, planned to bunk in the lodging provided by the outpost, she found she was in no mood to be around so many others and opted to spend the night aboard the *Sentinel*.

Rivulets of warm water ran down her back and along the tense muscles of her arm while she showered, all the way to where her hand was wedged deep between her thighs. Her body went rigid. She shuddered convulsively as a tidal wave of pleasure washed over her, but it still wasn't enough. She craved more. She wanted to feel the press of hot yielding flesh against her. The insides of her thighs were coated with a satiny sheen that had little to do with the water cascading around her, but this didn't concern her as much as the intense, almost overwhelming yearning for release that had preceded it.

Why was this happening to her now? It was too soon for the effects of Pompeilo to have worn off completely, yet she was beginning to feel like a sexually potent Valori. She wondered if all Valori felt this way, or if it was withdrawal from Pompeilo extract that had her on edge. Many years had passed since she last allowed herself to masturbate, and even then the desire for release hadn't been nearly as compelling as it was now. A Paladin's duty was too important, too revered, for the Valori in question to behave like anything less than a celibate priestess. Therefore she, like all other Paladins, took Pompeilo extract to ensure sterility and repress sexual feelings year round.

She knew some viewed the custom as harsh, but the use of Pompeilo wasn't nearly as cruel as an earlier practice prevalent in the more turbulent times when the Supreme Matriarchy was beginning to establish rule over Aria and the High Matriarchs' lives were more perilous. In those days, the Paladins were permanently sterilized, both to ensure their undivided devotion to their position, and to prevent undesirable breeding with the High Matriarchs they were sworn to protect. Now that the Paladins were more of a tradition than an actual defense force as a result of less tumultuous times, they weren't subjected to such extreme measures.

Kitani had been grateful for that small grace. At least the herbal remedy prevented a Paladin from being made a neuter permanently. During the breeding cycle, a Valori's sex glands swelled to nearly three times their normal size. Kitani already felt the effects of the change coming on her, a dull throbbing ache in her lower abdomen accompanied by the frequent mood swings she had been experiencing lately.

Placing her fingers over the source of the pain, she pressed down. The two internal glands were indeed swollen, she discovered, and the pressure from her gentle prodding made her long for another release. Normally, she wasn't so easily aroused. This was the reason for her concern. What was causing her to become sexually potent?

Her increased aggression and irritability were definitely withdrawal symptoms from the Pompeilo. But that didn't explain the intense sexual longing. It felt as though her loins were on fire, and if she didn't find release soon, she feared she might explode.

Rinsing between her legs brought to mind the powerful climax she had experienced only moments before. The mere memory of the sensation was enough to cause her sex to become engorged again. She stepped out of the shower, squirming every time the towel's coarse fabric came into contact with the sensitive area as she dried off. The dark blue pants she put on weren't comfortable either, since each time the crotch of the trousers brushed against her, it sent shivers coursing through her body.

Is it always like this without Pompeilo? Kitani lay face down on her bunk, wriggling to find a position which didn't stimulate her. The whoosh of the hatch sliding open caused her to spring up from the mattress.

She saw Sierra standing in the doorway, looking as cheerful as ever. The lieutenant had removed her Cipher armor in favor of a black jumpsuit. She noted with mild irritation how nicely the jumpsuit clung to Sierra in all the right places.

"I thought you might want some company," Sierra said, sitting down on the bunk across from Kitani. "You looked lonely sitting all by yourself in the mess hall."

With maddening acuity, Kitani became aware of every subtle nuance of Sierra's presence, down to the slightest scent. The fact that her heightened senses could detect, just beneath the mask of sweet perfume, the unmistakable scent of arousal only fed her hunger.

"If you must know, I prefer solitude," Kitani said, almost an outright lie, and the lieutenant would know it, she thought. After her life as a Paladin, as Leara's constant guardian and companion, she barely knew what it meant to be alone.

Sierra acknowledged her understanding with a sly grin. "Well, I thought I'd drop in to check on you anyway. How are you enjoying being with Cipher so far?"

"Thus far, I've only been present among your squad when it was fleeing or stealthily traversing the galaxy," Kitani replied. "However," she added mischievously, "I'm eagerly anticipating our next move. Bringing an end to Midas has long been a personal goal of mine." She sobered. "Midas has caused a great deal of distress, both to me and to Leara."

"It's been a source of worry for Cipher as well. For years, we've tracked Midas's spies from one planet to another, all the while allowing ourselves to be led on a wild goose chase. Now that we've obtained all the incriminating evidence we need to act, we cannot let the enemy out of our sight."

"I'd like nothing more than to charge into that base and tear it apart with my bare hands." Kitani clenched her hand into a fist for emphasis.

"Settle down," Sierra said as she reached across the distance between them and lightly covered Kitani's hand with her own. "You'll have your chance in due time. There's no need to go rushing off into a battle you have no hope of winning."

Kitani stiffened.

Sierra lightly traced her fingers along the tense muscles in Kitani's forearm. "Promise me you won't do anything crazy if I leave here tonight. If something happened to you, I... well, I'm not sure I could take it."

Sierra's sincerity made Kitani force herself to look at the human. "You shouldn't involve yourself with me. I'm dangerous," she said, gently brushing Sierra's fingers from her arm.

"And you think I'm not?" Sierra replied, laughing. "For the past eight years, I've lived among Cipher, the toughest, most lethal bunch of secret agents the universe has ever known. I've seen horrors that would make even the worst intergalactic badass blanch."

Kitani didn't doubt this was true. She had seen horrors herself. The training Paladins received was brutal although they were little more than ceremonial guards.

"You said earlier that you weren't afraid of me," Sierra said, leaning closer. "Well, Kitani Veldina, it takes a lot more than a Paladin to frighten me." She slid forward until her knees were touching Kitani's.

Kitani tensed further as Sierra reached up to stroke her hair, but she didn't move out of Sierra's reach. Instead, she inclined her head to one side, her movements stiff and apprehensive as she ever so slightly leaned into the gentle touch, allowing Sierra to caress her thick hair.

She sensed Sierra seething with sexual tension. The scent permeating the air was so alluring, she was tempted to give in to her desire. Would it be such a crime if she did? After all, Sierra was practically begging for it. There was no harm in giving Sierra what she needed, and a good tumble might even take some of the edge off her anxiety before the battle. She wished she could go about things as nonchalantly as she imagined, but she liked Sierra, and she didn't want to use her so casually. Even thinking such things made her blush.

"Tell me," Sierra began, pausing to moisten her lips with her tongue, "what do you think of Commander Duran and the crew? Working with humans is a new experience for you, from what I understand. I hope the crew hasn't been giving you too much trouble." She hesitated, swallowing hard before asking her next question. "What's your opinion of your human allies?"

Kitani closed her eyes as Sierra's fingers were still entangled in her hair. "They are so very... human," she replied. Perhaps humanity's ways would always be confounding to her, incomprehensible and alien. The cultural barrier between their species might be too great to ever be crossed.

Sierra looked sullen.

"However, I believe in time I may develop a greater appreciation for the company of the fairer sex," Kitani continued.

Sierra slid her hand from Kitani's hair and caressed her cheek. Kitani bristled with excitement at the sensation of smooth, cool flesh. Taking Sierra's quiet chuckle as an invitation, she rose from her bunk, moving forward until she had Sierra pinned against the opposite bed.

As Kitani ran her fingers through Sierra's rich sable hair, she inhaled the sweet aroma of shampoo. Sitting back on her knees, she smiled, and in that moment she found Sierra's gaze. Their eyes met for a split second. Her hunger was mirrored in Sierra's expression.

Kitani knew Sierra wanted this, wanted her, but something was holding her back as strongly as a physical restraint. Her sex was tight, aching for release, yet somehow she couldn't bring herself to take Sierra as a mate. Perhaps, she thought, her hesitancy stemmed from her many long years of being denied such a simple pleasure, or perhaps she merely feared the consequences should she actually reach sexual potency. There had been no successful breeding between a Valori and a member of another species recorded so far, but theoretically it wasn't impossible. Sierra undoubtedly thought of her as no more than an ordinary human woman, although a Valori, especially a sexually potent Valori, was in fact much different.

Taking Sierra lovingly in her arms, Kitani warned, "Be wary what you wish for, lieutenant. It may turn out to be more than you can handle." She bent her head forward, claiming Sierra's mouth in a kiss far more passionate than she should allow in her current state.

"The time isn't right," Kitani said, ending the kiss. Using her primal needs as an excuse to take advantage of Sierra was unforgivable. She would only feel guilty about it later. "Perhaps someday," she added, feeling tears in her eyes. It took every ounce of her self-control to disentangle herself from Sierra's limbs and rise reluctantly from the low bunk.

Sierra fell back limply on the bunk. Kitani turned and made her way toward the lavatory.

"I hope you're satisfied," she called over her shoulder as the hatch slid closed behind her.

Inside the lavatory, Kitani leaned her head back against the closed hatch. "I hope you're satisfied, indeed," she muttered. In the brief eternity that their bodies had cleaved together, she had come to realize that it would be wrong to use Sierra only to forsake her company later. Not only that, she also had her position as a Paladin to consider. Taking a human lover would not only be foolish, but if her actions ever reached the ears of the High Matriarchs, she would never be allowed to commit such an indiscretion again. Too bad her body couldn't be as reasonable as her head. Feeling her sex swell and pulse at the recollection of their encounter, she turned to press her forehead against the cool metal of the door.

Damn Pompeilo and its accursed side effects! It was difficult to focus on anything other than the lovely and willing Sierra Callaway sitting in the next room.

Chapter 19

The next morning, Commander Duran outlined her plan as she paced slowly and purposefully in front of the people gathered at the outpost. The commander never looked more imposing or more pretentious, Cybil thought, as when she stood before her assembled crew. Nevertheless, she had to give Duran credit for knowing how to make a dramatic appearance. She had donned a black cloak for this special occasion. The dark fabric matched the dark Cipher uniform perfectly, flowing behind her like a living shadow when she moved.

"Today, my brave warriors, we face our enemy in its own territory, and hopefully we will end its tyranny once and for all," Duran said. "Once again, I would like to thank everyone for the risk you're taking. Midas is a formidable foe, and in facing it we should take every precaution." She held up a helmet that matched the Cipher combat armor. "It's highly advisable to wear your protective helmet at all times during this mission, along with activating your suits' life support functions. This should keep out any foreign contaminants you may encounter in the facility."

The information was met with nods of approval from the gathered crew.

Cybil knew that in addition to the usual crew, members of other Cipher squads had volunteered their services to the cause, doubtless the reason why Duran was in such a cheery mood considering the somber occasion. With the new volunteers, the commander's crew totaled fifty at least, with quite a few aliens, she noticed as she scanned the faces in the crowd. No wonder Duran was stressing the importance of using the suits' life support systems, and the volunteers were eager to comply.

Undoubtedly, these men and women knew the treachery of which Midas was capable, and with so many alien faces among the Cipher agents, Cybil was sure a few of them harbored deep fears and reservations about journeying into the facility. Any safety measure, no matter how small, would be welcome for them.

"Two of us will go in undercover in order to infiltrate Midas Pharmaceuticals' headquarters," Duran went on. "Don't look so smug, Reynard, I'm not referring to you. This mission is crucial. I can't afford to have a loose cannon blowing our cover."

Cybil glared at Duran but made no protests. She was a wanted woman. Charging into the heart of the enemy's territory would be foolish. Even she wasn't too stubborn to admit the sense in Duran's precautions.

At a nod from Cybil, Duran continued. "My informant, Rex, tells me that the daily routine is pretty regular. Employees check in and out of the complex using a special ID card. Rex also informs me that he should be able to obtain several of these cards by this evening at the latest. With our undercover agents in place, the plan can move to its next phase."

"Pardon me, commander," Kitani interrupted, the ferocity in her eyes giving lie to the polite formalities, "but I thought now would be the best time to bring to your attention the fact that Leara and I have been involved in a similar operation. We have successfully infiltrated Midas before. I would gladly volunteer my services again if it would help."

"Thank you Paladin Veldina, but that won't be necessary," Duran replied.

Kitani hesitated a moment, and then said, "If Leara and I are to be exempt from this mission, then who, may I ask, will be included in this party?"

Duran returned Kitani's stare with equal intensity. "I've given it some thought, and the most suitable agents for the job are Lieutenant Callaway and Officer Banks."

Cybil noted that Sierra did not appear in the least surprised when her name was called. Quite the contrary, her friend seemed to be rather proud of the commander's selection. The pilot Amy Banks, on the other hand, seemed torn between whether she should be honored at her inclusion, or appalled at being chosen to venture into the corrupt heart of Midas Pharmaceuticals.

She very nearly felt sorry for Banks. After all, the young woman was a quiet person with a gentle disposition, not at all like her former image of a cruel and cunning Cipher agent.

"Only those two?" Kitani blurted out. "Two humans?"

Duran gave the Valori a stern look. "Two highly trained Cipher agents," she said firmly. "Remember, Paladin Veldina, that our enemy has a penchant for causing pain and suffering to aliens. I imagine they'd be rather ecstatic to get their hands on you." She smiled when Kitani narrowed her eyes threateningly. "I'm doing this for your own good. Please try to accept my generosity more graciously."

Kitani did not look delighted with Duran's suggestion that she remain at the outpost while her allies risked their lives. Cybil considered that as a warrior, the prospect of losing her life for the greater good did not bother Kitani.

"Commander Duran, it will take more than Midas's threats to keep me from performing my duty," Kitani said. "Remember, this is as much my fight as it is anyone's."

Duran sighed.

Talking sense into the Valori warrior was not for the faint of heart, Cybil thought, feeling a slight sympathy for Duran, but, she also had to admit that Kitani had a point. The alien plague, if successfully completed, would affect the Valori and other nonhuman races. If anyone deserved to thwart Midas's plan, it should be the nonhumans.

"I see your point, Paladin," Duran said. "You desire so badly to be a champion of your people, and I have no right to stifle that ambition. You'll be able to join us in our midnight infiltration of the compound. Tomorrow night," she added pointedly. "If I catch you trying to sneak away on your own, you can count yourself out."

"Out of the mission?" Kitani asked.

"Out of Cipher," the commander stated firmly.

Cybil watched the emotions flickering in the Valori's eyes like firelight and wondered what kind of response Duran's statement would generate.

When Kitani finally spoke, her voice sounded strained and hollow. "This is most unsatisfactory." She sounded ready to burst with pent-up rage.

Cybil sensed Kitani's frustration as the Valori stormed away. She thought Duran would certainly have her work cut out for her if she believed she could order Kitani around so easily. Suddenly, she noticed that Leara wasn't running after her friend, but remained at her side.

"Should you go to her?" she suggested softly.

Leara met Cybil's gaze with an icy stare. "I fear that going to Kitani now would not be the appropriate thing to do. It isn't me she wants. I think Kitani needs some time to herself more than anything right now. Kitani is a warrior. She'll be fine."

"I suppose you're right," Cybil said, her curiosity not really satisfied.

"Maybe we should do our part in preparing for the trials to come," Leara suggested in her gentle voice. "Even if we aren't permitted to be on the infiltration team, our contributions may be of use to those who are."

"Of course." Cybil wanted to say more, but couldn't. She felt like kicking herself for her standoffish behavior toward Leara since the evening before. The sexual potency phases and the ensuing breeding cycle were natural for the Valori. She should be honored that Leara would even impart such intimate information to her at all, considering the Valori's strong reservations toward other species.

Cybil found the Valori breeding cycle and its various phases to be quite practical. It ensured the race would continue to thrive, while at the same time preventing overpopulation. Hearing about it from Leara's lips had just seemed so… unexpected. Leara had a childlike innocence about her, and hearing her speak so frankly had been somewhat startling. Honestly, she had been shocked that Leara would discuss such a sensitive subject with her when not so long ago, she had refused to reveal information pertaining to the Valori's reproductive abilities.

Perhaps the most surprising thing to Cybil was that Valori reproduction didn't disturb her, nor did she find it particularly strange, as she once would have. She no longer viewed Leara and Kitani as mere aliens, outsiders to be feared and mistrusted. Somewhere along the line, she had come to think of them as people. Not even Leara's confidential disclosure or Kitani's current predicament could alter her opinion.

Poor Leara, she thought. She had probably shared the knowledge with Cybil in the hope of attaining understanding, maybe even assistance should the need arise. And all Cybil had done was withdraw into herself again. She was lost so deep in her own thoughts she had failed to realize the tremendous amount of trust Leara placed in her by willingly baring the secrets of her people.

She cares for you, idiot. Stop behaving like a narrow-minded fool, and tell her how you really feel. The mental reproach for her actions prodded her into speaking, but just as she was preparing to offer a sincere apology to Leara, the boom of Duran's voice broke her concentration.

"If there are no questions, the operation shall commence immediately." When no one offered comment or inquiry, Duran continued, "Lieutenant, you and Banks are to accompany me back to command so Rex and his men can brief you on your objectives. As for the rest of you, do all that you can to aid this mission without causing too much trouble."

Duran seemed to focus her gaze on Cybil as she made the last statement. She finally turned and retreated to the command center.

Cybil snorted. As if she would intentionally do anything to thwart their mission to overthrow Midas and put an end to the genocide campaign before it had a chance to begin. Just this once, Cipher's goal happened to coincide with her own. The future of galactic society was riding on the outcome of this mission. She would gladly set aside her differences in order to preserve that future.

Everything was changing so fast, but she didn't want to give it up. Life was just starting to get interesting, even if she didn't understand all the changes taking place between her and Leara or within herself. These matters would be resolved in the future.

As long as there is *a future*, she thought. The unspoken words strengthened her resolve.

Gently, she reached out and took Leara's hand, lacing their fingers together she made a silent vow: *No matter what happens, Leara, I will protect you. I promise.*

The next day passed slowly for Cybil and everyone else awaiting news of the infiltration team's progress. That night the waiting paid off.

"The operation was a success!" she heard Rex shouting from the command center. "Your officers successfully fooled everyone into thinking they were Midas employees, and the infiltrators have remained behind to secure entry for the rest of the team. I must say, Eris, you've trained your people well."

"Would you expect anything less?" Duran sounded offended at Rex's jest. Her tone lightened as she continued, "These women are Cipher, the greatest warriors in the universe. Surely you didn't believe a simple infiltration mission too much for them to handle?"

Rex laughed. "I haven't forgotten your warped sense of humor. Nor have I forgotten that you can be a rather cruel taskmaster when proper training is involved. I can only say that I'm glad you're on our side instead of the enemy's."

Cybil listened to the friendly banter between the commander and Rex with half an ear; her mind was more focused on storming the complex and bringing an end to their enemy's foul plan before it could do any more harm. She glanced sidelong at Leara, who stood by her side.

"Is it almost time?" The familiar voice, made strange by the strain behind each word, interrupted Cybil's thoughts. She turned to see Kitani standing at her other shoulder. The Valori was tense, her body rigid as she stared intently at Cybil.

Sensing Kitani was on the edge of violence, Cybil spoke carefully when she replied. "The commander seems to think so. With Sierra and Banks in place, we should be able to enter the facility tonight."

"Good," Kitani said, her lips parting in a grin that clearly showed her sharp canines. "I've been aching for some action, and it looks as though this is to be my only form of release." She leaned closer. Cybil flinched away as she felt the heat emanating from the Valori's body. "Better this than nothing, I suppose. Wouldn't you agree, Cybil?"

When Cybil made no reply, Kitani laughed sharply and walked away from the command building.

"Will she be all right? Kitani felt as though she was on fire with fever, and I wasn't even touching her," Cybil said to Leara.

"That's also a side effect of Pompeilo withdrawal. Perhaps the battle tonight will help to assuage some of the aggression she's feeling," Leara replied.

"Is it safe for her to join in the fight?" Cybil asked, recalling the fierce, half-mad gleam in Kitani's eyes.

"I fear Kitani wouldn't have it any other way." Placing a hand on Cybil's arm, Leara went on, "Don't worry so much. Kitani will be fine; I just know it."

Cybil wished she could share some of Leara's certainty, but all she could manage was a weak sounding, "I hope you're right."

Sierra stood guard by the door while she and Amy awaited the arrival of their teammates. *And Cybil.* She smiled to herself, knowing that her old friend would never allow her to tackle this challenge alone. Leara and Kitani would also be joining them, their honor as Valori preventing them from being anywhere else. It warmed her heart to know that she had so many trustworthy people watching her back.

"Here they come," said Amy, monitoring their surroundings with a portable scanner. "At least, I hope it's them." She chuckled lightly, and added in a more serious tone, "Doesn't it seem like it was too easy? I mean, Midas is a powerful empire with a lot of secrets to hide. Shouldn't the main base be more heavily guarded?"

"You worry too much, Amy," Sierra said, although she'd been thinking along the same lines. Their plan had gone swimmingly so far, but it almost seemed like Midas had been expecting them, like the enemy was playing along with their little game until the perfect time to strike. Her grip tightened on her pulse rifle. Someone was fast approaching their position.

Thankfully, Duran and the rest of their teammates appeared.

"How goes it, lieutenant?" Duran asked.

"The researchers here are working on horrors from beyond your darkest nightmares," Sierra said.

"Then I suppose we shall have to put a halt to their precious research," Cybil said, stepping forward from the crowd.

Noting that Leara stood right behind Cybil, affection gleaming brightly in her eyes, Sierra smiled.

Sierra's smile faded when she realized that Kitani wasn't among those in the group. When she voiced her concern, Cybil started, and Leara froze in horror.

"She was with us a minute ago," Cybil said, scanning the nearby area. The others followed her example and began searching for their missing teammate.

Leara, Sierra noticed, was whispering excitedly to Cybil, each of them glancing around nervously for any possible eavesdroppers. When she drew closer, she thought she heard Leara mention Kitani's name. Sierra strained her ears in an attempt to make out some of their words. Did they have some idea where Kitani might be?

"What's going on?" she asked, walking over to join Cybil and Leara. "Did Kitani say anything to either of you before she disappeared?"

Cybil shook her head. "Not a word."

"She's been behaving strangely lately," Leara added. She spoke slowly, clearly choosing her words with care. "All her life, Kitani has been trained to fight and protect others. She knows nothing else. Now that we're in the enemy's stronghold, I suppose she could no longer restrain herself. I should have watched her more closely."

Sierra sensed that Leara was hiding something and seemed reluctant to go into the exact details of Kitani's behavior. Why? Surely Leara wouldn't hold back any information that might help

Kitani. She decided not to press her further. Now was neither the time nor the place.

She squared her shoulders. “We have to find Kitani,” she announced. Though she doubted the former Paladin was accustomed to being in need of rescue, she thought it likely that Kitani hadn’t realized the dreadful danger of the situation. She was Valori, and Midas enjoyed conducting cruel research on nonhuman subjects.

Duran regained control by saying, “Everyone should split up in pairs, that way we can cover more ground faster.”

Knowing this had been a part of Duran’s original plan, Sierra nodded.

“Remember, in addition to setting the explosives to incinerate this accursed complex, we’re also searching for Paladin Veldina,” Duran went on.

Duran divided the squad into pairs, no doubt hoping that the members wouldn’t forget about Kitani in their zeal to complete the mission, Sierra thought, though the commander had to know she would never allow the Valori warrior to be forgotten. Lacking a partner, she started to set off on her own, but hesitated on seeing Cybil and Leara standing close together, still speaking quietly. She moved back within listening distance.

“This is Midas Pharmaceuticals’ most important research facility,” Leara said, “the place where its most heinous experiments are undoubtedly conducted. Who can say what dangers may be lurking within these metal walls?”

Cybil frowned. “Are you worried about the alien pathogens Midas is working on?”

“Don’t forget that Midas employees are usually human, especially here on Earth, so there’s no need for them to take extra precautions.” Leara’s brow furrowed. “There’s something foul about this place. I can smell it. A sickly sweet aroma, like the stench of death. It’s faint, but it’s definitely there.”

“I’ll speak to Duran about it, if you wish.” Cybil’s expression remained calm, but Sierra knew her friend well. Beneath the façade, her mind was no doubt swirling with the possibility that Leara’s fears were correct.

What if the very air within the research facility was dangerous for Leara and Kitani to breathe? Sierra wondered. And many of the reinforcements were also aliens and potentially prone to any contagions within the laboratories. She grew even more alarmed. Would the filtration system built into their combat armor be enough to keep any harmful elements at bay?

As if summoned by her thoughts, Duran appeared. "Time to move out," she informed them softly. "We must find Kitani quickly."

Stepping forward, Cybil said, "Commander, may I have a word with you? I'm concerned about what dangers we might run into in this facility. Are you sure these helmets are enough to protect against Midas's infectious diseases and poisons?"

Duran crossed her arms over her chest. "So now you're afraid?" she asked.

"Not afraid," Cybil corrected. "Just cautious. How do we know the filtration systems in these suits will work here? Have you tested them before?"

Sighing, Duran said, "Cipher's armor is built airtight. All you have to do is click your helmet into place and rely on the integrated life support system to do its job. Besides," she added, rolling her eyes at Cybil, "it is too late to turn back now."

"She's right, Cybil," Leara interjected. "I feel as though I've played a part in this mission since the beginning. And don't forget, Kitani needs us."

Sierra saw that Cybil looked uncertain.

"Maybe you should wait on the ship—" Cybil began, but Leara cut her off.

Leara took Cybil gently by the shoulders, looking her in the eye. "My place is by your side," she said. "I couldn't live with myself if I ran away and left you to face this peril alone."

"If that's what you truly wish," Cybil replied, "then I have no right to deny it. I only hope you realize what you may be getting yourself into."

Leara nodded gravely, "I was aware of the dangers when I asked permission to come along." She locked her helmet into place with a click. Cybil followed her example, switching on her suit's life support once her helmet was secure.

"Take care, Reynard," Duran said. "Be extra vigilant. Not all dangers may be as tangible as you think." She turned to go.

Seeing no need to remain any longer, Sierra stormed through the complex, her much anticipated mission all but forgotten in her haste to locate Kitani. She checked her handheld scanner again for any signs of life. *If I were a Valori warrior with raging hormones, where would I be*?

Although she had known the truth behind Kitani's sudden irrational behavior, she had decided it best to keep it from her teammates. Humans could be judgmental and narrow-minded about such things, even the human members of Cipher, and she hadn't wanted Leara and Kitani to be subjected to further prejudice.

As a high-ranking Cipher agent, Sierra had been educated in the customs and physiology of all the intergalactic races. She had immediately recognized the change in Kitani as signaling the beginning of a Valori's sexual cycle and couldn't understand why Kitani had rejected her. Hadn't she expressed her interest clearly enough? Maybe she had come on too strong and frightened Kitani away. She had learned that the bond formed by mating was sacred to the Valori, and choosing a mate was never a thing to be taken lightly.

As a Paladin, Kitani had been denied the privilege of bonding. Perhaps she was still unaccustomed to having such freedom over her own life, Sierra thought. *Or perhaps she simply doesn't wish to have you for a mate*, a nagging little voice chided her. She immediately dismissed the disheartening possibility, going back to worrying over the current dilemma.

It suddenly dawned on Sierra that, if she were in Kitani's shoes, the most important objective in her agenda would be to alleviate some of the tension that had been building over the past several days. With none of the more obvious methods available, the next best thing would be to get as close to the action in the research facility as possible.

As if to confirm her suspicions, a faint blip suddenly appeared on her scanner. Its coordinates pinpointed somewhere deep within the sub-level's chambers. *The labs!* The word rang ominously in her mind like the tolling of a massive funerary bell.

With the information provided to them by Rex and his spies, she and Amy had been granted scientist status, allowing them access to the laboratories where the most heinous research was conducted. During the infiltration, it had taken every ounce of her self-control to maintain composure in the face of Midas's nightmarish creations and their plans to employ them. Right now, she knew the corporation's top scientists were on the verge of creating airborne versions of the lethal pathogens, intending to release them on all the space stations frequented by aliens. With their success so close, new fears awakened within her as she envisioned Kitani wandering unknowingly through the dark corridors of the labs.

I have to get to her before she does something drastic! She rushed down the stairwell leading to the sub-level laboratories. The yellow dot on the scanner's small screen pulsed strongly now, which meant she was nearing her goal. Flinging open the double doors at the bottom of the stairs, she ran several steps inside the lab and paused to allow her eyes to adjust to the dim lighting.

A thousand years would not be sufficient time for her to adjust to the atrocities stored in the facility's basement, she thought numbly, forcing herself to continue walking. Row upon row of glass tubes stretched in front of her, each cylinder containing the cryogenically frozen remains of plague victims. On each of the tubes a date had been inscribed, categorizing the subjects by the pathogen's success rate. As she strode through the gallery of horrors, she noted the more recent subjects had undergone the most severe effects.

Sierra shuddered, nearly balking at the unnerving expressions on the subjects' frozen faces, but she knew she had to find Kitani before the Valori witnessed these abominations and blasted the cylinders to bits, possibly exposing herself to contaminants.

The yellow dot on the handheld scanner flickered brightly, accompanied by a steady hum. Whatever lurked in the laboratory with her was close, perhaps just around the next corner. After taking a moment to steady her nerves, she rounded the end of an aisle of tubes and was met by a hauntingly familiar voice.

"It's a beautiful sight to behold, is it not?" the voice said.

The owner of that voice had plagued Sierra's dreams and nightmares for many years. Listening to it now, she began to tremble.

"So much death and suffering, all so that humanity may prosper. It almost brings tears to my eyes."

Sierra couldn't stand it any longer. Staggering forward on wobbly legs, she stumbled in the direction of the lilting cadences and casual coolness she had always known. *This can't be happening.* The face she envisioned accompanying the woman's voice no longer belonged in this world, or any other in the known universe for that matter. *It just can't be...*

But it was, Sierra found. Rounding a corner, she came upon the source of the voice. The scanner slipped from her slack grip and slid across the floor, the hum it was emitting almost continuous. Finally, her legs would no longer support her weight. She crumpled to the floor as her gaze locked onto the woman standing by one of the glass chambers, admiring its contents almost lovingly.

The woman appeared not to notice Sierra choking on the words she wanted so desperately to speak. At last, she managed to croak, "M-Mother." The world around her reeled and threatened to go dark. "Mother, it is you," she went on, clutching at the sides of her head. “Please, tell me I’m not going crazy, and that you’re actually here.”

“You aren’t crazy,” the woman said, facing Sierra.

Melinda Callaway was the same stoic, rigid woman Sierra remembered from childhood. Her expression was still unreadable. Twenty years had not aged Melinda much, granting her an even greater dignity than she had already possessed.

“I thought you were dead,” Sierra said. Unable to fight back the tears any longer, she let them roll down her cheeks. “I don’t understand. Why didn’t you try to find me? Where have you been all this time?”

“I’ve been here,” Melinda replied, gesturing toward the laboratory, “in one of humanity’s greatest institutions. Midas Pharmaceuticals saw great potential in me, so my life was spared after Touchstone Cybernetics was destroyed.”

Sierra tensed. Carefully, she asked, “Mother, what exactly are you doing here, in Midas Pharmaceuticals’ stronghold?”

Her mother flashed a dangerous smile. “If not for Midas Pharmaceuticals’ generous offer, I would have met my end in the explosion just like the others.”

“You betrayed them?” Sierra couldn’t believe what she was hearing. It had to be a lie. It must be! How could her mother sell out to the enemy, leaving her friends and colleagues to die?

Melinda continued to regard her with cold, unblinking eyes. She finally said, “The real question is, dear daughter, what are *you* doing here?”

Gasping at the malice in her mother’s eyes, Sierra’s shock turned to terror, driving all thoughts of Kitani out of her mind as she acknowledged the bitter truth. Her mother was not a victim. Her mother was working for Midas Pharmaceuticals. Melinda Callaway was the enemy.

“Since you admit to having no prior knowledge of my survival,” Melinda continued, “what other business brings you all the way to Earth and to an off-limits laboratory, no less?”

Unable to frame a believable reply, Sierra gaped at her mother, thinking there was no escape. So soon after their reunion, she and her mother were destined to be separated again, only she feared that this time, the absence would be more permanent.

“Do not fear,” her mother said. “I won’t call the guards just yet. Too much time has passed since I last had the chance to converse with my only daughter, and I’m not as cruel and uncaring as many would believe.”

"What do you want to talk about?"

"Why, the future, dear, and the vast opportunities it holds. But first," Melinda narrowed her eyes, "I would discuss the intelligence of your career choices."

Sierra swallowed hard around the lump forming in her throat. Somehow, her mother knew about her ties to Cipher, meaning she must also know of Cipher's intentions on Earth.

Kneeling on the cold, hard laboratory floor, unable to flee from the mother she believed she had lost, Sierra felt panicked, well aware that her mother had become quite dangerous. Melinda Callaway was the enemy, she repeated to herself—a fact she found impossible to assimilate, despite the dire situation in which she now found herself.

Chapter 20

After peering cautiously around a corner and scanning the area for any signs of danger, Cybil motioned that all was clear. Immediately, Leara moved behind her, feeling awkward and uncomfortable as she clutched the plasma pistol in her hand.

Despite Cybil's tutelage, the pistol still felt out of place in her hands. Clearly, she wasn't the warrior her mother had been.

Mother. Leara shuddered when she envisioned Dallia's reaction to learning her daughter had serious doubts about her odds of survival. This mission was critical to the Valori, perhaps to everyone. No nonhuman, Valori or otherwise, would be safe as long as Midas continued its heinous work Unless Cipher succeeded in its mission of crippling the corporation by destroying its main base, Midas would very likely become unstoppable. Not to mention any additional bases Midas might have located throughout the universe, such as the secret research facility on Kronos. This was the enemy's main base. She simply couldn't give in to her fears now. The Valori were depending on her, and she vowed not only to return to Aria, but to return in victory.

"Something doesn't feel right," Cybil said. "The complete lack of opposition in a supposedly well-guarded facility is disquieting."

Smiling, Leara said, "Are you saying you'd rather face all manner of resistance as we make our way through the dark? Because it seems to me we're making much better progress unhindered by security officers and gunfire."

"Firefights I can handle," Cybil said, narrowing her eyes at the darkness. "It's the threats I can't see that have me worried."

Duran's words of warning rang in Leara's mind. By now, she was becoming familiar with Midas's atrocities, and the knowledge didn't sit well with a seemingly empty research facility. As Cybil had pointed out, it was too quiet. What was Midas up to? The organization may have grown arrogant in regards to its plans of genocide, but wasn't that all the more reason for it to take every possible precaution in safeguarding its research? Something wasn't right.

With each step Leara took, it felt more and more like she and Cybil were walking into a trap. "Uh, Cybil," she said, looking at her portable scanner, which had begun humming steadily.

Cybil nodded, reaching out to take the scanner.

Leara tilted it so Cybil could view the screen. "I think you may get your wish very soon."

Cybil studied the screen. Leara knew what she saw: a cluster of flashing blips gathering at the upper left corner, only several yards from their location and fast approaching.

"Battle drones! Take cover!" Cybil insisted. No sooner had the words passed her lips than the corridor erupted in flashes of red and blue light.

Leara flung herself at a narrow niche in the wall where the metal frame of a large hatch would provide some cover, while Cybil wedged herself in an alcove of the structure opposite her.

Leaning out of the alcove, Cybil fired a series of short bursts into the crowd of battle drones at the far end of the hall and then leapt back into cover to wait for her pulse rifle to cool.

"If we could get this door to close," Cybil called to Leara over the noise of the drones, "we could buy ourselves a little more time."

Leara saw Cybil fidgeting with the door controls for a few seconds, and finally pounding her fist against the keypad in clear frustration.

"Damn it!" Cybil exclaimed. "Someone has entered security codes to override manual input, like they were expecting us. I guess I was right."

"Maybe if I have a look at it," Leara offered despite being aware that the door controls were on the opposite side of a corridor filled with hot energy beams.

"Do you think you can handle it?" Cybil asked, her expression grim in the flickering light of the drones' fire.

Leara looked briefly at the hovering drones, which were beginning a slow descent down the long hallway, and then returned her gaze to Cybil and nodded solemnly, though her mind was filled with uncertainty. Would she be able to make it to cover in time? If not, would she be able to retaliate as the drones pressed them further?

Cybil said, "I'll cover you. On the count of three, we switch. Ready? One, two, three!"

On cue, Leara leapt out of the protective niche as Cybil aimed the Banshee pulse rifle at the approaching drones.

The scene in the corridor was a blur to Leara as she flew across the space, exchanging places with Cybil. The air was filled with the heat of plasma fire. Ducking into the alcove, she panted and trembled from her efforts, though her passage had been only a few scant seconds. She noticed Cybil, true to her word, remained in the center of the hall, drawing the brunt of enemy fire to herself. Her aim with the Banshee was true. Two of the drones sputtered and crashed to the floor while bursting into flames, leaving six more to continue their assault.

I will succeed, Leara swore a silent oath. She began working at the door controls. Now more than ever, she was determined to prove her worth to Cybil.

She smiled when Cybil's triumphant shouts heralded the destruction of another drone. How fond she had grown of this woman! Her heart sang in victory as Cybil dispatched two more drones, but a glimpse at the handheld scanner showed there were many more on the way. Too many for the two of them to deal with on their own.

Stay strong, Leara. Cybil needed her. During this most crucial moment, she vowed she wouldn't fail. She continued working. A few scant seconds before the reinforcement drones were upon them, the lights above the door frame lit up and power returned to the door.

"I did it!" Leara exclaimed, genuinely surprised at her own abilities. Her months spent undercover at Midas Pharmaceuticals had provided her with many new skills, including the ability to override almost any command. There had been times when necessity had demanded it of her. In order to get to the information the Valori so desperately needed, Leara had been forced to learn how to infiltrate just about every type of electronic safeguard imaginable.

After firing another burst of plasma into the fleet of security drones, Cybil ducked beneath the door as it slowly descended to the floor, joining Leara on the other side. Her brow glistened with sweat, but she wore a big smile on her face.

"Nice work, Leara, but I don't know how long this door will hold them. Our location has doubtlessly been pinpointed by now. It won't be long before every security drone in the place is after us. We should finish our assignment as quickly as possible," Cybil told her.

Leara nodded. “That looks like a lab over there.”

Duran had ordered the crew to plant explosives throughout the complex, particularly near areas where vital data might be contained. Leara knew the success of their mission depended on the complete elimination of any material regarding the plans for the biological weapons, therefore, not so much as a shred of information could be overlooked. Not in this facility or any others their infiltration might uncover.

While working on the explosive device Duran had given her, Cybil glanced over her shoulder, hesitated, and asked, “Is there something wrong? Are you hurt?”

Knowing she had been staring in the distance, Leara shook her head, smiling slightly at Cybil’s concern. “I was merely thinking of Kitani, wondering if she’s been found yet.”

Cybil’s expression softened noticeably. “You’re worried for her safety. Well, you shouldn’t fret too much. Sierra won’t leave this facility until she finds her.”

Taken by surprise, Leara stammered before managing, “I suppose you’re right.” In her heart, she knew Cybil must be right. Sierra did not seem like the type to give up easily.

Cybil rose and took Leara gently by the hand. She continued to hold her hand while leading her through the meandering corridors to the relative safety of the world outside this asylum of madness and despair.

Kitani stalked along a darkened corridor, the atmosphere reminding her of the research outpost on Kronos where she and Leara had stumbled upon Cybil. Perhaps that had been the point where this mad chain of events began unfolding, or maybe it had started long before they ever met the human mercenary, or even before they left Aria. Whatever the source, Fate had dropped her into a sea of change and like most Valori, she found herself unable to swim. Now here she was, on a decidedly hostile alien world, surrounded by members of the same species that would see her proud race brought to its knees.

But not all humans were blinded by hate and discrimination, she reminded herself. Cybil and Duran seemed truly committed to protecting the universe and preventing potential alien genocide by the plague. And there was Sierra, a strange little human who had so clearly expressed her desire to be more than just friends.

The thought brought a smile to Kitani’s lips. A part of her wanted to be with Sierra. Longed for it, in fact. As much as she had tried to convince herself the desire was only a side effect of her developing sexual potency, she knew better.

Guiltily, her mind wandered to thoughts of Leara and the others. No doubt they were worrying themselves sick over her sudden disappearance, but there had been no other way. She was currently in no mood for company.

She knew without a doubt that she couldn't handle another confrontation with Sierra. The sexual tension surrounding the human had led her to the decision to leave the group and go off alone. She could cover more ground alone than as part of a pair. Her keener senses enabled her to detect any signs of a threat long before the humans. Her teammates should thank her, really, for by surging ahead, she was ensuring that their path was cleared of peril.

And the path was, indeed, clear, Kitani thought. Since her departure from the group, she hadn't detected even an inkling of danger within the deserted complex. Did Midas truly conduct its most heinous research within these walls?

Kitani sighed. With no enemies lurking in the shadows, she was growing rather bored. Part of the reason she had left the humans was to quell some of her tension by finding a fight or two, but the vast structure seemed oddly abandoned. Something in the otherworldly silence disturbed her more than any ambush, though she couldn't say why. To make matters worse, her libido refused to allow her to forget about her desires, making it very difficult to concentrate.

She paused to lean against the cool metal wall. Suddenly, she heard a shrill scream coming from one of the floors below.

Sierra! The voice, though unmistakably Sierra's, held a note of fear and despair she had never heard from the usually calm lieutenant, prompting her to take action. Homing in on the direction of the cry, she rushed to the nearest stairwell leading to the sub-level chambers and raced down the steps at breakneck speed.

Getting closer, she heard a second voice, one unknown to her, speaking loudly enough for her to follow. The pitch underlying the harsh tones definitely belonging to a female, she decided. She battered open the door at the bottom of the stairs and charged forward, but her confidence wavered when she stumbled upon a nightmare: aisle after aisle of cryogenic chambers stretching out in front of her, each chamber filled with its own frozen horror.

Her shock pierced by the sound of Sierra's voice, Kitani ignored the horrendous experiments. Whoever Sierra spoke to, the human's fear and distaste were quite evident.

"You seriously have the nerve to make such a request?" Sierra was saying as Kitani crept along a row of glass tubes, pointedly averting her eyes from the misfortunate souls within.

"It's not like you have much of a choice, my dear," the other woman replied sardonically. "Either you join me and fight for our cause..."

"Or?" Sierra asked.

By now, Kitani could see the other speaker: an older human woman with features as harsh and untouched by sympathy as her words. Despite the cold, uncaring glare in the woman's eyes and the deep scowl that furrowed her brow, a definite beauty underlay the stern features.

"Or," the woman continued with a sneer, "I could call the guards right now. The decision is yours. Please choose wisely."

Kitani watched silently, waiting as Sierra appeared to carefully weigh the decision. Who was this woman, she wondered, and what sort of hold did she have over Sierra?

"Never," Sierra said grimly at last. "I'm sorry, but I can't allow myself to stoop so low as to join Midas. To do so would be to go against all I have fought for so many years." Tears glistened in her eyes. "Please forgive me."

The woman didn't seem amused. "So you prefer the company of that band of rogues over that of your own mother?" she said, the rising inflection of her voice marking the statement as a question rather than an accusation. The woman didn't appear in the least surprised at Sierra's answer, nor did she appear shocked by her daughter's next words.

"What you're doing is wrong, Mother."

Kitani stifled a gasp and ducked behind a glass cylinder. Her mingled desire and rage were all but forgotten as she listened intently to the disagreement between mother and daughter, unsure what she ought to do.

"So you think I'm wrong?" Melinda asked, her words sharp enough to cut through Sierra's defenses.

Sierra couldn't accept the monster her mother had become, but anger, shame, and a tangle of other emotions stilled her tongue.

As if reading her thoughts, Melinda went on, "You think I'm some sort of monster because I work on manufacturing biological weapons capable of eliminating entire species?"

"How could your work be considered good when you've already exposed hundreds, possibly even thousands of innocents to your terror? Look around you, Mother. Were these poor souls ever a threat to anyone?" Sierra indicated the glass tubes surrounding them.

"They certainly won't be anymore. Or maybe they're more of a threat now than they ever were. The pathogens are still active within the frozen corpses of the subjects and able to wreak havoc among unsuspecting alien colonies. In fact, I suggested dumping the dead bodies on alien worlds where their taint could cause extensive chaos and destruction," Melinda said proudly.

"Why do you want to do this? You used to take your work so seriously, dedicating your own life to developing ways to improve the lives of others. What happened that changed you so drastically?"

"What happened?" Melinda fumed. "You, of all people, should know what happened!"

Taken aback by her mother's sudden rage, Sierra shook her head.

"I lost everything to those alien bastards," Melinda continued. "My parents and my brother were all killed in the First Contact Wars. Your father died in the insurrections that followed in the wake of the war. All were victims of the aliens' cruelty."

Sierra had known her mother had been made a widow during the insurrections, but she'd never known the true extent of her hatred and resentment. "Humanity would have been lost if not for the intervention of the Federation," she tried to reason with her mother. "We owe the Federation races for securing our lives, our future. Why can't you leave the past behind you and end this madness?"

"Mad?" The gleam in her mother's eye when she spoke made Sierra take a step back. "After seeing how humans are treated by the galactic races, you dare to call our plan mad?"

"Not all aliens are bad," Sierra argued. "I know the years following First Contact were grim, but that war is over. Let it go."

"Let it go?" Melinda asked incredulously. "I've devoted my entire life to my research so people like you can prosper, and all you can say to me is let it go? Ungrateful whelp! As far as I'm concerned, the war will never be over. Not until humanity has claimed its rightful place."

"The aliens aren't our enemies, Mother. If you would only open your eyes, you would see that. The Intergalactic Federation races have done much to ensure humanity's fair treatment. Do you want their noble efforts to be in vain?"

Melinda snorted. "These fools weren't so noble when they pleaded for their worthless lives." A wave of her hand indicated the glass chambers containing the test subjects. "Garbage! The sooner we dump these twisted carcasses and get them out of my sight, the better." A devious smile touched the corners of her mouth. "Perhaps we'll dispose of them in the wilds of Aria and give those arrogant hermaphrodites something to distract them for a while."

In spite of her desire to appear unfazed by her mother's casual cruelty, Sierra gasped aloud. If Melinda had her way and the contaminated bodies were deposited in the forests of Aria, then the entire Valori population could be endangered. Sierra knew the Valori wouldn't allow an unidentified spacecraft access to Aria. But if an unmanned vessel crashed on the world, they would certainly be there to investigate, exposing themselves to the unknown dangers in the process. Undoubtedly, her mother was aware of the consequences. Perhaps she was even aware of Sierra's fondness for the planet and its inhabitants.

"What do you plan on doing when your plan backfires?" Sierra asked, trying a different angle with her mother. "These pathogens you're manufacturing could just as easily be turned against humans. If your own people start becoming infected, what will you do then?"

"We've already prepared for that inevitability," Melinda replied. "By the time the airborne variations are released on heavily frequented space stations, colonized worlds, and other densely populated areas, we'll have gone underground."

"Underground?" Did Midas intend on sending its top researchers into hiding once the plan was set in motion? "So you're targeting humans as well as aliens?"

"Not targeting, precisely, but if there are any who are misfortunate enough to get in the way, then what other choice is there?" Melinda grinned cruelly. "Their sacrifices will not be forgotten."

"You're willing to let them die!" Sierra exclaimed. "I can't believe you could sit back and watch while millions of your own people wither away. And after you so proudly proclaimed yourself to be some sort of savior to humanity."

"Midas will be humanity's salvation," Melinda insisted. "Once the plagues have run their courses through the various species, the universe will be purged of the alien scourge. Humanity will be free to begin anew."

"Humanity will be extinct," Sierra snapped.

"Not all humans will be affected. Those who have chosen to accompany Midas and support its ideals will be spared. It may take centuries, but eventually the chosen ones will repopulate the universe and humanity will thrive again."

"Thrive? I wouldn't necessarily call cowering away in some underground bunker thriving. That is what you are planning, isn't it? Hiding away in some impenetrable place until the plague pathogens have had time to die out? Hardly sounds like a life to me."

"What will you do, Sierra?" Melinda asked, watching Sierra keenly. "You could join us and be among the chosen. Don't you want to be among those to witness the dawning of a new era? You can go public with your information, just as you've threatened to do. In fact, I encourage you to do so. See how your beloved alien allies view humanity then."

Sierra's head snapped up, her mind filling with rage. "You'd like that, wouldn't you?" she said. "Turn every sentient species in the universe against humanity. That way our only option would be to fight and die while Midas sits back and laughs." Her mother made no attempts to deny this accusation, only smiled coldly. "Why, Mother, why do you hate with such intensity? If your plan succeeds, it will seal humanity's fate. How do you think we won the First Contact Wars? Without the aid of the Federation, we wouldn't even be here today."

Melinda said nothing, just continued to glare coldly at her.

Sierra felt her heart breaking under her mother's implacable calm. Although her mind still refused to admit Melinda had become the enemy, in the depths of her soul, she knew she had already lost her mother, and nothing she could say or do would ever bring her back.

From the shadows, Kitani watched the scene between Sierra and her mother. Once or twice, her hand strayed close to her sidearm. If that insane woman attempted to harm Sierra in any way, she wouldn't hesitate to act. At any rate, she couldn't allow this madwoman to wreak mass destruction on her homeworld or anywhere else for that matter. She might not agree with all the old rules and regulations restricting the Paladins, but she would die—or kill—to defend her species.

She noticed Sierra's hand also rested on her gun and admired her for her courage. As much as the thought of firing on her own mother must have pained her, it was clear Sierra wouldn't allow Midas to carry out its plans.

"Mother... Melinda... I'm afraid I can't let you succeed," Sierra said hoarsely, confirming Kitani's thoughts.

"Do you truly value those aliens over your own mother?" Melinda sighed. "If that's how you feel, then I'm afraid this conversation is over."

Before Kitani realized what was happening, Sierra's mother reached into the pocket of her lab coat and produced a gun of her own, aiming the blaster directly at Sierra's heart.

"Move!" Kitani shouted, knowing the time had come to act.

She leapt from her cover as Sierra ducked aside.

Apparently stunned by the unexpected turn of events, Melinda kept her weapon trained on her daughter for several more seconds until she realized the more imminent danger came from Kitani. Hands shaking, she quickly pointed the gun toward Kitani, who found herself directly in the line of fire. The force of a point-blank blast never came. Instead, the floor beneath her feet began shaking until the entire complex began to tremble.

"The explosives!" Sierra shouted.

Kitani kept her gaze fixed on Melinda, not daring to look away.

Sierra continued, "The commander's mission must have been a success. That means the whole place is about to blow!"

"This isn't over," Melinda said, a murderous gleam in her eyes. Before Kitani could stop her, she turned, quickly disappearing down the rows of cryogenic storage chambers.

"We have to go after her," Sierra urged, taking a few steps in the same direction.

"There's no time. If we don't get out of here and fast, we'll be burnt to cinders along with this accursed complex," Kitani said, gritting her teeth as another explosion rocked the underground laboratory, bringing with it a power malfunction. She muttered a mild curse as they were plunged into absolute darkness, but luckily, a light was mounted on the barrel of her pulse rifle. She flicked it on, focusing the beam so she could see Sierra's face.

Sierra stood in place, her expression agonized yet determined. Obviously, she couldn't bring herself to divert from her course, Kitani thought, feeling some sympathy for Sierra's situation. As much as she loathed the idea of sharing her enemy's fate, Kitani knew Sierra would never walk away now she knew the truth.

"All right," she said with a sigh, "but we have to act fast." She turned away from Sierra and cast about for any signs of Melinda

Callaway. Picking her way through the darkened lab, she began in the direction Melinda had taken. "Your mother couldn't have gone far. All we have to do is apprehend her—"

A muffled cry made her pause mid-sentence. When she turned around, Sierra was gone.

"Sierra?" Kitani ventured forward a few tentative steps, searching for her companion. From somewhere within the shadows cast by the cryogenic tubes, she thought she heard a soft rustling.

Standing as still and silent as a statue, she strained her eyes against the darkness surrounding the thin light beam from the device on her rifle's barrel. Although she could see better in the dark due to her elliptical pupils, she detected nothing out of place. She was ready to chalk up the vague rustling to her own paranoia when she heard the sound again, followed by an almost undetectable whistling.

Her eyes flying open wide, she caught a glimpse of a blurred object streaking out of the darkness and moving past her head, missing by a few scant inches. She heard the muffled sound again, and whirled in the direction the projectile had originated. Again, it was followed by whistling as an unknown object soared through the air.

Kitani leapt to one side in an attempt to dodge the attack, but the whistling ended in a hollow thud as the strange missile struck her left shoulder. The force of the impact wasn't as great as she had expected, not even enough to make her lose her footing as she recovered from her evasive maneuver, landing firmly on her feet in a crouching position several paces from where she had stood just seconds before.

Her senses heightened by the unknown threat, Kitani saw the outlines of shapes that hadn't been there earlier. The rustling in the shadows sounded louder now, confirming the enemy's location almost as surely as a shout. Like a great Korvallian wildcat stalking its prey, she leapt forward, prepared to fire her pulse rifle, only to halt when she noticed a light weight on her left shoulder.

Kitani looked at her shoulder. The projectile which had struck her appeared to be a small missile or a dart of some sort. Upon closer inspection, she saw that it was actually a syringe. To her horror, she realized the needle had successfully pierced her armor.

Grabbing the device by the barrel, she felt it compress beneath her grip, releasing more of its contents as she dislodged it from her shoulder. She flung the dart to the floor. An arc of clear fluid was briefly illuminated against her pulse rifle's light. She ground the syringe beneath the heel of her boot. It would take more than a tranquilizer dart to bring her down, she thought savagely. She was a Valori, not some animal to be hunted.

Cold sweat covered her body. She began advancing forward once again. The pulse rifle quivered in her hands. The floor seemed to fall away beneath her feet. Stumbling a few more steps, she dropped to her knees, the pulse rifle slipping from her grasp and falling to the floor, forgotten. The world reeled around, her vision warping and distorting.

Trying to shut out the confusion, Kitani squeezed her eyes closed. She clutched at the sides of her helmet. Her head pounded in rhythm with her rapidly beating heart, possibly in reaction to whatever substance now coursed through her body. She wondered absently what exactly had been contained in the syringe.

She slid to the floor, the cool metal offering little relief for her suffering. Her head pounded so hard, it felt like it might explode. The sound of footfalls rang somewhere close by her head, and then she knew nothing more as she lost consciousness.

Leara remained outwardly impassive as she watched their enemy's lair burst into flames, although her mind wasn't at ease. Both Kitani and Lieutenant Callaway were still unaccounted for. Beside her, Cybil also stared into the fire as it raged against the darkness, doubtless every bit as apprehensive as she was over their missing companions.

A blast of hot air buffeted her as another explosion erupted somewhere within the complex. The situation didn't look good for their friends and was becoming worse with each passing minute. Leara was nearly beside herself with worry as she stared helplessly at the blazing inferno. Kitani couldn't die, she insisted to herself. It simply couldn't be true.

"Where could they be?" Cybil asked

Leara shook her head in dismay, tears welling up in her eyes.

"They should be here by now." The blunt statement came from Duran, who had come to stand next to them. "Lieutenant Callaway has never botched a mission before."

"Commander!" Banks came running toward them across the field, frantically waving a handheld scanner above her head. "I have readings of a large star frigate lifting off close by. It seems the enemy had an escape plan."

"Let me see." Duran took the scanner from the panting pilot and began pressing buttons in rapid succession. "Just as I suspected," she said after a moment. "The readings match perfectly." Her expression was grim as she met the eyes of Leara and Cybil in turn. "Lieutenant Callaway and Paladin Veldina have been abducted by the enemy."

Leara froze in terror. Kitani wasn't dead, not yet anyway, but she feared that the situation she and Sierra had found themselves in might prove to be a fate worse than death unless Cipher reached them in time.

Back on the *Sentinel*, Cybil, Duran, and Leara had gathered in the communications room to discuss what to do next.

"This latest development changes everything," Duran said, shaking her head in frustration. "When we destroyed Midas Pharmaceuticals' stronghold on Earth, I expected to eliminate the bulk of its heinous research. What I didn't expect, however, was that one of my best agents would go missing and fall into the hands of our enemy."

"It's horrible!" Leara exclaimed. "Knowing the atrocities Midas is capable of, I can't bear to imagine what sort of danger Kitani and Lieutenant Callaway face."

"How do we even know Sierra and Kitani are still alive?" Cybil interjected. "For all we know, they could have been obliterated in the blast."

"I'm afraid not." Duran remained uncharacteristically serious. "I have tracking software installed in all my agents' armor. For security purposes," she added when she noticed Cybil glancing suspiciously at her own borrowed suit. "A necessary precaution. Without it, we wouldn't be able to trace their signals and follow the enemy vessel. Without it, Sierra and Kitani would be lost."

"You have a point," Cybil conceded with reluctance. "Furthermore, if I've learned anything at all about our foe, it's that they relish torture and torment. Sierra and Kitani are most likely alive." *But for how long*? The idea made her flesh crawl.

"Which is precisely why we must apprehend that frigate as quickly as possible," Duran said.

"Do you think Midas has moved its research to another secret base somewhere?" Cybil asked, rising from the table and leaning across it as she spoke. The thought that those cruel bastards still lurked somewhere in the universe with their horrible plans of devastating galactic civilizations made her want to lash out at something, anything, or anyone. She was calmed by Leara, who placed her hand lightly over Cybil's, quelling the anger bubbling inside her. No matter what happened next, she decided, she couldn't stand idly by and watch as innocent people like Leara were put at risk. Now calm, focused, and less likely to explode with frustration, she returned to her chair.

"No," Duran replied. "More than likely the handful of scientists who escaped Earth are using the frigate as a sort of mobile lab, for the time being, at least. However, given enough time and resources, they might be able to set up a new facility. That ship must not leave our sights."

"Commander," Navigator Jacques called, startling Cybil. "Enemy vessel at twelve o' clock. Awaiting further orders."

Rising from her elevated chair at the head of the bridge, Duran clutched the metal railing surrounding the raised platform. Cybil noticed a curious gleam in Duran's eyes as she leaned forward, staring into the blackness of space through the view port.

Duran's expression was determination mingled with fierce cunning, Cybil thought, and a peculiar sense of hope.

The commander sounded bold and unwavering when she said, "All hands on deck. Take out any defense system that ship may have." The space around them lit up as the *Sentinel* bombarded the vessel with fire from its plasma cannons. Satisfied, Duran shouted orders to the pilot. "Bring us around port side, Banks. Prepare to board the enemy frigate."

Grabbing a pulse rifle to augment her personal arsenal, Cybil held tightly to the metal railing surrounding the bridge. This was it, she told herself, the decisive battle that could very well affect the outcome of the war against Midas.

Chapter 21

Kitani woke to a dull throbbing in her left shoulder. When she tried to move it, intense pain lanced through her body, threatening to steal her consciousness again. With some effort, she was able to open her eyes, but the images she saw appeared distorted and out of focus.

She became aware of the faint murmur of voices, distant and hollow as if they spoke at the end of a long tunnel. No matter how hard she strained to hear, the meaning of the words wouldn't register in her mind, as though she was stuck in a dream. Unfortunately, she knew all too well that her situation must be closer to a nightmare.

Slowly, the world around her began to come into focus. She was lying on her back, on a hard, cold surface. There were people in the room with her. She could see them moving at the edge of her field of vision. She sensed another figure standing behind her. As the voices lost some of their indecipherable, hollow quality, she recognized the woman from her nightmares… or more precisely, from Sierra's nightmares.

Melinda Callaway spoke harshly to one of the other people in the room. Kitani knew the speaker was Sierra's mother long before the woman came into sight, leaning over her as she lay motionless on the cold slab of metal.

"So you're awake," Melinda said, her tone emotionless and cold. "Interesting. This could mean we'll have to increase the dosage for the pathogen to be effective." She smiled cruelly. "You should be honored, really. Although we've run a few tests on your kind before, you're the first Valori we've managed to capture alive. Such a stubborn, arrogant race. The others were defiant to the end."

Was this woman referring to the two murdered Paladins? Kitani wondered.

"What an excellent specimen," Melinda continued, holding a syringe with a long needle aloft for inspection. "Far better than some of the other species we've acquired."

Kitani's blood boiled as Melinda casually surveyed her body, making notes of her condition. The evil human woman looked at her as though she were nothing more than another virus to be examined under the microscope, which infuriated her. She pulled her lips back in a defiant snarl, but her throat was so dry the only sound that came out was a rather pathetic croak.

She realized she was strapped down, her arms and legs bound securely to the table. Even the movements of her head were restricted. Part of the reason for the dryness in her throat was a thick leather strap encircling her neck. Enraged by her confinement, she struggled against the straps, but her attempts were futile. Even without the bindings holding her down, she found herself too weak to put up much resistance. She was completely at this madwoman's disposal. For the first time in her life, she felt truly frightened.

Kitani swallowed hard against the strap constricting her throat, desperate and aching for even a sip of water, but she doubted her captor would be merciful.

Melinda examined her eyes, holding her eyelids open with the fingers of her gloved hand. Kitani held still, wary of damage to the delicate organs, but started when a voice rang out from across the room, loud and clear, and heartrendingly familiar.

"Why have you brought us here, Mother?" Sierra asked, no love in her voice when she addressed Melinda Callaway. "What have you done to Kitani?"

Releasing Kitani, Melinda glared daggers in Sierra's direction. "It isn't often I receive a chance to study a specimen so rare, so exquisite, as a Valori warrior. You won't spoil this for me." After nodding to two of her assistants, she returned to her examination.

Kitani struggled to resist, writhing against the restraints in vain, but the poison she'd been injected with left her too weak to move. She was trapped here, she realized with horror, trapped with a madwoman who would use her to test the effects of her pathogens and toxins, and then toss her aside like garbage. She shuddered in fear at the thought, but the fact that she could only lie there and do nothing while this vile woman threatened her and Sierra also infuriated her.

Sierra cursed to herself as she watched Melinda examining Kitani. She knew she had to act fast before her mother came to suspect Kitani's waxing sexual potency. If information of the Valori's reproductive system or their period of sexual latency was discovered, then a means to alter that already delicate cycle could be developed. Perhaps even Pompeilo extract could be modified and used as a weapon against the Valori. She couldn't allow that to happen.

"Let me go, you monsters!" she shouted, struggling against the two lab assistants. Head-butting one of her captors, a frail young man, squarely in the forehead, she swiftly used her restraints against the second assistant to jerk the woman forward as she tried to hold her in place. The unexpected maneuver caused the woman to stagger and bump into her colleague, who was clutching his head with both hands.

Sierra swayed unsteadily as she tried to regain her balance, her head pounding from the blow she had given the lab assistant. Despite her splitting headache and wavering vision, she rushed forward, charging at the two assistants while they were still distracted. She had taken no more than a few steps when the world around her erupted into chaos. A thunderous boom echoed through the cargo hold—an energy blast, she thought, staggering when the ship suddenly and violently pitched to one side.

"What the hell is happening?" Melinda demanded. She struggled to remain on her feet.

"Did you honestly think you could get away with it?" Sierra asked, realizing the source of the attack. "Commander Duran will never stand idly by while two of her subordinates are subjected to your cruel methods."

Melinda gave her an incredulous look. "But how?" Her gaze sobered. She seemed to notice the armor Sierra and Kitani were wearing for the first time, and she added, "You! It was you, wasn't it? You've been transmitting signals somehow, perhaps with those suits."

Sierra smiled. "I'm surprised it never occurred to you before, Mother. Don't get me wrong, I'm glad that you overlooked our armor once you confiscated our weapons. If you had removed or destroyed our armor, Commander Duran might have never located us."

Cursing, Melinda clutched the side of the operating table as another blast sent violent tremors throughout the ship. "At this rate, we'll be pounded to rubble," she said, narrowing her eyes at Sierra. "How does you precious commander intend to reclaim you if this vessel is reduced to no more than space debris? Haven't thought that through yet, have you?"

Sierra stared her defiance at Melinda as the world around her shuddered. Taking advantage of the distraction, the female lab assistant made as if to grab her, but she turned around and punched the woman in the face. Holding her bloody nose, the woman glared.

"Enough," Melinda said with mild amusement, but a moment later she scowled, her patience clearly beginning to fade. She addressed her subordinates harshly as she went on, "Unless you want to be killed by this ruthless Cipher rogue, you should relent in your fruitless struggles. I need you alive now. All hands report to battle stations. If it's a war Cipher wants, then a war Cipher will get."

The two assistants scrambled to their feet.

"I have more important business to attend to at the moment, but I'll return," Melinda continued to Sierra. "Remember, you're no longer of any use to me. There's no escape from this vessel, so don't get any bright ideas. If you don't exhibit improved behavior upon my return, dear daughter, I may have to jettison you into space. Think on that for a while."

Fury burning along her every nerve, Sierra watched Melinda go. When her mother and the two lab assistants were gone, she turned her gaze toward Kitani, her heart nearly breaking at the sight of the proud warrior bound and helpless, too weak to move.

"W-why?" Kitani rasped in a thin whisper, so different from her usual musical alto. "Why did you allow yourself to be captured along with me? You could have escaped."

Sierra smiled and walked over to the operating table where Kitani had been strapped down. The straps were thick, the buckles difficult to manage with her hands still bound. "And leave you behind? Leara would never forgive me. Besides, I could never live with myself if I ran away when an ally needed me. When I joined Cipher, I vowed to protect those who need it."

Kitani turned her head as far as the tight straps would permit, locking gazes with her. "Cipher is incredible," she said, her speech somewhat slurred, possibly a side effect of the drugs and poisons coursing through her system, Sierra thought. Kitani shook her head, almost as if trying to physically dislodge an unpleasant thought.

"All my life I've wanted to make a difference," she continued. "To stand for what's right and just. My status as a Paladin is both honored and revered among the Valori, but really, what have I done to change the universe? What can I do?" Kitani was close to tears now. "I can do nothing. Tradition will not allow it."

Unsure whether Kitani was delirious from the poison or if her behavior was a product of the strong sedatives Melinda Callaway had given her, Sierra listened to Kitani's ranting in thoughtful silence. Whatever the reason for Kitani's unusual talkativeness, Sierra didn't think it could be entirely attributed to the drugs.

"Perhaps I can help you," Sierra said. When she knew she had Kitani's undivided attention, she went on, "If you truly desire to make a change, maybe you should resign from your position as Paladin and join Cipher."

"Quit being a Paladin?" Kitani had a half-mad gleam in her eye as she spoke. "Nobody ever quits being a Paladin."

"Not even if that Paladin violates one of the oldest laws governing the Matriarchal society?" Kitani grew silent, her eyes round as she settled her gaze on Sierra. Was it fear in her eyes, Sierra wondered, or simply shock at such an implication? She knew this was a touchy subject for Kitani, so she decided to tread lightly as she continued.

"You've been on the move almost constantly for months now, your only other Valori companion being Leara Sorani. On top of that, you've allowed your supply of Pompeilo to expire. Even now, your body is racked with the side effects."

A look of horror crept into Kitani's features.

Speaking in a nonthreatening manner, Sierra said, "I've been with Cipher for eight years. Surely you didn't believe me completely ignorant of the customs and behaviors of those I serve?"

"They teach you about Valori biology in Cipher?" Kitani asked. Sierra thought she sounded slightly appalled at the idea of aliens having intimate knowledge of her species.

"Only the basics," she said, hoping to reassure Kitani that not all of the Valori secrets were in the hands of potentially rival species. "I know about the use of Pompeilo and its possible side effects, and I even know a little about the Valori sexual cycle. But back to the earlier discussion. You've been alone with Leara for months, and your stock of Pompeilo was abandoned and forgotten in the snows of Kronos. While I suspect you of no wrongdoing, how will your actions look to the High Matriarchs? Will Dallia Sorani be able to overlook your indiscretion?"

Apparently mortified at the thought of going before Dallia Sorani's harsh judgment, Kitani shivered against the restraints holding her in place. "I will very likely be permanently sterilized," she said. "In addition, I'll also be demoted. My oversight will cost me my status as Leara's personal bodyguard. And all this is if I'm lucky. If charges are brought against me of violating the trust placed in me to personally guard Leara, then I may be sterilized and exiled to the wilds of Aria, to live among the wild beasts and apostates that roam the deep forests. A fitting end, I suppose."

"None of that has to happen," Sierra interjected. "Cipher can protect you. All you have to do is accept its help."

There was genuine interest in Kitani's eyes, but when she spoke, she still seemed doubtful. "How will it help me?"

"You can be conscripted into the services of Cipher. Conscription is not a common practice, but I've heard of it being done before."

Kitani laughed. "Will Cipher have me, I wonder? A Paladin, who in haste to prove her worth, so casually forgot to adhere to one of our oldest laws?"

"An evaluation of your skills will definitely be in order," Sierra said. "You can't expect to start out on top. It will certainly be different than what you're used to, but with your training and dedication, I think you'll climb high in record time. What do you say, Kitani? Do you want to become a Cipher agent?"

"It's something to consider. It's an honor to even have the offer extended to me," Kitani replied, making no secret of her admiration for the shadow organization. "Since I was a child, I've heard legends of its warriors. Never did I imagine I would someday have the opportunity to be among its elite." Tears filled her orange eyes. "I'll do it. I accept Cipher's offer. After all, I'm no stranger to conscription."

Another blast caused the ship to rock dangerously to and fro.

"That's great. First, we have to survive this," Sierra said, clutching tightly to the table as the vessel was pounded by another barrage from the *Sentinel*.

"We will survive this," Kitani said, struggling against the straps with renewed vigor.

"Let me help you," Sierra said, wishing she had a knife to cut the straps. An idea struck her. "I'll see if there's a locking mechanism." She ran her fingers along the bottom of the table. "Got it!" With a loud snap, the strap holding Kitani's head loosened.

Kitani moved her head, turning it slowly from side to side, and then watched Sierra as she continued to work feverishly on the remaining straps.

Beaming brightly, Sierra said, "That should do the trick," and the last strap unfastened.

"Your mother had a valid argument," Kitani said as she unsuccessfully tried to stand. "What's the purpose in rescuing us if we're to be blasted to bits in the process?" As if to prove her point, the ship lurched beneath their feet.

Sierra looped an arm around Kitani's torso to provide support. "I believe in Commander Duran. She would never allow any harm to befall one of her own." As a volley of fire pummeled the port side of the ship, she braced herself and Kitani against the operating table.

"How was the commander able to find us so quickly?" Kitani asked.

Tapping her armor's breastplate, Sierra said, "The commander had a hidden microchip embedded in our combat suits. It's been sending signals to the *Sentinel* the whole time."

"Your commander is a remarkable woman." Kitani gave Sierra a lopsided grin and hunkered down with her under the operating table. "I have to admit, at first I was skeptical about humans being allowed so high a position within Cipher, but now I actually look forward to serving under her command."

"You may come to regret those words."

"I'm undaunted by a good challenge." Although Kitani tried to appear unfazed by the changes that awaited her, Sierra detected a trace of unease in her actions.

Another loud boom echoed through the makeshift lab, immediately punctuated by an eerie hissing sound. A miasma of white steam began spilling out into the cargo hold.

"Life support's been hit," Sierra said, her first instinct to activate the built-in life support features in her armor. Her efforts were in vain. Melinda Callaway and her assistants had left them with their armor but their helmets had been removed. She cursed at their misfortune.

"We only have a limited supply of oxygen, and that's rapidly dwindling," she said, nodding toward the ruptured pipe at the side of the room. "At the rate that air is leaking out, we won't last more than a half an hour at the most." She looked at Kitani crouched next to her. "Are you good to walk?"

Nodding affirmation, Kitani began to rise unsteadily to her feet. Her movements were slow and deliberate. Sierra suspected that if she were to release her hold on the operating table she would fall on her face. She noted also how Kitani's breathing seemed more labored than usual.

This was taking too long, Sierra thought in dismay. If she allowed the proud Valori to walk out on her own, they would never make it in time. Without saying a word, she rose from her position and looped her arm around Kitani's waist.

"Try to hold on for a while longer," Sierra said, concerned by Kitani's pallor. "Commander Duran is on her way."

Cybil rushed forward, her pulse rifle drawn and ready. So far there had been no sign of opposition aboard the Midas frigate, but she knew the enemy was lying in wait in the shadows. In addition, Sierra and Kitani were somewhere within the confines of the ship, alone and no doubt afraid as they suffered at the hands of their captors.

"Stay close," she instructed Leara, who had stayed right on her heels every step of the way. She couldn't bear the idea of Leara being separated from her and falling victim to the same monsters holding their friends.

"No need to tell me twice," Leara replied, her gaze darting back and forth nervously as she scanned their surroundings. "The frigate lacks the subtle reek of death and decay the Earth facility possessed, but I still sense danger hovering about us." She paused. "Do you believe Kitani and Lieutenant Callaway are still alive?" she asked hopefully as they made their way through the eerily silent corridors.

"The enemy seeks vengeance on those who have made it sweat for so long. However, I don't think killing Sierra and Kitani would be enough. Not until Midas has made them suffer. And perhaps," Cybil added darkly, "Sierra and Kitani have been brought here for interrogation."

Leara shuddered. "We must hurry," she said in a hushed whisper.

Cybil nodded in agreement.

For a long while, she heard only the sound of their footsteps against the metal grating covering the floor of the ship, and then Leara held up her hand, motioning for silence.

Tilting her head to one side, the Valori listened to the corridors ahead. Cybil strained her ears, but heard nothing until she caught the faint but unmistakable sound of footsteps ringing in the distance. Someone was coming their way. Leara looked at her. She nodded, satisfied when the Valori readied her plasma pistol.

Cybil pressed onward. Edging their way along an intersecting corridor, Leara remained behind her at a relatively safe distance, just as they had agreed before boarding the Midas frigate. She had made Leara promise not to involve herself in combat unless it was absolutely necessary. Leara was a fast learner, but she had doubts about the Valori's ability to handle herself in a real crisis. Content to have the brunt of enemy fire aimed exclusively at her, she pressed onward, heading straight toward the source of the footsteps.

Rounding the corner, she came on a woman clad in a white lab coat. Caught off guard, the woman staggered back a few steps, her eyes widening in shock.

"Freeze," Cybil commanded. "One more step and I'll pump you full of plasma."

Recovering from the surprise, the woman glared coldly at her but didn't resist.

"Cybil," a familiar voice called from somewhere beyond the cornered woman. A few seconds later, Sierra appeared, supporting a very obviously weak Kitani against her.

Although Cybil's attention was only diverted for a second, the woman used the distraction to her advantage. In the blink of an eye, she produced a plasma blaster of her own, pointing the muzzle at Sierra's temple while she glowered triumphantly at Cybil.

"It seems the table has turned," she said. "Drop your weapons."

"Conniving Midas bitch," Cybil spat as she slowly lowered her pulse rifle. "Is this the only way you can win? By threatening me with the lives of my friends?" She placed her pulse rifle on the floor, using the action to mask the tiny advancing step she made toward the woman.

"That's close enough," the woman stated, clearly noticing Cybil's desperate attempt to regain the upper hand. "I'm alive and would like very much to remain so. I'm familiar with the type of work you do. You took out one of my best agents. Ah, well, it was inevitable, I suppose. N'arex was a diligent worker, but he was a Zulian. In the end, he was expendable, as is the rest of his race. Perhaps I should thank you for making my job easier."

Cybil stared. She had loathed N'arex herself, but for sound reasons. This woman seemed ready to dispose of him simply because of his species. Would she have eventually become like this obsessed madwoman if her prejudices had been allowed to go unchecked? She was suddenly more grateful than ever for her fateful meeting with Leara and Kitani.

"Let her go, Mother," Sierra interjected. "Cybil isn't a Cipher agent. She has nothing to do with this situation."

"You know perfectly well that's a lie. Isn't she the one who infiltrated the outpost facility on Kronos, leading to the destruction of some of our most valuable research?" The woman returned her attention to Cybil, who regarded her in sheer bewilderment. Could this really be Sierra's mother, long presumed dead?

"Were you working with those accursed hermaphrodites from the beginning?" Melinda Callaway asked.

Cybil did not reply, continuing to stare at the woman in disbelief. "I don't understand," she said, her remark aimed at Sierra. "This woman is your mother? How can that be? She was killed in the explosion at Touchstone Cybernetics years ago."

"Apparently, Midas Pharmaceuticals saw her as an asset to its team and made her an offer she couldn't refuse," Sierra answered. "Once the opportunity presented itself, Mother betrayed everyone she worked with to spare her own life. She obviously took much of her research with her to Midas Pharmaceuticals. Its plans to develop an alien plague were in the infancy stages then, I suppose. Perhaps the plan only lacked a sharp mind."

Melinda Callaway beamed proudly. "You flatter me, dear daughter, but I'm afraid your efforts are a little too late."

"Exactly what kind of mother are you?" Cybil interrupted. "Your daughter believed you were dead. Why didn't you attempt to contact her?"

"Don't waste your breath, Cybil. Clearly, she was too busy conducting her torturous experiments to care about what had happened to me," Sierra said bitterly.

"Torturous experiments?" Melinda mocked. "Do you truly disagree with my work so much as to condemn it as torture? I always thought that you would grow into a wiser woman than that, dear Sierra. But then again, I see that you've made quite a few unwise career decisions over the years, like choosing to go against the infinite power that is Midas." She wrinkled her nose in disgust as her gaze slithered over Kitani, still at Sierra's side. "Not to mention siding with those repulsive hermaphroditic creatures."

Something inside Cybil snapped at this insult to Valori. "They are not repulsive," she said, fighting back the urge to throttle this contemptible woman. "And they don't enjoy being labeled as hermaphrodites by narrow-minded fools like you."

Melinda sneered. "Ah, an alien sympathizer. You're no better than they are. Since you're so fond of these creatures, perhaps you won't mind dying alongside them."

“Don’t do it, Mother,” Sierra pleaded. “It’s not too late. If you surrender peacefully, your life may be spared.”

“Surrender?” Melinda snorted in contempt. “I will never surrender, not to Cipher, not to anyone. Least of all to a rogue mercenary who can’t complete even a simple job. Just look at all your failure has caused.”

Cybil’s eyes widened at the accusation. “You were the anonymous client, weren’t you? The same one who wrought so much havoc on Eden IV’s alien population.”

Melinda replied, “I’m truly impressed. I wouldn’t have guessed you to possess the brain power to arrive at such an accurate conclusion. Think about it. None of this would be happening if you had just killed these two creatures and retrieved the data as I expected. Retrieving the data was all that ever mattered. I thought I made myself perfectly clear to your employer on this point. But alas, here we are. Your friends will lose their lives because of you. It’s all your fault.”

“Enough, Mother,” Sierra said angrily. “Kill me if you want, if it makes you happy, but leave Cybil and Kitani out of this.”

Melinda was enraged by Sierra’s boldness. “You’re in no position to negotiate with me. Tell me, Sierra, why should I give in to your demands? If I do as you suggest and kill you now, these two will only come after me again to avenge their fallen comrade.”

“Wrong.” The hoarse voice belonged to Kitani.

Cybil noticed that Kitani, her arm slung over Sierra’s shoulders as a means of support, had placed herself very close to Melinda Callaway.

Melinda’s eyes flew open wide when Kitani’s strong hand grasped her wrist.

“I would much rather end this now than endure the torment of losing Sierra,” Kitani said, twisting Melinda’s arm until she was forced to drop the blaster. Melinda struggled to pull away, falling to the floor and nearly dragging Kitani down with her. She tried to reach her blaster with her free hand, but Kitani managed to kick it away from her fingers.

Melinda’s blaster skidded across the floor and stopped just out of reach of Cybil, who watched the entire exchange with an expression of disbelief.

Kitani panted heavily from her exertion. Cybil could tell it was all she could do just to remain on her feet, yet Kitani refused to give in. Holding tightly to the struggling Melinda’s wrist, she managed to prevent the woman from escaping. Valori were stronger than humans, Cybil remembered. Even in her weakened state, Kitani was able to overpower Melinda.

A look of horror flickered in Melinda's eyes when she realized she had so blindly stumbled into a trap, but Kitani's ruse succeeded in giving her companions the opening they so desperately needed.

While Melinda's attention was focused on Kitani, Cybil reclaimed her pulse rifle and plasma pistol. She rushed forward, hoping to apprehend her friend's crazed mother.

Melinda made her next move, going for Sierra as she tried desperately to regain control of the situation. Grabbing Sierra roughly by the hair, she yanked her surprised daughter forward, forcing her to release her hold on Kitani. Caught off guard by the sudden lack of support, Kitani lost her balance and collapsed to the floor in an exhausted heap.

Sierra continued to struggle with her mother while Cybil advanced, hoping that getting closer to the fight would give her a clearer shot at Melinda. She feared that if she fired a shot now, she might miss and hit Sierra instead.

"Sierra, get down!" she shouted, hoping she would move out of the line of fire.

Pivoting on her heel at the sound of Cybil's voice, Melinda released her hold on Sierra enough for her daughter to wrench out of her grasp.

Cybil leveled the plasma pistol at Melinda's head but before she could fire, Melinda fished in the pocket of her lab coat and brought out a shiny, metallic object. She turned and began advancing on Sierra, seemingly oblivious to everything else.

A syringe, Cybil realized in horror. Raising the plasma pistol once more, she took aim at Melinda, who had come dangerously close to Sierra. If she missed her mark, she might end up taking out both women. But what other choice did she have? She couldn't stand by while this madwoman threatened the lives of her friends.

"Sierra, watch out!" she cried, but her voice was drowned out by Leara's frantic cry as the Valori leapt from cover.

Hearing Melinda Callaway's derogatory description of the Valori, Leara cringed. Valori didn't like being labeled hermaphrodites by other species, and it was considered a great insult to refer to one as such. She smiled when Cybil immediately spoke in the Valori's defense. Growing tired of waiting in the wings, listening to the conversation from afar while Cybil faced whatever horrors the Midas frigate housed alone, Leara edged her way closer to the action.

Cautiously peering around the corner, Leara was met by a scene that made her gasp. Kitani's usually olive complexion was ghostly pale, yet she continued to struggle valiantly against a human woman in a lab coat. She must be Melinda Callaway, Leara decided. At last, the woman grabbed Lieutenant Callaway's hair and pulled her away from Kitani. Having no one to help her keep her balance, Kitani staggered to one side and fell.

Concerned for her friend, Leara wondered what was wrong with Kitani. Clumsiness was not a characteristic of Paladins, nor was Kitani usually so unfocused and disoriented. She dared not imagine what Midas might have done to weaken a Valori warrior.

The woman's attention remained focused on Sierra.

Leara saw Cybil watching anxiously from several feet away. For some unknown reason, her pulse rifle and plasma pistol lay on the floor, but she quickly reclaimed the weapons.

Watching Cybil slowly advance toward the woman, Leara felt tightness in her chest.

Sierra and the woman struggled, their closeness making it difficult for Cybil to get a clear shot. She inched closer. Her shout caused the woman to turn, her grip loosening on Sierra. Leara's eyes widened when she saw the woman remove a syringe from the pocket of her lab coat and whirl back toward Sierra.

Leara knew she must act now although her instincts screamed at her to remain hidden.

Everything Cybil had taught her about armed combat came rushing back to her, drowning out all other thought. Leara couldn't bear staying in the shadows while her friends and Cybil risked their lives. How could she ever face them again if she cowered in a dark corner until the danger was over? She might not be a Paladin or a mercenary, but she was a Valori, and she was the daughter of the fierce and revered Dallia Sorani.

Lunging forward, Leara rushed toward the woman in the lab coat. She had never felt so alive, so powerful, as she hurried to protect Sierra.

The woman never saw her coming. Her attention was directed solely toward Sierra, who still stared defiantly despite being unarmed. Leara saw that Sierra had placed herself between Kitani and the menacing woman and stood in place with an implacable expression.

"Lieutenant, look out!" Leara cried in alarm.

Everything seemed to move in slow motion. The woman sprang forward, the syringe in her hand. Launching herself, Leara intercepted her at the last second.

The deafening sound of the plasma pistol rang in Leara's ears as her finger squeezed around the trigger, followed by a horrible, strangled scream. The woman's limp form toppled over on Sierra, who for some reason reached out and embraced her in her arms. The syringe slipped from the dead woman's fingers, bouncing and rolling across the floor.

Leara collapsed several feet away, hitting the unyielding floor hard on her right side. The lights overhead seemed to flicker briefly, and then everything went dark around her.

Snapping out of her daze, Cybil sprinted over to Leara, who lay motionless on the floor, not responding to her calls or gentle prodding. To her horror, Leara continued to lie where she had fallen, the plasma pistol still clutched in her hands. Kneeling next to Leara, Cybil felt her barriers break, and she began to cry.

Taking Leara in her arms, Cybil cradled the unconscious Valori against her chest, debating whether or not she should remove Leara's helmet. She soon realized Leara had come to.

"Leara?" she asked, her voice choked with emotion.

Slowly, Leara extended her hand, reaching up to entwine her fingers with Cybil's. "I'm here, love," she whispered.

Cybil mumbled, "So you are." After taking a deep breath, she said, "I thought I'd lost you, like I've lost everyone else who's ever meant anything to me."

Leara smiled. Sitting up and taking Cybil's face in her hands, she said, "Don't worry, it's just a scratch. I have no intentions of leaving you anytime soon."

"Promise?" Cybil asked, a rakish grin touching the corners of her mouth. This was all so new to her, but she didn't want it to ever end. She had realized, in a sort of grim epiphany as Leara lay motionless, that she couldn't bear to face the universe without her. Even though she and Leara were from different worlds, she vowed to never let that stand in the way of her loving again.

Leara laughed lightly when Cybil took her hand. She said, "I promise, Cybil, I'll stay by your side forever if you want."

"Sounds like a deal," Cybil said. She leaned forward, kissing Leara more passionately than ever before.

Sierra watched Leara and Cybil with dull fascination. People lived, people died. She returned her attention to her mother's lifeless body. Hatred was a bitter entity, she thought, warping and corrupting the mind and heart until all reason was consumed. It was a blight upon the galaxy, and as much as she wished to see it end, she was too wise to believe the struggle against Midas could be over with a single strike.

From the corner of her eye, she caught a slight movement. Kitani, who seemed somewhat recovered, now struggled to return to her feet. Witnessing Kitani's fruitless efforts to stand was heartbreaking, prompting her to wriggle out from beneath her mother's body.

"Kitani," she whispered, not wanting to believe the weak, nearly helpless Valori was the same proud warrior she had come to know. "Are you all right?"

"This is nothing," Kitani said as Sierra helped her to her feet. Once she regained her balance, she smiled. "Nothing at all..." Her voice trailed off. She began swaying unsteadily.

Sierra caught Kitani and held her fast, too afraid to let go for fear of dropping her.

"I can't breathe," Kitani said with a muffled laugh. When Sierra relaxed her hold somewhat, Kitani settled more comfortably in her arms. "Not to worry. I'll be fine. It will take much more than a little fever to keep me down."

Sierra put her cheek next to Kitani's forehead, appalled by the fire burning beneath the Valori's skin. Kitani was trying to be brave, but clearly whatever her mother had done was taking its toll. She looked at Melinda Callaway's body, her eyes clouding over.

"I'm sorry," Kitani said softly. "It's a shame your reunion with your mother had to end this way. I truly am sorry."

"Don't be. She was a madwoman, a murderer. She doesn't deserve your sympathy." In spite of the truth, Sierra couldn't vanquish her intense sorrow.

Leaning against Sierra, Kitani said, "I know this mission didn't end the way you envisioned it, but remember that whatever happens, you've won. "

"Wise words. It will be hard to move on with the knowledge of the madwoman my mother became," Sierra replied, "but I will try. I am a Cipher agent. I will persevere."

Sierra felt a heavy burden lift from her soul. At long last she knew the truth of her mother's fate. She was free. Burying her face in her hands, she allowed the tears, so long denied, to finally fall.

A warmth at her shoulder alerted her to Kitani's presence. When she looked up, Kitani was watching her, sympathy shining in her fiery eyes. Taking Kitani in her arms, Sierra embraced the Valori as though she were holding on for dear life. They remained in this position for several minutes, until Sierra saw Duran and the crew entering the room.

She quickly disentangled herself from Kitani and wiped a tear from her eyes when Duran came toward them, followed by at least half the Cipher agents involved in the mission.

"What the hell happened in here? Lieutenant, why did you fail to contact me at your last checkpoint?" Duran demanded. When she caught sight of Sierra holding Kitani in her arms, her expression went blank. "Get a medic over here on the double!" she shouted to the closest agent. In moments, a medical officer scurried over to aid Kitani.

After practically tearing Sierra away from Kitani, Duran took her aside. "Don't worry. Kitani will be fine," Duran reassured her. "These officers are the best in their field. Do you honestly think I would embark on such a dangerous mission with two Valori in tow without taking all necessary precautions?"

Sierra shook her head. She knew Duran was no fool, and no novice, either. She saw Duran's gaze drift to Melinda Callaway's body.

"Who's that?" Duran asked.

Sierra replied bluntly, "My mother."

Duran stared at her for several minutes. When Kitani had been secured on a gurney and prepared to be transported to the *Sentinel*'s medical bay, she gently nudged Sierra. "Go to her, lieutenant. She'll want you by her side more than anything."

Sierra gave Duran a confused look. Was her attraction to Kitani truly so clear to those around her?

"I'm sorry for your loss, Sierra," Duran added, the personal address making her condolences all the more genuine. "I'll see to it that you mother receives a proper funeral."

"She doesn't deserve it, Commander," Sierra said. "She became a ruthless and calculating mastermind on every level."

"I'm not honoring her achievements, Lieutenant, merely disposing of the body in a civilized manner. I will never be as callous as Midas Pharmaceuticals, regardless of her crimes."

"Forgive me. In my current state I must have allowed my emotions to get the better of me. It would be rather cruel to simply jettison the body into space." Sierra swallowed hard past the lump that had suddenly formed in her throat. It felt odd referring to her mother as a body, another casualty of war. "My mother mentioned Midas constructing a fortified bunker in an undisclosed location," she added. "Supposedly, this is where the chosen ones would live until the plagues died down and it was safe to surface again."

"I'll have the two scientists we captured questioned," Duran said. "We uncovered the locations of two more outpost facilities during our infiltration of the Earth complex. With this information, we should be able to shut Midas Pharmaceuticals down once and for all. You're dismissed, Lieutenant. See a medic, just in case you've been exposed to any hazardous materials."

"Understood. Thank you, Commander," Sierra said after a pause, giving Duran a proper salute before moving off to join Kitani as the medics wheeled the Valori away from the madness her mother and Midas had created.

Chapter 22

Cybil and Leara returned to the *Sentinel* with Sierra, waiting anxiously for news of Kitani's condition. After what seemed an eternity, a Valori medic emerged to inform them that Kitani would make a full recovery. Apparently Melinda Callaway had injected Kitani with a prototype version of a plague being developed for Valori. Luckily for Kitani, the pathogen was in the developmental stage and not as effective. Kitani's body temperature was somewhat higher than normal, but that could be a side effect of her withdrawal from Pompeilo, Leara told Cybil.

"The massive amount of toxins that have been pumped into her via the tranquilizer was the main cause for concern," the Valori medic informed them. "The blood agent was designed to spread at an alarming rate, and all that moving about on Kitani's part did little to help matters. Never fear," she added when silence settled over the waiting area. "The medical team has given Kitani a cure developed by Cipher that should counteract the pathogen's effects completely. A similar cure has been developed for other species, and doses have been distributed to the residents who were attacked on Eden IV."

Cybil sighed with relief. "I was beginning to wonder what happened to the Zulians on Eden IV. It's good to know they will be fine."

"Yes, we currently have medical officers standing by to monitor the situation." The medic continued, "Immediately upon the ship's arrival at Cipher headquarters, Kitani will be moved to the medical deck where her progress can be further monitored."

Relieved at the good news, Cybil retired with Leara to the private quarters granted them by Commander Duran. While they were making their way to their rooms, a strange figure approached them: a Cipher agent clad from head to toe in a black combat suit. The armor covered the person completely, so not even gender could be discerned.

"Cybil Reynard," the figure said, the voice scrambled by an electronic device integrated in the helmet. "If you will accompany me, I believe we have some rather important business to discuss." The figure turned toward Leara, offering a humble bow. "I apologize, *Si'rah* Sorani, but I'm afraid I must borrow Cybil for a few moments."

Leara acknowledged the bow with a slight nod and said, "If you must."

Sighing, Cybil said to the mysterious figure, "All right, lead the way." To Leara, she said, "I'll be back as soon as I can, I promise." Taking Leara's hand, she lifted it to her mouth, gently pressing her lips against Leara's knuckles. "Wait for me?"

"Forever and always," Leara replied with a sweet smile.

"I have no intention of taking that long, no matter how important this business may be," Cybil assured her.

Leaving Leara, she allowed herself to be led to a private room, knowing the person with the scrambled voice who led her there could be none other than the entity spearheading Cipher's every action. When her host appeared thoroughly satisfied they were alone, she spoke the name aloud to confirm her belief. "Enigma."

The person leaned casually against a control panel, arms crossed over the armored chest, and said, "It's been awhile, Cybil."

Beneath the helmet, Cybil sensed Enigma smiling at her obvious discomfort. Not knowing the speaker's real identity only maddened her further. *Not long enough*, she wanted to quip, but instead said, "What did you wish to discuss? What could possibly be so important that you would come here to speak with me in person?" She hoped Enigma would understand from the surly tone of her voice that she wasn't pleased by the honor.

Enigma chuckled. "I apologize for the disruption, but I wanted to personally thank you for all your contributions in this mission."

"You want to thank me?" Cybil was confused.

"Thanks to your interference in this case, Commander Duran and her team have managed to track down the remaining forces behind Midas. The two outpost facilities have been successfully eliminated, as well as the underground bunker where the chosen ones were planning to flee during the biological attacks. If you hadn't accepted the mission to track down the missing data and obtain proof of Midas's activities, Cipher might have been met with another dead end. Thank you, Cybil, for excellent work. As always."

Something in the voice seemed familiar, Cybil thought.

"Also," Enigma continued, "there is the matter we discussed earlier. Are you prepared to undertake perhaps your most daunting quest ever?"

During the excitement of breaking the Midas conspiracy, Cybil had nearly forgotten about the invitation to join Cipher. As rare a privilege as that might be, she was afraid she would have to decline. Now that she had put her past behind her and found a new reason for living, she was contemplating putting her days of wild and reckless adventuring behind her.

"I'm afraid I'm not Cipher material," she said finally. "I've flown solo for so long, I don't think I could handle a commander barking orders at me all day."

Enigma laughed. "When I asked you to consider a position among Cipher, I wasn't referring to joining the ranks of the paramilitary organization. I have far bigger plans in mind for you, Cybil."

"You intend to make me a commander, then?" As startling as she found the prospect, it wasn't entirely unwelcome.

"Not a commander, Cybil. Something much better. How would you feel about a position in the Senate?"

"The Senate?" Cybil gaped at Enigma. Had she heard correctly?

"For the first time, humanity is being considered for a seat in the Senate," Enigma went on. "Think about it. What better way to further humanity's cause than on the inside?"

Gathering her wits, Cybil pondered the implications of Enigma's offer, unsure if she was ready for it. "What makes you so sure I'm a qualified candidate for this position? I have no experience in politics. Quite honestly, I'm not even sure if I'd want to. I'm a mercenary. My way of getting things done involves action, not words. Aren't you concerned I'd be completely out of my element in the Senate?"

"You wouldn't be acting alone," Enigma replied. "Cipher has a profound interest in this matter, as it does in all matters which will have a deep impact on galactic society."

"So you're saying I'll be your puppet?" Cybil asked, indignant at the proposal. "All I have to do is sit in the Senate and look presentable while Cipher pulls the strings, is that it? How, may I ask, will that be considered an advancement to humanity? Cipher is a Valori organization, and the Valori call enough shots as it is. So how will anything be different for humans? Other races have never looked out for us before, particularly the Valori. Generally speaking, they're only in it for themselves. No offense," she added as an afterthought. Despite how she felt about this proposition, she owed Enigma much in regards for her life and her freedom. She didn't want Enigma to think her ungrateful.

"Anyway," Cybil continued, "you've read my files. You know about my past record as a space merc. Let me ask you one other thing: Knowing what you know about me, why would you even trust me with such an honored position? One little slip and I could ruin it for the rest of humanity."

"Oh, Cybil," Enigma chided, "don't you realize that I've been evaluating you for years?"

Cybil was certain she recognized something very familiar behind the scrambled voice.

"Haven't figured it out yet? Maybe this will help." Slowly, Enigma reached up and unfastened the straps holding the helmet in place.

Cybil gasped as wisps of cobalt blue hair shook free, and the face behind one of the universe's most elusive figures became visible at last.

"Kashmir?" she asked quietly. "Is that really you, or just another disguise?"

"I go by many names," Enigma replied. "And Kashmir is indeed one of them. But I think it would be best if we kept this knowledge between us, don't you agree?"

"Of course." Cybil had always known that Kashmir was the kind of woman who could have someone eliminated with a simple order, but she'd never realized the true extent of Kashmir's power. Agreeing to keep her employer's secret was more than just a polite gesture. Besides, having information that even Duran herself didn't possess would be extremely satisfying, she decided, even if no one else knew the reason for her smugness.

"Now you know, Cybil," Kashmir said. "You've seen beneath the helmet and you know I'm no Valori. I speak with the interests of humanity in mind when I offer you this role. Think it over, Cybil. Being an unofficial agent of Cipher isn't such a horrible life. And guiding humanity to its rightful place in the universe is a noble act, even if you aren't actually at the helm yourself. I won't let you fail." Kashmir's words sounded to Cybil like a solemn vow.

Cybil grew thoughtful for a moment, reflecting on all her past encounters with Kashmir. Why had she never suspected there was more to the blue-haired woman than what she already knew? After all, Kashmir was an information broker, the leader of Eden IV's vigilantes, and a former vigilante herself. There must be so much more to her history for her to not only attract the attention of Cipher's elite, but to actually become Enigma. Kashmir was certainly hiding a thing or two, but Cybil doubted she would ever tell.

"You know what?" Cybil said, feeling a sudden gush of courage well up inside her. "I'll do it. I'll become a senator, if you really believe you can get me in."

"Oh, there won't be any problems there," Kashmir said. "I'm Enigma. My word is law. You're practically a senator already, as far as I'm concerned."

Cybil took a moment to allow everything she'd learned to sink in. If someone had told her only a short while ago that her employer was the secret head of Cipher, and that she would seriously be contemplating a seat in the Senate, she would have laughed in their face.

"Is everything all right?" Kashmir asked, bringing her mind back to the present.

"I still can't believe that you're Enigma." Cybil shook her head. "All this time I've been working for you, I never suspected a thing."

"I am Enigma, but I'm not Enigma," Kashmir added cryptically. "Enigma is not one, but many. My power goes far beyond that of the Supreme Matriarchy or even the Federation, but there are still others I have to answer to."

"So Enigma is an organization, a separate branch of Cipher?" Cybil mused aloud. Somehow, she didn't find the truth all that surprising. Enigma's duty was too important to be handled by one individual.

Deliberately ignoring Cybil's question, Kashmir said, "In many ways, this won't be much different than your usual life. You'll still be working for me, and you'll still be fighting for what you believe in. Only the means by which your objectives are accomplished will change. Using a plasma pistol during a Senate meeting isn't advisable," Kashmir added jokingly.

The universe worked in mysterious ways, Cybil thought, and so did Enigma. She didn't know if she was ready to take such a giant leap, but she sincerely hoped she could live up to Enigma's high expectations.

Leara waited for Cybil in the sitting room of the guest quarters. From this vantage point, there was no way Cybil could sneak past without Leara seeing her.

It seemed to Leara that she spent a small eternity sitting on the large sofa facing the main door before Cybil at last emerged through the sliding hatch. Cybil looked tired, she thought, but beneath that weariness she detected a certain edge. Something was on Cybil's mind.

Waving at Cybil to get her attention, Leara wondered what the mysterious person had said to her to put her in such a disconcerted state. Upon seeing her, Cybil nodded a greeting and came over to sit next to her.

"What did the Cipher operative wish to discuss with you?" Leara asked.

"Not just any Cipher operative," Cybil said. "That was Enigma."

"Enigma? Really?" Leara found it difficult to believe that the almost mythical figure had been standing right in front of her. "What did the two of you discuss?"

"Politics," Cybil replied after a brief pause.

Not understanding, Leara shook her head. Cybil seemed reluctant, almost embarrassed to speak openly about her discussion with Enigma.

"Never mind," Cybil said. "It's not important."

"I believe this is the second meeting you've had with Enigma. You must be more important than you realize to keep attracting so much attention from Cipher."

"Lucky me," Cybil said, but she didn't sound very convinced.

"Well, I think you're important," Leara added. "Important to me, anyway."

Cybil had been a little distant since their return to the *Sentinel.* The tension that had developed between them was almost tangible, and it was driving her mad.

"Cybil, we need to talk." Leara glanced about the spacious room. Currently, there were no other passengers around, but she was still not satisfied. "Not out here, though. Follow me," she said, rising from the sofa.

Cybil stared after her for a moment more and then obediently complied.

Leara smiled to herself at Cybil's confused expression, but inside she felt as awkward and uneasy as Cybil looked.

When they reached Leara's room, she paused outside the door, uncertain if she had the nerve to go through with this confrontation. Behind her, Cybil stood close, so close that she could sense the warmth emanating from her body. Drawing a deep breath, she swiped the ID card across the scanner and waited for the hatch to open.

Once inside the room, Leara sat on the edge of the bed while Cybil remained standing just within the doorway.

"Well," Leara began, wanting to break the silence, "we've certainly been through a lot lately. I expect that Mother will be anxious to hear my report on Cipher's handling of the Midas case." She regarded Cybil thoughtfully for a moment. "What about you? What are your plans now that Midas's plans have been thwarted?"

"I haven't given it much thought, actually," Cybil replied with uncertainty. "The mercenary business is never slow, and my employer was so impressed by my performance in this mission that she's offered me a special contract to work for her indefinitely."

Cybil was avoiding the issue and Leara knew it. "But you're not certain you want to take it, are you?"

"Let's just say the work is a bit different than what I'm used to."

Deciding it was best to change the subject before Cybil became too uncomfortable, Leara said, "I still can't believe Kitani has decided to join Cipher."

Cybil arched an eyebrow. "The way I hear it, she didn't exactly join."

"Commander Duran conscripted her into the ranks based on her skills as a fighter, but regardless of how you explain the situation, Kitani seems thrilled at the prospect of remaining with Cipher."

"Duran definitely has an eye for talent. With the proper training, Kitani will make a damn good agent."

"So true," Leara said, feeling a stab of sorrow at the idea of losing her constant companion. "Kitani will go far in Cipher, but she'll be missed. My mother won't be pleased at having to select another Paladin for my personal service."

"Are there any candidates for the position?"

"Matriarchal Paladins are carefully selected based on their loyalty, combative abilities, and dedication to their duty. Finding a warrior with as much honor and prestige as Kitani won't be an easy task." Leara sighed. "I miss her already."

Clearly sensing the melancholy that had crept into Leara's expression, Cybil came over and sat next to her. She draped an arm loosely around Leara's shoulders and held her close.

Leara drew comfort from the small gesture, but so many questions were still left unanswered. Leaning into Cybil's embrace, she tried to push them out of her mind, but to no avail. "Cybil," she said, "what's happening between us? Or am I wrong in assuming that there is something?"

Cybil withdrew for a moment. "No," she said, leveling her gaze at Leara with confidence. "There is something. I've never felt this way before, like I'm drawn to you. It's hard to explain, but whatever force is between us is a very powerful one."

Leara's heart nearly leapt from her chest in joy. "You can feel it! I thought you could before, but I was too afraid to say anything for fear of frightening you away."

"So you know what this is?" Cybil asked.

"It is the mating bond, *rah'xenoji*."

"*Rah'xenoji*," Cybil mused aloud. "What does it mean?"

"Loosely translated, it means 'passion in the heart.' It's the link that binds two Valori together physically and emotionally. Every Valori experiences *rah'xenoji* when she finds a suitable mate."

"But I'm not Valori," Cybil said, obviously concerned.

"I'm aware of that, just as I'm also aware that I'm not human." Leara hesitated, now uncertain. "Are you all right with the differences between us, between our species?" She wasn't at all sure she wanted to hear Cybil's reply.

"I have no problems with the way we are, but are you sure you can live with this decision? You're destined to become a High Matriarch, one of the most powerful among the Valori. Shouldn't you be seeking a mate from among your own kind?"

"Is that what *you* want?" Leara asked suddenly. "Could you stand idly by and watch, should I choose to take a Valori mate? And could you honestly wish us well in our new life together? Is this what you wish, Cybil?"

Startled, Cybil stammered, "N-no, I just—"

"Nor do I," Leara cut her off firmly. In a much warmer tone, she added, "Oh, Cybil, I know my decision won't be easy for everyone to accept. I'm ready to face the consequences, no matter what they are. We're treading in unexplored territory, but as long as I don't have to face the future alone, I'm not afraid."

"I'm not frightened," Cybil said, gently taking Leara's hand in her own. "For a time, I thought I was, but now I see that I was merely afraid of loving again. It wasn't easy for me, you know, losing my family as a child. Ever since then I've kept my distance from everyone. It felt safer not letting anyone get too close. The betrayal I experienced at my parents' deaths hurt too deeply. I never wanted to feel that pain again."

"It must have been very hard for you. Being orphaned at such an early age is a tragedy I can't even begin to fathom, but you're safe now. You don't have to be afraid anymore." Leara encircled Cybil's waist with her arms. "I will never betray you."

"I just want you to be happy," Cybil said.

"I've never been happier than I am right now at your side." Leara smiled and leaned further into the embrace. "I couldn't bear the thought of never seeing you again. I know what I want," she added, staring deeply into Cybil's eyes.

Leara knew how difficult this was for Cybil and that she should be grateful for how nicely their relationship was going, but her heart longed for something more, something deeper. She yearned for the bond that would unite them as one, both spiritually and physically.

Cybil wanted it too, she thought, since the tension in the air between them was nearly palpable. If only Cybil weren't so afraid of her own feelings and could abandon her restraint. Cybil was so focused on what differentiated humans from the Valori. If she could see how alike they were, perhaps it would dispel some of her deeply held fears.

Why did everything have to be so complicated? She wanted Cybil, and it was quite clear that Cybil wanted her, so why could neither of them tear down the barriers holding their desires at bay?

Leara laid her head on Cybil's shoulder and tried to think of some way around her predicament. The solution presented itself rather unexpectedly when Cybil decided to voice some of her frustrations aloud.

"How do I deal with this, Leara? This burning desire building up inside me every time I'm near you threatens to consume me. I've tried to fight it, but can't." A shudder racked Cybil's body, though she continued to hold Leara.

"That is just the bond," Leara reassured her. "Don't fight it. Embrace it, listen to your instincts." When Cybil ceased trembling, she added, "Trust your instincts, Cybil. The bond will guide you. Open your mind and listen." She paused while Cybil took a series of deep breaths. "Can you hear it, the power of our bond?"

"I can," Cybil replied, her eyes still closed.

"What is it saying? What does your heart want?" Leara gasped when Cybil opened her eyes and bent her head down, capturing her mouth in a fierce kiss. She clutched tightly at Cybil's shoulders as desire flooded into her, overwhelming her senses.

Once the kiss ended, Cybil smiled rakishly and said, "I know I've been hard to deal with at times, but I promise I'll try to be less frustrating in the future. Can you ever forgive my brash, impetuous human ways?"

Raising her hand to cup the back of Cybil's head, Leara said, "Come closer and see just how willing I am to forgive you."

This time Leara initiated the kiss, pulling Cybil down and claiming her mouth fervently. Taking care not to nick Cybil's tongue as she had done in their first kiss, she parted her lips ever so slightly in silent invitation as she deepened the kiss.

"I've been a fool," Cybil muttered, panting heavily as she pulled away. "Now I know better. I know what my heart longs for and can finally see the truth for what it is. I love you, Leara. I want to be with you, always."

Shocked by the sweet sincerity in Cybil's voice, Leara swayed a bit unsteadily. Instantly, Cybil was there to support her, her arms encircling Leara and holding her close. She felt the beating of Cybil's heart through the fabric of her jumpsuit and drew strength from the power behind its pulse. Raking her fingertips lightly over Cybil's bare arms, she traced an outline of her well-defined muscles from her forearm to her shoulder, where the thin fabric of the sleeveless shirt prevented her from venturing any farther.

Cybil shivered beneath Leara's touch, gooseflesh rising along her arm.

Their eyes met. Leara felt something click inside her, the final piece of the puzzle at last falling into place. In that instant, she knew that she and Cybil were destined to be together, and no amount of running and pitiful excuses would drive them apart. She was beyond the need for excuses. Cybil inclined her head forward and brushed her lips lightly over hers.

"Are you sure this is what you want?" Cybil asked, nibbling her way down Leara's throat. "If we don't stop soon, I'm afraid I won't be able to."

Gently taking Leara's head in her hands, Cybil tilted her head. Their eyes met. Cybil trembled, staring at Leara almost imploringly through hooded eyes. "Please," she said, "Tell me what you want. I can feel the power flowing between us, but I need to hear it from your own lips."

Leaning her forehead against Cybil's, Leara replied, "I want you to make love to me. Claim me as your mate, your lover. Please, complete the bond. I need you, Cybil."

Complying with Leara's request, Cybil continued to kiss her as Leara leaned back against the pillows.

Taking the zipper of Leara's jumpsuit between her fingers, Cybil slowly pulled, revealing the creamy smoothness of Leara's skin inch by inch. Leara leaned her head back as Cybil kissed her way along her throat, but looked up when Cybil paused uncertainly, having reached the point where the jumpsuit dipped down between her breasts.

Sensing her hesitation, Leara regarded her questioningly.

"You're beautiful," Cybil said, her voice thick with passion.

Leara smiled and placed a hand on Cybil's cheek. "As are you. It's hard to believe this is really happening, and not just a pleasant dream."

"Oh, this is real all right." Apparently recovering from her earlier uncertainty, Cybil laid her head between Leara's small breasts. Leara felt her heart skip a beat, its tempo increased by excitement and desire when Cybil unzipped the jumpsuit to her waist.

The garment slid from her shoulders and glided down her back. Cybil reached forward tentatively, hesitating just before she made contact with Leara's bare skin. Taking Cybil's hand in her own, Leara guided it to her left breast, where she cupped Cybil's fingers firmly upon her flesh. Her nipple immediately tightened beneath the touch.

"See? We're not so different, are we?" Leara asked, her gaze focused on Cybil's chest.

Through the fabric of Cybil's shirt, Leara saw how her nipples had become taut peaks. Cybil laughed softly as Leara slid a hand beneath her shirt and began caressing her tight abdominal muscles, and then she assisted Leara with the task of undressing. The cinch belt at her waist only needed to be loosened before the jumpsuit continued its descent to the floor, where it joined Cybil's discarded tank top and pants in a little heap.

Leara stood apart from Cybil for several minutes, admiring and exploring Cybil's body with her eyes. Her own nearly flawless alabaster skin was a contrast to Cybil's tanned skin, marred and silvered in places by scars collected from missions gone awry, she supposed. She paid no heed to these imperfections, however, and stepped once again into Cybil's embrace. Unhindered by clothing, she could feel the heat of desire emanating from Cybil's skin and found she could barely contain her own wanton needs.

Taking Leara in her arms, Cybil lowered them to the mattress, where they lay tangled in each other's arms. Cybil trailed her fingers over Leara's stomach and dipped between her slightly parted thighs. Leara groaned sensually when Cybil's fingers found the ridge of her sex.

Leara suddenly grew tense. Until that moment, she had not realized just how close to the edge she actually was, how her body yearned for release.

"Please," she begged. Cybil continued to caress her swollen sex. "Please, Cybil, make me come."

Cybil's eyes widened briefly at her request.

Raising her head so she would be closer to Cybil, Leara said, "I need you inside me."

A tidal wave of ecstasy rushed over her as Cybil's fingers filled her. Leara rode the waves of pleasure that followed Cybil's penetration, relishing the way she seemed to know exactly where and when to touch her. When her body could take no more, when she was so close to the edge she might topple over the brink, she confidently plunged headlong into the abyss, knowing that Cybil would be there to catch her.

Leara tossed her head back and cried out in ecstasy, her fists bunched in the sheets as her body was racked with the aftershocks of their lovemaking. Cybil remained inside her, gently caressing her until her body ceased to shudder.

"Is it always so intense?" she asked once Leara opened her eyes.

Feeling suddenly shy and insecure, Leara stammered, "I-I'm not sure. To be honest, this is the first time I've ever experienced it."

"You're joking," Cybil said.

Leara felt like shrinking beneath her gaze. Cybil seemed so much more experienced. Realizing she knew next to nothing about the art of lovemaking, she could think of no reply.

Cybil must have sensed her unease, for her gaze softened and she said, "You're serious, aren't you? There's nothing to be ashamed of. It's just a little surprising that someone who's a hundred and twenty-three years old has never… well, you know."

"Valori take the bond formed by mating very seriously," Leara said. "Although there are some exceptions, Valori tend to be monogamous. Until I met you, I'd never really given finding a mate much thought. No one has ever awakened such desires in me before." Trying to explain the mating bond long held sacred to the Valori was harder than she expected. She wondered if Cybil would ever truly understand how much their union meant to her.

"That's beautiful," Cybil said, the suddenness of the statement startling Leara. "Finding someone you love enough to spend centuries of your life with is really amazing."

Leara smiled. "I love you enough to share the rest of my life with."

Laughing, Cybil said, "I'm not so sure I'll last that long. Especially considering my line of work. Although," she added, a twinkle lighting her eye, "that could change in the near future."

"What do you mean? Are you retiring from the mercenary business?"

"Maybe I should. Now that I've been made a better offer, I see no need to risk my neck time and again."

"A better offer?" Leara was genuinely interested. What exactly did Cybil have in mind?

"You asked what Enigma wanted to discuss with me earlier," Cybil said. "How would you feel about being mated to the first human senator?"

"A senator? You're joking."

"It's no joke. Enigma has offered me the position, and I'm seriously considering it, even though I'll actually be little more than Cipher's pawn in this game, I think I could make a difference for humanity. My presence in the Senate alone will have an impact on humanity's future, one way or the other."

Propping herself up on her elbows, Leara said, "This is wonderful, Cybil. If you become a senator, you could change the way galactic society views humans forever. You might very well become the hero your race needs. What are your chances at being elected to the Senate?"

"According to Enigma, I'm as good as in already. All I have to do is say the word." Cybil laughed a little hysterically and covered her face with her hands. "What am I thinking? I must be insane to believe I can actually pull this off. I know Cipher will be behind me every step of the way, but I've never been good at taking orders. What if I make a complete mess of it?"

"You know that I'll always support you," Leara said, wrapping an arm around Cybil's shoulders. "I think you should pursue this. You were right earlier. You can make a difference. Give yourself more credit, Cybil. You're an unsung hero already. Your contributions in the Midas case were integral to Cipher's investigation. You're a fine leader, and I know you'll always put your people's interests first."

Cybil peered through her fingers at Leara. "You're right. Opportunities like this don't come around every day. It's nice to have someone to talk to," she added, leaning her head against Leara's.

"Glad I could be of service." Leara nuzzled her way along Cybil's neck.

Cybil reciprocated by taking Leara in her arms, melding their still-naked bodies together in a heated embrace.

"Talking with you is wonderful," Cybil huffed between kisses as she kissed a trail along Leara's throat.

"It can wait until later," Leara finished for her, tilting her head back to allow Cybil to trace a path across her collarbone with her tongue. "Right now, talking isn't what I need."

Cybil mumbled in response, the sound vibrating against Leara's sensitive flesh. Cybil's tongue extinguished the fires ignited by her fingertips, yet Leara was still burning for her. Their bond was still new, the desire that drove them together still growing. At that moment, she wanted nothing more than to strengthen the bond between them.

Cybil lay across Leara, her body almost completely covering the smaller Valori. Never in her life had she felt this way. Her insides were like fire, and in spite of the intensity of her earlier orgasm, the press of Leara's flesh against hers was enough to set her ablaze with desire again.

Settling herself between Leara's legs, Cybil felt the heat of the Valori's sex against her. She shifted until her clitoris was slotted against Leara's. Leara moaned with desire at the intimate contact, spreading her legs wider in invitation. Kissing her way along the smooth flesh of Leara's neck, Cybil began a slow descent, intermittently interrupted as she tried to take in every inch of Leara's body.

As she paused at Leara's chest, taking one taut nipple between her lips, Leara raised her head from the pillows and gasped, "Your attentions are agonizing, love."

Relenting in her exquisite torture, Cybil continued downward. She felt Leara's fingers tangle in her hair as the Valori urged her onward. Leara groaned in sheer rapture when Cybil reached her destination and gripped the headboard for dear life.

Cybil knelt on the floor next to the bed. With Leara's legs draped over her shoulders, she explored more deeply the nature of Valori anatomy than any human probably had in the past. She was grateful that Valori physiology greatly resembled that of a human woman, and the external features responded similarly to stimulation. Relishing the sounds of pleasure her simple ministrations elicited, Cybil ran her fingers along Leara's swollen sex.

Cybil was acutely aware of the firm organ at the anterior of Leara's sex, similar to a clitoris but longer. It felt heavier, thicker to the touch. She brushed her thumb over it, surmising the organ was designed to enable easier penetration. Since this was only her first intimate encounter with a Valori and she had only limited knowledge of the subject, she could only imagine how the organ might be used during a breeding cycle. Taking it gently between her lips, Cybil stroked her tongue across it. Leara's sex stiffened until it was nearly as hard as stone, extending beyond the hood covering it.

Cybil could feel the effects of *rah'xenoji* now as never before, and it was amazing, as though she could sense exactly what Leara wanted and what she needed as clearly as if Leara had asked for it. This unspoken understanding between them felt incredible, like some deep void she hadn't even known existed had been filled.

Leara began to writhe and wriggle with need, her sex dilating with blood. Her tongue working feverishly, Cybil sucked the organ into her mouth, delighting in how the slightest pressure to this highly erogenous area brought Leara a step closer to release. She felt her own need bubbling up inside and slid her free hand between her thighs. Leara's powerful release gushing over her hand and exploding in her mouth sent her over the edge, and her body spasmed with waves of pleasure powerful enough to make the universe shimmer around her.

Once Cybil caught her breath, she climbed into bed beside Leara, settling back on the pillows. Leara curled alongside her body, her head resting on her shoulder.

"I had no idea Valori could come twice at the same time," she said, running her fingers through Leara's silken hair.

"Just one of the perks of being a Valori," Leara replied with a suggestive smile. She stared up at Cybil drowsily through half-closed eyes.

A strong sense of protectiveness crept into Cybil as she held Leara, watching as her lover drifted off into a peaceful slumber.

I received more than I bargained for when I accepted this mission, Cybil thought, watching Leara sleep contentedly next to her. *And certainly far more than I ever dared hope for.*

Epilogue

All was quiet aboard the starship *Integrity*, the serenity a far cry from the chaos and peril so prevalent in Cybil Reynard's former life. Having been elected the first human senator a few weeks ago, she was growing accustomed to her new life.

Surprisingly, she was having an easier time adjusting than she initially thought. Taking orders from Enigma was really not so different than her career as a mercenary. Her acceptance was likely due to the fact that her former employer was still dictating her actions from somewhere within the shadows. She smiled to herself at her thoughts, knowing that she could rest easy as long as Enigma was in charge. And no matter who actually made the major decisions, all the power and prestige of the senatorial status belonged exclusively to her, at least as far as the general public was concerned. She was currently one of the highest ranking humans in the known universe; her status was second only to Kashmir.

As much as Cybil hated to admit it, she was actually enjoying her career change. Her new life was exhilarating. Everything from the respect her position garnered to the simple luxury of living aboard the *Integrity* itself excited her in a way she never knew possible.

A vast starship armed with a photon cannon capable of penetrating the surface of a planet, the *Integrity* served as lodging for members of the Senate and the councilors. Being the first human assigned such a prestigious position, naturally Cybil was something of an outcast among her peers. She didn't let that bother her. Having the full support of Cipher wherever she went had its advantages. The strong sense of foreboding which accompanied the elusive organization and all its affairs was among them.

Cybil reclined in an overstuffed chair in her private suite, reflecting on her years as a mercenary. Sudden warmth on her hand made her look up. Leara Sorani sat next to her, her eyes filled with love and affection as she covered Cybil's hand with her own. Leara was so beautiful, so captivating, that Cybil could barely resist touching her any time she was near.

Leara had arrived one day shortly after Cybil was accepted into the Senate, sent by none other than her mother, the High Matriarch Dallia Sorani. Life aboard the *Integrity* consequently became less lonely and much more interesting for Cybil with her beloved Leara by her side once again, but Leara had claimed that it was business that brought her there.

In order to be reunited with Cybil without causing controversy among the Valori, Leara had volunteered to assume the role of the official ambassador of the Supreme Matriarchy, a rather prestigious position among her people. Cybil suspected that Dallia knew her daughter's true reasons for voicing such a request, though thankfully, she chose to remain quiet on this subject and honor Leara's wishes.

From what Leara had told her, Dallia was rather pleased that her daughter was finally showing an interest in politics and granted Leara permission to carry on with her plans for the wellspring of knowledge and experience she would gain aboard the *Integrity*. But Cybil knew the truth. She could feel the deepening bond between them tugging at her insides whenever Leara was absent, and it was likely Leara felt the same way. Becoming an ambassador for her people was a small price to pay so they would have an excuse to remain together.

Cybil had been elated at the news that Leara would be joining her. Her new life was centered around a tight schedule, which didn't allow for many planet-side visits with a lover.

Now contented by her lover's presence, she couldn't help thinking that perhaps Kashmir had something to do with Leara's decision, a suspicion further confirmed when she received an encrypted message from Enigma. Going into the bedroom to receive the transmission, she sealed the door behind her for privacy.

"How are you handling your new position?" Enigma's voice was once again scrambled beyond recognition. "I trust your colleagues aren't giving you too much opposition?"

"Nothing I can't handle," Cybil replied with vigor. "Everything is just great, Enigma. And I have you to thank for it all."

"No thanks are necessary. I'm merely doing my job." Enigma was silent for a moment, and then said, "I believe you'll be happy to hear that your friends are doing well, also. Kitani has made a full recovery and is settling in quite nicely among Commander Duran's crew. Not a trace of the alien plague remains, though she's been warned to avoid strenuous activity until she's had a chance to recover her energy completely. Lieutenant Callaway has also been informed of this precaution," Enigma added suggestively.

Cybil laughed at the innuendo, the joke confirming that this was her friend Kashmir speaking and not some anonymous agent of Enigma. The uncertainty remained each time she held a conference with the elusive figure. After all, Kashmir herself had said that Enigma was comprised of several different people.

"Keep an eye on Sierra," she said. "I fear this whole ordeal with her mother has been more taxing on her than she's letting on. Watch over her for me, all right, Enigma?"

"Absolutely. As I've said before, Cybil, you are more valuable as an ally than a foe."

"The same goes for you," Cybil replied with a roguish grin.

"Well, I imagine you're rather anxious to get back to your business," Enigma said. "That reminds me, I believe further congratulations are in order. I hear you're happy with the little surprise I sent you. So happy, in fact, that you sprang a surprise of your own." Cybil blushed although she knew Enigma couldn't see her. "I only hope that you'll remember to invite me to the wedding. I can only imagine the look on the High Matriarch's face when you declared your love for her daughter. Just imagine the shock of it… Leara Sorani married to a simple human woman. Tell me, Cybil, how is Dallia taking the big news?"

Cybil grunted. "She'll get used to me in time. Or at least that's what I'm hoping."

"I'm sure she'll learn to love you," Enigma said. "Your charisma can conquer even the hardest of hearts. But I've taken up too much of your valuable time already. Best of wishes to you and Leara, Cybil."

"Thank you."

Cybil slowly rose from her chair, Enigma's words echoing in her mind. Although she hadn't noticed before, she was eager to return to her new life and her new lover—eager and slightly nervous as well. This was a new beginning for her. For the first time in many long years she felt truly alive and whole. Her former reservations forgotten, Cybil headed back to her room, where her beloved Leara awaited her.

Author Jennifer McCormick

About the Author

Jennifer McCormick was born in North Carolina in 1983. She's always had a fascination for space exploration and the unknown. She enjoys all things science fiction and fantasy, from books and movies to video games.

As a child, Jennifer was an avid reader and always had an interest for writing. Her interests are shopping, reading, and spending time with family and friends. She currently lives in beautiful northwestern North Carolina with her parrot.

The Midas Conspiracy is Jennifer's debut novel. She's currently working on her second novel, *The Withering.*

Make sure to check out these other exciting Blue Feather Books titles:

In the Works	Val Brown	978-0-9822858-4-8
Playing for First	Chris Paynter	978-0-9822858-3-1
Cresswell Falls	Kerry Belchambers	978-1-935627-95-1
30 Days Hath September	Jamie Scarratt	978-1-935627-94-4
Survived by Her Longtime Companion	Chris Paynter	978-1-935627-88-3
Soulwalker	Erica Lawson	978-1-935627-83-8
Lesser Prophets	Kelly Sinclair	978-0-9822858-8-6
A Kiss Before Dawn	Laurie Salzler	978-1-935627-89-0
Appointment with a Smile	Kieran York	978-1-935627-86-9
Confined Spaces	Renee MacKenzie	978-1-9356279-7-5
My Soldier Too	Bev Prescott	978-1-935627-81-4
Return of the Raven	Jamie Scarratt	978-1-935627-72-2
In the Now	Kelly Sinclair	978-1-935627-85-2

www.bluefeatherbooks.com

CPSIA information can be obtained at www.ICGtesting.com
Printed in the USA
BVOW070346121012

302804BV00001B/48/P